LEGACY

OF

DESIRE

Also From Larissa Ione

~ DEMONICA/LORDS OF DELIVERANCE SERIES ~
Pleasure Unbound (Book 1)
Desire Unchained (Book 2)
Passion Unleashed (Book 3)
Ecstasy Unveiled (Book 4)
Eternity Embraced ebook (Book 4.5) (NOVELLA)
Sin Undone August (Book 5)
Eternal Rider (Book 6)
Supernatural Anthology (Book 6.5) (NOVELLA)
Immortal Rider (Book 7)
Lethal Rider (Book 8)
Rogue Rider (Book 9)
Reaver (Book 10)
Azagoth (Book 11)
Revenant (Book 12)
Hades (Book 13)
Base Instincts (Book 13.5)
Z (Book 14)
Razr (Book 15)
Hawkyn (Book 16)
Her Guardian Angel (Book 17)
Dining With Angels (Book 17.5)
Cipher (Book 18)
Reaper (Book 19)
Bond of Destiny (Book 20)
Bond of Passion (Book 21)

~DEMONICA BIRTHRIGHT~
Legacy of Temptation
Legacy of Chaos
Legacy of Desire

~ MOONBOUND CLAN VAMPIRES SERIES ~
Bound By Night (book 1)
Chained By Night (book 2)
Blood Red Kiss Anthology (book 2.5)

~CONTEMPORARY/WOMEN'S FICTION ~
Snowbound
The Escape Club

LEGACY

OF

DESIRE

NEW YORK TIMES BESTSELLING AUTHOR

LARISSA IONE

Legacy of Desire
A Demonica Birthright Novel, Book 3
By Larissa Ione

Copyright 2026 Larissa Ione
ISBN: 978-1-963135-50-3

Original art used with permission from Steffani Christensen

Published by Blue Box Press, an imprint of Evil Eye Concepts, Incorporated

Acknowledgements

I hate to say, "as always," but truly, this is one of these moments. Liz Berry, *as always*, you were crucial to the process of writing this book…which turned out to be one of my favorites. To say I appreciate you and your friendship doesn't cover it. But thank you. Thank you *so much*.

Jillian Stein, you're another "as always." You go above and beyond, and I'm so, so blessed to be working with you and to have you as a friend. You're just swell. ;-)

I also need to thank Hang Le for these incredible covers. My anticipation for each one grows as the series progresses. I can never wait to see what you come up with! *As always*, you knock it out of the park.

Kim Guidroz, *as always*, you make my writing life easier. You're a joy to work with and to be around, and dammit, we don't get to do that often enough!

Chelle Olson, it's so very special to know the person who digs into my books, to know that you 'get it.' You belong to this world, and I hope you live in it for a long, long time!

Cheryl Johnson and Kat Daugherty, *as always*, thank you for holding down the group fort so I can concentrate on writing. You ladies are freaking awesome! Cheryl, I'm so glad we live so close! Let's hang again soon!

As always, Grace Wenk, I'm floored by how you know my books better than I do. Your contagious enthusiasm is a gift in every way, and I always love getting your on-point input!

Stacey Tardif, I'm so happy for that fateful day, way back then, that brought you into my 'verse. *As always*, I'm so thrilled that you're part of the process now, and there's no one I'd trust more to give my books that final stamp of approval.

And last, but not least…and *as always*, I need to thank my mom and husband for all the support. Without you, I'd never be able to get anything done. The pups thank you too!

Dedication

For Arlee Thompson. After all these years, to have you nearby and to be able to share this process with you has been priceless. Your journey is just beginning, and I'll be there with you every step of the way. I can't wait to see where it takes you!

For Jennifer Jennings. I'm in awe of all you do, and I'm so grateful to have you in my life. Our shared passion for animals brings me so much joy.

For Michelle Kudrick. Thank you for giving me a fun break from writing now and then. You bring out my 'outside self,' and I'm looking forward to lots of seasons on the trails!

Love you ladies!

For my readers. Thank you for your patience while my broken arm healed enough to finally be able to finish this book! I hate that it had to be delayed, but we're back on track now, and I hope you love this one as much as I do! And a special thanks to Pollyanna Stewart for helping my characters survive (mostly) Alaska!

Glossary

Aegis, The — Society of human warriors dedicated to protecting the world from evil.

Agimortus — A trigger for the breaking of the Horsemen's Seals. An agimortus can be a symbol engraved or branded upon the host person or object, or it can be an event.

Camborian — The human offspring of a parent under the possession of a demon at the time of conception. Camborians may or may not possess supernatural powers that vary in type and strength, depending on the species of demon inhabiting the body of the parent at the time of conception.

Council — All demon species and breeds are governed by a Council that makes laws and metes out punishment for individual members of their species or breed.

Decipula — A marble-sized trap designed to capture and contain the souls of dead demons until Sheoul-gra can be rebuilt.

Daemonica — The demon bible and basis for dozens of demon religions. Should they come to pass, its prophecies regarding the Apocalypse will ensure that the Four Horsemen fight on the side of evil.

Dermoire — Located on every Seminus demon's right arm from his hand to his throat, a *dermoire* consists of glyphs that reveal the bearer's paternal history. Each individual's personal glyph develops at the top of the *dermoire*, on the throat.

Fallen Angel — Believed to be evil by most humans, fallen angels can be grouped into two categories: True Fallen and Unfallen. Unfallen angels have been cast from Heaven and are earthbound, living a life in which they are neither truly good nor truly evil. In this state, they can, rarely, earn their way back into Heaven. Or they can choose to enter Sheoul, the demon realm, in order to complete their fall and become True Fallens, taking their places as demons at Satan's side.

Guardians — Warriors for The Aegis, trained in combat techniques, weapons, and magic. Upon induction into The Aegis, all Guardians are inked with an enchanted Aegis shield tattoo. Each tattoo is tailored to its wearer, imparting gifts such as night vision or the ability to see through demon invisibility enchantments.

Harrowgate — Vertical portals, invisible to humans, which demons use to travel between locations on Earth and Sheoul. Very few beings own, or can summon, their own personal Harrowgates.

Ligorial — Binding thread for angels. Restricts the use of their powers. Worn loose but will physically bind an angel at the whim of the Ligorial's user.

Marked Sentinel — Humans charmed by angels and tasked with protecting a vital artifact. Sentinels are immortal and immune to harm. Only angels (fallen included) can injure or kill a Sentinel. Their existence is a closely guarded secret.

Memitim — Angels assigned to protect humans called Primori. Once earthbound until they completed their duties and ascended to Heaven, all Memitim now belong to their own Order and may reside in Heaven or on Earth.

Primori — Humans and demons whose lives are fated to affect the world in some crucial way. Their status is kept hidden from most, even in Heaven.

Radiant — The most powerful class of Heavenly angel in existence, save Metatron. Unlike other angels, Radiants can wield unlimited power in all realms and can travel freely through Sheoul, with very few exceptions. The designation is awarded to only one angel at a time. Two can never exist simultaneously, and they cannot be destroyed except by God, Satan, or the Heavenly Council of Orders. The fallen angel equivalent is called a Shadow Angel. See: Shadow Angel.

Regent — Head of the local Aegis cell.

ReSpawned — Demons whose souls were returned to their former bodies and released from Sheoul-gra when Azagoth destroyed the realm. The freshly respawned demons were sent into Azagoth's war with the fallen angel, Moloch. Millions were killed, their souls free to wreak havoc, but those who didn't die became known as ReSpawned.

S'genesis — Final maturation cycle for Seminus demons. Occurs at one hundred years of age. A post-*s'genesis* male is capable of procreation and possesses the ability to shapeshift into the male of any demon species.

Shadow Angel — The most powerful class of fallen angel in existence, save Satan. Unlike other fallen angels, a Shadow Angel can wield unlimited power in all realms, and they possess the ability to gain entrance into Heaven. The designation is awarded to only one fallen angel at a time, and they cannot exist without their equivalent, a Radiant. A Shadow Angel cannot be destroyed except by God, Satan, or the Heavenly Council of Orders. The Heavenly angel equivalent is called a Radiant. See: Radiant.

Sheoul — Demon realm. Located deep in the bowels of the Earth, accessible only by Harrowgates.

Sheoul-gra — Until its destruction, it was a holding tank for the souls of evil humans and demons. A purgatory that existed independently of Sheoul, it was overseen by Azagoth, also known as the Grim Reaper. It is currently under reconstruction.

Sheoulic — Universal demon language spoken by all, although many species also speak their own language.

Ter'taceo — Demons who can pass as humans either because their species is naturally human in appearance or because they can shapeshift into human form.

Quanimus — The part of the soul that can connect with the energy around it, including from other dimensions. According to some, everyone—including humans and animals—possesses a *quanimus*, but not everyone can access it. The access point for all magical and supernatural abilities, it is an organ unseen but capable of great power, similar to the heart, except that it circulates spiritual energy instead of blood.

Ufelskala — A scoring system for demons based on their degree of evil. All supernatural creatures and evil humans can be categorized into five Tiers, with the Fifth Tier comprised of the worst of the wicked.

Demonica Family Tree

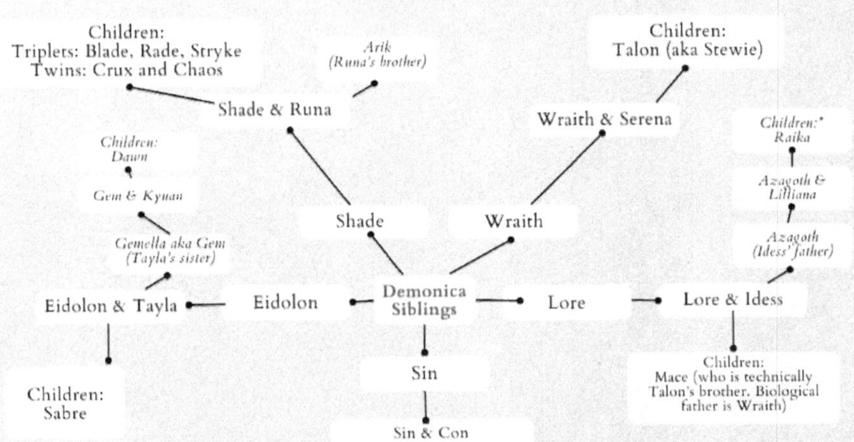

Four Horsemen Family Tree

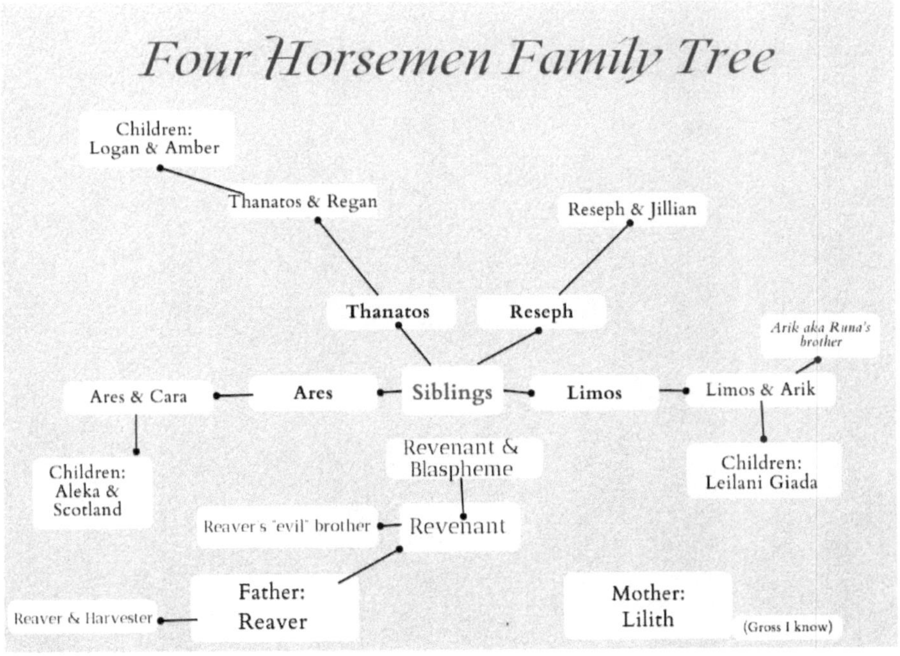

Prologue

A mere century ago, if someone had told Harvester she'd enjoy baby-sitting, she'd have decapitated them and impaled their head on a pike.

But damn, she loved her grandchildren, and she volunteered to watch them whenever she got the chance. Her only regret was that she wasn't their biological grandmother. No, their bio-granny was a twisted, evil succubus, and the very *thought* of Lilith brought bile to Harvester's mouth. That skank didn't deserve such delightful children in her life.

Watching Aleka and little Scotland play, their red heads bopping in their mother's flower beds under the watchful eyes of a couple of hell-hounds, warmed her heart, which had been frozen for so many centuries. She just wished Reaver could be here. But no, he'd been restricted to Heaven while the angelic leadership contemplated punishment for his *minor* role in the destruction of Sheoul-gra, the underworld realm that'd once held the souls of dead demons and evil humans.

Fools. Reaver, one of the most powerful angels to have ever existed, shouldn't have to explain his actions. The ruling body needed to get over itself. It had been nearly a decade since Azagoth destroyed Sheoul-gra, and Heaven hadn't dished out judgment or punishment yet.

Well, there had been judgment. Lots of it. The holier-than-thou crowd, which consisted of the majority of Celestials, excelled at looking down their perfect noses at others.

Angels were the worst. Which was why Harvester didn't count herself as one of them, even though she'd recently had her wings and

Grace restored. Before that, she'd spent most of her thousands of years of life as a fallen angel, and frankly, it was hard to shed that past. She'd been powerful. And fearful of nothing—except her father, Satan, anyway.

Now, she was a full-fledged Heavenly angel again, but her halo was tarnished and mangled—something other Celestials never let her forget.

Which gave her some insight into Revenant's plight. Like her, Reaver's brother had been born an angel. But unlike her, he was born in Sheoul, the demon name for Hell, and raised at Satan's side. He'd never even set foot in Heaven until a few years ago. But thousands of years of living in the demon realm had corrupted him, and he wasn't welcome there. The joke was on Heaven, though, because Revenant ran Sheoul now, and he held a grudge.

Harvester couldn't stand the guy, but she could sympathize with his position. He was an angel…yet *not* an angel…and scorned by those in Heaven *and* Hell. He was, in fact, trapped in Sheoul the way Reaver was trapped in Heaven. But hopefully not for much longer. Surely, the Council of Orders would give Reaver and Revenant stern warnings and leave it at that.

"G-ma!" Scotty shouted and waved from where she sat in the crook of a tree, much higher up than most five-year-olds could achieve. The child was part monkey. "Can I have a cookie?"

"What did your mom say?"

A warm breeze ruffled Scotty's hair, which probably hadn't seen a comb today. She reminded Harvester of Scotty's favorite Disney princess, Merida, with her unruly locks and rebellious nature. Aleka, as different from her sister as night and day, favored the free-thinking Disney princess, Belle, with her curiosity and love of books.

The old Harvester would have hated that she knew anything about Disney princesses. The new Harvester enjoyed watching the movies with her granddaughters. She always rooted for the villains. Somehow, she could identify with their plights.

Except for Cruella de Vil. What a cunt.

"Mom says we can have as many cookies as we want," Scotty said matter-of-factly.

Suspicious, Harvester glanced over at seven-year-old Aleka, who was as bad at lying as Scotty was good at it. "Is that true?"

Shaking her head, Aleka kneeled to pick a couple of flowers that lined the boundary surrounding the island's Harrowgate. "Mom said we can have one after lunch and one after dinner."

Scotty stuck out her tongue at her sister before turning a sugary smile on Harvester. "Pretty please?"

Harvester couldn't resist any of her grandchildren, but she tapped her chin and pretended to think about it. "Hmm, I don't know…"

"Pleeeeeease?" Scotty clutched her belly with the dramatic flair of a stage actor. "You don't want me to die of hunger, do you?"

"You won't die of hunger. You're immortal, sweetheart." The breeze picked up, stirring the gardens with a fresh wave of fragrant marine air. Harvester had always loved the way Greece smelled like sand, sea, and herbs, layered over the peppery notes of an ancient, bloody history. "I suppose you can have *one*. But you have to promise to eat all your dinner."

"Even if it's yucky?"

"Even if it's yucky."

"Okay, I promise," Scotty swore solemnly. The girl had inherited Ares's faithful conviction to keep his word when he gave it. She might be admirably skilled at lying, but when she made a promise, she kept it.

Standing, Aleka swept dirt off her skirt. "I don't want one. I told Rath I'd help him polish his horns this afternoon." She clapped her hands in excitement. "They grew another inch! The left one is still shorter, though, and he's all emo and sensitive about it. So, if you see him, don't mention it, okay?"

Ares and Cara had adopted the goatlike Ramreel demon as a toddler and raised him as Aleka and Scotty's older brother. He was a randy teen now, proud of the horns that had just started to emerge at his temples.

"I won't say a word."

Aleka darted off toward the guard quarters, where Rath had recently moved when the first nubbins of his horns had come in. He'd grown up in the main house with his sisters until, in accordance with Ramreel tradition, he'd "joined the herd," leaving to reside with the other Ramreel warriors on the island to begin training as a member of the island's elite security force.

"G-*maaaaaa*!" Scotty swung her little legs in frustration, her sandaled feet clicking against the tree trunk. "You said I can have a cookie."

"I did say that, didn't I? Hop down, and we'll get one."

"Can't I eat it here?"

Harvester sighed. Of her five grandchildren, Scotty was the most precocious. Fiercely independent, strong-willed, and mischievous, she kept everyone on their toes. Aleka was the curious, studious one. Leilani was the outgoing, social girly-girl who loved fashion and cameras. Logan was easygoing, steady, and reliable. Amber was contemplative and observant, wise beyond her years and, frankly, a little unsettling. You never knew what would come out of her mouth.

You never knew what would come out of Scotty's mouth, either, but for entirely different reasons. Harvester loved the spontaneity of the child's unpredictable behavior. Harvester figured that if she ever had a daughter, she'd be like Scotty.

"Fine. I'll get you one." She gestured at the two hellhounds lurking nearby. "You two mutts keep an eye on Scotty for a second."

Scotty giggled. "Grams, I don't need protection."

No, she didn't. This island was as safe as anywhere in all the realms. Besides belonging to the Horseman known as War, it was defended by hellhounds, Ramreels, and hundreds of earthbound angels known as Memitim. Scotty was as safe as she could be.

Harvester headed toward the house, and to her surprise, Scotty gathered her toy bow and leaped out of the tree.

"Are you coming inside?" Harvester asked.

"Nuh-uh," Scotty said, chin up in defiance. "I'm going to the beach."

"Not alone, you're not," Harvester told her with a stern wag of her finger. "You wait here, and I'll be right back." She hurried inside the mansion, found the freshly baked cookies Lilliana had set out, and grabbed a couple. She paused at the refrigerator, wondering if she should take drinks to the beach as well. Scotty loved orange soda—

A bloodcurdling scream shattered her thoughts.

Scotty.

Harvester flashed outside. Her granddaughter wasn't there. Neither were the hellhounds.

"Scotty?"

Fear made her voice shrill as she called out again. "Scotty!"

In the distance, snarls and pained yelps mingled with the crash of ocean waves. The beach! Terror ripped through Harvester as she darted to the edge of the rugged cliffside, where Scotty's little footprints ended.

Harvester's heart stopped. A swarm of ghastbats blackened the view of the sandy shore below, the gaps between their leathery bodies revealing a couple of hellhounds, their snapping jaws and massive claws violently snatching the leathery demons out of the air.

Ghastbats? Here?

Didn't matter. The mystery of how they'd accessed the island would have to wait. All that mattered right now was finding her granddaughter.

"Scotty!" she screamed again.

Frustrated by the churning horde obscuring her view, she popped her wings and lifted into the air, desperately scanning the water, the cliffs, the sand.

To her left, a hellhound roared in agony as some hideous creature lit into it in a flurry of claws and teeth. What *was* that thing?

Wait. No. It couldn't be.

But it was.

A *mordaemon*. A monster that stole immortality with a single bite, they were one of only a handful of creatures that struck terror into the hearts of every immortal. Including Harvester. But why was it here? And how had it accessed the island?

It hurled itself away from the fallen hound, its sickly pale, spiky wings creating whirlwinds of sand. A chunk of hellhound flesh hung from its gaping maw.

Sensing weakness, a hundred ghastbats descended upon the injured, newly mortal hellhound, their claws and razor-sharp fangs tearing it apart as it shrieked in the kind of soul-deep agony few understood.

Poor bastard.

Reaching for one of her most powerful weapons, she blasted the *mordaemon* with a stream of molten Heavenly lightning. The air went still and heavy with electricity as the demon lit up from the inside, its skin sizzling, its eyes smoking. The thing's body swelled, vibrating the atmosphere so violently that stones broke free from the cliffs and tumbled to the shore. Then, in a whoosh of flame, it winked out of the human realm and back to Hell, where it belonged.

In the distance, the island's alarm bells rang out. Reinforcements would arrive within seconds. But that was too long.

Oh, Scotty, please, please be okay…

Frantically, Harvester scoured the beach for any sign of the child, picking through the broken bodies of the dead and dying ghastbats and the shredded remains of the unfortunate hellhound.

Nothing.

Nothing, dammit!

But over near an outcropping of boulders, another hellhound crouched on the beach, injured and bleeding, snapping at the eagle-sized bats as they attacked from above. And sticking out from beneath the hound's massive body, a skinny, pale arm, lying limp on the hot sand.

No!

Harvester banked hard and crash-landed on the beach next to the beast. It swung its shaggy head around with a surprised snarl, its jaws dripping with ghastbat blood and ragged bits of their black flesh.

"It's just me, you mangy mutt!" Hastily, she zapped ghastbats out of the sky with bolts of lightning, clearing the airspace for a protective force field. It only took a couple of heartbeats to secure an evil-proof dome above them, but it wouldn't last for long.

The hellhound, whose name she thought was Ogre, lurched to his feet on unsteady legs, lifting his body off the tiny one he protected.

Scotty lay lifeless on the ground, the sand soaking up her blood as it drained through dozens of deep, gaping wounds. Shattered bone and organs spilled out of the gashes. But as bad as all the injuries were, one wound stood out, filling Harvester with icy fingers of dread.

The ragged punctures in her ribs, oozing with green fluid, were from the *mordaemon*.

A cry escaped Harvester as she fell to her knees and gathered the child's limp body into her arms. Scotty's life force, so weak that Harvester could barely feel it, faded to almost nothing and began to flicker.

There was no time. Not even enough to get Scotty to Underworld General. Not that they could do anything.

She was going to die. The *mordaemon* had seen to that.

"No, baby," Harvester croaked. "I won't let you."

Ruthlessly ignoring the sounds of battle all around her, Harvester reached deep inside herself and seized her very essence. What she was about to do was forbidden. A grievous offense.

She didn't care. There was nothing she wouldn't do for Reaver and his family.

Tears rolled down her face as she drew out a tiny strand of her Grace and channeled it into Scotty.

For a moment, nothing happened. The Grace seemed lost, meandering around inside the girl's spiritual body, unable to connect with her soul. Was it too late?

A hellhound released a mournful howl, its haunting call sending a chill up Harvester's spine. Was it sad about its dead packmate, or did it sense that Scotty was on the verge of death?

Please, no. Please!

As if she'd heard Harvester's plea, Scotty gasped, and her bloodless face filled with color. *It worked.*

A sob of relief escaped Harvester as she cut off the flow of Grace. She'd given Scotty a minuscule amount—a mere hundredth of a percent of Harvester's total well of power, perhaps.

Not enough for any other angel to sense it inside the girl. She hoped.

Reaver would likely sense the loss inside Harvester, but he'd approve of what she'd done. Scotty would have died without the infusion.

Now, Harvester's Grace was part of her, woven into her life force. Scotty would be more powerful and resilient than before.

But…and it was a big *but*, should Harvester's Grace ever be taken from Scotty, she would die. A *mordaemon's* bite was always fatal.

In Harvester's arms, the child stirred as her body healed. Loud groans turned to soft whimpers as her bones knitted together, and the gashes in her flesh sealed. Harvester knew too well that the healing process was sometimes more agonizing than the initial injury, and she held Scotty tightly, doing her best to ease her thrashing.

Eventually, Scotty quieted, and her big, hazel-green eyes blinked open.

"G-ma?" Scotty looked around, seemingly confused by the sight of ghastbats dive-bombing the hellhound reinforcements charging down the cliffside. "What happened?"

"I don't know, sweetheart. But we're safe." Even more hellhounds phased onto the beach to join the massacre, so many that the sand disappeared beneath the writhing, slashing beasts. Screeches of rage and pain filled the air as the hounds tore the ghastbats apart, though not always before losing a chunk of flesh or suffering a pierced eyeball. How *had* the ghastbats and *mordaemon* gotten here? "Can you tell me what happened?"

Scotty wriggled out of Harvester's arms and scrambled to her feet, her little fists clenched defiantly, as if she wanted to take on the creatures herself. "The monsters came. What are they?"

"They're called ghastbats." Harvester watched two hounds rip one in half during a round of tug-of-war. "They normally live in Sheoul. I don't know why they're here or where they came from."

Scotty's face turned bright red, and she looked down at her feet.

Shit. Harvester reached out and took the girl's hand. "Scotty?"

"They…they came out of the Harrowgate," she whispered.

Alarm stabbed Harvester right in the heart. A gate malfunction could expose the entire island to the worst kinds of demons. Her family would be in incredible danger.

"They flew out of the gate by themselves?" That shouldn't be possible. Ghastbats couldn't operate the controls.

"It's not my fault," Scotty cried, yanking her hand out of Harvester's. "She told me to open it. I thought it was going to be a surprise!"

The hair on the back of Harvester's neck stood up as her wings shot out and lifted her to her feet. Fear made her voice harsh. "Who told you to open it?"

Scotty buried her face in her hands. "My friend," she mumbled between sniffles.

"Your invisible one?" At Scotty's nod, a frisson of suspicion skittered across the surface of Harvester's mind.

Dammit. This was exactly why she'd told Ares and Cara to get a handle on the invisible-friend situation. Invisible friends might be common coping mechanisms for human children, but immortal children, especially those with powerful parents, were at high risk of being targeted by supernaturals with evil intentions.

"Listen to me, Scotty," she said. "This person is not your friend."

Scotty started bawling, and Harvester, who rarely experienced guilt, felt her heart squeeze painfully hard. "I'm sorry, sweetie. But she's not—"

"I know!" Scotty shouted. "She made those things attack me. I jumped off the cliff to escape, but I don't remember what happened after that."

She sniffed and wiped her nose with the back of her hand. "Lilu said…she said, 'Goodbye, you snot-nosed insect.'" Her lower lip trembled. "She's mean."

She was also as good as dead once Harvester got a hold of the bitch. This Lilu person must—

Harvester's train of thought took an abrupt detour at a sudden, devastating suspicion. "Did you say, Lilu? That's her name?"

Scotty slapped her hand across her mouth. "She told me not to tell," she mumbled.

Of course, she had. *Lilu* wouldn't have wanted anyone to research that foul name. A name that harkened back to Mesopotamian demon times. A name whose female form, Lilitu, was eventually translated.

Into Lilith.

Lilith.

Fury steamed through Harvester's veins. But it didn't make sense. Lilith had died years ago, and her soul was sent to Sheoul-gra a couple of years before the purgatory's destruction. Yes, Azagoth had demolished Sheoul-gra and released billions of demonic spirits to wage war, but surely he hadn't been stupid enough to release *Lilith*. Not when the responsible thing would have been to destroy her soul.

But then, the Grim Reaper had been inconsolable and irrational when his very pregnant wife disappeared, kidnapped by an enemy bent on vengeance. He would have used every powerful demon he controlled to get her back…including Lilith.

Shit. If Lilith was alive—corporeal—again, that bitch would want to take revenge on her Horsemen offspring. And how better to torture them than to kill their children?

Harvester thought about the time her grandson, Logan, son of the Horseman known as Death, had been attacked by a demonic storm. If not for a hellhound protector, he might have died.

Had that been Lilith's work as well? Had she found a way to contact Scotty through some sort of telepathy? She could have been tricking the girl for months. Maybe even longer, if Scotty hadn't been truthful about how long she'd had an "invisible friend."

"It's okay, Scotty." Harvester sent a wave of lightning bolts at a swarm of ghastbats, watching them fall from the sky. "I'm going to get rid of Lilu for you, okay?"

The green flecks in Scotty's eyes glittered darkly. "Are you going to kill her?"

My, my, she was a bloodthirsty little thing, wasn't she? So like Harvester.

"Eventually, my dear. I promise you, she will die for what she's done. But right now, I'm going to block her from your mind." She started to reach into Scotty's head, but the little girl grabbed her wrist in an iron grip.

"Please don't tell Mommy and Daddy."

Harvester rarely experienced moral dilemmas. She'd spent too much time as a fallen angel to waste her energy on deciding what was wrong or right. She just did what was best for her and those she loved, ethics be damned.

But in this case, she didn't know what was best.

She desperately wished Reaver were here to help, but wishing was a waste of time. She could spare a few seconds to curse the angels who had confined her mate to Heaven, though.

"Please," Scotty begged. "I don't want them to know I'm so dumb."

"You aren't dumb, sweetheart."

"Yes, I am." She wiped her runny nose with the back of her hand again. "Aleka's the smart one. That's why I must be good at fighting, like Mace and Blade. I need to protect Aleka while she reads her dusty old books." When she blinked her big, watery eyes at Harvester, her heart melted.

"Please, G-ma. They can't know I opened a gate."

They couldn't know Harvester had given Scotty some of her Grace, either. Grace, in very small amounts, was only to be sacrificed to humans. Too much could go wrong when an angel's essence was injected into supernaturals. And if the recipient of the Grace turned evil, it could provide a conduit for evil into the donor angel, and even into Heaven itself. If anyone learned of the truth, Scotty would be targeted by angels who would steal the Grace for themselves, or by demons who prized Grace as one of the rarest, most powerful spell-casting elements.

It was such a tiny amount. Undetectable. No one will know. And she'll be stronger for it. So, it's a good thing.

"I'll tell you what," Harvester said. "They're going to know something happened. That can't be changed. But they don't need to know that you got hurt, okay?" At least, they didn't need to know the full extent of Scotty's injuries. She was fine, and there was no sense in freaking them out.

Scotty's eyes narrowed as she considered her options. "They're going to be mad at me for opening the gate."

"Perhaps," Harvester murmured, but she knew they'd be far more upset that someone, probably Lilith, had gotten to one of their daughters.

Maybe Harvester should put a mind shield on all her grandchildren.

Because if Lilith really was responsible, she wasn't going to give up.

Not ever.

Chapter 1

13 years ago.

This is it.

Scotty, her face streaked with blood and her clothes shredded by demon claws and teeth, stared down the last obstacle in the test she needed to pass to join the Demonic Activity Response Team's Special Forces Division. If she took out the ogre in front of her, her dream of working with Blade and Mace in their elite unit would come true.

What if they don't want me?

She shook her head clear of that idiotic thought. Sure, it had crossed her mind a few times over the last twenty-four months, pretty much from the very first day she'd begun regular training with the two. Unfortunately, she had still been in school, while they'd been employed by DART for years, so she hadn't been able to do anything but train. No missions, no real battles. Also, no pay.

You're too young, they'd all said. From her parents to her aunts and uncles, to even Mace and Blade, they told her she wasn't ready. Didn't matter that she was trouncing trained Ramreel warriors twice her size by the age of fourteen. Everyone insisted she needed to finish school and turn eighteen. Her father had flipped out *hard* that one time she'd said she was going to drop out of school and join DART.

So, the very day she graduated from Hellmouth Academy, she'd moved out of her parents' island manor and into her own private residence next door and applied to DART.

Obviously, they'd hired her. That had been the plan since she was old enough to say, "I don't wanna be a dumb doctor or astronaut. I wanna be a DART agent."

But a spot in the Special Forces Division wasn't a given. There were tests, and if she failed, she'd be washed out of the running and sent to a different DART department.

Screw that. She didn't want to push paper, work in a lab, or be put on a low-risk investigative team. *Bo-ring.* She wanted to be on a special forces team. She wanted to be on *Mace and Blade's* team. They were the best of the best. Seminus demons with extraordinary fighting skills and innate healing—and killing—abilities. And she wouldn't settle for anything or anyone less.

"You gonna take down that ogre, or just stare at him?" Mace called from the spectator area.

The ogre, a pretty decent guy who worked for her father and volunteered now and then to play the big-boss-final-battle role for DART trials, tapped his foot impatiently. Each tap in the arena's sand made the ground beneath her quake.

"Me does not have all day," he grunted.

She grinned. "Me, either. I have a victory party to attend."

They met in a clash of training swords and mallets, and two hours later, Scotty finally won the match by putting the ogre on his back.

Everyone who'd come to watch flowed down from the bleachers to congratulate her. Her aunts and uncles, cousins, family friends, pretty much everyone. Even her mother's hellhound protector gave Scotty a gross, sloppy kiss.

After she showered, there was cake, balloons, streamers, and all the expected celebratory nonsense—which she appreciated. But when Mace and Blade took her for the promised video game marathon at their place, well, *that* was what she'd been waiting for. An all-nighter with pizza, popcorn, and energy drinks.

It would be her first time spending the night with them.

Butterflies flitted in her stomach at the thought. Of course, nothing inappropriate would happen. They were all just friends. The boys had never even looked at her sketchily, which she'd assured her father over and over.

But what if they did? What if, while she sat between them on the sofa, they reached over and took her hands? What if one of them leaned over and kissed her? How would the other one react?

Heat flooded her cheeks as she set their drinks on the coffee table and grabbed a game controller.

"You sure you're not too tired for this?" Mace asked. "You had a long day."

She loved how they looked out for her, even if she didn't need it.

"So did you," she pointed out. "You guys went through the first six hours of the trial with me." The guys had been part of the teamwork evaluation portion of the tests, designed to ensure they all worked well together.

"I still think it was stupid to make us go through it," Blade said. "They know how well we work together."

True. All of them, along with their brothers, sisters, and cousins, had been training for the End of Days since they could pull themselves up in a crib. Heck, the very first toy she remembered getting was a plastic sword. Then, when Scotty was ten, she'd been paired up with Mace and Blade during a training session, and within minutes, it had been clear that the three of them were special. Individually, they were all excellent fighters, but together, they formed one powerful, well-oiled unit, each with unique abilities that synced with the others. Their strengths complemented the others' weaknesses. They were a dream team.

Their first mission would exceed DART's expectations. She just knew it.

A door slammed, and a moment later, heavy footsteps grew louder, until one of Blade's triplet brothers, Rade, entered the room, his dark, unnerving gaze fixed on her.

"I heard you're officially on DART's payroll now," he said in his signature deadpan voice. "Congratulations on being stuck with those two."

"Hey," she said, annoyed. "I'm happy to be part of their team."

Rade nodded absently. He wasn't a team player, and most attempts to force him to work with others ended in disaster. But what made him difficult to be around also made him DART's best interrogator. "You guys gonna set some ground rules?"

"Ground rules?" Mace chugged half a can of an energy drink. "What kind of ground rules?"

"Like, the romantic kind."

"We're going on missions, not dates, bro," Blade said. "I doubt we have to worry about Scotty demanding to mate bond with one of us while we're investigating the gory site of a brutal demon massacre."

"Exactly. That would be ridiculous." She grinned. "I'd have to bond with *both* of them while we're investigating a brutal demon massacre."

She'd been joking—she loved messing with Rade, who was as humor-impaired as one of his other brothers, Stryke. But her joke must not have landed right, because Blade and Mace looked startled. Rade just gave her a dead-eyed stare. She could never tell if he thought she was an idiot, or if it was just Rade being Rade.

"Two Sems can't bond with one female." Rade's voice was flat as his gaze.

"I was kidding. Sheesh." But seriously? She'd have to choose only one of them? No way. That would be impossible. Call her greedy, but she would want them both. "Just curious, but how do you know that?"

"I know Sems who've tried. All three did the ritual, and fate only chose one of the males."

Ah, fate. Her father always said that strong leaders made hard choices and didn't leave anything to fate.

But her grandpa, Reaver, had pulled her aside once, after her father had given her the choice-fate lecture *again*. "Scotty, someday you're going to face an impossible decision. There will be no winner if you choose. So, let fate make the choice." He'd lifted her off the ground and hugged her tightly. "Sometimes, the right decision is the one you don't make."

He was apparently such a strong believer in fate that he'd sent Mace and Blade gifts of daggers with the word *FATE* engraved in the hilts when they were hired by DART.

Rade looked at each of them in turn. "Maybe you guys should make an agreement not to get involved now. Save yourselves the trouble later."

She was about to say it wasn't necessary when both Mace and Blade nodded.

"Probably smart," Blade said.

Mace responded with an agreeable, "Yup. We gotta swear to be friends only."

They both gave her expectant looks, and her heart sank. She'd kind of thought that they'd all just…be together. Always. For everything. In every way.

She'd been a fool. She was exactly what Aleka always said she was. A silly girl who lived in another reality.

"Yeah," she muttered. "Friends only."

Mace produced his *FATE* blade and slashed his palm before handing the knife to her. "I swear…"

Chapter 2

Present day.

The stench of blood, pain, and evil hung in the air like an acidic fog as Blade crept through shadowy rooms and narrow halls, his boots making the old church floorboards creak. Ahead, the outline of a mystical doorway beckoned him with a flickering glow, promising an epic battle with supernatural creatures and—

"I think I'm ready to lose my virginity."

Blade tripped over his feet at Scotty's announcement. The concealed doorway in the basement of the abandoned church forgotten, he wheeled around to face her. His cousin and DART teammate, Mace, popped upright from where he'd been bent over the body of a demon, his knife dripping with the monster's blood.

Mace glanced over at Blade. "Did she say what I think she said?"

"You heard right." Scotty made her summoned sword—also dripping with greasy, inky demon blood—disappear. "My birthday is only two weeks away. I don't want to be a thirty-year-old virgin."

Unsure what to say, Blade and Mace just stared at her as she stood in a dust mote-infested beam of sickly light that squeezed between the slats of a broken, boarded-up window. They'd been sent to root out a nest of demons causing trouble for the new property owners, but given the rundown condition of the building, Blade figured the demons were the least of their problems. Black mold and the possibility of the roof collapsing in on them seemed like more pressing concerns.

Huffing, Scotty jammed her fists onto her hips, her bare, toned arms streaked with gore. She looked like a badass in black, from her leggings made from the impenetrable, flexible scales of a Sobek demon's head, to her combat boots and form-fitting tank that showed off her sleek, muscular physique. A weapons harness and various sheaths criss-crossed her body, ensuring she always had a killing tool at the ready for every occasion, every species of demon, or, in the rare event that her ability to summon a sword failed.

"Well?" she prompted. "Will you guys help me?"

Help her? Lust flushed through Blade's body. He'd fantasized about being with Scotty for years, and what she'd just asked for was basically his dream come true.

There was only one problem with that.

Years ago, Mace and Blade swore an oath that they would never—*ever*—have sex with their best friend. The three of them had been tight since they were kids, first playing together, then training together, and now working together. Their bond was too important to fuck up with sex.

But he couldn't help imagining what it would be like to be with her just once. To agree to her shocking request. His hands would probably shake as he peeled off her clothes, and his heart would race at the sight of her naked, hard body. He'd seen her in a bikini a million times, but he'd sell his soul to know what secrets she hid under the stretchy fabric. Were her breasts sprinkled with as many freckles as her nose and cheeks? Was she smooth between her thighs, or were her curls as red as her fiery mane?

Would she let him worship her with his mouth and tongue before he sank into her willing body?

Or would Mace be the one who got to be with her for her first time?

A hot surge of jealousy tore through him, followed by instant shame. They'd sworn their pact for this exact reason, long before Blade had developed feelings for her. He was a jackass for hoping for something that couldn't happen.

He looked over at Mace, who slowly, methodically, wiped the blade of his knife on his pants and slipped it into the sheath at his hip.

"Scotty," Mace said, his voice low and rough, "we swore an oath. We can't help you."

She blinked, confused, and then laughed. "Oh, my gods. I wasn't asking you guys to help me like *that*." She made an *ick* face, which was kind of insulting. "I want you to help me pick the right guy. Maybe someone from DART, but not our Brussels office. If things don't work out, I don't want to have to see him all the time afterward, you know?"

Okay, so that was an icepick to the heart. Blade had wanted Scotty for so long and had suffered through watching her date, even though she'd never actually slept with any of the guys. Now, she wanted him to find someone for her to fuck? To take her virginity?

Hell, no.

"Uh…" Mace swallowed, making his personal Seminus symbol on his throat, an eagle in flight, appear to flap its wings. Like his biological father, Wraith, the male was never at a loss for words. But he looked absolutely gobsmacked now. "I don't…I mean, shouldn't you be the one making that decision?"

"Come *on*." She rolled her hazel eyes so hard she probably got a glimpse of her brain. "I have the worst taste in males. You've seen the idiots I've dated. Remember Shawn? And Adam?"

Oh, yeah, Blade remembered. She'd met Adam, a human, in the produce section of a grocery store and liked that he hadn't known who she was. When she told him, three dates in, he'd freaked out and ghosted her.

But Shawn…*that* fucker had known full well that she was the daughter of Ares, the Horseman of the Apocalypse known as War. They'd met at a friend's party, and as a half-demon who ran a vodka distillery, he'd been enamored with her. Unfortunately, his fascination had turned to obsession, and it had taken a visit from Blade and Mace, a few broken bones, and the threat of all four Horsemen knocking on his door to convince him to leave her alone.

Sure, she would have destroyed the guy herself, but they'd beaten her to it.

Blade waffled. "I don't know, Scotty." On one hand, it would kill him to know that he'd played a part in selecting a guy to fuck her. On the other, he could make sure the guy wasn't an asshole. She deserved someone worthy. Someone who would cherish every second with her.

Someone Blade might not be tempted to kill afterward.

Riiiight. Who was he fooling? He'd crave the destruction of any male who took what Blade desired. He was kinda like his dad, Shade, in that way. No one touched what was important to him.

Scotty jammed her fists onto her hips again, as if this time she'd look less cute and more serious. "What's the matter? You owe me. I've hooked you guys up with a million females. Remember Sasha? And Triska? My friend Lushus?"

"Ah, Lushus." Mace grinned. "She was always game for anything."

Blade grunted in agreement. The curvy, insatiable half-succubus had been hot for both. They'd barely kept up with her, and they were freaking incubi who needed sex with a female to survive.

"Whatever happened to her?" Blade asked. "She up and disappeared about a year ago."

"Ugh." Scotty shook her head in dismay. "She decided to 'embrace her human side,' so she joined a cult and now only gives it up to the nine leaders. They're trying to fuck the evil out of her or some shit. I'm sure it's totally legit," she said dryly. "Now, back to my problem. Are you guys going to help me, or what?"

No way.

But, man, she had that muley look on her face that said she'd get what she wanted, one way or another. Mace saw it too, and his expression was resigned as he glanced over at Blade.

Shit.

"Yeah," Mace muttered as he delivered a brutal kick to a dead demon's skull. "I guess I'm in."

Not wanting to seem petty or raise questions, Blade nodded woodenly. "Same."

Scotty gave them a bright smile. "You guys are the best."

Mace practically preened at the compliment. Dude soaked up flattery like a sponge. But Blade only felt sick to his stomach because he knew what would happen.

His dream female was about to plunge him right into his worst nightmare.

Boom.

The rhythmic thump of hard-rock music reverberated through the upper level of the complex Mace shared with his cousins, making his head pound and his body pulse.

Boom.

Dammit. His *cock* should be what was pulsing right now.

He pulled away from the gorgeous, ebony-haired, dark-skinned female he'd been *this close* to stripping naked. Cursing, he swiped up the *Deadpool* T-shirt he'd just dropped to the floor.

"Sorry," he told her. "I'll be right back."

Alayna pouted prettily and sank onto the bed, her lime-green miniskirt hiking up her thighs enough to reveal a tantalizing hint of pink silk panties. "I'll wait. But hurry. You promised me all night."

"Feel free to get started without me." Summoning his most dazzling grin, he shot her a flirty wink that charmed the pants off all the females. "Check out the toys in the corner chest if you need inspiration."

The thumping got even louder, the beat more grating, and Mace lost his smile *and* his erection. He donned his shirt so violently that he ripped a couple of the seams as he stormed down the industrial-wide hallway in search of the source of the racket.

All the rooms in what used to be a technical innovations complex were soundproofed, but for some reason, music was dampened in parts of the main building and amplified in others. *Others* being the upstairs living quarters.

As expected, the doorway to his youngest cousin's room was where noise went to die. You'd never know Crux lived here unless he was playing video games in the game room or raiding the fridge. No sounds came from Rade's room, either, but that guy never made any noise. He was like a lone hellhound on a hunt: watchful, patient, and silent...until he attacked.

And then, it was his prey that made the noise.

Mace didn't bother glancing at the doorway to Logan's room. Logan, son of the Horseman known as Death, had moved in with his fiancée, Eva, a while back.

Which left two occupied suites: Blade's and Sabre's.

Mace put his money on Blade. Sabre's taste in music ran a lot less annoying. And yep, the metal frame around Blade's doorway, painted in the red and black of his favorite football club, rattled with every beat. Just like Mace's bones and teeth. What the ever-loving hell—

"Mace!"

Startled, he wheeled around, cocked and locked, ready to kick some ass. Then he felt like an idiot when he saw Crux, hunched over in the hall, his hands covering his ears. His bed-mussed, tawny hair stuck up in matted tufts, and he was wearing baggy sweats, his face pale and contorted in pain.

"Are you going in there? Tell Blade to turn down his music. My head's killing me."

Mace dropped his fists to his sides. "Still? Didn't you go to bed early last night because your head hurt?"

"Yeah."

Crux winced at a series of deep, booming drumbeats, somehow losing even more color. He now had the corpselike pallor of an *obhirrat's* maggoty insides.

Mace threw a gentle arm around his cousin's bony shoulders and guided him toward his room. "Go back to bed. I'll handle this."

With a weak nod, Crux ambled through his doorway. Poor kid. Mace remembered the hellish weeks leading up to his transition, thinking things couldn't possibly get worse. They had. Much, much worse. And any day now, the first of two maturation processes would begin for Crux, and his world would become a tsunami of misery.

Boom. Boom. *Boomfuckingboom!*

Mace pounded on Blade's door. "Yo, Blade!"

No answer. No surprise, either.

Mace threw open the door.

Blade's apartment was dark, illuminated only by the weak, rainy-day-afternoon light from the windows overlooking the backyard. His shadowy form blocked the kitchen window, where he stood motionless, palms braced on the counter, his gaze focused on something—or nothing—on the tennis court below.

Mace thumped his fist into the sound system controls on the wall. Silence. Blessed silence.

Startled, Blade tore himself away from the window, rounding on him with an angry curse. "Mace. What the hell? What do you want?"

"Peace and quiet would be nice."

"You could have just lowered the volume."

Mace shrugged. "Could've but didn't want to."

He glanced around at the living room, decorated in rich browns and mahogany, his cousin's leather furniture draped with a cream afghan that his mother made to "brighten up the place." Also brightening up—and cooling down—the place was a gleaming blue coffee table of non-melting ice, crafted by demons from Sheoul's Frigidoom region. Masumi's ornate jade vase sat on top of it, and since the bathroom door was closed, Mace assumed she was inside. Nothing unusual about any of that.

But…Blade had tossed his battle gear across the back of the sofa instead of hanging it on the rack on the wall. The guy was a neat freak— more like Stryke than he'd ever admit—so yeah, something was up.

"What's going on?"

"Nothing." Blade strode over to the bar and poured a shot of whiskey. The good shit from a demon-run distillery that produced spirits formulated to give Seminus demons a good buzz. Regular alcohol didn't usually affect them at all.

"Bullshit. You don't blast music and get all moody for no reason." This had family trouble written all over it. Mace got that. He had a dickhead of a brother, too, but the animosity between them was nothing even close to what Blade had going on with Stryke. "What did Stryke do now?"

Stryke had been estranged from the family for years, but Blade's relationship with him had been especially strained. Now, Stryke was back in their lives, and Blade was tolerating it about as well as a vampire tolerated holy water. Even his choice of alcohol was a statement. The whiskey was from one of the very few distilleries unaffiliated with Stryke's StryTech empire.

"Fuck Stryke." Blade threw back the shot of whiskey. His personal symbol, a sword broken in half, writhed angrily beneath his jaw as he swallowed. Heck, his entire *dermoire*, a paternal history of glyphs that ran down every Seminus demon's right arm all the way to the fingers, seemed to thrash in irritation.

"That doesn't answer my question."

The bathroom door swung open, and Masumi stepped out, wearing high-heeled combat boots, a naughty smile, and nothing else.

Mace stared, unable to drag his eyes away…but not because she was nude. He'd seen her naked a thousand times. Hell, she was naked more often than not. What struck him now was that Masumi, a succubus who usually sported lush black hair, deep-tan skin, and dark eyes, had assumed Scotty's red hair, milky skin, and hazel-green eyes. She'd even gotten Scotty's freckles right. Mace knew, because he'd memorized them. The ones on her left cheek that looked like Yoda were his favorite.

"Both of you tonight?" she asked, anticipation turning her low, sultry voice even huskier.

Blade gestured at the door with his shot glass. "Mace was just leaving."

"Mace was *not* just leaving." He folded his arms stubbornly across his chest. He wasn't going anywhere now that he knew what—or *who*—

was behind Blade's shitty music and shittier attitude.

Masumi's glossy red lips puckered in a sassy pout. "I see. Summon me when you're ready, Blade." An instant later, her body morphed into a stream of pearlescent liquid that arched high before pouring itself into the jade vase.

Mace never got tired of watching that. And he'd never *not* be grateful to Stryke for freeing her from her cruel master. Now, they had to find a way to free her completely. Until then, though, their mutually beneficial arrangement kept her—and the males in the house—alive.

When you were a species of demon that would die without sex, agreements like that were game changers.

"So." Mace turned back to Blade. "How long have you been fucking Masumi while she looks like Scotty?"

Blade's cheeks went slapped-ass crimson. "She doesn't look like Scotty."

"You've always been a shitty liar."

"What?" Blade shot back, temper jacked up at being called out. "You telling me she's never worn red hair for you?"

"Sure, she has." Masumi's ability to sense her summoner's moods allowed her to tailor her appearance to the situation every time. Last week, he'd needed a pick-me-up, and she'd given him a hot sci-fi fantasy by doing herself up as a green-skinned, short-haired Orion from *Star Trek*.

Blade turned back to the alcohol. "Then shut the fuck up."

As if. Shutting up wasn't a trait Mace was known for. "Do you have a thing for her?" The question came out like a demand, but Blade didn't seem to notice.

"For Masumi?" He set his empty shot glass on the counter and reached for the whiskey bottle again.

"Don't play dumb." Mace crossed the room, wishing that, for once in his life, he could let shit go instead of confronting it head-on. "I'm talking about Scotty, and you know it."

"We made a pact, Mace." Blade opened the bottle and started pouring.

"A pact only keeps us from sleeping with her." Mace slapped his hand down on the table. "It doesn't keep us from wanting her."

"Do *you* want her?" Blade asked, his tone defensive, his pour paused.

Mace shifted uncomfortably. This wasn't a topic he allowed himself to ponder. Sure, if they hadn't made that pact, he'd have gotten Scotty into his bed years ago. But they *had* made the pact, and his respect for their friendship kept him from so much as even thinking about being with Scotty. He *couldn't* think about it. Couldn't picture her naked or fantasize about watching her come. If he ever allowed himself to do any of that, he wouldn't stop. He'd want her with a fierceness that would destroy him and everyone around them. So, he ruthlessly suppressed all inappropriate thoughts.

"No," he said, with as much honesty as he believed himself capable of. "Do you?"

Please say no.

"Hell, no. No way." Blade practically threw the bottle onto the counter. "But Scotty—" He cursed and jammed his hand through his dark hair. "She's making a mistake."

"Because she wants to lose her virginity to some rando?" The very idea made Mace want to strangle someone. "I don't see any way to stop her."

"We can talk to her. Convince her to wait until she finds a guy she wants to be with."

That would almost be worse. A one-night stand was one thing. A lover, a potential mate, even…fuck, the very idea gave him hives.

Selfish piece of shit.

Yup, that was him. He had to either inject himself with a sexual suppressant or have sex all the time, but dammit, he didn't want Scotty to be with a male. To his credit, that attitude was a recent thing. Before the incident on Stryke's oil rig a couple of months ago, he hadn't given a hellrat's ass who she dated. Well, mostly. He did extensive background dives on any guy who so much as looked at her.

But on the rig mission, she'd nearly been torn apart in demon-infested waters. He'd almost lost her to Death's icy grip. And now, it occurred to him that he didn't want to lose her to another male, either.

"That's not going to work," Mace said. "You know how stubborn she is. It should be one of us. She's ours." The moment the words fell from his lips, he regretted them. Blade's eyes shot wide, reflecting Mace's own shock at having said them. "I didn't mean it like that," he said quickly. "I just meant…I don't know." Shit. He sounded like an idiot. "I guess I just don't want to see her get hurt." There. That sounded noble and crap. It was also true.

Wow. He was a paragon of honesty today, wasn't he?

Blade nodded as if he understood. "I also don't want her to fall in love with some asshole and ruin what we've got." His long pause ended with a bitter laugh. "Is that fucking selfish, or what?"

It was selfish as shit, but Mace had no room to judge. He was a passenger on the S.S. Selfish right there with Blade.

And yeah, Scotty falling in love would suck. The three of them had been a team for over a decade, friends for longer. Inseparable and synced. How would they be able to fit anyone else into their tight circle?

Suddenly, Mace's wrist comms vibrated, saving him from thoughts that would only make him want to join Blade in drinking himself blotto. A screen flashed in front of his eyes as the comm's NeuroLink connection to the chip in his temple completed. Blade glanced down at his comms and back up, and Mace knew his buddy was seeing the same holo-missive from Kynan.

New mission. My office. One hour.

An hour. Perfect. Gave Mace enough time to do his thing with Alayna and for Blade to finish with Masumi.

Would she still look like Scotty?

The question weighed more heavily on him than he'd like, but at least they had a mission to concentrate on. Nothing kept problems on the back burner like a dangerous assignment.

Blade must have been thinking the same thing, because the tension fled from his body. "I'll meet you downstairs in forty-five." He offered his fist. "Team up."

Tapping knuckles, Mace nodded. "Team up."

Team Selfish was on the move.

Chapter 3

The relentless Greek sun beat down on Scotty as she crossed the arena, her combat boots kicking up pristine, freshly groomed white sand.

Crap. She and her sister were the first to train today. Aleka had to be thrilled, but Scotty preferred to spar on battle-churned ground. Every footprint, every rutted skid mark, every bit of blood, told a story that Scotty could learn from. Even the stench in the heat spurred Scotty to fight harder to keep her own blood from splashing onto the parched ground.

Not that she had to worry about bleeding while sparring with Aleka.

Their father hadn't arrived yet, but Aleka was pacing anxiously in front of the weapons racks. And, of course, she was wearing body armor. She had an entire collection of slash-resistant clothing that also absorbed the power of blunt blows. Today, she'd gone with khaki leggings and a form-fitting, long-sleeved olive top.

Aleka was such a wuss. They were freaking *immortal*. She'd heal from minor cuts and bruises in seconds.

"Hey, sis." Scotty stopped in front of the short swords. "Haven't seen you in a while. I was surprised when Dad hit me up at the last minute to train with you." She hefted one of the swords, a straight, double-edged blade made for thrusting. Aleka's protective clothing was practically useless against jabs and stabs.

If Aleka had even an ounce of battle smarts, she'd choose a shield and a long weapon to counter Scotty.

Scotty would bet a million bucks that she wouldn't.

"It was my idea. I've skipped training three months in a row, and I needed to get Dad off my back." Aleka tied her long, wavy hair into a high ponytail, and Scotty watched in envy. Unlike Scotty, Aleka had gotten silky, strawberry-blond waves that wouldn't dare get frizzy or move out of place. G-ma used to joke that Scotty's hair was as fiery and wild as she was. "I also wanted to talk to you and figured here was as good a place as any." She dropped her hands to her sides. "I have a lead on the location of Harvester's blood."

Scotty nearly fumbled the sword. "Holy shit."

They'd been looking for answers for months, with little success. All they knew so far was that there had been an incident in Heaven that had resulted in their grandfather, Reaver, being taken captive, and their grandmother, Harvester, being killed when she tried to escape.

But not all hope was lost. Harvester's angelic Grace had found its way into Scotty's cousin Logan's fiancée, making Harvester's resurrection a possibility.

If they found her blood.

The day she died, Harvester's blood had rained down to Earth in two places: Aunt Limos's house in Hawaii and a mosque in Jerusalem. After coating everything within a fifty-yard radius, the blood had disappeared as if it had never been. But, according to some witnesses, the blood at the mosque had formed a stream that drained beneath the Foundation Stone at the Dome of the Rock.

So far, Aleka had been unable to find it, and time was running out. Harvester's Grace couldn't remain in Eva for much longer without killing her.

"What's this lead?"

"I found evidence of a previously unknown room underneath the chamber we searched," Aleka said, her eyes bright, and her voice giddy with excitement. She loved solving mysteries, especially when they were archaeological in nature. Or, more accurately, demonological in nature. As a leading expert at the London Museum's Centre for Demon Anthropology and Archaeology, she totally got off on poking around dusty, ancient shit. "I'll be heading back to the mosque as soon as I can get permission. Want to join me?"

Scotty might not share her sister's fascination with history and old, useless crap, but she did share Aleka's obsession with finding out what had happened to their grandmother. Scotty missed her badass, devil-may-care G-ma every single day.

Aleka fidgeted with her ponytail as she waited for an answer. She'd never liked wearing her hair up. Scotty rarely let hers down.

She and her sister were opposites in pretty much everything.

"Wouldn't miss it," Scotty said.

"Good." Aleka flipped her ponytail over her shoulder. "You always had a special connection with her. It's probably a long shot, but I'm hoping you can sense her or something." With a reluctant sigh, she glanced over at the weapon racks. "I can always use your muscle too."

Scotty tested the tip of her blade. It was a training weapon, so the edge was predictably dull. "Maybe if you trained more, you wouldn't need my muscle."

Aleka huffed with annoyance. "You sound like Dad."

Yeah, she'd been accused of that more than once. She'd take it as a compliment. Where Aleka had taken after their mother, Scotty was definitely a daddy's girl.

And she had the freckles to prove it.

She watched her flawlessly skinned sister scowl at the weapons. "Is he still trying to get you to train more often?"

"Every time I see him."

"Then maybe you should do it," Scotty suggested. "He knows what he's doing, and he just wants us to be safe."

"I work in a museum," Aleka said, as predictable as a sunrise. "It's not like I'm getting attacked on a daily basis."

Scotty hated that stupid argument. "It doesn't matter where you work or how safe you think you are in a public building. We're a target for every evil scumbag who wants revenge on our family. You need to be prepared for anything."

"Yeah, yeah." Aleka waved off Scotty's lecture the way she would an annoying gnat. "Good thing I have my little sister to protect me." She crossed her arms over her chest, which Scotty also envied. Aleka's favorite joke used to be that she'd gotten their mom's chest, and Scotty got their dad's.

It was *not* as bad as that.

It wasn't.

"So, what's new with you?" Aleka asked.

Scotty cast a surreptitious glance at the arena entrance to make sure their father wasn't nearby as she considered whether to confide in her sister. They'd always been as close as Scotty would want, but their differences often made it hard for them to relate. On the other hand,

Aleka was also older and had more experience with males.

So, what the heck?

"I've decided to lose my virginity." There.

"Wow." One manicured eyebrow climbed up Aleka's forehead. "I didn't even know you were dating someone."

"I'm not."

Scotty waited for Aleka's judgy attitude, but all she said was, "Okay, so why now?"

"My thirtieth birthday is coming up." She pointed her sword at her sister in a quasi-menacing manner. "And don't give me the lecture Dad did, about being immortal and waiting for five hundred years or some shit. Sex looks fun, and I'm missing out."

"Missing out?" Aleka barked out a bitter laugh. "Sex is overrated."

"Really? Even with a Seminus demon?"

Suddenly fascinated by the selection of truncheons and maces next to the axes, Aleka drifted over. "I wouldn't know."

"Liar." Scotty followed her sister, refusing to give her an escape route on this topic. "You can deny it all you want, but I know you hooked up with Sabre."

Aleka halted mid-step and wheeled around, her pale cheeks burning with outrage.

Ooh, there was definitely a juicy story here.

"What did he say to you?" she demanded.

Scotty paused dramatically, mostly to watch her sister squirm. She blinked a lot when she was anxious.

"He didn't say anything," she finally said. "He doesn't need to. Everyone saw you leave Aunt Limos's party with him."

"I told you before, we didn't leave together. He left first." Aleka huffed in annoyance. "Anyway, it doesn't matter. Nothing happened. So, drop it."

"Come on, sis," Scotty begged. She, Mace, and Blade had spent weeks trying to figure out what had gone down that night. Aleka and Sabre had flirted all day, putting their heads together as they laughed at private jokes, exchanging sneaky touches, and eye-fucking each other when they thought no one was looking. The sultry Hawaiian air between them had practically sizzled with erotic energy. "You can tell me. Obviously, *something* happened, because you both get all grumpy and evasive when the subject comes up."

"Well," Aleka said, pivoting crisply back to the weapon racks, "maybe you shouldn't bring it up, then."

Hmm. Probably not going to happen. Scotty was way too nosy. She wanted the dirt. All of it. Must have been juicy to make Aleka and Sabre miss the event that had rained their grandmother's blood down on the party.

"If you want to know what sex with a Sem is like," Aleka continued, as she perused the top row of close-range weapons, "I'm sure Mace or Blade would be happy to show you."

Unfortunately, that wasn't an option. And deep down, she was still a little bitter about that. She'd told Aleka that she didn't want to be a thirty-year-old virgin, but really, it was more about moving on with her life. Maybe finally being with a guy would make her quit pining for what she couldn't have.

"I told you. We all swore an oath to protect our friendship and our team. I can't sleep with either of them. Also, you really should choose a longer weapon. Try a spear or a halberd. And something small you can throw."

Ignoring Scotty, Aleka ran her finger over the worn wooden handle of a war hammer. Long or short, she preferred crushing weapons over slicing and penetrating ones.

"*They don't cause as much blood,*" she'd once said.

To which their father had answered, "*It depends on what you hit and how hard you strike it. Once, I knocked a guy's head clean off with nothing but a tree branch. Crushed it like an egg. And you should have seen the geyser—*"

Aleka had retched. She'd always had a weak stomach.

"I know about the oath," Aleka said. "But come on. It was a verbal oath, not a magical one. You can break it anytime. And you're trying to tell me that neither of them has *ever* made a move on you? Really? Not even Mace?" As if to make a point, she lifted the spiked mace off its hook. "That guy will nail anything with a pulse. And honestly, I doubt a lack of a pulse is a deal-breaker."

Scotty scowled. People always misjudged Mace. Yeah, he could be an egotistical playboy with absolutely no filter, but he was also generous, loyal, and reliable. If he said he had your back, he did. One hundred percent.

Scotty would enjoy kicking Aleka's ass in Mace's name today.

"They're honorable males," she shot back. "If they make a promise, they keep it."

"Take it easy, sis." Aleka held up her hands, the mace in one fist. "I didn't say they weren't honorable. But they *are* lust demons. They need sex a gazillion times a day, or they'll die. I'm just a little shocked that their instincts have never overridden their brains around you."

Her sister made a good case, and Scotty had probably overreacted, but she'd always been protective of her teammates. Besides, it wasn't as if Aleka had any room to talk, given that their evil grandmother was a succubus.

"*You're* part sex demon," Scotty pointed out, still a little irritated by her sister's *lack of a pulse* comment. "Do you have problems controlling *your* instincts?"

"No. Do you?"

Scotty frowned. She'd never really thought about it. She was what she was, and the why of it didn't matter. She lived in the now, didn't need backstories, didn't care about history. Which was funny, because her sister was the opposite. Obsessed with history, backstories, and getting answers to all the questions that came with them.

"I don't think I have any sex-demon instincts," she said.

Heck, she had never felt so much as a stir of arousal on any date. Which was why she'd never had sex. She'd kissed guys, even copped a feel now and then, but…ugh. So unexciting.

So far, she hadn't noticed even a hint of Lilith in her genetics. Thank the gods. But Mace and Blade had said that her succubus traits might not manifest until they were triggered by a specific event, like having sex or reaching a certain age. The latter seemed unlikely, though, because puberty usually brought on those kinds of changes, and she was well past that.

"You said you can control your instincts," Scotty mused. "But are they like, normal? Like the birds-and-bees stuff Mom talked to us about? Or does weird succubus shit happen?"

Aleka shifted her weight and took a sudden, keen interest in the spikes at the tip of the mace. "Dad's coming."

Scotty wheeled around to the arched entryway, only to find that Aleka had been messing with her. "Bullshit."

"Well, he'll be here any minute." Aleka swung the mace in a wide arc. "We should start practicing."

Scotty easily, almost lazily, blocked Aleka's sideways blow with her sword, and the comforting, thrilling clang of weapons echoed through the arena. "You are the queen of avoidance."

Aleka grinned as she sidestepped Scotty's half-hearted return jab. "And you're the queen of asking too many personal questions."

That was fair. "Let's switch to summoned weapons."

Scotty's sword materialized in her left hand, and its power surged through her body. Man, she loved the buzz she got from holding it. Craved it, even. When she fought with the thing, the thrill she got was almost sexual. Better than anything any male had ever done for her.

Oh. Was that how her succubus DNA showed itself? By giving her a lethal sex toy?

Lame.

Aleka hefted her weapon into attack position, broadcasting her next move, as usual. No matter how much training she did, she couldn't break that habit. Good thing she had a dull desk job. She wouldn't last a day in Scotty's world. Of course, Scotty wouldn't last a day in Aleka's, either. She'd die of boredom.

"I want to practice with a mace today," Aleka said.

"You can manifest one."

Which had always irked Scotty. She could only manifest a sword, and while she could charge it with the powers of nearby elements, a double-edged longsword was the only weapon she could summon. Aleka could conjure up almost anything without mechanical moving parts.

"I like the feel of *this* mace."

That…seemed unlikely. "You *never* want to practice with summoned weapons," Scotty pointed out.

"So?"

"So, it's weird."

Aleka swung the mace, and Scotty danced out of the way. Her sister really wasn't great at fighting. "You sound like Dad. Again."

"He wouldn't get all over your case if you'd just do it." Scotty went on the offensive, swinging her manifested and physical swords in a form her father called Skinning Trolls. "He probably thinks you're being stubborn just to piss him off."

Aleka retreated, ducking and blocking as she went. Her form was *so* sloppy. "If he wants me to attend these stupid fighting lessons once a month, he'll have to deal with it."

Seriously, what the hell was the problem? Aleka hadn't conjured a weapon during training in over a year. She always chose something from the rack and refused to change it up, no matter how hard Scotty pressed her. Frustrated, their father had confronted her about it a few months ago, and the confrontation ended with Aleka storming home. Then, their mother had scolded their father, and no one had spoken of it since.

Scotty swung her blade, pulling back at the last second so she didn't slice through her sister's unprotected neck. Still, the tip nicked Aleka, leaving a thin red line spreading across the top of her collarbone.

"Ouch—"

Scotty nailed her with an identical cut on the other side. As their father liked to say, "Injure one side of the body, then strike the other while they're guarding the first one. Symmetry. It's artistic, and evil hates it."

"Scotty!" Aleka slapped her hand over the second cut. "What the hell?"

"Sorry." She shrugged. "First one was an accident."

"And the second?"

"Symmetry."

Aleka threw her hands up in frustration. "Even when Dad isn't here, he's here."

"I'm sure he'd love to know you actually pay attention to his lessons—" Scotty broke off at the sensation of her comms vibrating on her wrist. A heartbeat later, a message from Kynan popped up.

Yes! Looked like there'd be some real battles in her future, not just lame sparring lessons with her sister.

"You're going to have to get another sparring partner," she said. "I gotta go."

"Duty calls?"

"Yep." Scotty made her summoned sword disappear. "Want me to ask Rath to spar with you?"

Aleka racked her mace. "He's on guard duty."

Rath, their adopted older brother, *lived* for guard duty. He'd grown up with Aleka and Scotty, but he'd joined his Ramreel demon herd several years ago, becoming part of Ares's island security team. The warrior race excelled at battle, and their size and vigilance made them natural, formidable sentries.

Scotty returned the practice sword to the rack just as their father entered through the main archway. The living glyph on his forearm, his trusty warhorse, Battle, stomped its hoof as Ares stepped out of the shadows. The high sun made the red highlights in his hair glitter, bestowing him with a coppery crown that only added to the kingly air he bore like a mantle. A warrior nearly as old as time itself, he feared nothing.

Nothing except losing a family member. Which was why Scotty, Aleka, and Rath had been training to fight since they could walk.

"Sorry, Pops." Scotty moved to meet him, planting a kiss on his grizzled cheek. Apparently, their mother liked him with a five-o'clock shadow. "I have to go to work. But Aleka tells me she's *super* excited to train." She shot her sister an impish wink, and Aleka shot her the finger.

"Be safe," he said, hauling her back in a one-armed bear hug.

"Hey," Aleka called out. "How come whenever I cancel a session, you make me reschedule?" She flung her arm at Scotty. "But she just gets to walk away?"

"Scotty constantly practices," he said, his deep voice rumbling off the arena walls. "You constantly avoid it."

Scotty laughed and waggled her fingers at her sister. "Toodles. Have fun!"

That earned her another flip of the finger and a glare that promised retribution. Aleka would probably guilt Scotty into a shopping trip—or worse, Scotty would have to help her dig through musty museum crates.

But what Aleka didn't know was that Scotty didn't always mind spending time with her sister. They had so little in common that they struggled to find stuff to talk about, so when Aleka asked for a favor, Scotty usually agreed. Maybe they couldn't bond over deep conversation, but they could share experiences now and then. They regularly got a laugh out of the time Scotty got stung by a petrified demonic scorpion when she'd stupidly reached inside a three-thousand-year-old crate. Scotty preferred the story about Aleka spilling coffee all over a hot fire-fighter in a bookstore café she'd dragged Scotty to, though. While she stammered out an apology, she spilled the rest on his buddy.

Scotty chuckled as she jogged toward the island's Harrowgate. She loved her sister, but sometimes, the woman needed to loosen up. Or lose herself in a bloody battle. Or steamy sex.

Not that Scotty was experienced with steamy sex. But Mace and Blade swore that it was the best way to relieve stress. Even better than battle.

Scotty wasn't so sure about that, but if she had her way, she'd find out in the next two weeks.

Kynan Morgan loved his damned job.

Who would have ever guessed that he'd go from dedicating his life to killing demons…to marrying one *and* running an agency that employed them.

Yeah, his young, dumb, demon-hating, thirty-year-old self wouldn't recognize his sixty-three-year-old self, even though he didn't look a day older than he had back then. If anything, gaining immortality had shaved off a few years. He looked twenty-seven, tops. And thanks to the amulet around his neck—a literal, tiny piece of Heaven itself that had been charmed by angels—he'd live forever...as long as he didn't do something stupid, like get his head chopped off by a fallen angel.

Reflexively, he reached up and brushed his fingers over the thick scars across his throat, a reminder that he *had* almost lost his head once. His first encounter with a demon back in his military days had left him with a damaged voice and a new career path.

Kynan glanced to his right at Tayla, his half-demon sister-in-law and DART's Special Investigative Unit Director, before addressing the trio sitting across the table from him in the building's main briefing room.

Scotty, Blade, and Mace lounged in their chairs, looking deceptively chill, but Ky estimated that between the three of them, they were in possession of at least a dozen knives, nine feet of garrote wire, a couple of shock sticks, and too many supernatural weapons to count. They were the best of the best, freakishly in sync, and his most capable and trusted team across scores of DART locations around the world. If they couldn't handle a situation, no one could. At least, no one on his payroll.

Tay slid mission packets toward the three special forces operators, who snatched them up like kids scrambling for cupcakes.

He'd seen them do that before too. A couple of weeks ago, in fact. They'd scarfed down two dozen cupcakes between them.

"I can't wait to see where we're going." Mace's sun-streaked dark hair hung in his face as he dug into the envelope. "Somewhere hot with beaches, I hope. Warm sand, killer surf, chicks in bikinis..."

"Not...exactly," Ky said, amused. Call him sadistic, but he got a kick out of sending Mace to places that forced him to work hard at having fun. The guy needed to be taken down a peg or two now and then.

Tayla wore her I'm-about-to-fuck-up-your-day smile. She also got a kick out of pushing Mace out of his comfort zone and forcing him to be more serious. "You," she said, all classic Vanna White with a flourish, "have won an all-expenses-paid trip to wild, buggy Alaska."

Deflated, Blade groaned and tossed his packet back onto the table. "I hate the cold."

"It's summer there," Kynan said, and Blade perked up. "Expect sudden rainstorms and mosquitoes the size of pterodactyls."

Blade slumped back down in his seat. "Even better."

"Stop whining." Scotty perused the packet. "I like Alaska. You got mountains, bears, and kick-ass breweries."

"You're not on vacation," Tayla reminded them. "This is a mission."

Mace looked up from flipping through the photos included in the briefing materials. "What kind of mission?"

The eager glint in his coffee-colored eyes matched Scotty's. Those two liked the dangerous and weird assignments and were always ready to go tearing into a situation. Blade was the cautious one, so, instead of a glint, his dark gaze held wary shadows.

Tayla turned on the room's main 3D holoscreen, and it hung over the table between them. "It'll be a joint operation with two special-ops agents from our Seattle office. You already know Skoll, so you know he's a werewolf with extensive training in tracking and survival. And, thanks to his dad's job as a paramedic at Underworld General, he's also trained in advanced first aid. The other agent is Jon. Former Green Beret and a bear shifter with specialized knowledge of multiple Indigenous languages and mythologies."

The trio exchanged glances.

"Okay," Blade said slowly. "So, what, exactly, are we doing with them?"

"You'll meet at a hotel in Fairbanks," Kynan said, "and then you'll set out for a cabin in the Yukon-Charley National Preserve, where you're going to be investigating reports of a wendigo."

"A wendigo?" Mace jacked upright in his seat. He loved shiny new things. "What the fuck are those? Demons?"

"Good question." Tayla tucked a long strand of auburn hair behind her ear. She was also around Kynan's age, without a single gray hair or wrinkle, thanks to the bond she shared with her Seminus demon mate, Eidolon. "Jon'll be able to tell you more about them, but basically, they're cannibalistic beasts. The Aegis and DART have always assumed they were mythical, but several people have gone missing near the preserve, and a credible source gave a description that resembles the wendigo myth."

Mace grinned. "Awesome. We could be the first to confirm them as a new known species. We'll be famous. Plastered all over *Underworld News Today.*"

"So, are they demons?" Scotty asked, ignoring Mace and his delusions of fame and fortune. "Or no?"

Kynan shrugged. "We don't know. That's what your team is going to determine. Read your packets for more information, and the Seattle boys will fill you in on the rest."

Mace nodded, his body language morphing from devil-may-care to serious-as-a-heart-attack as he shifted into mission mode. The guy was a wildcard in social settings, but as reliable as the tides on an assignment. Ask him to do it, and he did it. His methods of achieving the goal, however, tended to be unconventional and, as often as not, against the rules. "When do we leave?"

"You have six hours to prepare," Tayla said. "Your packets contain addresses, names, and essential information you'll need to get you started. Pack light. You'll be hiking a lot."

Kynan reached into a drawer and withdrew a box. The team watched, spellbound, as he plopped it down on the desk and lifted the lid.

"This," he said, "is a prototype of the weapon we contracted with StryTech."

Scotty's eyes shot wide. "Is that…a Reaper?"

"Yep." Kynan lifted the sleek object from the box, its polished horn grip conforming to his palm as if it were made for him. He couldn't wait to get into the field and try it out for himself. He'd been stuck behind a desk for far too long, and he was itching for a fight. "Stryke delivered it to me yesterday, and you guys are going to be the first to test it out."

Scotty practically bounced in her seat. Her sharp eyes missed nothing, though, and she zeroed in on the weapon's grip. "Is that Ramreel horn?"

Kynan nodded. "Don't worry, no innocent Ramreels died for this. A male from your father's herd donated it."

"I wasn't worried about its origins," she said. "Most Ramreels are evil bastards. I'm just wondering why Ramreel horn is part of the construction."

Kynan ran his thumb over the smooth, oddly warm demonic material. "Stryke said it can sense the intentions of whoever is holding it. Increases accuracy."

"Awesome." Mace's dark eyes gleamed with excitement, while Blade's went wary and cold. Any mention of his estranged brother did that to him. "How does it work?"

Kynan pressed a button near the barrel of the pistol-sized weapon. Two wings popped out, and a cable snapped into the retention spring.

"Cool," Scotty said. "It looks like a miniature crossbow."

"It works a lot like one too," Kynan said. "But there are some key differences." He handed the weapon to Tayla and held up a bolt. "First, the projectile is smaller and thicker."

"Why?" Scotty scowled at the bolt as if personally offended. "That's clumsy. The circumference will slow it down."

Leave it to Scotty to instantly zero in on the weapon's weakness. She was just like her father.

"The shaft has to be larger than a typical bolt because it contains a *decipula*," Ky explained. "StryTech couldn't shrink the soul traps down any smaller."

Blade glanced up at Ky. "But won't that make it less lethal?"

"The point of this weapon is to capture souls, not kill," Kynan said, although Stryke assured him that his company's continuing research would find a way to make the Reaper as lethal as possible. "As long as the bolt is embedded in the demon when it dies from any injury, the *decipula* will capture its spirit."

With the destruction of Sheoul-gra, the souls of deceased demons had nowhere to go and had been wreaking havoc in both the human and demon realms. StryTech had developed traps to catch and store the souls until Hades could rebuild Sheoul-gra, but deployment of the traps required the ability to see the souls. With the Reaper, anyone could catch a demon spirit.

"What about humans?" Mace asked.

"The Reaper will definitely kill humans," Kynan said, "but it won't capture their souls. This weapon is designed to work against demons only."

"Okay," Blade said. "But how will we know if the bolt has trapped a soul?"

He plucked another bolt from the container. "This one contains a soul. You can tell by the glowing symbols etched into the shaft." He carefully replaced the projectile inside its velvet-lined case. "They're equipped with a guidance system, so no matter where you aim the Reaper, the bolts will seek out the most injured enemy demon."

Tayla turned the weapon around and showed them the pencil eraser-sized white button on the right side. "If needed, push this, and you can deactivate the guidance system."

"Why would you ever do that?" Scotty asked.

"To protect the good guys." Tayla placed the weapon on the table and gestured to a flat panel on the handle grip. "Before a battle, everyone in your party needs to touch the panel to identify themselves as allies. That'll prevent the projectile from seeking out any injured associates. But let's say there are civilians around, or more help arrives on scene, and you don't have a chance to get their energy signature imprints. You'll need to disable the guidance system, so the bolt won't seek them out as the most injured person in the fight."

"Ah." Scotty toyed with her ponytail. "Makes sense."

"Anyone else have any questions?" Tayla looked between the teammates. "No? Then get ready for the mission." She placed the weapon back in its case and slid it across the desk. "I know you don't need it, but good luck."

No, Kynan thought as the team filed out, all swagger and cocksure attitudes, they didn't need luck. They had more talent and skill between them than the entirety of most nations' armies. And they were attuned to each other, so tight that not a single molecule of oxygen could get between them.

And that was what concerned Kynan from time to time. For all the trio had gone through, their friendship had never been tested. It had never even been strained.

What if something *were* to happen to test their bond? He knew all too well how quickly shit could fall apart when cracks formed in a foundation.

"Hey."

He looked over at Tay as his office door closed behind Blade. "Yeah. What's up?"

She cocked her head, the pink streak in her hair dipping behind her shoulder. "You look worried."

"Worried?" He scoffed. "Nah. They've faced worse. I was just thinking about the old days."

"Which ones?"

The worst ones. "Our Aegis days."

She drew in a long, heavy breath. "Oh."

"Yeah." He threw his head back against his chair, his time as a demon hunter in charge of an entire cell of slayers flashing through his mind. Tayla had been one of his best fighters…until she hooked up with the demon doctor who ran the hospital she'd been tasked to destroy. "We thought we knew it all."

She snorted. "We didn't know jack shit. But hey, we're both in a good place now. We have amazing mates, the best kids, and awesome jobs."

"We rose from the ashes," he murmured.

They'd been fortunate. So many who burned never came back. His dead first wife being one of them.

"Do you ever think about what's next?" Tayla asked.

He cocked an eyebrow. "For whom?"

"Us." She shrugged, a slow roll of the shoulder that bore her mate's *dermoire*. "The world. I mean. Shit's been quiet for a while. We haven't faced an apocalypse in like, thirty years. It's kinda freaking me out."

"You forgot about the hell rift beneath Stryke's oil rig in the North Sea a couple months ago."

"Oh, yeah." She grabbed the leftover documents on the desk. "Since Stryke handled most of it and the damage was minimal, I never remember to include it."

She seemed disappointed.

"Don't worry," he said cheerily, "I'm sure there's something catastrophic right around the corner. And I think you're forgetting that Azagoth destroyed Sheoul-gra and released millions—maybe billions—of evil souls. The worst ones have yet to be captured. I predict lots of potential apocalypses in the future."

"Thank you." Grinning, she started for the doorway. "You always see the bright side in any situation."

He just shook his head. Demons. Kill them or marry them, you'd never understand them.

Chapter 4

They arrived at the Fairbanks hotel a few minutes after six p.m. local time. The wilderness-themed establishment was busy with summer tourists, but the two Seattle-office DART guys had reserved a conference room just off the lobby.

Scotty had known Skoll for most of her life, but mostly as an acquaintance. His father, Luc, was a paramedic at Underworld General, so Blade and Mace had spent more time around him than she had. A tall, tawny-haired male with broad shoulders and intense, crystal-blue eyes, he turned all the girls' heads.

Scotty had never seen the other guy, Jon, before. He was maybe an inch taller than Skoll, with dark hair and a bullish build that reminded her of her father. She'd bet that when he shifted into a bear, he was massive.

Skoll was friendly enough, offering handshakes and sticks of his cinnamon gum, but Jon was warier, hanging back to study them as if they might be the enemy and not colleagues.

But then, Blade did the same thing. Not Mace, though. Nope, he made himself the life of the party right away, buying a round of tequila shots and ordering moose meat nachos and fries smothered in elk gravy.

"Good to see you guys again," Skoll said, after a few minutes of catching up and small talk. And maybe it was her imagination, but she swore his gaze lingered on her for longer than her teammates. Of course, he *had* been a little flirty the last time she'd seen him, a few weeks ago at Runa's birthday celebration. "Harrowgates are scarce here, so we got a rental vehicle to get us as close to the cabin as possible. We'll give you the basics right now and will fill you in on the rest during the drive."

"Kynan mentioned a cabin." Mace yanked a chair out from under the table across from her and plopped down on it backward, using the back to prop up his arms. "What's up with that?"

"Belongs to the guy who first reported the wendigo activity. Nathan Mitchell. Former Aegi. It's his place. We lost contact with him a week ago."

"Aegi?" Blade took a seat at the table next to her like a normal person. "Why did he report this to DART instead of The Aegis?"

A server came over with their food and drinks, and Jon waited until the guy was gone before replying. "He did report it to The Aegis, but they didn't believe him. Told him to contact us, because we 'love wild goose chases.'"

Sounded about right. The Aegis was full of assholes.

"Kynan said people have gone missing." Scotty frowned at the taxidermized dead animals mounted around the room. Demon heads would look better. "Did Nathan know them?"

"He knew two of the missing. They were off-grid prepper buddies. Ironically, they moved up north to avoid demons." Skoll took a couple of photos out of a file and slid them into the center of the table. "Jason Steele and Gary Lewis. Steele was an Alaskan native who returned a few years ago after separating from the army, and Lewis moved here from Missouri after his divorce."

Scotty glanced at the photos of the men, both of whom appeared to be in their late forties or early fifties. Outfitted in survival gear and carrying rifles, they looked like they could take care of themselves.

"And Nathan is the only person who has seen a wendigo?" Mace plucked a nacho off the serving plate. "How do we know he didn't off his buddies and make up the wendigo story to cover his tracks?"

"We don't." Jon's deep baritone echoed through the room, and Scotty shivered in feminine appreciation. Blade's voice was similar, rumbling and gruff. Mace's too, but usually only when he was injured, hungover, or lusting after a female. "That's why we're investigating."

Scotty snagged a fry dripping with dark-brown gravy and shredded meat. "How long will it take to get to the cabin?"

"It's an eight-hour drive to the trailhead." Skoll popped a jalapeño into his mouth.

"And then a three-hour hike to Nathan's cabin," Jon added. "It's going to be a long day."

"What about supplies?"

Coughing a little, Skoll reached for his water glass. "We already loaded the truck with enough carry-in rations to last a week. The cabin should be stocked too."

"Let's get going, then." Blade shoved to his feet. "We don't want to be traipsing around in a strange forest in the dark."

"Chill, man." Skoll made an encompassing gesture with his arm, taking in the chainsaw-art grizzly in the corner, the Native paintings on the wall, and everything else in the Alaska-themed room. "We're in the land of the midnight sun. This time of year, it'll be light until ten, and we'll only have partial darkness for a couple of hours."

Scotty had to push the fries aside before she ate the entire plate. "Seems like an odd time of year for creatures like wendigos to be out. From what little research I managed before we came, they're more of a cold-weather-and-darkness monster."

"They are," Skoll agreed. "That's why this is so strange."

"So, you believe they're real?" Blade's question was more of a challenge than a genuine query. He'd been skeptical from the beginning. "Not a myth?"

"They're real." Jon's voice was a bear-like growl.

"How do you know?" Blade pressed.

Jon gathered the files on the table. "The stories were passed down in my family for generations."

"Ah," Blade said. "So, anecdotal evidence."

Jon chucked the folders into a box with enough force to nearly knock it over. "My great-great-grandfather was killed by his brother, after he was turned into a wendigo by an evil spirit."

Blade's struggle to not roll his eyes was making him twitch, so Scotty quickly drew Jon's attention. "Any idea why a wendigo would be active in the middle of the summer?"

"There are a couple of theories." Jon looked between the three of them, but mostly at her. He had gorgeous eyes. Sea green and clear, like the water surrounding her father's island. This guy might be a pop-the-cherry contender. "It's possible that it was summoned. Maybe by someone wanting revenge on the missing men or to protect the land. It's also possible it was awakened from hibernation after a recent earthquake. We don't know. But that's what we're going to find out."

Skoll tossed some more files into the box. "Our supe says you have some sort of new weapon to test on these things?"

"It collects souls." Scotty gestured to Blade's backpack, where he'd stowed the Reaper. Out of the three of them, he was the best shot with a firearm or crossbow. Scotty could kick all their asses with every other kind of bow, though. "But it'll only work if the wendigos are demons."

Jon lifted his jacket off the back of his chair. "We brought flame-throwers and flammable arrows. Fire's the most effective weapon against them."

Skoll, having nearly drained his ice water, paused with the glass near his mouth. "Disagree." He had nice lips. Not as full as Jon's, but less cruel. More like Mace's. And he had a crooked smile like Blade. "Decap-itation kills everything."

"Scotty is amazing with a sword," Mace said, and she nodded, because yeah, she was. "So, we got the decapitation thing covered."

"Good. Because wendigos don't fuck around." Jon paused, and when he spoke again, his tone was dark. "I've fought a lot of demons and not much scares me."

Blade cocked a dark eyebrow. "You're afraid of something that's probably a myth?"

"They're cannibals," Jon said gravely. "And they want you alive when they start eating you." Jon threw on his jacket and scooped up the box of files. "You'd better hope they're myths, because if you aren't afraid, you're an idiot."

The ride to the trailhead in the Land Rover took forever. Mace hated taking forever to do anything. When he wanted something, he wanted it *now*. If he wanted to go somewhere, he wanted to be there *right now*. And when he wanted a female, he wanted her *right fucking now*.

This sitting-in-a-vehicle shit was for humans. But since Alaska had few Harrowgates—what lunatic demon wanted to haunt frozen tundras and uninhabited forests?—they had no choice but to spend hours on shitty roads, with Scotty squished in the back seat between him and Blade.

Some of the roads could barely even be called such. Rutted dirt trails met with cracked and buckled pavement, and they often narrowed into single, overgrown paths.

They used the time to get to know each other or sleep. Mace had managed to catch a few winks, and Blade had slept almost the entire way. At least his eyes had been closed. Still, Mace suspected the guy had kept track of everything going on around him. Scotty, always a chatterbox, kept the conversation going by asking Skoll and Jon questions about their work and lives.

Mace wasn't sure he liked how chipper she was, and he *definitely* didn't like how much they flirted with her.

She soaked it all up, laughing at their stupid stories. Her words from yesterday kept flashing in Mace's mind.

I think it's time to lose my virginity.

Fuck. She'd better not lose it to one of these idiots. Skoll was okay, but the bear shifter was a dick. Way too serious and lacking appreciation for Mace's jokes. Reminded him of his half-brother, Talon. Still, Scotty giggled and batted her eyes like a teenage groupie mooning over a rock star.

Scotty never giggled. Or mooned. And when had she learned to do anything with her eyes besides roll them? What the fuck?

"We're a few miles from the trailhead." Skoll squinted into the early morning sun rising behind some snowcapped mountains. "We should get to the cabin a little before noon. That'll give us time to get some sleep and plan our hunt."

"What time is sunset?" Blade asked, his eyes still closed, his head propped against the window.

"Around nine p.m." Jon steered to avoid a pothole, but managed to hit a different one. Mace's ass would be broken by the time they stopped. "Darkness at about ten. Sunrise is at six. So, basically, we'll have about nine hours to hunt this thing."

"Hopefully, we won't need all nine," Blade said, his voice utterly flat. "Because I'm ready to kill something."

Me, too, Mace thought, as he stared at the back of Jon's head.

Me, too.

Chapter 5

It seemed like a million years before Skoll finally pulled over at a trail-head, and they all bailed out of the stuffy truck into the cool morning air. How did humans stand being in vehicles for so long?

Scotty would never take Harrowgates for granted again.

The trail to the cabin was surprisingly well-maintained and wide enough to accommodate a small car. Jon said the cabin's owner, Nathan, kept it up for his truck, UTV, and snowmobile.

Scotty took in the beauty of the landscape as they walked, so mesmerized by a crystal brook running alongside the trail, its shallows gurgling over smooth river rock, that she nearly tripped over a gnarled root.

"How well do you know Nathan?" she asked the guys, hoping no one had seen her nearly faceplant.

"I came out here once to interview him." Skoll nimbly avoided the root that had almost done her in. "He picked me up at the trailhead in a five-seater Polaris. Nice rig. Like, he lives in a shack with no running water but has a fifty-thousand-dollar UTV." He shook his head in disbelief. "He'd have given us a ride if we hadn't lost contact with him. One of us would have had to ride in the bed, though."

"I'd have volunteered to run behind you." Scotty peered down an embankment at the babbling brook. "After that long-ass ride, I could use the exercise."

Mace snorted. "She never gets tired, either."

"That's right," Jon said, shooting her a lazy grin that must come straight out of the manual on how to seduce females, because Mace had the same smile. She'd seen it a million times…just never directed at her. "Your dad is one of the Four Horsemen of the Apocalypse. Did you inherit his immortality?"

She nodded, still watching the creek, the water sparkling in patches of sunlight that penetrated the thick tree canopy. This place was gorgeous. She'd always loved mountains and wild forests. Beaches were nice, but there was something so tranquil about the woods.

When they weren't infested by monsters, anyway.

"I mean, I can be killed," she said, "but not easily." She shot him a look she hoped he took as playful and not creepy. "And I have crazy good stamina."

She wasn't great at flirting, and what little she knew, she'd learned from her cousin, Leilani. That girl made a sport of getting attention.

Jon's lips twitched in amusement, and his gaze practically smoldered before he turned back to the trail. "I'm sure you do."

Skoll gave her a quick glance and a wink. "I'm not surprised, either."

Yes! Confidence boosted. Her cousin Leilani would be proud.

Blade rolled his eyes, and she caught Mace silently mimicking Jon's words. She gave him a sharp jab in the side and then laughed at his indignant, "Oof!"

"How far are we from the cabin?" Blade sounded irritated.

Jon drew to a halt, stopping them as he studied his wrist comms—a 3D map, most likely, but he didn't activate share mode, so she could only guess.

"According to this, twenty minutes away." He gestured ahead, where the trees thinned, and the trail snaked along a rocky hill. "Should be around that bend."

Mace pushed past Jon, his attention on an ancient fir just off the trail. "Are we on Nathan's property?"

Jon glanced up at the cloudless sky, his gaze following an eagle soaring overhead. "Have been for an hour now."

"Guys." Mace moved toward the tree, its gnarled trunk twisted into a display of arboreal agony. "Check this out." He stopped at its base, his fingers tracing a swirly pattern carved deeply into the bark. "It's a symbol. An Aegis ward against evil."

"They're probably everywhere." Jon's eyes narrowed as he scanned the surroundings. "Be careful. Aegis wards don't usually discriminate."

That was a lesson they'd all learned too well. To The Aegis, all supernatural beings—except angels—were enemies, from demons and vampires to werewolves and shifters.

"There's another on that rotten stump." Mace leaped over a fallen log with panther-like grace and started up the slope, whipping aside scraggly brush as he trudged closer. "The symbol is different."

Skoll turned in a slow circle, his sharp gaze raking the forest and the trail ahead and behind. "The music changed. It's ominous now. Be careful."

Blade scowled at the werewolf. "What?"

"His music is like an early warning system," Jon explained. Except his explanation didn't help at all.

"I always have music in my head." Skoll's fingers skimmed over the machete at his hip as he continued to monitor the area. "Like an earworm, except the music changes depending on the situation. It's like my life has a soundtrack."

That would be awesome.

Blade disagreed. "Sounds annoying."

Jon shifted to the rear, keeping an eye on the trail behind them. "You seem like the type who gets easily annoyed."

"You seem like the type who gets punched in the face a lot," Blade shot back.

Ooh, things were getting spicy. Scotty loved a good conflict, but maybe they should wait until they got to the cabin.

Skoll halted mid-step, alarm etched in his expression. "The tempo's picking up. Music's getting louder. More intense." He spun around to Mace. "Mace. Don't!"

Too late. Mace's boot crunched down on a mossy log, and in a silent explosion, he went airborne. His pained yelp was cut short when he struck a tree with the sickening crack of both branches and bones. He slid down the trunk and hit the ground with a thud, leaving a trail of blood behind on the bark.

"Mace!" Scotty raced toward where he'd crumpled into a mangled heap in the ferns, fear clawing at her with icy fingers. They'd all been injured before, had gotten way too intimate with near-death close calls. But something about the way Mace lay like a broken, discarded doll terrified the hell out of her.

She crashed to her knees next to him. "Hey." Holy shit, so much blood.

"I'm…fine," Mace groaned, struggling weakly to roll onto his back.

"Hold him still." Skoll shrugged off his backpack. "He's going to make it worse." He grabbed a first aid kit from one of the pockets and crouched next to her, just as Blade took a knee across from her.

"Blade," she begged. "Do something."

Their gazes met over their teammate's writhing body, and her gut sank. Blade's grim expression confirmed her fears. This was beyond bad.

He clamped his right hand down on Mace's wrist, and a hot glow lit up his *dermoire*, starting at his personal symbol and flowing down the dark lines all the way to his fingertips. Mace hissed through clenched teeth as Blade's healing power reversed the damage.

Tossing aside his useless medical kit, Skoll watched in fascination. "I spent a lot of time at Underworld General as a kid, but I've never seen a Seminus demon in action before."

"*I've* never seen a trap that can do this kind of damage." Sweat beaded on Blade's brow, and his breath came in shallow spurts. The process wasn't easy on him, either. It sometimes left him drained for days.

Scotty contemplated the trap and the utter destruction it had wreaked on Mace. Not an inch of his body had been spared.

"It was a bone-crusher spell," she murmured. "Had to be."

Clearly, Nathan meant business. She gave Mace's hand a gentle squeeze and had to bite back a cry at the way it felt less like a body part and more like a bag full of the D&D dice the guys were always playing with.

"Blade," she croaked, "how many bones are broken?"

"All of them," Mace groaned. "Feels like all of them."

"He's not wrong," Blade muttered under his breath. He glanced up at Scotty and mouthed, "*This is bad.*"

Oh, gods.

"Can't…can't believe I didn't see the trap." Mace groaned again.

"S'okay, buddy," Blade said, calmly and confidently, in a great imitation of the deep, reassuring paramedic voice his dad used with patients. Patients he liked, anyway. Shade was more than happy to let evil demons suffer. Scotty had always appreciated his form of vigilante justice.

Blade slid his healing hand over Mace's ribs. "Bone crushers are almost impossible to detect."

Scotty glanced over at Skoll. "Please, tell me Nathan gave you a map of all the ward and trap locations."

Jon answered from where he'd remained on the trail, keeping watch as they tended to Blade. "It's at the cabin. We'll have to be careful until we know where they all are."

Closing his eyes, Mace swallowed sickly. "Think…I'm gonna pass out."

"Stick with us, man." Jaw tight, tendons in his neck straining, Blade poured more energy into Mace's injuries. "This'll only hurt for a couple more minutes."

Hurt? Scotty had been the beneficiary of Sem healing several times in her life, and it didn't *hurt*. It was straight-up torture. The worse the injury, the worse the pain. Her stomach churned with empathy for what Mace was going through.

"Are all Seminus demons able to heal like that?" Skoll asked.

"No." Scotty gave the standard spiel for Blade. At this point, she knew almost as much about their species as they did. "All Sems are born male, and during their first transition, they develop one of three abilities. Blade's ability can heal injuries, but not his own. Mace has a different ability. He can't heal, but he can tweak bodily functions in others. Like, he can trigger the release of endorphins or slow down a heartbeat. Blade's brother, Rade, has the rarest gift. He can get inside your head and make you see things or snip memories."

Rade's gift was seriously scary.

"I've heard about Rade," Skoll said. "He—no. No, no, no!" He lunged to his feet. "Fight music."

Ear-splitting screeches filled the air, and a chill shot up Scotty's spine.

Demons.

Jon cursed and ducked, barely avoiding being brained by a hatchet. By the time the weapon hit a tree with a lethal thunk, he'd already launched in pursuit of the hatchet's owner.

"Dammit." Skoll took off after Jon, a machete in one hand, a throwing star in the other. So much for being careful.

"Go," Mace breathed. "They need help. I'm better. I'm fine."

His color *was* better, and most of his visible wounds had at least partially healed. But he was in no way *fine*.

"I've done all I can," Blade said to her. "You stay. I'll go."

He stood, but she grabbed his wrist before he could take off. "Be careful."

His dark, intense eyes locked with hers, a familiar promise swirling in their depths. His response would, unfailingly, be, "Always," a counter to Mace's perpetual, "Never."

Blade didn't disappoint. "Always." With an almost cocky wink, he took off after Jon and Skoll.

Mace wrapped his arm around his midsection, cringing as he shifted his weight. He was pale with shock and blood loss, his lips nearly white. She had never seen him this anemic.

"I don't need a babysitter."

"Maybe not." Gently, she brushed a sun-kissed dark lock of hair away from a half-healed cut on his forehead. "But you do need blood."

Most Seminus demons didn't drink blood, but Mace's birth father, Wraith, had passed on his vampiric needs to both Mace and Talon. Neither required blood to survive, but feeding increased their strength and helped them recover from injuries.

Mace threw his head back against the tree and closed his eyes. "I could use a hit."

In a couple of quick motions, she rolled up her sleeve and held out her wrist. "Take it."

His eyes popped open. "What? You? No."

"Don't be an idiot. You need it, and I have it. Besides, where else will you get it? I doubt some crusty, grizzled gold prospector is going to show up anytime soon and offer you his vein."

"Grizzled gold prospector?" He started to laugh, but ended up coughing. "What"—cough, wheeze—"what century do you think we're in?"

Scotty ignored his sarcasm and thrust her arm in his face.

Clearing his throat, Mace dropped his gaze to her wrist. Hunger put hollows in his cheeks, and a glimmer of gold in his eyes, but a heartbeat later, he turned away. "I can't."

"Bullshit. Since when have you ever turned down a female offering something?"

"You're not…you're not one of those females."

"Knock it off." She thrust her wrist upward, closer to his mouth. "Stop being an idiot."

"I can't, Scotty," he breathed, but his fingers curled around her forearm, drawing her hand to his lips. Lips that had probably touched a thousand females in ways she didn't want to think about.

It's finally my turn.

It was a thought she shouldn't have. But right now, she didn't really care.

For a long, drawn-out second, she worried he'd refuse, but then his fangs sliced downward into her wrist, and she sucked in a harsh breath at the abrupt, sharp sting.

A heartbeat later, the sting morphed into a surprising, pleasant tingle that radiated from where his mouth worked her wrist. Oh, sweet sin. The effect was intoxicating. Warmth flowed through her, tingling and effervescent. It was like bathing in sparkling wine, the bubbles bursting against all her erogenous zones, and she could imagine—

Mace released her, shoving her hand away with such force that she almost tipped backward.

Blinking, swaying on her knees in a drunken stupor, she struggled to regain her composure. "What's wrong?"

He dropped his head back against the tree with a sigh. "Your body's healing my bite too quickly. It's like sucking ice cream through a straw. Juice ain't worth the squeeze."

She cursed and glared down at her wrist. Stupid immortal genes. "Shit."

"It's okay."

"It's not okay," she insisted. "You're too weak to walk, let alone fight if we get attacked while the others are gone. You need blood."

Mace opened his mouth to protest, but whatever he'd been about to say was silenced when she straddled his thighs and brushed her hair away from her neck.

"Take it from here. The jugular won't heal as quickly as the vein in my wrist."

"Are you serious?" He gaped at her. "No. Fuck, no."

Baffled, she stared back at him. "Are *you* serious? You just tried with my wrist. What's wrong with my throat?"

He averted his gaze, dropping his eyes to where her legs bracketed his. "It's different," he murmured.

Still baffled. "How?"

"It just is."

People said Blade was the stubborn one. But no. Of the three of them, Mace could out-mule anyone. Blade dug in his heels out of careful thought and didn't generally let emotion play a role—except in the case of his brother, Stryke. But Mace's stubborn streaks were irrational as hell and often born of ego or pride.

She'd learned to weaponize those weaknesses a long time ago.

"You scared?"

His dark eyes snapped up. "Of what?"

She shrugged. "You tell me."

He stared at her, his ego battling his conscience. "I'm not scared of anything."

"My. Ass." This decision should be a no-brainer, so why was he waffling? She leaned in so close their noses nearly touched. "I know when you're scar—"

He struck with the savage growl of a predator. His fangs penetrated her throat, and she gasped at the unexpected intensity of both the pain and the pleasure.

Her entire body tingled, and warmth spread through her breasts, then lower, until it pooled between her thighs. Unexpected sensations made her squirm, chasing the pleasure as it intensified all over her body, even as she tried to corral her scattered thoughts.

This was arousal, wasn't it? After all this time, why now? And how could this feel so good…and at the same time, bad? Mace was her friend, and she shouldn't be turned on by an act meant to help him. This was basically a clinical procedure. It meant nothing. It never would.

It couldn't.

But as a low, rhythmic purr erupted from deep inside his chest, she lost her ability to contemplate her guilt. It was as if the very air around her became a mantle of desire, weighing her down until she melted against Mace's body. She dug her fingers into his shoulders as she clung to him. Between her legs, the hard ridge of his erection pressed into her, and she had to summon every ounce of self-control not to rub against it.

Wow. She got it now. Got why Mace tried to resist feeding from her.

This *was* different. This…was playing with fire, and gods help her, she'd never learned to keep her fingers out of the flames.

They didn't find any demons. Just blood from the single shot Jon had gotten in from his handheld crossbow before the thing outpaced them. The beast had left a trail for miles, but eventually, Blade decided it was no longer feasible to track it.

"We need to keep going." Jon peered intently into a ravine, the winding trail to the bottom showing clear signs of recent use but no blood. Either the thing had stopped bleeding, or it had evaded them.

"You guys track it if you want to," Blade said. "I'm not leaving my teammates alone. For all we know, this was a trap to lure us away, and they're in trouble."

Now that he'd voiced the possibility, anxiety flared in a sudden, hot rush. Scotty and Mace were both lethal warriors, but in his weakened condition, Mace wasn't at full capacity. Hell, he'd lost so much blood, he'd probably be as capable in a fight as an untrained ten-year-old human boy. He needed to feed, and soon. Preferably from a human, but as non-demons, Jon and Skoll would make suitable donors if worse came to worst. Blade just wished his demon blood could help.

Then there was Scotty.

Not an option.

Skoll shot his buddy a look. "Blade's right. Fight music is over anyway. My head's full of shitty, reflective emo tunes. Let's get to the cabin and plan our next move from there. We're not prepared to deal with the wendigo yet."

Blade swatted at a mosquito. Kynan was right; they were big bastards. "You don't think what we were chasing *was* a wendigo?"

Jon's gaze scoured the landscape, his body still tensed for battle. Blade might not like the guy, but he could admit that the male appeared well-trained and competent.

"Wendigos are almost as allergic to daylight as vampires," he said. "But they attract low-level demons like flies. Whatever we were chasing was probably a bottom feeder drawn to the wendigo's evil." He cast a forlorn glance into the ravine before shrugging in defeat.

Blade took the lead, fear for his teammates spurring him on as he jogged along worn animal trails and leaped over fallen logs. Forest critters scattered ahead of them, and birds yelled at them from the branches above.

Jon slowed, looking into the forest canopy. "The noise is a good sign. Animals know evil. They'd be silent if there was a demon nearby."

Thanks, Captain Obvious. Blade picked up the pace, afraid for his friends, despite Jon's assurances. *Hurry, hurry...*

He burst out of the brush and onto the main trail. Mace and Scotty should be right over ther—

He came to a stunned, breathless halt. Skoll crashed into Blade's back, but he was too numb to care.

What. The. Actual. Fuck?

Mace and Scotty were locked in a writhing, moaning tangle of arms and legs. Mace's face was buried in her neck, her long, thick ponytail wrapped in his fist. His other hand rested on her hip, his fingers digging into her jeans.

As Blade watched, Scotty arched, her breasts thrusting upward and testing the fabric of her camo T-shirt, and Mace tugged her tighter against him.

They were fucking with their clothes on.

Hot, stinging envy drilled into Blade from the top of his skull to the bottom of his feet, pinning him to the ground. But his lust demon instincts warred with jealousy, gradually dulling the edges with the intoxicating warmth of arousal.

Skoll and Jon flanked him, and while their bodies weren't wired for sex the way Blade's was, they sure as shit were susceptible to the lust pheromones billowing off Mace and Scotty in radioactive blasts.

Blade's jealousy went next-level as the guys observed Mace and Scotty with a mix of curiosity, surprise, and arousal.

Mine.

Scotty wasn't his, of course, but his primal brain didn't care. No one was allowed to lust after Scotty. All that mattered was getting Scotty away from these males.

Mace included.

"Mace!" His roar echoed through the air, and the forest went still as death. *Hey, look at that, Jon. There's a demon in the forest, after all.*

Mace's eyes, glazed over with bloodlust and plain, old-fashioned carnal lust, didn't seem to register what was happening. Not even when Blade tore Scotty from his grip. He hauled her off Mace's lap and dropped her to her feet.

Blood spurted from Scotty's throat in a crimson gusher.

Oh, shit.

Shit, shit, *shit!*

They hadn't been making out. Mace had been feeding.

Scotty slapped her hand over the bite marks on her neck. "What the hell, Blade?" she snapped. "Mace needs blood."

And he couldn't have waited half an hour for Jon or Skoll?

Instantly shamed by the thought and withering under Scotty's fury, Blade stepped back.

"Sorry," he grumbled as he fired up his healing ability and reached for her. Yeah, she'd heal quickly on her own, but his guilt wouldn't let him wait.

Scotty had other plans. Furious, she jerked away and offered her hand to Mace.

Mace waved off her help and came unsteadily to his feet. "Not cool, man."

"So not cool." Scotty scowled at Blade, accusation and indignation burning in her eyes. "What did you think was happening?"

Wiping her blood off his mouth with the back of his hand, Mace braced himself against a tree. "He thought we were gonna fuck."

Scotty rounded on Blade, a bundle of redheaded fury. "How dare you!" She punched him in the shoulder hard enough to make him stumble. He'd always admired how she never held anything back, but maybe she could have pulled that punch a little.

"I'm a sex demon, Scotty. I know lust when I see it." And smell it. He paused, inhaling the last, fading notes of the lust perfume lingering in the air. His voice was a little lower, rougher when he spoke again. "And especially when I feel it. It was coming off both of you like radiation from a nuclear power plant."

Scotty shuffled her feet, and Mace averted his gaze. Good. Blade had struck a nerve. Which assuaged his guilt a little. Then Mace shoved his other shoulder, knocking Blade back to where he'd been standing before Scotty had pounded on him.

"Dickhead." Mace shoved him again. "It didn't mean anything. You fucking know what happens when I feed. When any vampire feeds."

Yeah, okay, he knew. Arousal came with the territory, even more so when the vampire was also a sex demon. It was instinct, and something Mace couldn't help. Hell, had the guy fed from any other female, he'd have been inside her by now. No doubt Mace had used a lot of restraint with Scotty.

It must have been torture.

An image of Scotty rocking on top of Mace popped into Blade's head, and he imagined himself in Mace's place. Could he have withstood the feel of Scotty's body rubbing against his? Could he have resisted the taste of her skin or the sound of her moans?

I could do it.

Liar.

It wouldn't take much for his spark for her to explode into an uncontrollable inferno.

Scotty raked her fingers through her Mace-ravaged ponytail. "And it wasn't my fault that I got into it a little. It's the stupid sex-demon pheromones. So, stop being a whiny bitch. Nothing happened, and nothing would have happened even if you hadn't barged in."

"I know." Chastised into submission, Blade sighed. "Sorry. Seriously."

Mace and Scotty glanced at each other and shrugged. "It's fine," Mace said. "I'd have flipped out too."

Blade doubted that, but it was cool of Mace to try to make Blade feel less stupid.

"Are we done with the drama?" Jon slung his packs over his shoulder. "We need to get to the cabin. We're wasting precious daylight."

"Yeah." Mace hissed as he put his full weight on his left leg. That one had taken the brunt of the crushing spell, and Blade wasn't sure his attempt to repair it had been enough. "Shit. This hurts."

Skoll cast Mace a concerned glance. "Does your species heal fast?"

"Faster than most." Mace limped over to his pack, but Blade hauled it up and added it to his load. Mace gave him a grateful nod. "Feeding helps too. I should be a hundred percent by tonight."

Mace was full of shit. The damage had been catastrophic. Fatal, if not for Blade. But still, Blade wasn't a talented, respected physician like his uncle, Eidolon. He wasn't even as skilled as his cousin, Talon—also a doctor at Underworld General Hospital. No, Blade chose to craft his abilities into weapons instead of tools for healing injuries.

He could shred organs and pop arteries with a mere touch, but putting someone back together was a lot more difficult than taking them apart.

Jon seemed to contemplate what Mace had said as he started up the trail. "Do all Sems need to drink blood to heal?"

"Nah." Mace fell in with Blade and Scotty, his gait slowing them all down. "My biological dad is part vampire. I inherited his fangs and the occasional need for blood."

Jon frowned. "Like, an actual vampire? How? Vampires don't breed, and they only turn humans, not demons."

"Long, ugly story, dude." Scotty was still dragging her fingers through her ponytail, as if doing so would contain her curls. Especially now that they'd been tangled in Mace's fist.

Blade had to tamp down a wave of envy.

"You know his dad?" Jon asked her.

"Everyone knows him." At his questioning stare, she explained. "Ever heard of the demon named Wraith?"

"Seriously?" Jon wheeled around, managing to keep pace while walking backward. "That guy's a legend."

"And he'll remind you of it every chance he gets," Blade muttered, but no one could miss the fondness in his tone. His uncle *was* a legend. The legitimate, saved-the-world kind. He'd been the cool uncle when

Blade and his brothers were growing up. The one they all worshiped—well, everyone except Stryke. Stryke had followed Eidolon around like a puppy since the day he could crawl after him.

Jon and Skoll peppered them with more questions as they headed toward the cabin. They were especially fascinated by Scotty's family, but who wouldn't be? The Four Horsemen of the Apocalypse were either loved or hated by everyone on the planet. Even before the truth of their existence became known, they were known.

Gradually, their questions grew more personal and blatantly flirty. Blade hoped Scotty saw through their BS interest, but whatever. As much as he didn't want her hooking up with either of them, most of his concern was for Mace. His gait was off, and he was too pale.

No matter how close the cabin was, it wasn't close enough.

Chapter 6

The hike to the cabin took longer than expected. Normally, Scotty could appreciate a good hike, but this time, she just wanted to get off the trail. Shit had gotten so weird and awkward after Blade's sudden appearance while Mace was feeding. And it wasn't as if they could hurry. Mace's injuries limited them to a crawl.

Making it all worse, Jon eventually stopped asking questions and started prepping them for tonight's wendigo hunt.

Wendigos hate water.

Wendigos prefer to eat their victims while they're still alive.

No, it's not wendigoes. It's wendigos. No e.

Blade shot Mace an I-told-you-so look for asking Jon that particular question.

"What?" Mace asked, waving off Blade's offer of help to get up an incline, the way he waved off the ghastbat-sized mosquitoes harassing them. "I'm gonna have to write reports. Need to know how to spell wendigos."

"Let me fucking help you, dammit." Blade slipped under Mace's arm and forced the male to lean on him.

Blade looked over at Scotty. "Maybe you should open a gate and get him to Underworld General."

"Don't you fucking dare," Mace growled. "I'll be fine after I get some sleep."

Skoll swung around to Scotty. "You can do that? You can open gates like your dad?"

"Wait." Jon shortened his stride, letting her catch up. "If you can open gates, why did we just spend hours getting here?"

"The Horsemen can open destination gates almost anywhere," she explained. "But I can only connect to other Harrowgates. That's why I didn't gate us to the cabin."

And she'd been secretly glad there were no Harrowgates anywhere near the cabin. She *hated* opening personal gates. Hated the nausea and panic that gripped her every time she summoned one. Hated making up excuses to avoid using her ability to transport her team quickly. How many times had they been forced to go miles out of their way to find a Harrowgate when she could have just zapped one open?

A pit expanded in her gut at the thought of opening a gate for Mace. Would she get him to Underworld General if necessary? For sure, one thousand percent.

But she hoped she wouldn't have to.

"There." Jon pointed across an expanse of forest that had been cleared of underbrush. "There's the cabin."

Oh, thank gods.

Built into a bend in the stream they'd been following, the cabin was well-concealed, its weathered beams faded and patchy with moss. A couple of deer watched them warily from the other side of the creek, bounding away as they approached the cabin's worn porch.

Wise animals, she thought, as she took in the obscene number of deer skulls and antler racks decorating the rickety railing. A rusted metal folding chair was the sole furniture on the deck, its seat padded with the pelt of some unfortunate animal.

"You said someone actually lives here?" Mace coughed, sounding too winded for comfort. "Even in the winter? This is crazy remote."

Skoll gestured to a nearby shed that was bigger than the cabin. "He's got a snowmobile and a UTV, but I doubt he lives here during the winter." He shrugged. "But who knows? People who live off the grid are nuts, but they're hardy nuts."

Scotty eyed the werewolf. "Didn't you grow up off the grid?"

Apparently, his parents, Luc and Kar, kept a low profile for their family's safety. Scotty didn't know much about it—she didn't know Skoll or his sister, Luca, that well—but she'd heard things.

"Yep," Skoll said. "That's why I can speak with authority on the subject."

Mace, who was more of a hotels-over-tents kind of guy, glanced around in disgust. "This is messed up. Bet there's not even a coffee maker."

Jon's get-serious look was a waste of time. Mace was rarely serious. But she doubted he was joking about the coffee maker.

"Quiet," Blade murmured, one hand dropping to his favorite combat knife. "Door's ajar."

It took less than a heartbeat to read the situation and each other. By mutual, silent consent, they all drew weapons like a smooth, well-oiled machine. Nice. Scotty, Mace, and Blade didn't always get to work with other teams that synced well with theirs.

Blade nudged the door open with his boot, its ominous creak sounding too loud in the peaceful surroundings. She wasn't getting any evil vibes from inside, but some creatures could suppress their sinister aura.

"Trust your instincts," her dad liked to say. *"But don't be an idiot."*

Blade and Jon burst inside. Scotty and Skoll put their backs to the doorframe and kept watch outside, ready to back up the others if needed.

Mace slumped onto the chair and studied a pair of bald eagles soaring overhead.

Damn. That was so not Mace. He wasn't one to bird-watch if he could be in the middle of the action.

"Clear!" Blade's deep voice called out. "There's some blood on the floor."

Scotty and Skoll helped Mace inside. She expected a murder scene, maybe an overturned chair and some broken glass. But aside from a few drops of dried blood, the place was clean and neat, smelled of the wood used to build the cabin, and was much cozier than she'd expected. The furniture was simple and utilitarian, consisting of a futon, a rocking chair, and a sturdy, four-person table, but plush blankets were draped over the seats. The wood stove on the far wall had seen better days, but it looked inviting, thanks to the bearskin rug spread on the scuffed wood floorboards.

Bunks built into two of the walls could sleep four, but the tiny bathroom would struggle to fit *her*, let alone any of these big guys. The heavy, military-issue green blanket serving as a door was a sad attempt at privacy.

Almost as disappointing was the kitchen. The best that could be said was that it had a large pantry filled with canned goods, military rations, and pouches of freeze-dried meals—real prepper stuff that always tasted like reconstituted crap. The knives and cookware were in good shape, though. The guy obviously wanted to cook his tasteless survival food in the best pots and pans on his propane stove. Then he got to wash them in the sink rigged with a foot pump that brought water in from the stream, where she'd just seen an eagle take a dump.

She grimaced. "I hope we're not expected to drink from that."

Jon tossed his duffel onto one of the bunks, claiming a bottom bed. "We brought purifiers, but Nathan brings in drinking water. He said there's twenty gallons in the closet." He gestured to the bathroom. "It's a camp toilet, so you gotta take the bucket out and bury it in the woods every day. If you want to shower, there's one out back that draws from the stream."

Ugh. There were very few things Scotty and Aleka agreed on, but one of them was their dislike of camping. They were both big fans of warm beds, hot showers, and flushing toilets. She definitely didn't judge Mace for his hotels-over-tents stance.

Skoll glanced at his comms. "We should get some rest. Sunset is in a few hours. Who wants to take the futon?"

"I will," Scotty tossed her pack onto the floor next to it. "I'm the shortest. You guys would have to sleep folded up like tacos."

Jon bent to untie his boots. And wow, he had a nice ass. "I could go for a taco right about now."

Everyone murmured agreement as they staked out their beds, Mace taking the remaining bottom bunk, and Blade grabbing the one above him.

Scotty wandered over to study the blood, but now she just really wanted Mexican food. "Looks fresh. Animal or human?"

A growl and whoosh of air startled her so badly that she summoned a sword, spun around, and prepared to fight.

But *holy shit*, she wasn't prepared to fight *that*.

A massive bear, its paws twice the size of her head, stood on all fours where Jon had just been standing. Deep brown with a silver saddle stretching between its heavy shoulders, it grunted and put its nose to the floor, inhaling in deep, loud chuffs.

She'd seen bear shifters before, but not one like this. Usually, their size matched their wild-animal counterparts. This bear filled the cabin and couldn't have stood on its hind legs without punching through the roof. Even Blade and Mace were taken aback.

A moment later, the bear morphed back into Jon.

"It's human," he said, shaking off the transformation, his mid-length, dark hair swinging wildly.

"I could have told you that without the drama," Mace muttered from where he'd plastered himself against the log wall to avoid being squashed.

Jon snorted. "How?"

"Vampire," Mace said flatly. "Dumbass."

Jon might have forgotten, but Scotty hadn't. Her neck prickled, throbbing where Mace had buried his sharp fangs. Her fingers skimmed across the bite, but it was long gone, leaving only a hypersensitive tingle and some dried blood as evidence of the most sensual thing that had ever happened to her.

Now, when she glanced over at Mace, her breasts felt heavy, and an unbearable tension began to build between her thighs.

She caught Blade staring at her, his hooded gaze disturbingly blank, yet it pinned her in place like a big ol' spike of guilt. She jerked her hand away from Mace's bite like she'd been caught with her fingers on the lock to her father's armory.

Which had happened more than once as a child. The difference was, she'd been able to charm her dad into forgiving and forgetting. Something told her that what'd happened between her and Mace, no matter how innocent, would never be forgotten. At least, not by her. She'd replay today over and over, seeking to recreate the remarkable sensations and feelings Mace had sparked inside her.

Innocent, my ass.

Yeah, nothing about what had happened felt innocent. Was that what it was supposed to be like when a female was with a male? And why now? Why with *Mace*, of all people? One of only a handful of males on the planet who were off-limits.

Was Lilith's succubus DNA finally rearing its evil head?

Shaken and desperate for an escape from her thoughts, she glanced around the room for something—anything—that would give her a reason to change the subject. But she couldn't avoid the way Blade regarded her from behind an impenetrable wall that hadn't been there before. Mace watched her as well, his gaze locked on her throat, the banked heat in his eyes making her sweat.

He'd been affected too. She shouldn't have liked that fact, but she did.

Jon and Skoll—proving they had great instincts—read the room, their speculative, questioning gazes sliding between Mace, Blade, and Scotty.

People were always trying to suss out their unique relationship. They wanted to know if sex was involved. If they squabbled. If there was ever friction between them. Jealousy. Competition.

The answer to all their questions had always been *never*. Well, competition, yes, but it was friendly, complete with ribbing and pranks.

But this was new. Disturbing. Not friendly at all.

Her frantic gaze lit on the notebook propped on the counter. Perfect. She hurried over and flipped it open, hoping there'd be something interesting inside. More interesting than her inconvenient sexual awakening with a guy she couldn't have anyway.

But nope. Supply lists. Spell recipes. Oh, wait. *Jackpot.*

"Hey." She waved everyone over. "It's the map of Nathan's traps." According to the key, hashtags indicated magical traps, asterisks marked physical devices, and checkmarks signified the placement of wards.

Blade eased next to her and pointed to one of the hashtags. Heat billowed off him like a furnace. Had he always run so hot? Or was it because he was angry at her? Or was guilt making her sense something that wasn't there?

"That's the one that caught Mace," he said.

She forced herself to focus on the notebook and not Blade's proximity. It would be easier if his hip wasn't brushing hers. And if he didn't smell as earthy as the forest.

"Nathan placed everything in a layered web pattern, with the cabin in the center." She flipped the page and drew an uneasy breath at the chicken scratch and smears of blood on the back. "Guys. This was the last thing he wrote."

Mace sank down hard on his bunk, as if his legs had given out. "What's he say?"

"He was attacked by a wendigo while checking a trap." She squinted, struggling to make out the last sentence. Despair and pain bled into the paper, along with his blood. "It tore up his chest and arms. He barely escaped."

Jon cursed. "No one *barely escapes* a wendigo."

"What do you mean?" Blade shifted his stance, no longer touching her, and she wasn't sure if she was relieved or not. What she did know was that she hated that she'd noticed at all. She'd stopped being hyperaware of their every touch the moment they swore their oath and had accepted that neither of them wanted her the way she wanted them.

But their dynamic seemed to be shifting, which couldn't be a good thing.

"It's kind of like lycanthropy. If they get a hold of you, you turn." Jon's voice turned even more somber. "If the thing didn't finish him off, Nathan's a wendigo now. And he knows this land."

Okay, yeah. That was a problem. Now, there were potentially *two* wendigos. And if Nathan was a monster who could evade his own snares…they were sitting ducks.

Chapter 7

Mace woke up in agony. Half the reason was that his eardrums were pulsing to the tune of Ozzy Osbourne's "Bark at the Moon." But Blade's stupid alarm did what it was supposed to do. It made you want to get out of bed, even if it was to beat the crap out of him so he'd turn it off.

For once, though, Mace didn't want to get out of bed. The mattress was lumpy and uncomfortable as hell, but he'd rather suffer in the bunk than put weight on his left leg.

And because the fun just couldn't stop there, his cock ached too. The bastard throbbed painfully against the fabric of his sleep shorts, pointing directly at Scotty as if she was true north and his dick was the needle of a compass.

It wasn't often that he hated being a lust demon, but right now, he'd give anything to not have to deal with the life-or-death consequences of his sex drive.

Groaning, he fumbled through his pack for the injector that would suppress the desires and keep him from dying for a little while. He and Blade had brought a three-day supply and a two-day emergency backup. With any luck, they'd be out of here long before they had to reach for their reserves. Things started getting dicey by the end of day three as the lack of real sex made them strung out, grumpy, and fighting to stay focused. Then there were the health risks, which included atrophied organs, fever, heart failure, and death.

So, yeah. Best to avoid using the injections often.

With that happy thought, his fingers found an injector pen just as Scotty sat up on the futon, her sleep-mussed hair floating around her bare, slender shoulders. He rarely saw her with her hair down. It brushed against her black tank top and mesmerized him, holding his gaze as he wondered what it would feel like to run his hands through the curls.

She stretched like a lean, graceful cat, the fine muscles in her arms and back flexing beneath smooth, freckled skin. Skin he'd tasted when he'd penetrated her throat with his fangs and swallowed her sweet, life-giving blood.

He'd fed from countless, nameless females, but what he'd done with Scotty had been more than feeding. It had been an experience. A strengthening of their connection. He hadn't thought it possible to feel closer to her, but the sense of rightness left him reeling.

So did the guilt. He could tell Blade over and over that being with Scotty had only been about feeding, but eventually, he had to convince himself.

It's natural to get turned on during feeding.

Scotty's blood is only half human. She's also a quarter angel and a quarter succubus, so, of course, his desire would be amplified. He'd basically been plugged into a supercharged battery.

There's nothing to be ashamed of.

Remember the oath.

Fuck.

With a snarl, he jabbed the injector pen into his right thigh. Mercifully, the lust flowing through his veins eased. Finally, he could tear his gaze away from Scotty and the sexy curve of her neck as she absently traced the site of his bite with one finger. Was she thinking about what they'd done? Had she dreamed of it the way he had, turning the feeding into lovemaking on the forest floor?

"Get up, lazy asses," that dickhead, Jon, barked like a drill sergeant.

He must have stripped off his T-shirt at some point in the night, because he was now parading around in front of Scotty in nothing but his sleep shorts. When he crouched down in front of his bag to dig out some MREs, she stared at him so hard the guy had to feel her gaze like heated lasers on his skin.

"Sunset is in an hour." Jon tossed the Meals Ready to Eat onto the old, rickety table. "We need to go over the map and our game plan."

Mace really did not like that guy.

"Put on a fucking shirt," Blade muttered as he shuffled his way to the bathroom.

Jon snorted and ripped into the plastic MRE bag with his teeth.

"I'm a big girl," Scotty called after Blade. "I've seen bare chests before. Also, don't hog the bathroom."

"Don't worry, Scott," Mace said. "We all know hogging the bathroom is your thing." He swung his feet off the bunk. The moment his left foot hit the floor, a thousand kilotons of pain dropped on him like a bomb.

"Sonofa—!"

Scotty was there in an instant. "What is it?"

"My leg," he hissed through gritted teeth.

Scotty peeled the blanket away. "Oh, my gods."

He told himself not to look. But he often gave himself advice he didn't heed.

He looked.

Instant. Regret. And not a small amount of nausea.

His lower leg was a blackened, pulsing mass of flesh, like a charred hot dog on the verge of bursting. Sinister crimson streaks ran like fractured glass from his toes to his knee, and as he watched, they spread upward into the healthy flesh as if driven by hunger.

"Blade!" Scotty shouted. "Blade, get out here. Hurry!"

Blade nearly ripped the blanket doorway off its nails as he tore out of the bathroom, his jeans still unbuttoned. He was there in three strides, the cabin trembling with every heavy step on the scarred wooden floor.

"Bro," he breathed. "Shit. Why didn't you say something?"

"I was sleeping," Mace ground out as a fresh wave of pain shot through him. "Musta been out of it."

"I checked on him during my watch a couple of hours ago," Scotty said. "He looked fine."

Mace vaguely remembered both Blade and Scotty taking turns checking on him, but he hadn't been in pain. Not like this. This had happened fast.

Blade wrapped his hand around Mace's ankle, his touch light, as if he was afraid too much pressure would pop Mace's leg like a water balloon. His *dermoire* lit up, from the broken sword glyph beneath his right jaw, all the way to the swirls at the tips of his fingers. Then the hot sting of Blade's power stabbed into Mace's muscles. His head swam, and he no longer gave a shit about the symbols of their male ancestry.

"You can fix it, right?" Scotty gave Mace a comforting smile and a pat on the hand, like, "*Of course, Blade can fix it.*" He could fix anything. He was always patching them up.

Mostly, he patched up Mace, though. Scotty usually healed too fast to need his help.

"Sorry, man." Blade heaved a heavy breath. "This is out of my league. You need to get to Underworld General."

"Hell, no." Mace struggled to conceal a particularly agonizing slice of pain, but he couldn't hide the way he spoke through clenched teeth. "Try harder."

Blade's eyes narrowed, shadows flickering in their dark depths. "I did. I'm telling you, this is more than I can handle." He turned to Scotty. "You'll need to cast a gate."

Closing her eyes, Scotty let out a deep breath. She hated opening gates. Not that she'd ever admit it. She denied it every time, but she had tells. "No problem."

Mace hated making her do it. Hated watching her bleed. Hated that it turned him on, even as he despised himself. She clearly didn't enjoy hurting herself to open a gate, and he was a jackass who had to control himself at the tantalizing aroma of her blood. And now that he'd tasted it…

He only wanted more of her.

And not just her blood.

"Whatever." Mace breathed through a burning spike of pain that skittered upward, all the way to his hip. "Let's just do it so I can get back here. Eidolon will have me patched up within the hour."

He allowed Blade to help him to his feet and keep him standing upright as Scotty stepped into the center of the room.

"Someone toss me the knife under my pillow."

"What for?"

Jon's question was merely curious, but Mace, pissed off at the situation and struggling to control his pain, snapped, "Because she said so."

Scotty gestured to Skoll, who was standing nearest the futon. "Because I need my blood to power the gate."

"Can't you summon a blade?" Skoll flung aside the pillow and found the dagger Scotty had slept with since her sixth birthday. Blade had been at the birthday party when Ares gave her the dagger. She'd been delighted, swearing she'd never part with it. Her mother, Cara, had been less thrilled. Ares probably didn't get any that night.

"My summoned blade won't cut my own flesh." She made an

impatient sound and thrust out her palm. "Hurry."

Skoll handed her the dagger, hilt first, and she deftly flipped it into the air, caught it, and sliced open her palm in one smooth, practiced motion. Didn't matter that she did that kind of thing all the time. Mace winced. He really did hate seeing her bleed, especially for him.

Except earlier, when she bled onto your tongue.

Right. Except that. That would provide him with fantasy material for a long time. Masumi could do the red-haired thing like she did for Blade, and—

Stop it! Scotty was off-limits, and there was no point in fantasizing about her. In fact, it would be *stupid* to fantasize about her. Especially now. He was probably dying, and all he could think about was getting Scotty on his lap again, her throat exposed, vulnerable.

Fucking stop!

Scotty's blood dripped to the floorboards, forming a thick pool that glistened in the faint light from the propane lanterns. With a wave of her hand, the blood spiraled upward into a thin, vertical line about eight feet tall. It spread, becoming a four-foot-wide shimmering curtain.

Jon let out a low whistle of appreciation. "Awesome ability."

"Sure," Scotty said, as she reached for the roll of paper towels on the counter. "If you like pain."

Jon looked over at her. "Depends on the pain," he said slowly, and Mace felt the sudden urge to punch the suggestive smile right off his face. "It's not all bad."

And wouldn't you know it, Scotty fell for that husky-voiced delivery and his smoldering, fuck-me eyes, giving him a flirty smile right back.

Mace muttered obscenities under his breath as he limped over to the newly formed Harrowgate. Blade had better keep an eye on this situation while Mace was getting patched up.

"We'll go with you," Blade offered, and Mace almost agreed, for no other reason than to get Scotty away from the other two males. But ultimately, they had a job to do, and he wasn't going to let Kynan down.

"You guys handle the assignment," he said, "I'll be fine. There's nothing you can do anyway."

Scotty pressed a paper towel into her palm. "Bullshit. You're the one who says that splitting up the team always ends badly."

He gestured to his leg. "It already went bad." He swallowed a little nausea and hoped they didn't notice. "You know I'm right."

Yeah, they did. The mission came first. Besides, if they went with him, they'd just end up hanging around a boring-ass hospital while Skoll and Jon got to do all the fun shit and get all the credit.

"We'll check on you later," Scotty promised.

"I know." He popped Blade a fist bump, but Scotty bypassed his fist and went straight to a hug, clinging to him, her lips brushing his ear.

"Remember the blood on the floor when we first came inside?" she whispered. "You didn't really know it was human, did you?"

He grinned. He should have known she'd call him out.

"No," he whispered back. "But Jon's an ass."

Her laughter followed him into the Harrowgate, cutting off when the door closed and left him inside a black box with glowing symbols and a map on the wall. Next to the map, Underworld General Hospital's caduceus pulsed. The moment he touched it, the box opened, and he limped into the demon hospital's Emergency Department.

Chu-Hua, a Guai demon nurse he'd known since he was an infant, hurried over, her piglike feet clacking on the obsidian floor.

"Hey, Chu." He braced himself on the corner of the reception desk before he fell over. Man, he felt like shit. He hadn't felt this bad since his transition. "I need to see Eidolon."

"Dr. E is off today," she said in her high-pitched squeal.

"Lucky me," came a familiar voice from behind him. Fuck. Groaning, Mace turned to see his half-brother sauntering over, looking as cocky as ever in black scrubs embroidered with the UG caduceus and *Dr. Talon.* "Today, you're my problem."

Yep. Splitting up the team *always* ended badly.

Blade didn't like this. Didn't like sending Mace to the hospital while he and Scotty remained behind. And judging by the expression on Scotty's face, she didn't like it, either. She was still pale and shaky from opening the gate, but the worry in her eyes was for Mace.

"You sure you guys don't want to join him?" Skoll asked. "We can start the search without you."

"We stay on mission." Blade grabbed a long-sleeved tee from his pack. "Mace is in the best hands now. There's nothing we can do."

What he'd said was true, but Blade didn't have to like it. Especially because, as Mace always pointed out, every time the team split up, bad shit happened.

It's bad luck to separate us, man. You know it is.

He'd told Tayla and Kynan that a million times.

We're a team. You can't break up a team. It's bad juju.

Skoll nodded and flicked his finger across his wrist comms. A glowing 3D map popped into the air. As Blade shrugged into his shirt, Skoll manipulated the image, zeroing in on the area surrounding the cabin.

"Sightings of the creature were reported here, here, and here," he said, tapping red markers indicating multiple areas on the map. He gestured at several spots tagged with black dots. "And these are the last known locations of the men who went missing." He flicked off the map. "We should split up into two groups. Since Jon and I are both more familiar with this area and case than you two, I suggest that Jon pairs up with Blade, and I'll take Scotty."

I'll take Scotty.

That was a hard no.

"Kynan sent us because we work best as a team," Blade said. "Scotty and I will pair up."

"But—"

"We can communicate via the comms or handhelds if we have questions." Scotty started toward the bathroom with an armful of clothes. "This isn't about not wanting to work with you guys. It's just that we're a package deal. We operate as a unit."

Skoll shrugged and let it go, but Jon shook his head and rolled his eyes, muttering something uncomplimentary under his breath.

"You got a problem?" Blade asked quietly.

"No problem." Jon swung around to him, his broad shoulders blocking the view of the entire north wall. "Unless wondering how over-rated your *legendary team* is happens to be a problem."

Before Blade could put Jon on his ass, Scotty changed course and thrust herself between them like a pissed-off cat.

"Overrated?" She was at least a foot shorter than Jon, but she got all up in his grill, somehow seeming to tower over him. It was hot, and Blade couldn't find it in him to feel shame about thinking that. "Wanna put our record up against yours?"

"Sure," Jon said, baring his teeth in a cynical smile. "But you can't count the times you got help from all your Horsemen and angel buddies."

What a dick. "You think we need help to do our jobs?"

The dick shrugged. "Guess we'll find out, won't we?"

Fuck that guy. Scotty and Blade were going to locate every wendigo out there and put them out of commission before Skoll and Jon needed to take their next piss.

"Okay," Scotty said, jamming her finger into Jon's sternum. She could never let shit like this go. Also…hot. "Why do you think we're overrated?"

Amused, Jon looked down at her finger. He wrapped his big hand around hers and gently pushed it away. But he didn't release her. "Maybe not *overrated*. Privileged, I guess."

Privileged? Scotty's family history was one giant tragedy. Mace had a tricky history with two fathers, a mother who was once an angel, a grandfather who was the Grim Reaper, and a bitter half-brother.

And Blade…his insides ached just thinking about it. His brother, Rade, had been traumatized as an infant by a psycho demon, and his baby brother, Chaos, had been slaughtered while in Stryke's care. Their family had been torn apart, and Stryke only made it worse by walking away from them all. Now, he was back, and everyone acted as if nothing had happened.

Blade wasn't ready to forgive and forget. So, naturally, now *he* was the bad guy. He was about to tell Jon where he could shove his opinion when the guy started blathering again.

"Let's face it," he said, "you guys grew up in palaces, with servants and guards. You were trained to fight from the day you were born. You're like, blessed by angels and crap."

"Not all of us." Scotty jerked her hand away from his. "And fuck you. We've gone through some bad shit. Our lives haven't all been *privileged*."

"Really?" Jon snorted. "Ever gone hungry for days because one of your parents worked three jobs and the other was an addict? Ever been sold for drug money? Ever been hated just because someone in your family is the wrong color or wrong breed?"

"Seriously?" Scotty blinked, taken aback. "I can't even imagine."

"We have a sun bear in our lineage," Jon said. "Sun bear shifters are small and considered cowardly and weak in the bear-shifter community. They've nearly been hunted to extinction. Soon, they'll be as extinct as the pandas."

"There were panda shifters?" Scotty got that look on her face, the one she got when she saw a kitten. "Aw, they must have been adorable."

Jon's gaze turned inward, his expression sad. "They were a gentle people."

"That's awful." She moved one of the lanterns to the bathroom, gathering clothes and speaking as she went. "Is it rude to ask what bear species you are? Because whatever you turned into was huge. Bigger than any grizzly I've ever seen."

"And shaggy," Blade said. "I didn't think grizzlies were that shaggy."

"My family is from a rare, ancient line of prehistoric bears." Jon started pulling stuff out of his pack and rearranging it.

"You mean, like a cave bear? Or a short-faced bear?" Scotty called out from where she was changing behind the curtain. "Aleka was always shoving pictures of dinosaurs and woolly mammoths and crap in my face during her paleontology phase."

Blade remembered Aleka going through many phases before settling on demon archaeology. Growing up, she'd been one of the few people who could hold a conversation with Stryke. Hell, she'd been one of the very few who *wanted* to have a conversation with Stryke. Having brainiac siblings was something he, Scotty, and Mace all had in common, and something that came up often, since all their siblings were huge pains in the ass.

No one denied that Blade had it the worst, though.

"Wouldn't that make you royalty among bear shifters?" Blade asked.

Jon snorted. "And now you see why having a sun bear in the family would be a huge scandal. A dozen of my family members were run out of society and left penniless. But not before they sterilized us."

"That's insane, man," Blade said. Now, he felt bad about hating the guy.

But he still didn't want him sleeping with Scotty.

"Enough chin wagging," Jon said, clearly wanting to change the subject. He gestured to the supplies they'd brought. "We're wasting time."

He was right, and they got to work putting together light packs containing various supplies, water, purification tablets, protein bars, and one first aid kit per team. Then, as twilight stretched across the forest, turning the distant mountains gray, they weaponed-up and headed out.

"Let's take the main trail and then split up at the river," Jon suggested as they stepped off the porch.

Sounded fine to Blade. Scotty, dressed identically in black tactical pants and a turtleneck reinforced with ensorcelled, puncture-resistant thread, gave an affirming nod, too, and they slipped into the forest.

Dark shadows grew darker as they navigated the worn trail. Day creatures gave way to night creatures, and silence descended, save the occasional hoot from an owl and the drone of nocturnal insects.

One of the insects buzzed past his head. Fucking mosquitoes. He lit up his *dermoire*, and several of the bloodthirsty bastards popped as if they'd landed on an insect zapper.

Skoll looked at him in surprise. "I thought Sems needed physical contact for their power to work."

"They do," Blade said. "I'm special." Sure, zapping bugs was a sidekick kind of power, but it came in handy.

Jon looked back at them, his night eyes glowing with the faint yellow light common to most shifters. "How's your night vision?"

"Excellent. Both of us," Scotty assured him, but she didn't mention that hers was better than Blade's. "Blade can also blend into shadows."

Not as well as his father, but yeah, the ability to camouflage himself came in handy now and then. More often than Mace's ability to sense souls like his mother. But she could see them, and he couldn't.

"Great," Jon said. "But we still need to be careful."

"No shit," Blade muttered, remembering why he didn't like the guy. "Like we don't know to be careful."

"Wasn't *my* teammate who walked into a trap," Jon drawled.

Scotty barked out a bitter laugh. "He's got us there."

"Yeah, yeah." The guy was still a dick.

The trail dropped down into a muddy creek bed dotted with fresh moose and wolf tracks.

Crouching, Skoll studied the tracks. "It's a young moose. And lame."

"How many wolves?" Scotty asked.

"Six." Skoll looked off toward where the tracks disappeared into the woods. "That moose had better hope the wolves catch it before the wendigo does." He blew out a breath and stood. "And then the wolves better run too."

As if Skoll's words were a trigger, something screeched, and a shiver shot down Blade's spine.

Scotty summoned her sword. "What was that?"

"I don't know," Jon replied, "but it didn't sound friendly."

The forest went still. Unnaturally still.

Off in the distance, a wolf howled, a sound that spoke to Blade on a level so deep he couldn't explain it, even to Scotty and Mace. And while Stryke and Rade probably understood, he never spoke to either of his brothers about the werewolf part of them, inherited from their mother.

He hadn't spoken to Stryke about much at all over the last fifteen years, and Rade was…Rade. Getting him to string more than a dozen words together was hard enough when you *weren't* discussing something private and personal. And Crux hadn't shown any signs of having any werewolf DNA yet, but neither had Blade, Rade, or Stryke until after their Seminus transitions into maturity.

So, yeah. Blade had dealt with his inner beast alone for his entire life. Sure, he could talk to his mom about it, but she couldn't understand what it was like on the nights of the full moon, when his blood ran hot, and he was restless and feeling like his skin was shrinking…but he was trapped in his Seminus body and couldn't do anything about it.

As infants, he and his brothers had been immunized to prevent them from shifting into nightmare beasts with the prey drive of a werewolf but the sex drive of an incubus. Runa couldn't relate to that, nor could she relate to the psychic connection he had with his brothers—a connection Stryke had broken a long time ago. Recently, he'd repaired the link with Crux and Rade, but Blade had opted out.

He listened to the wolf again, and his hackles rose. The canine was sending out a warning.

Skoll sniffed the air, tension making the tendons in his neck stand out in stark cords. "Do you guys smell that?"

"Smell what?" Scotty asked. But right then, Blade caught a whiff of a familiar metallic tang.

Blade swung around. "Blood. A lot of it."

"Could be the moose." Jon's fingers curled around the hilt of the machete at his hip.

Skoll scowled. "Whatever it is, it's old. Has a hint of rot."

Blade caught the stench of decay as the wind shifted, bringing a breeze that also smelled of moss and water.

Skoll checked the map. "We're out of Nathan's trap boundary. This way." He gestured for them to follow, and they crept through the brush, leaving the worn wildlife trail behind them.

They moved slowly and carefully, Skoll in the lead, Scotty and Blade following, and Jon bringing up the rear. The odor grew stronger and more acrid, making Blade's eyes water. Scotty looked like she was about to gag.

"Don't move!" Jon hissed. "It's right the—"

Something big, with flashing claws and dagger-like teeth, exploded from a thicket and slammed into Jon. They tumbled down the embankment, crashing through the brush in a tangle of thrashing limbs.

Jon battled the creature as he fell, desperate to keep its mouth away from his throat. Ugly, formerly human, the thing's shredded clothes hung off its thin, skeletal frame, but that's where the resemblance ended. Its unhinged jaw gaped wide, its huge maw filled with sharp, blackened teeth that dripped with stringy saliva.

Blade half-jumped, half-slid down the slope after Jon. He body-slammed the thing, barely saving Jon from having his face bitten off. The monster snarled and lunged for Blade, but he was ready, armed with a branch as thick as Scotty's thigh. He struck out, knocking the creature into a tree with a satisfying crunch.

Scotty followed up with a throwing knife, catching the creature in a sunken, black eye. The thing screamed, and in the blink of its other eye, it disappeared into the brush.

"Son of a bitch," Scotty breathed. "Was that a wendigo? Did it bite you?"

Panting, his skin glistening with sweat, Jon frantically patted himself down for injuries. "I'm fine," he said, but his voice shook as hard as his hands. "I'm fine. Really. Couple of scrapes from the brambles is all."

Blade knelt next to him. "Let me check you out. Don't want you spontaneously turning into one of those fucking things."

"Right." Jon eyed a scratch on his hand. "You'd love to chop off my head."

Maybe a little.

"Wouldn't be the first time I've had to put down an ally after they changed."

The grim reality of what they were all facing settled over them like a shroud. But the good news was that Jon's wounds were minor and most likely caused by the tumble down the ravine. Blade had them healed within seconds.

Skoll returned from fetching Jon's pack from where it had gotten hung up on a tree limb during the fall. "I'm digging the healy-healy," he said, as he tossed the pack to the ground next to Jon. "Maybe we should get a Seminus demon on our team."

Blade snorted. "Like any Sem would want to work with you ass-holes."

"Other way around, man," Jon muttered. "Other way around."

"Hey," Scotty called out. "I found something."

Skoll and Blade helped Jon to his feet and joined Scotty at the top of the ravine, where the wendigo had attacked Jon.

"What the hell is th—?" Skoll recoiled, caught his heel on a root, and would have repeated Jon's tumble into the ravine if Scotty hadn't caught him.

Blade shoved a tangle of leafy branches aside. A partially eaten skull, one eye dangling from its socket, stared back at him. "It's a human head." He glanced at a lump a few yards away. "And a torso." That, too, had been ravaged, the internal organs strewn about, the ribs broken, the spine twisted.

"Ooh, lemme see." Holding her breath, Scotty got in close and poked the head with a stick. She loved the gory shit. "Must be one of our missing persons." She used her comms to get some images for later victim identification and reports.

"We need to find this thing," Blade said, but Scotty was already on the move, heading north in the direction the creature had gone.

They'd barely started after her when something ahead of them screamed—a grating, bone-chilling sound unlike anything Blade had ever heard.

The sound came again, this time from the east. Then another, this time from the northwest. And another from behind.

"It's four wendigos," Skoll said, his voice low. Shaken. "Fuck me, there are four of them."

Chapter 8

Gods, Mace hated Underworld General.

He'd practically grown up here, in the hospital that was basically the family business. His parents, Lore and Idess, worked here, too, although their jobs didn't really involve saving lives. In fact, both worked with dead people—Lore in the morgue as the medical examiner, while Idess spent most of her days guiding human spirits out of the place.

But with as much time as he'd spent here in his early years—first in the nursery and then later, roaming the halls with his cousins—he now avoided it like the plagues the staff treated.

Medical shit creeped him out. He didn't like the sickly odors of death and disease, the wailing patients, or being reminded of his mortality. A five-hundred-year lifespan probably sounded like forever to humans, but it seemed like a pathetically short amount of time to him. Especially when so many of his friends were immortal.

Like Scotty.

The thought of her living for thousands of years after he and Blade died sat in his brain like a tumor, metastasizing more on every passing birthday. One day, the malignant mass would consume him, and he had no idea what he'd do then.

"You need to tell me what happened," Talon said as he guided Mace to an exam room, and none too gently, either. "Instead of cussing me out under your breath. I have excellent hearing, you know."

"Obviously, not that excellent," Mace growled. "It wasn't aimed at you. Not everything is about you. I was cursing at the situation."

"Uh-huh." Talon gestured to the exam table. "Hop up. Do you need help?"

"I'm fine." Mace shrugged out of his brother's grip and hauled himself up onto the paper-covered pad. It hurt like hell, but he bit his tongue. No way was he showing weakness in front of Talon.

As Mace leaned back, Talon palpated his leg. "You going to tell me how this happened?"

Mace explained, mostly through clenched teeth, as Talon poked, prodded, and channeled his excruciating power into the spreading black flesh. It was nearly to his knee now, the dark veins stretching into healthy flesh all the way to his hip.

He hadn't truly been worried before, but the way Talon's mouth tightened into a grim slash was starting to freak him out.

"This is magic damage," Talon said. "You need a specialist. Stay here. I'll be right back."

Where the hell did Talon think Mace was gonna go?

Shaking his head at his jerk of a half-brother, Mace glanced down at his wrist comms. He tried pinging Scotty and Blade, but naturally, there was no signal coming from their units. Then he groaned as an avalanche of pain roared down his leg.

"You okay?" Talon's voice pierced the bubble of agony.

"No," he admitted. Begrudgingly. "Where's that specialist?"

"Coming. I sent for your dad, too."

"Which one?" Normally, when Mace said something like that, it was to get under Talon's skin. He hated reminders that they shared a biological father. But this time, Mace was genuinely curious. Hoping for Lore.

It wasn't that Mace didn't love Wraith. He did. Blade claimed Mace hero-worshiped him a little, and Mace denied that shit, but Blade was probably right. Mace and Wraith were so alike—more so than Talon and Wraith. More so than Mace and Lore.

But Lore had always been Mace's *dad*. Wraith was Wraith. Lore was Dad.

Talon's movements were a little jerky as he prepared a surgical tray. "Don't be a dick."

"Whatever, Stewie," Mace muttered, using Talon's childhood nickname, which usually annoyed the shit out of him.

Clenching his jaw tight, Talon tossed some scissors onto the tray. Then some syringes. And what was that one wicked-looking thing? Forceps? Catheter? A speculum, maybe? He'd heard those terms bandied about, but he'd never cared to learn medical terminology or how to use anything more complicated than a Band-Aid.

Mace relaxed as much as he could and tried to concentrate on anything but the pain. "Remember that time I crashed my bike, and you stitched me up with your mom's sewing needle and bright pink thread?"

A rare, faint smile curved Talon's mouth. "You were afraid you'd get in trouble because you were grounded. We both ended up in hot water. Eidolon thought I did a great job, though."

"His opinion was all that mattered to you back then," Mace murmured.

"And Wraith's was all that mattered to you."

That was fair, but there was more to it. Mace wasn't sure why— maybe it was the pain, or maybe it was the faintest tingle of fear that he wouldn't make it out of here alive—but he wanted Talon to know how he'd felt back then.

"Your opinion mattered," he said.

Talon's surprised gaze flicked up to Mace, but how could he be shocked? Mace had toddled after his big brother since the day his parents sat him down and explained how he'd come about. Lore was sterile, the result of human-Seminus DNA gone wrong, and all three of his brothers had donated genetic material to create Idess's pregnancy. When Mace was born, Wraith's symbol at the top of his *dermoire* had revealed the father's identity.

Mace had been thrilled to have another dad and a brother. But Talon hadn't been as enamored with the idea, and nothing Mace did ever won him over.

Talon started to say something, but was interrupted when Idess swept into the room, just ahead of Lore, and smothered him in a hug.

"Hi, Mom."

She pulled away, and his dad moved in to tug him into a brief embrace before focusing on his leg.

"Talon." Lore glanced over at Mace's brother. "Thanks for letting us know he was here. You said you paged Dr. Vale?"

"Vale?" Mace hadn't heard that name before. "Is he new?"

"He?" A statuesque, bronzed female stepped into the room, her metallic skin stretched over a sharp, angular bone structure that could have been carved from flint. Three curved, black horns burst from her skull, forming a hard Mohawk from the front of her head to the back. She gave him a stern look, her ebony eyes glittering with contempt.

"And I'm not new. I've been here two *sextas* now."

Sextas, a Sheoulic word that measured time in units of six years. So, she'd been at UG for twelve years, and he'd never once seen her? He'd have remembered seeing a *draak* demon. The dragon-shifters were rare, and even more rarely seen outside of the Draig region in Sheoul. Which was good, because they were assholes. The males *and* females.

"Dr. Vale specializes in treating injuries caused by spells," his mom said, casting Vale a smile, which was returned. At least, Mace hoped the baring of a million sharp teeth was a smile. "A vengeful spirit cast a spell on me last fall, and Dr. Vale broke it in about thirty seconds."

Mace cranked his head around. "You didn't tell me you were attacked."

"Please." Idess waved her hand in dismissal. "It was a wart spell. Beginner stuff."

Dr. Vale ran a scaly hand over Mace's leg and made a hissing noise. "This is definitely not beginner stuff."

The room's curtain swept open, and Logan, Scotty's cousin and fellow DART agent, stepped in, his expression a mask of worry.

Mace scowled at Talon. "How many people did you call besides my parents?"

"I didn't call him. Not everything's about you," Talon said, throwing Mace's earlier words back at him. He turned to Logan. "We're kind of busy right now—"

"Eva needs help." Logan shoved the curtain all the way back, showing where Eva stood, her face gaunt, eyes dull, and her skin a ghastly shade of dead-body gray. "We need Eidolon. Please. Hurry."

Idess's long braid swung against her navy sweater as she hurried over to Eva. Gently, she reached up to touch Eva's cheek. "No doctor can help this," she said softly. "Not even Eidolon."

Eva swallowed dryly. "Is it...Harvester's Grace?"

Idess nodded, her face almost as pale as Eva's.

Ah, damn. When Scotty's grandmother, Harvester, was killed, her angelic Grace had found its way inside Eva. But the human body wasn't built to withstand that much power, and unless someone found a way to remove it, Eva would die.

Eva swayed, her skin going waxy. Logan leaped for her, catching her before she hit the obsidian floor.

"Take her to Trauma Two," Talon barked, rushing out after them. He stopped at the threshold. "Vale, I'll need an update on Mace's condition ASAP."

She nodded crisply and returned her scaly hand to Mace's leg. It was agonizing, but his thoughts right now were with Logan and his mate. Mace hadn't liked the former Aegis spokesperson at first, but now she was family and working for DART's media team. It turned out she was pretty great.

"Is she going to be okay, Mom?"

He didn't like the worry in Idess's eyes, or the way she squeezed Lore's hand, her mouth drawn tight. "If Aleka can't locate Harvester's blood for a ceremony quickly, there's nothing anyone can do for her. She needs an angel."

"You're an angel," he pointed out.

"I haven't had any real angelic power for decades."

"But you have brothers and sisters. All the Memitim—"

"All my Memitim brethren together wouldn't be enough power to save her. She needs an Archangel. They have dominion over Grace."

"But aren't all the Archangels trapped in Heaven right now?"

"Yes," Idess said softly. "So, without Harvester's blood, Eva will die."

Chapter 9

Gabriel groaned as consciousness took hold and pain overwhelmed his senses. A dull, throbbing ache in his head competed with stiff joints, muscle spasms, and cramps in his gut. Grit scratched his eyes when he opened them, making his vision blurry as he tried to figure out where he was.

One thing was clear: his wrists were chained, and he was lying on a cold, hard stone floor.

Oh, yeah. He was being held prisoner. Sometimes, he forgot. Because who would want to remember?

"You're awake. Finally."

The female voice, as cold and sinuous as a serpent, sent terror slithering down his spine. And it was too late to pretend he was still unconscious.

Footsteps drew closer, and his already parched mouth went even drier. Black high heels appeared in front of his face, and before he could shift away, one of them smashed into his cheek.

Agony shot through his jaw, and blood spurted onto the ground. He watched in morbid fascination as the stone absorbed it, drinking it like a sponge.

Suddenly, she fisted his hair, wrenched his head back, and hurled him against the wall. More pain crashed through him, and he figured she'd just broken his pelvis. Definitely some ribs. And the thing that really sucked was that he no longer healed instantly. He'd lost that perk when the Thrones cut off his wings and booted him from Heaven. The only way to get it back was to enter Sheoul and become a True Fallen angel, complete with leathery wings, powerful abilities, and an evil soul.

No thanks. He'd rather be an Unfallen, stuck between realms and as helpless as a human infant. It sucked, but at least his soul would remain uncorrupted.

But is it? Really? After what happened to Hutriel?

Ruthlessly, he shoved the memory of his battle with the angel on Stryke's oil rig into the deepest recesses of his mind and concentrated on his current predicament.

His arms trembled as he pushed himself up until he was leaning on his side against the wall and staring at his tormentor. The worst of three females who had been torturing him for…how long? He had no idea. Months, probably. Felt like years.

"What are you going to do to me today, Lilith?" he croaked.

She crouched down on her heels, her legs spread wide to reveal… everything. As a succubus, the most infamous sex demon in history, and the mother of the Four Horsemen, she enjoyed showing off her body. And using it for both pleasure and pain. Mainly, she took her pleasure from others' pain.

Gabriel had given the bitch a lot of pleasure.

He shuddered, his body reacting to his thoughts and maybe out of dread of whatever she was about to do to him. At least she was alone. When the others joined in, the horrors were so much worse.

"I'm not going to do anything to you," Lilith said. "If you agree to enter Sheoul."

"This again?" He snorted, which turned into a cough that produced blood clots. Cool. Lung damage, too. When he recovered, he rasped, "It'll never happen. Never!" He slid down the wall a little, too exhausted to fight gravity. "Evil whore. You'll have to drag me to Hell."

In a flash of pale motion, her sharp nails flayed his cheek wide open. "Turning Unfallen angels evil by force is for losers. When the decision is made of one's own free will, their corruption is total. My rewards for convincing an Unfallen *Archangel* to willingly enter Hell will be beyond imagining. The Dark Lord is generous with those who please him." Her hand drifted between her legs as the prospect of being rewarded by Satan himself seduced her. "He will fill me with such… power," she moaned.

She would have a long wait. Two powerful brothers, Revenant and Reaver, the Horsemen's father, had locked Satan away for a thousand years, and there were still nine hundred and fifty odd years to go. In the meantime, Revenant ran Hell, and as far as Gabriel knew, he wasn't Lilith's biggest fan.

"I'm sure Revenant will have something to say about that," he said, reminding the bitch queen that, while she was incredibly powerful, she was also in hiding. Apparently, Revenant had called for her head.

She hissed, her shiny fangs glinting in the smoky torchlight. Her palm cracked against his injured cheek, her nails scoring more tears in his already damaged flesh. He tested it with his tongue, and…yep, it poked all the way through his cheek.

"Never say his name!"

"Ah." Okay, he got it now. "That's why you want me to voluntarily enter Hell, isn't it? If you drag me down there, you think I'll tell Revenant how to find you." Entering Hell by choice rather than against his will would embed the evil even deeper into his being and make him more likely to join Team Satan than Team Revenant. "And yet, you keep torturing me."

"Torturing you?" She threw her head back and laughed. "Pain isn't torture. It's pleasure." She reached down and wrapped her hand around his flaccid cock. "And this," she purred, "is the gateway to both."

His gut roiled at the feel of her palm on his sex, her hand pumping slowly up and down. He never got hard for her or the other two whores—at least, not without the potions they forced down his throat. Usually, he puked them back up, but they still did the job they were meant for.

Then he threw up again after they used him for their demented desires.

"You're going to submit to me, Gabriel," she said. "I don't care how long it takes. You *will* submit to me."

"Never," he growled. "I'm an *Archangel.* I will never kneel to a demon."

Her fingernails dug into his cock, and he hissed in pain. "You *were* an Archangel, until your Heavenly brethren betrayed and abandoned you. Now, you're mine." She pushed to her feet slowly, sensually. "Kneel between my thighs, Gabriel. Use that wicked tongue and your new fangs the way I like it."

He hated the reminder that his body was shedding angel attributes and replacing them with evil downgrades. His holy glow had been snuffed, and now he had baby fangs that kept cutting his lip. If he entered Hell, he'd get wings, powers, and even bigger fangs to slice up his tongue and mouth. "Fuck you."

"That will come after."

He closed his eyes and threw his head back against the wall in stubborn defiance. But he knew how this would end. She would either torture him into unconsciousness, defile him with her body and foreign objects, or she'd find an innocent to torture if he didn't pleasure her.

Either way, he was in for another nightmarish day that would make him that much angrier at the bastards who had kicked him out of Heaven. He would use everything Lilith did to him as fuel for the vengeance he planned.

His list was long. So long that even Lilith, whom he hated with every feather he'd lost, wasn't at the very top.

Chapter 10

The temple was delightfully creepy.

Dusty, its walls and floors stained with ancient blood, and cobwebs stretching between gnarled, desiccated roots, it was just the kind of place Raika would expect demons to hang out.

So cool.

She loved the underworld and all its weirdness. The gross, squishy textures intermingled with sharp edges and wicked spikes. The mysterious realms, shrouded in evil fog and given life by unholy wails and agonized screams. She loved all the things that made other people run away in terror.

Sure, she didn't love the cruelty inherent to evil, but something about the atmosphere that supported it was fascinating. But she also adored horror movies, so that tracked. And her father was the Grim Reaper himself, so...yeah. Her friends sometimes joked that she was a real-life Wednesday Addams.

She was okay with that.

Summoned blade in hand and a delicate orb of light floating in front of her, she crept along narrow passages, sometimes pausing to study the grotesque and erotic images carved into—or painted on—the uneven earthen walls. The scenes of butchery and orgies grew more graphic as she got closer to what she assumed was the main chamber. If she interpreted the symbols correctly, this was a Temple of Lilith. One of dozens, but unknown to Raika before now.

Why had her prey come here? The demon Raika sought wasn't a succubus.

As she slipped around a corner, her exceptional eyesight guiding her through the darkness that extended far beyond her *me-powered* light, her shoulder brushed some sort of painting nailed to the rough wall. Little more than a stretched piece of hide—or, more likely, skin—the hyper-realistic piece featured six hideous, horned demons feasting on what looked like a human male, his rib cage spread wide, his mouth twisted into a silent scream.

Strangely drawn to the detailed scene, Raika drew her fingertip along the edge, noting the smooth texture of the canvas and the sticky, almost wet feel of the paint. And maybe she was imagining it, but it seemed that, all around her, the air grew heavy. Oppressive.

The chamber spun, closing in on her.

She tried to back up, but something—one of the demons inside the painting—grabbed her hand.

A rare thread of terror shot up her spine as the beast tugged her so violently it nearly wrenched her shoulder from its socket. Its sharp-toothed maw gaped wide enough to swallow her entire head as it dragged her closer and closer.

Grunting with effort, she threw herself backward and sliced at the demon with her free hand. The blade caught the thing in its lower jaw, breaking bone and sinew with such force that the shockwave vibrated through her arm. It screeched, teeth and blood exploding onto the wall and coating her hand in gore.

With a whoosh, the demon retreated into the painting, and the malevolent tension in the air dissipated.

Fool! Raika berated herself as she fell back against a stone pillar to catch her breath. *You were caught off guard. So stupid!*

She should have recognized the *tableau sinistre*, an abomination that sucked unsuspecting admirers into the scenes. Once inside, there was no escape. You were trapped, living the horror of your death over and over for eternity.

She shuddered at the thought of being stuck in a painting of a demon feast.

Raika could appreciate the diabolical nature of the art, but that didn't stop her from shooting it a glare and giving it a wide berth.

The corridor narrowed just as she felt a warm bloom against her abdomen.

Yes!

Halting, she plucked a hot crystal shard from a pocket on her weapons harness. The tracking crystal glowed with heat and pulsed with a feeble, flickering orange light faster than it had before she entered the temple.

She was getting closer to her target.

Excitement drilled through her, and her breath practically burned with anticipation.

"I fucking love my job," she whispered to herself.

"And what, exactly, is your job?"

Startled, Raika wheeled around to the owner of the raspy, female voice. "Funny you should ask," she said calmly, hoping to hide the fact that she'd been caught by surprise. Again. "My job is to capture you."

"Me?" The demon, an eyeless, sharp-toothed, ugly-ass thing half-concealed in shadows, cocked its head. "Why me? You've been stalking me for weeks. Who are you?"

Raika slipped the little bead back into her pocket and summoned another blade. She fought best with two.

But she wasn't ready to fight yet. She liked it when her prey knew their fate. She liked…foreplay.

"Why you?" Raika purred. "Because you're a demon who escaped your fate when Azagoth destroyed Sheoul-gra and freed you."

"My fate?" The demon hissed in anger. "That bastard sealed me in a statue of agony for centuries. He freed me! My fate is now my own."

"Nice try, but that's not how Heaven sees it."

The demon retreated into the shadows. "You're an angel?"

"If only you were that lucky." Raika clanged her weapons together and grinned. "I'm a Reaper, bitch. And it's time to reap."

One of the best things about being an angel was being almost impervious to extreme temperatures. It was something Gabriel had taken for granted.

Because, as an Unfallen angel, he felt the cold. He felt the heat. He felt the fire Lilith liked to burn him with, even as she made him lie prone on blocks of dry ice.

Right now, he felt every inch of his blackened, scorched skin and frostbitten flesh. With the exception of one exploded eye, his face didn't hurt, but that was only because Lilith had healed his shredded cheek.

"I don't want to mar your beauty, my lovely Gabriel," Lilith had told him. "I like my lovers pretty."

Once, he'd been stupid enough to tell her that he wasn't her lover. She had a very loose definition of the word and had shown him, over and over in the most painful and vile ways possible, that he was, indeed, her lover.

Bile filled his mouth at the memory of the things she'd done to him and forced him to do to her.

Don't puke. Don't puke. Do. Not. Puke.

Desperate to avoid the misery of choking up vomit in his raw throat, he focused on two pieces of straw a few feet away. Not long ago, he could have blinked them out of existence with a mere thought. Or impaled them in the walls. Or transformed them into blades that would decapitate the horrid bitch.

But now, the little bits of straw just lay there on the stone floor, mocking him. Hell, he couldn't even make them move when he blew a breath at them. Not that he had any breath to spare. He could barely breathe through his agony, and what little air moved through his lungs felt like fire.

Everything hurt. Even his ears. His eardrums throbbed, sending pulses of pain into his brain. The rhythmic thumping grew louder, hurting more. It drove him crazy—so crazy he thought he heard shouts. Clanks. Strange thumps.

Wait… He lifted his head and concentrated. Footsteps? Curses? Battle?

The noises drilled into him, and excitement made his heart leap. He knew what fighting sounded like, and that was definitely the clang of blades on blades. Screeching. Bloodletting.

He opened his one good eye, but his eyelid was sandpaper across his tender cornea. Blurry images of what he thought were two females formed before him. By the shape of her body and the shock-white color of her short hair, he knew the one getting her ass kicked was Vanthora. But who was the curvy warrior in black? And why was she fighting the demon?

Not that it mattered. He'd root for anyone who could destroy Vanthora.

They danced a violent, bloody routine across the floor, weapons flashing, curses flying. The dark female controlled the battle, her movements graceful and effortless as she beat his tormentor to a pulp. Victory in increments. Death by a thousand cuts.

Vanthora went down, and excitement burst through him as the other female performed an exquisite, fluid routine that a ballerina would envy, almost mocking the prone demon before slicing her head clean from her body.

Who is this magnificent warrior?

Wings erupted from her back, arched in victory. Shiny black at the pointed, clawed arches, the feathers gradually turned crimson at the tips in a stunning ombre effect.

He coughed, and her wings flared as she spun around, her blades dripping blood.

His vision was still too blurry to make out her face, but her silhouette left an impression that would have had him thinking naughty thoughts if his brain and body weren't so broken.

Tucking her wings away, she approached, her boots striking the floor with light taps. A moment later, she went down on her heels, forearms resting casually on her knees.

One slender hand reached out to tip his face up. "Who are you?"

That voice! That smoky, deep voice that sounded like sex on a bed of hot coals.

"Raika?" he croaked.

Startled, she leaped backward into an aggressive crouch, a blade poised to punch through his skull. "Who are you?"

"Gabriel." He coughed, spraying blood. "I'm…Gabriel."

Silence. Then, "You're not Gabriel. Not the Archangel Gabriel, anyway. I've met him. He was way hotter than you. Smelled better, too."

She thought he was hot?

She thought he *used* to be hot. Now, she thought he was ugly and stinky.

"I can prove it." He swallowed, making a futile attempt to work up some saliva to relieve the dry pain in his throat. "Look at my hair. It's all the colors of humankind. It's unique, even among angels."

"It's shit-brown right now. All of it. You're filthy. Try again."

"I know your father," he wheezed. "He used to call me Jim Bob. I met you at his manor, remember? He made you change out of the bikini." He'd also threatened to make cocktail olives out of Gabriel's eyes if he didn't stop staring at his daughter.

"Oh, yeah. I guess you *are* Gabriel." Cocking her head, she appeared to think on that. "So, you were yeeted from Heaven?" At his nod, she added, "And Vanthora captured your pathetic, Unfallen ass?"

Pathetic? Kinda harsh. "Not Vanthora. Lilith. And another fallen angel named Fearr." Stifling a groan, he staggered to his feet. "You need to release me before she comes back."

"Lilith?" Raika casually flipped her blade into the air and caught it with two fingers, clearly unconcerned that one of the most powerful demons in history could return at any moment. "Hmm. Makes sense. This is one of her temples."

"Right." He thrust his bound wrists at her. "Quickly!"

Another agonizing moment of contemplation. "Lilith is one of the demons I'm tasked to capture." She strolled around the perimeter of the room, moving her hands in complex patterns as she weaved some sort of magic he couldn't see.

"What are you doing?"

"I'm setting a trap."

"Then you'll release me, right?"

Barking out a laugh, she swung around to him. "Why would I do that?"

He stared in disbelief. "You can't leave me here."

"Of course I can." She moved toward him, a malevolent smile lifting one corner of her luscious mouth to reveal a shiny, sharp fang. When she reached him, she crouched down and booped his nose. "You're the bait."

Chapter 11

Scotty couldn't remember the last time she'd felt so exhilarated by a chase. Maybe it was a release from the anxiety over sending Mace to the hospital. Or maybe it was the cool night air, invigorating her muscles and filling her lungs with energy. Or maybe it was the location. The rugged wilds of Alaska called to the huntress in her.

Whatever it was, she leaped nimbly over fallen logs and ducked through briars that made Blade curse as he tried to keep up.

She'd always been the fastest of their DART team, nimble and flexible. But it wasn't as if the boys were slouches. Blade was a powerhouse, strong and fierce, rock-steady in battle, while Mace was quick and light as a fox, with a creative and tricky unpredictability that kept his foes off balance.

"Scotty." Blade's voice, hushed and harsh, sounded extraordinarily loud in the eerie silence. "Did you hear me? We've been chasing this thing for hours. We should check in on Jon and Skoll."

"Just a couple more miles." She came to a halt at the edge of a clearing. To the west, the rocky mountainous slopes full of nooks and crannies would make great shelters for a wendigo. And according to the info packet Kynan had provided, the area had recently become known for its cave systems after being discovered by a geological survey team.

But to the north and east, forested land provided cover for anything that wanted to hide.

"Which way?" she asked. "I haven't heard the things screeching for a while now."

They'd given chase for two of the wendigos, but when the creatures split up, it forced Blade and Scotty to choose just one to follow. Now, they had to watch their backs as well as their fronts.

Blade pulled up next to her on the right. He always went right. Mace went left.

He lifted his head and inhaled. She'd always thought he looked so… wolfy when he did that. He didn't like her saying that, though. He didn't like talking about his werewolf side. It didn't often make an appearance, but it was something he despised. Blade had never liked being out of control, and the nights of the full moon left him grumpy, anxious, and a little feral.

"It went into those hills," he said. "I can't believe you can't smell it. It's like rotting meat and demon feces."

"I smelled it earlier." She forced down a shudder. "You're not wrong."

They took off after the thing, Blade in the lead, sniffing the air like a hellhound after wounded prey. His sense of smell got stronger with a waxing moon, and she gave silent thanks that it was nearing its Waxing Gibbous stage for this mission. And not just because it aided Blade. The illumination provided ample light for their hike to the mountain foothills.

Figured, though, that as they paused to plot their next moves, clouds strangled the moon from out of nowhere, and the scent of rain grew heavy in the night air.

Blade looked up at the sky and growled. "I hate Alaska."

As if in response, the sky opened up. The downpour crashed down on them in a shockingly furious deluge.

"Way to go!" she yelled over the roar of the rain blasting the trees and hillside. "Insult the host!"

"Ha. Ha." He made a beckoning gesture. "This way."

They ran toward a rocky outcropping and ducked inside a shadowed crevasse. Water dripped down her face and plastered her hair to her skull. Using her sleeve to wipe her eyes, she assessed their situation.

"Well, shit," she said. "We're going to lose the scent and the tracks."

Blade shrugged out of his backpack and tossed it to the ground. "On the bright side, we got a shower."

"Hmph." She unloaded her pack, too, since it looked like they could be holed up for a while. "Might as well use the break to call Skoll and Jon."

Their comms were unreliable out here, and sure enough, she didn't have a good signal. So, she plucked the old-fashioned relic of a radio from her mission kit.

Skoll responded immediately, his voice hushed. "Everything okay?"

"Yeah. We're in the foothills to the northwest, taking shelter from the rain." She gave him the coordinates. "How are you guys?"

"It's not raining here yet," he replied. "But we're close to our target. We'll let you know when we've bagged him. Good luck."

"You, too."

Blade watched her put away the radio, his eyes glinting with speculation.

"What?" She zipped up her bag. "Why are you looking at me like that?"

His gaze skipped away, focusing on the rain and the stream of water forming in the gully below. "No reason."

"Stop lying."

"Do I need a reason to look at you?"

"Stop stalling."

He reached back to massage his neck and sighed. "I'm just…wondering."

"About what?" She braced herself against a slab of mossy stone, grateful for a break. "And stop making me drag information out of you." He could be so frustrating. Mace talked too much, and Blade didn't talk enough.

He sighed again, but at least he looked at her. "Are you going to sleep with Skoll or Jon?"

She blinked. "Wow. Okay. A little out of the blue."

"You asked."

"You're right." This shouldn't be a difficult topic. Not when she'd just asked her two best friends to help her lose her virginity.

But now, every time she thought of losing it to either Jon or Skoll, her brain misfired, and all she could think about was how she'd felt in Mace's arms with his fangs buried in her throat and the hard ridge of his erection rocking against her core. Even now, her cheeks heated at the memory, and she couldn't look Blade in the eye.

Because the much more uncomfortable truth was that she was thinking about Blade differently now too. Mace had awakened something inside her, and she was seeing them both in a new, sexy light.

"Well?" Blade prompted. "Now who's stalling?"

Right again.

"Sorry," she said, waving her hand in dismissal. "I haven't really thought about it much. We've been kinda busy."

"Stop lying."

Guilt burned in the pit of her stomach. Damn him. Continually throwing her words back at her. A gust of wind howled through the mountains, giving her a second to think. Jon and Skoll were both hot. Any female would be lucky to get them into bed. But the truth was that she felt nothing for them. Not sexually, anyway.

Not like what she'd felt with Mace.

"I'm not sleeping with either of them," she said truthfully.

He seemed surprised—and a little pleased. But maybe that was her imagination.

"Why not? You could do worse. I mean, from what I know about Skoll, he's a standup guy. Jon's a dick, but I'm pretty sure he knows his way around a bedroom."

Must have been her imagination, after all. For some reason, she felt a little put out. Which was ridiculous, given their oath. No matter how much changed regarding her newfound libido, the pact remained, and she would have to get her shit together or risk losing the best friends anyone could ask for.

"So, you think I should proposition one of them?" And how would that even go? "*Hi, wanna have sex? I don't know what I'm doing, just FYI.*"

"Fuck, no." Blade shifted away from a rivulet of water flowing off the rocks next to him. "I'm wondering why you would say no, when you seemed so adamant about losing your virginity."

Shrugging, she stepped away from the growing stream on the ground. Geez, how much longer was this storm going to last? "Maybe I realized it's no big deal."

There was a brief pause. "Is it because of what happened between you and Mace?"

His words, spoken in a rigid, controlled voice, stole her breath. How did he know? A knot of panic formed in her gut. Panic and guilt and a fiery blast of heat.

"No!" she said quickly. Too quickly. Too *guiltily*. "Nothing happened. It was just blood. You know that." Gods, could she sound any more defensive?

"Right." Blade's voice was deceptively quiet. "Just blood."

A spark of indignant anger helped alleviate some of the guilt. "Yes, just blood. You know it was, and I don't know what's up your ass, but knock it off. You're just jealous that I was able to help him when you couldn't."

She regretted her words the second they left her lips, and once again, Blade called her on her crap.

"Are you serious?" He stared at her in disbelief, completely oblivious to the fact that water was pouring down his shoulder now. "You think I'm jealous of you because my skills weren't enough to fully heal him?"

Yes, she knew it was ridiculous. But *something* was up his ass. "Maybe you wanted to be the one to offer your vein."

He waited for a peal of thunder to fade away, but he still had to shout over the din of the rain and wind. "First of all, my blood couldn't nourish him the way yours did. Second, even if I had offered my vein, he wouldn't have been turned on by it."

So that was his problem? He was truly *that* bothered by the fact that Mace had gotten a little aroused?

"Blade," she said softly, "that's a dangerous path to go down. You can't be jealous of him. You can't. We swore an oath to prevent exactly that. Jealousy could tear our team apart."

"I know." Finally, he stepped away from the water, tucking himself closer to her, bringing his comforting warmth with him. "Believe me, I know—"

A simultaneous bolt of lightning and crack of thunder made her jump. Blade's arm came around her, tugging her against his broad chest. It felt good. Better than it should. Guilt bubbled up again.

Blade went taut, his already hard body going as rigid as marble. "Can you hear that?"

"I just hear wind and rain…"

She frowned. There was something else, too. A rumble. Like a pack of hell stallions barreling through a forest. It grew louder, but now she could hear splashes and gurgles.

Abruptly, the horrifying answer came to her. "Flash flood! Blade—"

The wall of water hit them with the force of a charging Gargantua beast, cutting their legs out from under them. The thrashing river ripped them from their shelter and swept them along with the current.

"Blade!" She screamed his name between gulps of breath. "Blade!" In the darkness, there was nothing but terror and pain as Scotty crashed into floating logs and slammed into boulders.

Then, in a rush of swirling water, she felt herself being sucked violently downward.

Then, she felt nothing.

Blade's head was pounding.

The sensation of dampness and grit on his skin and clothing grew more uncomfortable as consciousness pushed back the fog of confusion in his brain.

What happened? He blinked, but all he could make out in the darkness were blurry shadows. *Where was he?*

He sat up, groaning at the aches and sharp, stabbing pains that seemed to emanate from every muscle, every bone, and every freaking cell in his body. He shoved his wet hair away from his eyes. He was soaked and sitting in a puddle of mud.

The flash flood.

Scotty!

He lumbered to his feet, staggering a few steps before a hand snagged his arm and held him upright.

"It's about time you woke up."

"Scotty," he breathed, tugging her against him. "Thank the gods you're okay."

"I'm fine." Her words, muffled by his chest, comforted the hell out of him. "But I was worried about you." She pulled away and guided him over to a relatively flat-topped boulder, where he could sit. "You've been out of it for hours."

Hours? He sank down onto the rock and tried to get the lay of the land. Well, the *under* land. It appeared they were inside a subterranean tunnel system. It looked like two, maybe three passages extended from the small cave.

"I think the flood washed us down here." She gestured to a puddle a few feet away. "I woke up in that." She held up her left arm. "With a broken wrist and some busted ribs."

Instantly, he gripped her shoulder and fired up his healing gift. In his hands, her bones felt small and delicate. Birdlike. But this female was a powerful warrior, and the most delicate thing about her was absolutely nothing.

"It's fine," she said. "Everything was healed half an hour ago."

She was right. He didn't detect any residual damage.

"You look better too." She scanned him with a critical eye from head to toe. "You were pretty beat up at first."

He was still pretty beat up. Everything hurt, and his neck protested as he tilted his head up to take in the fissure in the cave ceiling. The gap was just wide enough to reveal a sliver of the moon and a handful of stars. "We must have dropped through that crack. That's a hell of a fall."

Scotty nodded grimly. "We got lucky. Sort of. Do you want the good news or the bad?"

He usually went for the bad news first, while Mace went for the good. Scotty chose depending on her mood.

"Good news," he said. "In honor of Mace."

"Aw, that's sweet. Okay, so I looked around while you were recovering. I'm pretty sure we stumbled upon a wendigo nest."

He blinked in surprise. "Awesome. That's some Wraith-level luck." Wraith was famous for his luck at finding shit. "You can gate us out of here, and once we find Jon and Skoll, we can ambush the bastards. It'll take a while to get back here, since there's no Harrowgate close, but—" He paused. "Wait. What's the bad news?"

She blew out a frustrated breath. "I can't summon a gate."

"What? Are you sure?"

"I tried." She gestured to a small pool of blood, evidence of her attempt. "Since we're not surrounded by water, and there's not a hellmouth nearby to block my ability, my best guess as to why I can't summon a gate is that there's a Morabuble somewhere in these tunnels. We might even be inside it."

Definitely bad news. Morabubles were incursions of the hell realm into the human one. Places where the veil between the realms was thin or unstable, allowing demons and humans to pass through—intentionally or accidentally. Worse, the twisted, untamable energy that seeped through the veil warped magic spells and innate abilities. Even if Scotty *could* open a gate, it wouldn't be safe to use it. They could end up in a troll's cookpot, on another planet, or shredded into confetti.

"That explains the demons," he said. "If wendigos draw demons, it would be easy for them to come through the incursion."

"That's what I was thinking."

"Okay, so we need to find a way out." He looked around for their packs. "We can call Jon and Skoll—"

"No, we can't. I think our packs got swept away. And I don't know about your comms, but all mine can do is keep time. Everything else is toast."

He glanced down at his wrist, taking in the shattered face of the unit staring back at him. Muddy water had gotten inside the device. So much toast.

At least his weapons had survived intact, if a little waterlogged. The harness itself was shredded in places, and he'd lost a couple of loops, but not a single knife or throwing star.

Oh, no. Frantically, he patted himself down. Shit, shit, shit!

"Blade? What is it?"

"The Reaper. It's not in its holster. I think I left it in the pack."

"Dude." A look of horror crossed Scotty's face. "Kynan is going to kill us."

"Nah." Blade swallowed dryly. "He's just going to be happy we're alive."

"He can be happy we're alive and still want to kill us, you know."

He laughed. It made his ribs hurt a little. "Come on, let's find a way out of here." He accepted her hand and allowed her to help him to his feet.

But the feel of her palm in his brought a new, horrible awareness. When she started to withdraw, he tightened his grip, keeping her there.

"We should hurry," he said gruffly.

"Agreed. I don't want to face more than one wendigo without backup." She frowned down at their hands. He knew he should let her go, but the feel of her skin against his felt too good, spreading through his arms, his chest, torso…groin. "Blade?"

"Sorry." Reluctantly, he released her, but the arousal remained. "How long did you say I was unconscious?"

"At least a couple of hours."

Oh, fuck.

"Blade? What is it?"

He unleashed a barrage of curse words. "My injections were in my pack."

Scotty's eyes shot wide. "How long?"

"Soon. If we don't get out of here soon…" He swallowed. He couldn't even say it. Not to her. Not to the one person he wanted more than anything. Not to the one person he could never have.

"You're going to need sex," she finished. "And you'll need it from me."

Chapter 12

You're going to need sex. And you'll need it from me.

Scotty's words rang through her ears in a loop she couldn't stop. For three hours, they'd searched for an exit, and it didn't matter if they were scaling treacherous inclines or crawling through claustrophobically narrow tunnels, her thoughts kept turning to the what-ifs.

What if they really had to do it? What if she hated it? Worse…what if she loved it?

Frustrated by the direction of her thoughts and the fact that they might as well be walking in circles, she stopped at a fork in the tunnel system.

"This is bullshit," she said. "We haven't found anything."

Well, that wasn't entirely true. They'd found bats, bones, and rotting corpses. They'd also dispatched three scavenger demons drawn by the wendigos' malevolence.

Once, they'd caught a draft of cool air and followed it, sure they'd finally found a way out. Unfortunately, it turned out to be coming from a narrow gap in the rocks at the top of an unclimbable cliff.

Blade's head swiveled from left to right, his nose flaring as he inhaled. "I smell fresh air from the right," he said, his voice little more than a grunt. "Fresher than from the left, anyway."

She turned to him, forcing herself not to look into his eyes. She knew better than to meet his gaze—or any Seminus demon's gaze—when they were fighting their needs. Their species was literally designed to be sex machines, and everything about them was made to seduce females. From their hypnotic, color-changing eyes and perfect, muscular physiques, to the pheromones that drugged every female in close proximity, they were sex on a stick.

And with every passing hour, his needs became more urgent, and her ability to focus on anything but her growing arousal tanked.

"How are you doing?" She focused on his broad chest, the way it expanded and contracted with his deep breaths.

He had so many muscles. Hard, thick muscles that flexed beneath his form-fitting turtleneck.

Stop it.

"I don't have much time."

The way he said it, with a simmering, velvety undertone, rolled through her like a caress.

Ignore it. Shake it off.

"We'll get out of here." She clapped him playfully on the shoulder, and he hissed.

"Don't," he growled. Startled, her gaze flew up to his, and her breath caught at the liquid gold swirling in his eyes. Warmth bloomed inside her chest, spreading through her breasts, making them so sensitive that her nipples tingled at the slightest rasp of her bra. "Don't touch me right now."

She jerked her hand away, but the languid sense of arousal, the same as she'd felt with Mace, remained. "I'm sorry," she croaked. "I just—"

"I know. Let's go."

He hurried down the tunnel, and she followed him as they wound through more narrow passages that sometimes forced them to crawl.

Man, he had a nice ass.

Stop. It!

Gritting her teeth, she concentrated on getting out. Not on his ass. Or his muscular legs. Or his powerful arms.

Gods, they had to get out of here.

Blade squeezed between the cave walls and waited as she easily slipped through and found herself in an open space, half of which was taken up by a shallow pool.

Her gaze lit on a canvas blob near the far edge of the pool. Could it be...?

Yes!

"My backpack! Yours might be nearby." While Blade searched the area for his—*please, please find it*—she dug through her pack for the radio.

She nearly shouted in excitement when she found it, intact and functioning.

Quickly, she sent a transmission to Jon and Skoll.

Come on, come on…

"Skoll here."

She sank against a rock in relief.

"Skoll, it's Scotty. We need your help." She explained what'd happened, and in a huge stroke of luck, the other team was near where they'd been swept into the caverns. In an even bigger stroke of luck, Jon had a rough map of the area.

Wraith-like luck, indeed.

"Stay where you are," Jon told her, as if they had much choice.

She glanced over at Blade, who was still searching for his pack, and lowered her voice. "What's your ETA?"

"A couple of hours, probably," Jon said, and her mouth went dry. Blade wouldn't make it another twenty minutes, let alone two hours. "You said you think the caves are where the wendigos are nesting? Dawn is coming. Watch your backs. They'll be returning soon. Jon out."

"Out," she murmured. Shit.

"I'm not going to make it." Blade's voice, dark and smooth, caressed her from across the space.

Desperate to end this…whatever it was happening between them, she fumbled for her dagger. "I'll open a gate. We must be far enough from the veil." They had to be.

Nervous tremors made the blade unsteady as she sliced into her hand. For the first time ever, she didn't dread opening a gate. The weird panic that usually gripped her was held at bay by the urgent need to get out of there.

Blood dripped to the ground. Drip, drip, drip. Too slow! Viciously, she slashed at her palm again. And again.

"Scotty!" Blade started toward her. "What are you doing?"

"It's taking too long." She slashed again, and the blood poured, way more than she needed. She didn't care. They had to get out. She had to get away from Blade.

Clenching her fists, she envisioned a gate.

Nothing. The pool of blood just sat there.

Fuck!

"Blade, I'm sorry—" Her words broke off at the sight of him standing a few feet away, his chest heaving, his golden eyes hyperfocused on her.

"Do you know about the Sem bonding ritual?" he asked, his voice husky, the tone vibrating in her core.

"I…kinda." Mostly, she just knew that two Sems couldn't bond with one female. Rade had made that very clear all those years ago.

Blade drifted closer, his gaze locked on her bleeding hand. "The male and female exchange blood. Not much, just a taste, really…"

Oh…gods. If it felt anything like what she'd experienced with Mace—

"Blade." She snapped her fingers, startling them both out of the sexual haze building around them. "Blade! Get your shit together."

She needed to get *her* shit tighter too. But thinking was becoming more and more difficult as his need pumped pheromones into the air.

"I'm sorry, Scotty," he croaked. "I'm…I'm not going to be able to control myself soon. I'm just going to…go."

"Go? Go where?"

"Somewhere. Anywhere." His voice was rough, tortured in a way she'd never heard. "I have to get away from you. I can't…I won't…hurt you."

"Oh, Blade," she whispered. "You could never hurt me."

"Not…physically…I don't think." The anguish in his expression made her heart ache. She'd rarely seen him so vulnerable. So miserable. "We took an oath. I won't betray you or Mace." He ducked into the tunnel.

She couldn't let him go. He didn't have much time left, and she wasn't about to let him die.

"Stop!" When he didn't, she panicked, unsure what to do. All she knew was that his life depended on her. She'd given Mace what he needed, and now it was time to give Blade what *he* needed.

Desperate, she shrugged out of her shirt. "Look at me. Blade! Look. At. Me."

He halted, hands clenched at his sides, his thick shoulders rising and falling with deep, rapid breaths. For a long, drawn-out moment, she thought he'd take off again. But just as she began to give up hope, he turned. Slowly.

"Ah, damn, Scotty," he rasped. "What are you doing?"

Good question. She unhooked her bra and tossed it to the ground. His hot gaze fell to her breasts, and in response, her nipples tightened and tingled.

"Did you read the oath's fine print?" Weird how her voice was steady, but her hands shook, fumbled as she unbuttoned her pants. "We're released from our vow if it'll save a life."

"We didn't—" He cleared his throat, but it didn't help the hoarseness. "We didn't sign a contract."

Before she lost her nerve, she shoved down her jeans and stepped out of them. "We didn't have to. The fine print is implied."

Releasing a tortured moan, he closed his eyes. "Scotty, don't."

By now, her hands shook so hard she could barely hook her fingers beneath the fabric of her panties to slide them off. In her chest, her heart pounded against her rib cage, and her gut got all twisty.

This was how she'd felt when Mace had been feeding from her. Excited. Afraid. Wanting.

She'd never experienced this before this assignment. Not with any male. Didn't matter how hot they were. How smooth their words. How skilled their kisses. Even her attraction to Jon and Skoll was shallow. Forced.

So why now? Why were the two males she couldn't have…the only ones who made her feel something she'd never felt before?

This couldn't happen. Yet it had to. She knew that. She'd be saving Blade's life.

But why did she feel so guilty about it?

Her panties slid to the ground, leaving her exposed.

She'd never been shy about her body, especially around Mace and Blade. They'd seen her in all stages of undress, and she'd seen them that way, too. No big deal.

But this? This felt like a big deal.

Resisting the urge to cover herself with her hands, she took a step closer. "Blade?"

He opened his eyes and moaned again.

"Please, Blade," she whispered as she lost the battle with her confidence and wrapped her arms around herself, as if that would hide anything. "I don't know how to do this."

"Do what?" His words were barely discernible, spoken between clenched teeth.

"Seduce someone."

Molten gold swirled in his eyes, hypnotizing her as he took a step closer. "Fuck, Scotty," he murmured. "You wouldn't ever have to—" He shook his head and stepped back. "This isn't right."

Obviously, her seductive skills failed, and he didn't seem to care about his own life. She was a little humiliated by the former but pissed enough about the latter to try from another angle.

"Listen to me, you stubborn ass," she barked. "Jon and Skoll are potentially hours away. If the wendigos show up, you can't fight like this. Your stubbornness will put me in danger. It'll put *both* of us in danger. We will fail our mission. Do you want that?"

"Never," he swore. "But—"

"But nothing." She was her father's daughter, and he'd taught her how to deal with a stubborn soldier. Hunger gleamed in his eyes as she strode over to him, putting a little extra sway in her hips. She probably looked ridiculous, but it got his attention. "I need you at full capacity, warrior." She unhooked his weapons harness and tossed it aside. Then she reached for his fly. Behind it, the outline of his erection strained the buttons. "You need to commit. Give me everything you've got."

There it is.

Blade's jaw hardened, and his eyes glinted with a new, fiery determination. She'd broken through to his inner sense of purpose and his willingness to face a challenge.

And also, to the lust demon that demanded he have sex or die.

Her fingers fumbled with the top button of his fly, and his hand came down on hers. For a heartbeat, she thought he might stop her.

But no.

He released his erection, his greedy gaze drilling into hers.

And she knew right then, for better or worse, nothing would ever be the same between them again.

This was so fucked up, in so many fucked-up ways.

Scotty had been Blade's fantasy for longer than he wanted to admit, even to himself. It was something only Masumi knew, and she'd never spoken of it. But on the days he longed especially hard for Scotty, Masumi would show up with red hair, hazel-green eyes, freckles, and sometimes, combat gear.

So, yeah, he'd wanted Scotty. But he'd been resigned to the fact that he could only have her in his fantasies. He'd *never* considered that it could actually happen. Now, she was standing in front of him, offering herself on a platter, and his brain was glitching.

Want. Can't. Oath. Mace. Want. Can't. Oath. Mace.

His body tensed, his balls cramping as fire shot through his cock, and his need went next-level. He didn't have much time. Soon, the cramps would rip apart his insides. Pain would feel like a clamp on his skull, and blood would start seeping from his nose. Then his ears. Then…other places.

Not long after that, he'd die. His family would have to deal with yet another loss. His parents would lose another son. Granted, Chaos's soul was back in play, safe within Stryke's mate's womb and soon to be born again as a baby named Chasm. But the trauma of losing him so brutally would forever remain an unhealed wound.

He had to do this. He'd deal with the guilt later.

"You're going to have to take the lead on this, Blade." Scotty's cheeks burned red as she stared up at him. "I'm not a moron; I know how this works. I mean, the mechanics. But the rest…"

His heart clenched at the fragility in her voice. She was one of the least fragile people he'd ever met, and to see her so off balance sparked a noble, protective instinct he didn't even know he had.

"I got you." He reached for her, but paused for just a moment, admiring Scotty in a way he'd never been able to before. The way he'd dreamed.

Her beauty stole his breath. She was naked perfection.

His mouth watered at the thought of running his tongue over every inch of her plump, high breasts. He dragged his gaze lower, to the neat triangle of red between her thighs, and he practically drooled. He wanted to part her legs and dive in, to taste her unique flavor. She'd be spicy. One hundred percent.

But his body was on fire, his cock swelling with as much pain as arousal, and it wouldn't be long before his primitive demon brain took over and drove him to mindless, rough sex with no consideration for his partner.

Scotty deserved more for her first time than this, but at least he could make sure *he* was in control. Not his dick.

He could *try*, anyway.

But his virtuous intentions died a quick death the moment she closed her hand around his cock.

Every Seminus instinct fired, and all he could think about was burying himself in her tight heat.

He seized her shoulders and tugged her hard body against his. She gasped in surprise, but he cut it off, swallowing it with his mouth on hers. The kiss was nothing like the soft, sweet kiss he'd always imagined they'd share. No, this was years of pent-up lust coming to bear, and he took her mouth hungrily as he ground his erection into her pelvis.

Mine.

The part of his brain that should have been thinking about going slow took a leave of absence, and in an unrestrained surge, he carried Scotty down to the ground. He kissed her even harder as he tucked her beneath him so his cock nestled against her center.

Take her.

Yes.

He reached down, somehow finding the presence of mind to test her readiness. He was dangerously close to losing himself to the drive, but the idea of hurting her managed—just barely—to pierce the hazy frenzy of need.

Scotty tilted her hips upward as he slipped his finger between her folds. He brushed her swollen nub, and her low moan was like an erotic whip, driving him out of his mind. He dipped his finger inside her, and then it was his turn to moan at the feel of her slippery tightness.

The demon inside him took control at that moment.

Nothing mattered except getting relief from the pain and riding a high of ecstasy.

"Now," he rasped. "Now." He sheathed himself in his fantasy.

Scotty cried out, and again, the thought of hurting her broke his sexual delirium, and he froze, grinding his teeth with the effort it took to remain still. The way she clamped around him, squeezing him with her silky channel, had him ready to burst.

"Scotty…I…sorry…"

"It's okay," she breathed. "I'm okay. Keep going—"

With a roar, he surged against her. Gripping her ass with one hand and anchoring them to the cave floor with the other, he pumped wildly. He threw back his head as pleasure swelled inside him, taking him to the very brink. His incubus senses told him she was close, too, and his heart sang. He was with the female he'd fantasized about for years. The one he'd have sold his soul to be with.

A twinge of guilt tried to ruin things, but he brushed it off because, dammit, while he'd willingly sell his soul, he wouldn't sell his relationship with Mace. This didn't count. This was nothing but sex to save his life.

Kinda like how Scotty's blood had healed Mace.

And this…this wouldn't happen again. Not ever.

But that didn't mean he couldn't enjoy every second of it right now.

"Blade." Scotty's breathy whisper nearly took him over the edge. "I didn't..." She panted and groaned, arching her pelvis to take him deeper. "I didn't expect...this."

Don't come. Not yet...

He dipped his head and growled against her ear. "Expect what?"

"The connection." Her hands framed his face to lift his head so he was staring into her brilliant, sexed-up eyes. "It's like...like we're one."

Yes. Gods, yes.

He'd always loved the connection of being with a female, skin to skin, their bodies intertwined, but it had never felt like this. As if their very *souls* were intertwined.

"I'm sorry," she said quickly. "That sounded stupid."

"Never." He dipped his head again, but this time to kiss her. To pour everything he had into her. Because gods help him, this felt so right. She was his. They might never make love again, but he would forever, secretly, consider her his. His beloved. His lover.

His *Lirsha.*

Pleasure quickly drowned Scotty's humiliation of sounding like a total sap, a virgin fool girl who fell in love with the first guy she banged. Scotty would apologize again soon. Well, soon enough. Right now, all she could think about was what Blade was doing to her.

Kissing her senseless. Caressing her butt and thigh as he moved between her legs. Every stroke of his cock sliding inside her brought her closer to the brink. Being with a male was so much better than she'd imagined.

Lately, her imagination involved Blade. Or Mace.

Quickly, she purged her mind of Mace. She couldn't think about him right now. About him and how he'd feel about this. It wasn't a betrayal...not really. Would he rather that Blade died?

She knew the answer to that, and yet, the guilt niggled at her.

Stop thinking!

Right. There was no room for anything except the pending explosion of ecstasy.

"Scotty," Blade gasped. He rammed his hips into her with such force that her spine dug into the earth and caught, holding her in place for his furious thrusts.

She couldn't withstand the storm that took him, and she cried out as her climax ripped through her. He shouted—her name, she thought—and warmth poured into her as he pumped inside her, throwing his head back in a primal roar of bared teeth and straining muscles.

He was magnificent, a creature of danger and desire, and beneath him, she felt both safe and savage, a warrior princess meeting her lover in a celebration after battle.

They writhed together as another orgasm took her. Then another, and another. Bliss consumed her like a wildfire in a drought-stricken forest, stealing her breath and all coherent thought.

She lost count of the episodes of ecstasy that racked her body, but Blade remained inside her the entire time. Kissing her neck when she gasped for a breath between orgasms and then holding her tightly when she had another. He surged against her every time she came, sometimes slowly, languidly, easing her through her peak. Other times, he thrust wildly, wringing pleasure out of her as he climaxed again.

"Holy shit," she breathed against his shoulder as she came down from the latest orgasm. Her legs flopped open, her muscles too weak to support them. She couldn't even lift her arms to hug him. "That…that was amazing." She swallowed dryly between panting breaths. "No wonder you guys never have a shortage of dates."

His mouth curved into a slow smile dripping with male pride. And he did, in fact, have much to be proud about.

"Females do love us," he said, his voice low and post-sex husky.

"And now I see why." She might have to find herself a Sem of her own. "Maybe I should be hanging out at Underworld General. I think half the world's Sem population works there."

"You need to stay away from incubi." He rolled to the side, taking her with him. "We're all horny assholes."

True. But she knew many Seminus demons, and for the most part, they were decent, loyal, and dedicated to their work.

"Is that why you're still inside me?" She reached up and brushed a lock of dark hair off his forehead. "Do you need more?"

"I don't…*need* it." His cheeks burned red, which was adorable. "I just don't want this to end."

Her heart stuttered at his admission. She didn't want it to end, either.

Back when the three of them had taken the oath, it had been hard, at first, to watch them pursue other females. She'd even walked in on them in the middle of banging some of them, which had been like pinpricks in her heart.

But she'd gotten over it. All those pinpricks became protective scars, and for years now, she'd understood that friendship was all they could ever have.

Now, something had changed for her. Something new stirred, and she wasn't sure she was ready to let go of the feeling quite yet.

"Scotty?" Blade pressed a lingering kiss onto her forehead. "I'm sorry your first time was…this."

Was he kidding? This was better than she could ever have hoped for. She'd thought she'd go on a date or two with Jon, or Skoll, or anyone who *wasn't* Blade or Mace, and they'd have hot sex, but a hella awkward time after that.

"This was perfect, Blade."

She rested her head on his shoulder, growing gradually more aware of the mud on her skin, the rocks stabbing her bones, and the chill in the damp air. An imaginary timer started, too, one that ticked down the few remaining minutes they would ever have like this. The last seconds of—

"I'm worried about Mace," Blade said softly.

Yep, there it was. Back to reality. An uncertain reality because, like it or not, things were different. And yet, nothing could change.

"Mace is in the best hands," she assured him. "We'll see him soon."

"I know." Blade withdrew, formally breaking their connection and leaving her feeling…empty. He sat up to gather her scattered clothes. "That's not what I meant."

Oh. He meant the sex. Her gut did a slow roll of dread. "He'll be okay with it," she insisted. He would. "You'll see."

"He'll *say* he's okay. And he might even understand." Blade dragged his hand down his face, looking suddenly tired. "But deep inside, he'll blame me for not injecting myself sooner, or for losing my pack. I only left it behind that once, but he's always jumping my shit when I take it off. It'll fester. You know how he is."

Yeah, she did. Mace didn't let much get to him, but when it finally did, he was completely irrational, and he didn't calm down for her the way Blade did. He'd say he was cool with something, but then, someday down the road, maybe even years later, he'd randomly explode over something small, and all his anger would erupt. And it was destructive. To himself and everyone around him.

Blade laid her clothes on a relatively dry boulder. "Maybe we shouldn't say anything."

If only it were that easy. "He can read us like books, Blade."

"Yeah, but he can't read us if there's nothing *to* read. Nothing has changed between us. We're still friends. This was a one-off, and it won't happen again."

No, it wouldn't, but she didn't like how the finality of his words made her chest tighten. "We have to tell him. There can never be secrets between us."

There was silence, broken only by the drip of water from the cave ceiling. Then, finally, "I know."

A deep heaviness sank into her belly as she sat up and reached for her clothes. This was it. She would go her way, and he'd go back to fucking a dozen females a week. Or Masumi, dozens of times a week.

Jealousy percolated as they cleaned up in silence, using the little pond of cool water to rinse. Not jealousy of Masumi. Not really. Scotty loved the succubus. Masumi had probably saved the life of everyone in the house. And she was genuinely a good person who cared about the entire family.

It was just too bad Masumi wasn't free to love. Her species had been bred specifically to fulfill the needs of Seminus demons, and without that, she'd die. Unless she mated with a Seminus demon, Scotty supposed. Was she even allowed to do that? She'd have to ask her someday.

Just as Scotty tugged on her top, a sound, like a snake slithering through ashes, froze her in her tracks. She glanced down at her comms. Sunrise.

"Blade," she whispered.

Instantly, he was armed and at her side, his nostrils flaring as he sniffed the air. "Wendigo," he said in a hushed voice. "Strike that. Multiple wendigos."

A shiver crawled up her spine, followed by a rush of adrenaline. Those things might be creepy as shit, but she and Blade had been born to slay monsters like that.

"We got this," she said.

He nodded, shooting her a sly smile. "Let's put them down before those two idiots show up. I want all the credit."

"Hell, yeah," she said, putting out her fist. "Team up."

"Team up." He bumped her knuckles, and just like that, things were back to normal.

Perfectly, perfectly normal.

Really.

Chapter 13

Gabriel was pissed.

Raika, who was supposed to be playing for the good guys, had left him, chained to the wall, in Lilith's torture chamber. He'd sat there, filthy, starving, and writhing in pain, for who the hell knew how long. When you were a prisoner, days were measured in...wait. They weren't measured at all. Time was one endless enema.

Blood rushed through his ears as he fumed. The thudding pulse sounded like footsteps.

They *were* footsteps.

Anxiety replaced anger as he lifted his head and watched the entrance with his one good eye.

Lilith stepped into the chamber, and his anxiety topped out. She was carrying a black dildo as thick as a softball bat and embedded with...what were those things?

His heart—and his ass—clenched when she held it up.

Razor blades.

"Hello, my delicious morsel of angel flesh—" She froze mid-sentence, going completely still, except for her gaze, which frantically shifted around the room. Suddenly, she hissed, her lips peeling back from grotesque, jagged teeth. She'd gone from an impossibly gorgeous, seductive temptress to a hideous, red-eyed demon in a flash. Evil was rarely subtle. "Who was here?"

"I don't know what you're talking about."

"Liar!" she spat, her eyes flaring wide with what he swore was panic. "It's a trap."

She hissed again, and in a blur of motion, she wheeled around and darted out of the chamber. Three heartbeats later, Raika burst inside, weapons drawn.

"You just missed her," he said.

Scowling, Raika turned to him. "How far into the chamber did she get before she sensed the trap?"

He shrugged, wincing at the crack in his shoulder. "About halfway."

"Hmm. I'll need to adjust the mana load and weaves in the spell."

He one-eyed her curiously. "You're using spells instead of natural ability?"

She disappeared her weapons and wings. They were glorious. Like his had been. Now, he just had bloody bone stumps that never healed.

"I use everything at my disposal," she said. "And in this environment, I was afraid she'd sense the use of angelic power."

Raika was probably right. And truthfully, he didn't know what special powers she'd been granted by Heaven when she reached maturity and had been tasked with capturing the evilest of the demons her father had set free. During Gabriel's restriction in Heaven, he'd been forbidden access to any information about her or her duties. He'd been forbidden access to almost everything.

"Well?" He held his bound wrists out. "You're freeing me, right?"

She appeared to consider his request, and he started sweating. He couldn't take another day in this place. He was starving and in pain—little more than a mass of well-tenderized meat at this point.

"I guess I might as well," she said, sounding distracted as she looked around the room. Clearly, his situation was of little concern to her. She was just like her father. But hotter. "Lilith won't return anytime soon. And now she knows she's being hunted. I fucked up."

"Yeah, that's too bad." He gestured with his hands. "Free me?"

She regarded him with the aloof gaze she'd also inherited from her father. That looking-down-her-nose thing belonged to her mother, though. "I'll take you to Underworld General."

"The demon hospital?" He'd considered going there when he first landed in the human realm, but only until he could figure out his next move. He'd had weeks to do that now, and his plan to get back into Heaven didn't involve demons. "You're kidding, right?"

"Look at yourself. Do you really think you'll survive more than a day without getting caught by demons or fallen angels?" Her mouth twisted in distaste. "You have broken bones punching out of your skin. You're so dehydrated you're not even bleeding from gaping wounds. And I'm pretty sure your right clavicle isn't supposed to be on the same side as the left. So, yeah, I'm taking you to UG."

The very idea of being treated by demons, inside a demon facility, was outrageous. Insulting. He was an Archangel, dammit. He should be taken somewhere far more appropriate.

"Take me to Ares." Gabriel and the Horseman weren't buddies or anything, but Gabriel had been to his island, and if anyone could help, it was Ares.

"I'm not your taxi service." She hauled him to his feet, uncaring of his agony. "You're going to be Eidolon's problem now."

Mace had known pain in the past. He'd broken about a million bones, had been nearly disemboweled a couple of times, and once, Blade had even had to restart his heart.

But the things Dr. Vale had done to him made all those other instances seem like minor scratches and contusions. At least his parents had stepped outside and hadn't—hopefully—heard his roars of agony.

Talon had, though. Figured his half-brother would be standing right there, using the excuse that he needed to monitor Mace's organs in case they exploded or melted or some shit. They hadn't, thankfully. Mace would have hated for Talon to have an I-told-you-so moment.

"Hey, kiddo."

Mace looked up from the video game he was playing in the 3D projection from his wrist comms. He'd needed to take his mind off Blade and Scotty, the mission he'd failed to complete, and the fact that he couldn't contact them.

"Hey." Mace shut down the game as Wraith sauntered into the room, decked out in battle gear and a worn leather trench coat, beneath which there would be dozens of weapons. Weapons he'd taught Mace to be proficient with by the time he was ten. "Who called you? I know Talon didn't."

"Idess sent me a message." Wraith moved over to the bed as quickly and smoothly as the creature that was his namesake. "How are you doing? Your parents said you could have died."

"They worry too much."

Wraith gave Mace's arm a fond squeeze. "It's what parents do."

"What do parents do?" Talon blew into the room like a storm cloud, no doubt pissed about Wraith's presence.

"They worry about their kids." Wraith turned his words into a challenge as he faced Talon. "Even when they're adults."

"Well, there's no reason to worry about Mace." Talon tossed his clipboard onto the counter. "He's doing great."

"What about you?" Wraith asked.

"Me?" Talon scoffed. "I'm not the one who was dumb enough to get caught in a bone-crush spell."

"Fuck off," Mace sighed. "Traps aren't always easy to detect. Because, you know, they're *traps*."

"Speaking of traps," Wraith said to Talon, in a voice that was definitely a trap, "you still messing with that fallen angel?"

The room's temperature dropped about ten degrees. Talon's relationship with an abhorrent, insufferable fallen angel was one of those subjects you brought up at the family dinner if you wanted to blow shit up.

Mace had been known to blow up a dinner or two.

"She has a name, you know," Talon said.

She sure did. Mace, Scotty, and Blade called her *Angelus Horribilis*. It did not amuse her.

"I'll bet she has many names." Wraith's lips peeled back in disgust, revealing massive fangs that Mace envied. Mace's weren't nearly as long. "And I'd bet she's never told you what they are."

"This might shock you, Dad, but I don't give a shit."

Wraith seemed relieved. "So, it's just sex. Why don't you—?"

"We're not discussing this," Talon snapped, and Mace hoped Wraith would let it go. At least for now. Everyone knew Talon was only dating the evil bitch to piss off his dad, but the more Wraith pushed, the more he shoved Talon closer to her.

When Wraith gave a reluctant nod, Talon turned to Mace. He still looked irritated, though. "You asked how Eva is doing. She's stable for now. As for you, Dr. Vale cleared you for discharge. But," he said, his voice taking on a note of doctorly gravity, "you have to keep your resting heart rate below fifty. That's pretty high for our species, but you still need to be careful. I'm going to send a monitoring application to your wrist comms. When your heart rate goes above fifty heartbeats per minute, the alarm will sound. If it goes above sixty, get to the hospital immediately."

"Uh…why? What'll happen if I don't?"

"Heart failure," Talon said bluntly. "The kind you're unlikely to come back from."

Not cool.

"He should stay here if he's in that much danger." Wraith looked over at Mace. "You don't have to go."

"Yeah," Talon said, sarcasm dripping from his voice. "Because he loves being here so much."

"For once, Talon's right. I'm going home." He looked down at his chest, as if he could see inside. "How long do I have to keep my heart rate down?"

"Give it twenty-four hours. Once your fever breaks, you're out of the woods. So, take your temperature every couple of hours, and don't do anything but rest. Have food delivered. And no sex. I'll give you a prescription for a couple of doses of the suppressant StryTech developed."

"Fuck that," Mace said as he threw his legs over the side of the bed. He was so out of here. "Isn't that drug dangerous? It nearly killed Stryke."

Stryke hadn't thought the suppressant Eidolon invented worked long enough, so he'd come up with a formula that allowed a Seminus demon to go up to a week without sex. But the side effects included restlessness, nausea, fertility, insanity, and death.

"Eidolon approved it for extreme short-term use," Talon said. "It can cause fertility, so either take one dose of the usual suppressant, or take precautions the first time you have sex with a fertile female."

"Oral only. Got it."

"Or Masumi," Wraith suggested. "She can't get pregnant."

"Speaking of Masumi," Mace said, feeling a sudden need to poke the hornet's nest, "she says she hasn't bedded Talon in months. He's been too busy with Scorn."

"You just had to do that, didn't you?" Talon snapped. "Like usual, you had to fucking insert yourself where you don't belong."

And that was the crux of the matter. Talon had never accepted Mace as his brother. Had always resented the fact that Wraith was Mace's father too.

"According to you," Mace shot back, "I don't belong anywhere."

"*Stop.*" Wraith's sharp reprimand echoed through the room. "Knock it off. Both of you."

Mace gestured to Talon. "He started it."

"Go to hell—"

"I said, knock it off," Wraith roared. "If I have to—"

"Hey!" Lore stuck his head into the room. "Raika's here. And you'll never believe who she brought with her."

Chapter 14

So, *this* was the infamous Underworld General Hospital.

It looked exactly as Gabriel had imagined, with Sheoulic words and symbols painted in blood on the flat-gray walls, gutters carved into the obsidian floors that ran with what he thought was blood, and chains and hooks hanging from the ceilings.

The only thing that surprised him was that it was clean. Chaotic, but clean.

Gabriel was aware of all the eyes on him as Raika ushered him—dragged him, really—out of a Harrowgate, past a registration and waiting area, and into an empty, curtained room.

Eidolon, the Seminus demon who, along with his four siblings, ran the hospital, strode inside just as Raika shoved Gabriel onto some sort of examination table.

"They called in the big guns for me, I guess," Gabriel said, because of course they had.

Even without his wings, he was a legend, an ageless warrior with the knowledge of the universe and the Creator's supremacy woven into his DNA. His presence would make waves and strike fear into the hearts of demons.

"I was actually just heading home," Eidolon said, tossing his white physician coat over the back of one of the chairs, "but I got stuck treating you because no one else wanted to."

Well, that burst his self-important bubble. "No one?"

"Angels give most demons the creeps."

Yeah, well, right now, angels gave Gabriel the creeps too.

"I'm not…" He cleared his throat. It wasn't easy to say the words. Even after all that time in Lilith's chamber of horrors, it was only now finally sinking in. "I'm not an angel anymore."

Eidolon snorted. "You still reek of all that sanctimonious goodness."

"Takes a while for the holier-than-thou stench to fade after losing your wings," Raika said.

He shot her a look. She'd propped her hip against the counter, its polished metal top catching glints of the row of jeweled cuffs around the shell of her ear.

"Interesting take on it," he said, "given that your parents are angels. Which makes you an angel. I'd think you'd be a little less hostile toward your own kind."

"I was born in the underworld. Tainted, according to *your* kind." An aura of darkness bloomed around her, undulating and twisting like a living thing. A few seconds later, it faded away, leaving a lingering sense of malevolence in the air. "My parents run the netherworld, and my father is the Grim Reaper. They're hardly angels." She raised her chin, her amber eyes glinting with arrogance. "And neither am I."

Her argument was valid, much as he hated to admit it. But they weren't fallen angels, either.

"They occupy a gray area," he conceded. "You all do. But I don't." Anger flared at the memory of being betrayed by his Celestial brethren. Of being called a traitor, when *they* were the ones who had led a coup to wrest control from the Archangels. "My wings were torn from my body, and I was cast out. *Me.* An *Archangel.* The last time an Archangel was booted—"

"It was Raphael." Raika shoved away from the counter. "And it wasn't that long ago." She started toward the door, her black-as-night hair billowing around her shoulders as if blown by a ghost breeze. "Compared to what happened to him, you have it pretty good. So, stop whining."

"Raphael deserved it. I didn't."

"He said, *whining.*" Raika swept out of the room like a queen discarding her lowly subjects.

What an infuriating female. She truly was the female version of Azagoth.

"I'm going to channel some healing energy into you," Eidolon said, now that she was gone. "There's a chance your angelic genetics and my demonic power won't play nice, but Unfallens usually respond well."

"What happens when they *don't* respond well?"

Eidolon reached for him, the markings on his right arm glowing. "It's not important."

Gabriel begged to differ, but the demon didn't give him a chance to protest. Eidolon gripped his shoulder, and instantly, a hot, oily sensation spread through him. Nausea flipped his stomach, and bile flooded his mouth. He'd never thought he'd ever let a demon channel its evil into him. Sure, he'd cozied up to many demons over the millennia, but that had been part of his job. Heaven had to win the battle between good and evil, no matter the cost. And if the price meant working with demons from time to time, then so be it.

But this was different. This was a demon injecting power into him. Could be helping. Could be doing the opposite. Seminus demons could make a heart start…or stop. They could stanch bleeding in the brain, or they could explode brain matter.

The only thing that comforted Gabriel was knowing that Eidolon was reportedly not a complete scumbag. In fact, he and his siblings were credited with helping to save the world once. Maybe twice.

Whatever.

"Can you tell me what happened?" Eidolon peered closely into Gabriel's wrecked eye. "Are your injuries a result of your expulsion from Heaven?"

"Angels took my wings," Gabriel growled. "Everything else is the handiwork of Lilith and her merry band of evil skanks."

"Lilith?" Eidolon's voice dipped low as he channeled energy into Gabriel's eye. "If it's the Lilith I think you mean, I have a lot of friends who'd be interested in any information you can provide."

Gabriel was counting on that. They'd also be interested to know about the fallen angel who worked with Lilith. Fearr, once a high-ranking commander in Satan's armies, had taken the number-two spot on the Horsemen and Underworld General staff's must-die list after a violent encounter in UG's parking lot. Apparently, her two accomplices had already met gruesome ends at the Horsemen's hands, but they'd been looking for Fearr for three decades now.

Eidolon frowned. "You've got multiple injuries in various stages of healing. Damn," he breathed. "Some of them must have been excruciating. How long were you—?"

"A million years," Gabriel broke in. That's what it had felt like, anyway. "A million damned years."

Gabriel had to give the demon credit. He took a hint and stopped asking questions about something Gabriel wanted to put behind him. Angels were highly resistant to severe mental trauma and skilled at compartmentalization, which meant locking shit away. And every time you opened the door to access a little information, you risked letting everything out.

Shadows flickered on the edges of his vision. "Doc? My eye—"

"It's almost healed," Eidolon said. "Just one second…"

There. Gabriel could see out of that eye again. He glanced around at the skulls and jars of grotesque things on the shelves and mounted on the walls and decided it had been better when his vision sucked.

"We done, doc?"

Eidolon nodded. "Find a safe place to hole up for a while. You'll probably fall into a light coma. You're only partially healed, and your Unfallen body needs time to adapt to its new status. Once it does, you'll be as good as new."

"Good as new would mean having wings," Gabriel said.

"True." The doctor reached for a clipboard hanging nearby. "You never said what happened to get you booted from Heaven."

"You're right." Gabriel left it at that.

The demon probably already knew far too much of what was happening inside Heaven than he should. Again, it appeared that Eidolon and his family were trustworthy, fighting on the side of Team Good. But while Gabriel wasn't beneath allying with them when needed, he refused to trust them.

Once again, Eidolon didn't press. That was the thing about this particular demon. He was calm, cool, and smart enough to know when to push and when to let go. Gabriel knew *angels* with worse temperaments and lower IQs.

"So, what's the plan?" Eidolon asked. "You don't strike me as someone who wants to enter Sheoul willingly, and once word gets out there's an Archangel Unfallen on the loose, you're going to be hunted to the ends of the Earth. So, how are you going to avoid being caught and forced to become a True Fallen?"

Gabriel had thought a lot about that. A lot. There hadn't been much else to do while he was being held prisoner, and right now, survival was his number-one priority. He'd resisted coming here, to this hospital run by evil degenerates, but Raika may have unknowingly provided him with exactly what he needed.

"Actually, I was hoping you could help me with that."

One black eyebrow cocked up. "You want a job? Reaver was a physician here back when he was Unfallen. Kept him safe for decades."

There wasn't a Celestial in Heaven who didn't know that story. Reaver was a legend among angels, loved by many, hated by more. Once an Unfallen with either no memories or false ones, he had been one of only a handful of fallen angels who had earned his wings back. His mate, Harvester, was the only True Fallen to earn hers, and together, the two formerly fallen angels made a formidable team.

Until a coup in Heaven resulted in Reaver being taken captive and Harvester being killed.

"I don't want a job," Gabriel said. No, it was not the time to hide. Right now was the time to fight. Heaven was in trouble, ruled by an extremist faction, and Gabriel had to find a way to take it back. That wouldn't happen if he buried himself in work—work healing *demons*. "I want you to help me get in touch with one of the Four Horsemen."

"Why would you think I can do that?"

He gave Eidolon an are-you-kidding-me look. "Don't bullshit me. I know you're all tight. You run in the same circles, and your kids all hang out together. Ares's daughter is practically chained to two of your nephews. So cut the shit."

Eidolon snorted in amusement. "Fair enough. Who do you want me to contact?"

"Ares."

"Why?"

"It's none of your concern, demon."

"You're pretty demanding for someone in your...diminished... position."

Gabriel growled. "I am the Archangel Gabriel, Lord of the King-dom of Chrystalis, Destroyer of Demons, Builder of Realms, and over two hundred other titles of such significance that your puny demon brain can't even begin to comprehend. You *will* contact him for me."

"I see. How about this?" Eidolon wadded up a sheet of paper and tossed it into the trash bin. "Show me your official Center of the Universe credentials, and I'll shoot Ares a message right now. Or, you answer my question and tell me why you want to talk to him. Your choice."

Insufferable fiend! But the fiend held all the cards, and Gabriel wasn't in a position to do anything about it.

Oh, how the mighty have fallen.

So humiliating. "I want him to grant me asylum."

"Interesting." Eidolon spun back to him on his stool. "What makes you think he'll allow you to stay on his island?"

"I've helped train his children—and yours—in battle. I can help the Memitim on his island in their dealings with Heaven. And," Gabriel added, "I have information he wants."

"Lilith." Eidolon's dark eyes sparked with hatred as he stood. Everyone despised Lilith. As they should. "I'll see what I can do."

Good. Gabriel had a plan B named Stryke, but Ares was in a better position to help him. Besides, if Heaven learned that Stryke was in any way aiding Gabriel, they would destroy him. But they would think twice about starting shit with the Four Horsemen of the Apocalypse.

As Gabriel shoved himself off the exam table, Eidolon's sister-in-law, Idess, stepped in, her eyes glued to Gabriel.

"It's true," she whispered, awe making her voice tremble. Finally, someone was revering him as he should be. "You're really here."

"Greetings, Idess." He'd only seen her a couple of times, back before Azagoth destroyed his realm, but she'd always been gracious. And adequately adoring.

"I can't believe it." She glanced at Eidolon, excitement sparking in her eyes. "We need to take him to Eva."

"Eva?" He frowned and then remembered Azagoth and Raika telling him a while back that the female—Logan's wife—was hosting Harvester's Grace. "Why do you want me to see her?"

Idess's eyes glistened with emotion. "She's dying."

Frankly, Gabriel was surprised that Eva was still alive. The human body couldn't withstand the radioactive power of an angel's Grace for long. Harvester had died months ago, her blood raining down on Earth, coating the Temple Mount and a small beach in Hawaii in splotches of crimson. Most in Heaven had considered it a suicide. Others, like Gabriel, called it murder, no matter that she'd entered an unsurvivable portal with intent. If she hadn't been forced to, she'd still be around, advocating for her imprisoned mate and stirring every angelic pot she could.

He sighed. "What do you want me to do about it?"

"We need your help to expel Harvester's Grace. And as far as I know, only an angel can do it. A powerful angel, like an Archangel."

Powerful? Gabriel almost laughed. He'd lost his wings, his power, and his dignity when those bastards booted him from Heaven. Bitterness coated his tongue and his words. "I can't help you."

"Can't you at least try?" Idess pleaded. "I'm not an angel anymore, but surely you can draw Harvester's Grace—"

He cut her off with a frustrated curse. "I said no." At the devastation in her expression, he tempered his tone. "There *have* been instances of dead angels being brought back and reunited with their Grace, as long as their Grace hasn't returned to Heaven."

"So, it *is* true?" Excitement bled into Idess's voice. "Aleka found an ancient ritual she thinks will do that, but we've had no real evidence."

Of course, Aleka had found the ritual. Ares's eldest daughter was useless with a weapon, but she could wield knowledge against evil as effectively as any blade.

"You'll need Harvester's blood. Just a drop will do."

Idess nodded. "Aleka's been trying to find some, but I fear we're running out of time."

"You say Eva is here? In the hospital?"

"She was brought in a few hours ago," Eidolon said. "She's weak. Her body is caving in on itself."

Damn. "Have her eyes turned white?"

Eidolon looked startled. "An hour ago."

Double damn. "She doesn't have much time."

"What are we talking here? Weeks? Days?"

"Days. She might rally and seem like her old self, but she'll crash fast after that," he said grimly. "Tell Aleka to hurry."

Chapter 15

Wendigos were hard as shit to kill.

Jon was right, not that Blade would ever admit it. The bastards were fast. And they were also already corpses. The bodies appeared to be animated by evil, so with no bodily functions, Blade's ability to stop heartbeats or collapse lungs was of no use.

Scotty cursed as her blade sliced through a wendigo's skull and didn't so much as slow it down. "What the fuck?"

Blade leaped over the screaming wendigo on the ground, one arm and leg severed by Blade's bone-cutter knife. He came down hard, burying the blade in the back of another wendigo's neck. It shrieked and swiped at him with one spindly arm, slamming Blade into a stone pillar.

They were getting their asses kicked.

"There's five of them," Scotty shouted. She hurled herself into the closest one, replacing her summoned blade with a smaller KA-BAR for hand-to-hand combat. Her timing was dead-on, and the fiend's head ripped loose from its neck and dropped to the ground, the open maw twisted in a silent scream. "Four!"

And several dead demons.

The demons weren't hard to kill, but they *were* distracting, attacking from all sides in overwhelming numbers that made it hard to fight off the wendigo assaults.

"We could really use Mace," he shouted back, as he kicked an imp so hard its spine punched through its paunchy belly. Simultaneously, he hurled a throwing star into a wendigo's eye.

Suddenly, a stream of fire and searing heat blasted through the cave. Blade and Scotty dove behind a pile of rocks, barely missing being toasted by Jon's flamethrower.

Demons and wendigos screeched as the fire engulfed them. The moment Jon tossed aside the flamethrower, they jumped back into the fray.

It was so much easier to decapitate wendigos that writhed on the ground, all charred and crispy.

"I love the smell of roasted evil in the morning," Skoll said, as he impaled an imp with a dagger.

Scotty barked out a laugh. "Sounds like something Mace would say."

Her smile faded, and her summoned sword flickered between being solid and transparent. She swore at it before making it disappear and replacing it with the dagger on her hip.

She'd always had trouble maintaining a summoned weapon when her concentration was divided. Blade got that. His mind kept jumping to Mace in the most inconvenient moments. Like now, as he finished off an injured demon as it skittered toward an exit.

Mace was most likely fine, healed by the best doctors on the planet. But until Blade got confirmation, he wasn't gonna relax. The not knowing for sure was a killer. Then there was the fact that he and Scotty needed to tell him what they'd done...

The caves, which had seemed so big and cavernous before, closed in on Blade. Dead and dying demons and wendigos littered the ground, their blood pooling or running in rivulets along the rock crevices. The place reeked of death, charred meat, and bowels, and Blade found himself wanting out. Now.

"Blade!" Jon shouted. "Behind you!"

He whirled around, but not quickly enough to avoid the razor-sharp claws of a skeletal fiend that had somehow risen from the ashes. It's crunchy, blackened skin rasped as it raked its claws across Blade's chest, slicing his weapons harness in half and taking some of his shirt and skin with it.

Scotty leaped across several dead bodies and stabbed the demon in the throat, dropping it to the ground. With a snarl, she whacked off its head and then rounded on Blade.

"What the hell was that?" She sounded just like her father when he was giving them a dressing-down. "You're not usually so sloppy."

"Trust me, I know." Angry at his own carelessness, he cursed. "I was thinking about Mace."

"Oh." She put away her weapons. "He'll understand, Blade." Scotty sounded confident, but the doubt in her eyes belied her words. She turned to the other guys. "Let's finish this, and I'll gate us to HQ. We can fill in Kynan on the mission and then head home."

Home. Where they would have to fess up to Mace about what they'd done.

His chest tightened as he glanced around at the carnage on the floor of the cave and couldn't help thinking that he'd rather go another hundred rounds with those wendigos than tell his best friend that he'd broken their oath with their other best friend.

Mace felt like shit.

Physically, he was A-okay. Sort of. Still had to keep his heart rate down.

Mentally, it was a whole other thing.

Like a jerk, he'd thrown fuel on the fire between Wraith and Talon. And between Talon and him. Not that he cared much what Talon thought of him. Not really. There had been a time, when he was younger and dumber, that he'd wanted a relationship with his brother. Had loved his brother. And maybe he still did. But Talon had made it clear that he didn't consider Mace a part of the family, let alone his sibling.

Still, the family drama accounted for only a fraction of his anxiety. He was also agitated by the situation in Alaska. He was sure his friends were all right, probably having the times of their lives battling freaking wendigos. But he hated being away from them. Hated not being a part of the team. Hated not partaking in the glory of a battle. Scotty liked to say he had major FOMO.

Fair enough. He supposed he did have a fear of missing out. But he also wasn't good at being alone. Unlike Blade, Mace didn't do the solitary thing well. He never had.

Making everything worse, he was sickened by what was happening to Logan and Eva.

Mace had lived with Logan at the compound for years before he met Eva, but even before that, Logan had been a friend. His parents, Regan and Thanatos, were tight with Mace's family, so he'd grown up alongside the son of the Horseman known as Death. They'd gone to school together, had trained on Ares's island together, and now, they worked together at DART. Mace hated seeing Logan's anguish as he hovered at Eva's bedside, counting every breath as if she didn't have many left.

And from what Mace had heard, she didn't.

His steps were heavy as he traipsed past the compound's pool on his way to the rear entrance. With the restrictions on his heart rate, he probably shouldn't even get in the hot tub. At ninety percent healed, he was almost as good as new, but his brother had been adamant about the low-heart-rate thing, and since Mace didn't want his ticker to blow up, he supposed he should follow the rules, no matter how much they sucked.

Maybe he could de-stress the way they did it back in the caveman days. On a Nintendo console, playing Super Mario Bros.

The kitchen and living areas were empty, but that wasn't a surprise. Mace had seen Sabre at the hospital, Rade was probably at work, and given that it was three o'clock in the afternoon, Crux was either training on Ares's island or in his room, taking virtual college courses. Assuming he was feeling better, that was. Poor kid's pre-transition episodes were getting more frequent and severe. Mace cringed just thinking about it.

He grabbed a bottle of sparkling water from the fridge, and as he twisted the cap off, Blade and Scotty filed through the back door. They looked exhausted but freshly showered, wearing their gym clothes from work. They often dragged themselves into HQ to report to Tayla or Kynan immediately after an assignment, and if they were in bad shape, covered in blood or guts or whatever, they'd shower before the debriefing. No one cared if they donned their gym clothes for meetings, because at least they were clean. And not smelling of sweat and bowels.

"Hey." He grinned so hard his face hurt. He didn't think he'd ever been so happy to see them.

"Hey." Blade's smile seemed forced, as if it was fighting the dark crescents under his eyes. He held up a plastic bag. "Brought you a souvenir from Alaska."

Scotty, her damp ponytail clinging to her neck, rolled her eyes. "It wasn't my idea, I swear."

"This ought to be good." Eagerly, Mace snatched the bag from

Blade and peeked inside. An eyeball, inside a clear globe attached to a fine silver chain, looked up at him. *Okaaay.* "What the hell is it?"

"Dunno," Blade said. "We found it inside the wendigo's lair. Probably some sort of talisman."

"And you thought bringing an unidentified, undoubtedly evil talisman here was a good idea?"

Scotty punched Blade lightly in the shoulder. "I told you we should have given it to Aleka to study."

Blade shrugged. "I just didn't want Mace to feel left out of the hunt."

"Um, thanks, I guess?" Mace tossed the bag onto the couch. He'd definitely give it to Aleka later. Keeping that thing around likely wouldn't be the smartest move. He knew from experience. A painful, embarrassing one. "So, how did it go?"

Blade and Scotty exchanged glances, but it wasn't playful or the kind that said, "*You go first.*" It was more…surreptitious, and Mace's Spidey-senses tingled.

Had something gone sideways?

"It went the way it usually goes," Blade said, sounding enough like his usual self that Mace figured he must have read more into their glances than there was. "We kicked ass."

"We did," Scotty followed up. "But forget that. How are *you?* We didn't get any news until Kynan filled us in. We were worried sick."

Mace glanced down at his calf. "No big. Leg is almost better."

"When did you get released from the hospital?" Blade opened the fridge and tossed a water bottle to Scotty before opening his own.

"I just got home." A low, throbbing pulse in his thigh told him he'd been standing too long, so he hobbled over to the couch before his heart rate ramped up from the pain. "And dude, you'll never guess who Raika brought into the ER."

Blade flung his go-bag onto the floor. "Who?"

He drew out the anticipation by chugging half his water. He'd always liked a side of drama the way everyone else liked a side of fries. "Gabriel."

Scotty's eyebrows shot up. "No way! The Archangel?"

"The very halo."

Blade, his dark eyes as wide as Scotty's hazel ones, paused with his bottle of water halfway to his lips. "But angels can't enter Underworld General."

"They can if they've lost their wings."

Shock lit their expressions, making the freckles on Scotty's cheeks stand out like a dusting of cinnamon on cream. "What? He's *fallen* now?"

"*Un*fallen, but yeah."

"Holy shit." Absently, she reached up to twirl her hair around her finger. She'd fidgeted with her hair since she was a kid. He'd thought it was cute when they were younger, the fierce little wildcat with a sword in one hand and a finger wrapped in a curl on the other. Now, he couldn't look at her doing that without thinking about how her ponytail had felt in his fist while his teeth were in her throat. "Was it because of what went down on the oil rig?" She gave her ponytail a frustrated tug. "I *knew* he killed Hutriel. No way a demon did it the way he claimed."

Mace had similar thoughts about Gabriel and the other angel. The battle scene on the helicopter pad, littered with demon and angel parts, had been sketchy as hell. The cut that had severed Hutriel's head had been oddly clean, unlikely to have been made by a demon's claws or teeth. But Gabriel's sword could have done it.

"Gabriel didn't say why," Mace said, "but it sounds like he got the boot right after that. And get this… Lilith caught him and held him prisoner. It was Raika who rescued him."

"Lilith." Scotty sank onto the couch as if her legs had given out. Her grandmother was a heavy subject. Blade moved as if to lay a hand on her shoulder, but seemed to think better of it at the last second, snatching his hand back like she was a hot stovetop. Made sense. Sometimes, Scotty was as prickly as her father when it came to physical comfort. Pricklier when it came to her demon granny. "Did Raika get her? Tell me she got her."

"Nah. Bitch got away." Mace threw his aching leg up onto the ottoman. The throbbing eased, but it only made the growing throb in his pelvis more noticeable. He needed an injection. Soon.

"Where was Lilith keeping him?" Scotty's eyes were bright now, the flecks of emerald embedded in the hazel depths having turned to shards, lit by the fire of hatred. "Where can we find her?"

"Chill, Scott." Mace fell back against the cushions. "It's not like I interrogated the guy. I didn't even see him. Just heard it through the FGC." The family gossip channel had a lot of fodder lately. "That's all I got for catch-up." He slumped as he thought of one more thing. The worst thing. "Did Ky tell you about Eva?"

"Yeah." Scotty stood again. She seemed oddly restless, more than usual when someone brought her grandmother up. "I'm going to help my sister find Harvester's blood as soon as I leave here. She thinks she's close."

"Let us know if you need help," Blade said.

"Will do."

The situation sucked, and Mace didn't like being mired in suck, so he changed the subject. "So, how did you guys get the wendigo?"

Blade snorted. "It wasn't just one. We took out six of the bastards in their lair."

"Six?"

"Plus demons." Scotty popped her foot onto a chair and bent to tie her sneaker. Mace forced himself not to stare at her legs. Toned and smooth, made to squeeze a male between them. He'd gotten a taste when he fed, and now he couldn't stop thinking about it. "Low-level hordes."

The hordes were the worst. Whether in video games or real life, he'd rather fight one powerful demon boss than a dozen scrappy minions bent on overwhelming their opponents.

"Where was their lair?"

"A cave system," Blade said. "The demons were coming through an incursion deep inside the mountains. We think it happened during a recent earthquake that awakened the original wendigo."

Scotty nodded. "Kynan's going to ask StryTech to seal the rift the way they did with the one at the oil rig."

"It's weird that we're suddenly finding a bunch of these things." Most rifts had existed for thousands of years, but for various reasons, they couldn't be easily used by most species. But when the veil was extra thin or torn, it allowed for demons and malevolent energy to pour out uninhibited.

Blade's voice took on the gruff tone he always used when his brother was the topic of conversation. "That's what Kynan said. He'll talk to Stryke about that too."

"Did you catch any demon souls with the new weapon?"

Blade glanced over at Scotty again. This time, Mace absolutely knew Blade looked contrite.

"I kinda lost the Reaper," he muttered. "We got caught in a flash flood and sucked down into a tunnel. Kynan was not happy." He glanced up the stairs to the second floor and their private living quarters. "Have you seen Crux yet?"

"Nah, like I said, I just got here. You might want to go check on him. He's probably in his room."

"I hope he's been eating," Blade said. "He needs to pound the calories before the transition starts, or it's gonna wreck him."

"Masumi will make sure he eats during it," Mace assured him, but they both knew the reality. A Sem's transition was a dangerous time, full of pain, dehydration, starvation, and, potentially, death. Crux needed to be as nourished and strong as possible before it began.

A few heartbeats passed. Then a few more. Then things got awkward. Which *never* happened. And was it his imagination, or did Scotty and Blade exchange a few more furtive glances? Nah. He was probably still suffering the effects of his injury and its subsequent, painful cure.

But he had to be sure. "Okay, guys. What's going on?"

This time, their looks lingered. He *wasn't* seeing things. Something definitely wasn't right.

"Stop fucking around. Talon says I can't let my heart rate get above sixty heartbeats per minute, or I'll die. And you're starting to stress me out."

Blade fumbled his water, spilling some onto the floor. "What'd you say?"

"You're kidding, right?" Scotty gaped at him. "Tell me you're kidding."

"Nope." Now that he had their attention, he folded his hands across his abs and soaked it in. Side of drama and all that. If he hadn't joined DART, he'd have been an actor. In school, drama class had been his favorite. Screw math. And science. And pretty much everything else. "He's making me sit around, because if my heart rate gets too high, it will stop. It's a side effect of the injury. Or of the cure. I'm not sure. They both sucked. But the cool thing? It's a prescription to play video games until I'm healed."

"What the fuck, Mace?" Scotty practically yelled. "Why didn't you say something sooner? We could have killed you with—"

"With what?" He scoffed. "Your wendigo hunt story? Come on."

"No, it's just..." Scotty's cheeks flared pink, and she averted her gaze.

Mace glanced down at his heartbeat monitor. Forty-three. "Just what?" Mace pressed.

Blade swore. "It's nothing." He shot Scotty a look that dared her to argue. Which made Mace even more curious. It also made his pulse pick up. Forty-seven. The alarm would sound at fifty. He could die at sixty.

Chill. Breathe.

"It's obviously something."

"It's about Skoll," Scotty said quickly. "I made a date with him."

Her words made his heart skip a beat. Which was probably better than the alternative.

Skoll? Mace knew something like that would happen, but he didn't want to have to think about it. Now, he had to pretend everything was totally cool when his only consolation was that at least it wasn't Jon.

"That's great," he said, all cheery and full of lies. "Why did you think that would upset me?"

"See," Blade said, giving Scotty the side-eye. "Told you it was nothing."

"Yeah. Totally cool." Mace fidgeted with his water bottle. "Skoll's a decent guy."

Fuck that. No one was good enough for Scotty. But he couldn't say that, and he had to stay calm, so he just took a gulp of his water and kept his mouth shut.

"Okay, then." Scotty hefted her bag to her shoulder. "I'm taking off. I'll see you guys later." She jabbed her finger at Mace. "You. Take it easy." She rounded on Blade. "You. Get some rest. We pushed some limits this week."

"Limits? You?" Mace asked, teasing. He knew how hard she pushed herself. "Never."

Usually, when he teased her, she fired back at him, even if it was just to shoot him the finger. But this time, her face turned red, and she stammered.

"I—I mean, not too bad. We just…we took a fall, and I was kind of out of juice when we fought the wendigo…and I'm going to go. See ya."

She rushed out of the house, and Mace looked over at Blade. "That was weird. What was that about?"

"You know how she is," he said with an exaggerated shrug. "She hates when she fucks up."

"How did she fuck up?"

"She didn't. Not really." Blade shifted his weight from one leg to the other as if dancing around the subject. "She was tired and worried about you. That's all. At times, she struggled to maintain her summoned sword." He gestured to the stairs. "I'm going to scoot too. See you later."

"Wait," Mace said, and Blade froze mid-turn. "Don't forget Amber's birthday party tomorrow. The decorators will be here in the morning."

"The party's still on?" Blade swung back around. "Even with what's going on with Eva?"

That had been Mace's concern as well. "Amber wanted to cancel, but Eva made her swear she wouldn't. She wants to be there if she can."

"I guess that makes sense," Blade said slowly, "but *we* need to cancel. They can have the party somewhere else. Your heart rate—"

"Talon says it'll be back to normal within about twenty-four hours. I'll be fine by then. And if I'm not, I'll just hang out in my bedroom. We're not canceling."

Blade scowled. "I just don't know why we're having it here instead of at Than's place. Or at any of the Horsemen's places."

"Amber wants to swim."

"Ares and Limos have miles of warm beaches."

"You know she hates the ocean. And we have an Olympic-sized pool." He grinned. "Come on, you know you love parties."

Blade still seemed troubled.

"Okay, man, what's wrong with you? You're like Mopey Mike at the HQ café."

Blade snorted. "I've never seen that guy smile. Scotty calls him Eeyore."

"Yeah, well, you're not Eeyore. So, spill."

"Nothing's wrong," Blade said, forcefully enough to be convincing. "Just tired. Some of us didn't get to lie around in bed for a couple of days."

Mace smiled, relieved to see his buddy back. "Go get some rest. And some Masumi."

Blade raised his hand in a brief wave and mounted the stairs.

Everything was back to normal.

Chapter 16

Scotty and Aleka didn't find Harvester's blood, but they *did* find a secret room beneath the Dome of the Rock on the Temple Mount that might be where her blood drained. As soon as Aleka deciphered the text on the seal, they'd check it out.

Hopefully, she'd do it within the next couple of hours and give Scotty an excuse to leave Amber's party.

Not that she didn't love her cousin or wish her the best, but until she and Blade came clean with Mace, Scotty didn't want to be around either of them. Keeping her mouth shut was too hard, and the moment it opened, stupid shit fell out.

Like, what the hell was up with the lie about making a date with Skoll? Thankfully, Blade had played along, but shit. Why couldn't she have come up with something less stupid and less…verifiable?

This day would suck. At least Mace had let them know that Eidolon had given him the all-clear to get back to normal life. Which was fantastic, but it also meant that she and Blade needed to tell him the truth, and soon. Maybe after the party.

Scotty pressed her hand to her queasy stomach as she walked across the expansive grounds on her way to the massive backyard. She could already hear people laughing around the pool and smell a variety of savory meats cooked either in the outdoor wood-fired brick oven, the roasting pit next to it, or the luxury grill area beneath the covered patio.

As the daughter of a Horseman and the niece of three others, she'd grown up with old-world wealth and extravagance. This, though…she glanced around at the building and the parklike surroundings…this was Stryke's construct. He hadn't acquired his wealth over the course of thousands of years. He'd made his billions—some estimated as much as a trillion—practically overnight, and then re-invested in his company and property, such as the modern, outrageously tech-appointed compound his brothers and cousins now called home.

Stryke's new headquarters, a few miles away in downtown Sydney, made this old one appear tiny.

"Scotty!" Amber waved from the poolside chair where she sat with her ever-present sketchbook and a pencil, her sunglasses uselessly perched atop her curly, dark hair.

Since Scotty wasn't yet ready to see Blade or Mace, she beelined over.

"Amber." She gave her quirky cousin a hug and pulled up a beach chair. "Happy birthday."

Tossing her book and pencil aside, Amber sighed. "It's just a day. I don't know why people make a big deal of it."

"You sound like Stryke."

She laughed. "He and I definitely agree on this."

Like Stryke, Amber had never liked being the center of attention, rarely even leaving her parents' keep in Greenland. When she did, it was only to go to places she knew well. Scotty had managed to get her out to lunch a couple of times, but only because they went to quiet cafés in small towns.

"Where are your parents?" Scotty asked. "I didn't see them when I got here."

"Over there." Amber gestured with her chin toward where her parents, Regan and Thanatos, were playing cornhole with their uncle Reseph and aunt Jillian.

"Where's the baby?" Regan had just given birth to Amber and Logan's little brother after a difficult pregnancy, and this was his first time out in the world.

"He's in the carrier."

Scotty squinted and then nodded. "Oh, right. It's hard to see with the hellhound in the way."

Amber reached for her glass of cola. "Cujo is obsessed with him. I told Logan that he and Eva had better hurry up and have a kid so the poor mutt has something to watch over."

Orphaned as a pup, Cujo had bonded with Logan when he was an infant, and they'd been inseparable ever since. That was the thing about hellhounds. Either they wanted to eat you, or they wanted to protect you. There was no in-between. None. If you weren't someone they loved and adored, you were food. Or worse.

"I just hope they get the chance," Scotty said, thinking of Eva. Logan had texted everyone this morning to let them know that she'd rallied and was doing so well that they planned to attend the party.

Amber gave a noncommittal nod that Scotty couldn't read. Her cousin…she knew stuff. No one knew how or why, but she just…knew. And if she didn't want to disclose something, no amount of pestering, badgering, or pleading could get it out of her.

Scotty didn't even try.

Amber's gaze narrowed and grew hot as Talon walked by with his demon Barbie girlfriend, Scorn. No one liked that bitch, but Amber had particularly strong feelings about her. Amber also had particularly strong feelings for Talon, but in a completely different way.

But her glare was hotter than usual today. A flare of heat even brought a tinge of red to her tan cheeks.

"Okay, cuz." Scotty lowered her voice conspiratorially. "What's going on?"

Evil Barbie's head swiveled as if she'd heard them speak, and she shot Amber a malicious smile. Wow. Brazen as fuck.

"I swear I want her dead," Amber growled, and Scotty blinked in surprise. Amber was the most mild-mannered, timid person she'd ever met. Those words were not something she'd have expected to come out of her mouth. Ever.

"Seriously?"

Amber tore her murderous gaze away from the fallen angel. "She cornered me in the kitchen just before you got here. Said she knows I want Talon. But she was gross and graphic about it. Then she said I probably sit around imagining him between her legs and wishing it was me he was with."

Anger, searing and hot, shot through Scotty's veins. "Are you fucking kidding me?"

Amber had inherited her father's pale-yellow eyes, and right then, they glowed like hot citrines. "She said if I so much as look at him again, she'll gut me and strangle me with my own intestines."

"She's dead." Scotty glared at Evil Barbie. "I'll kill her for you."

"Aw, you're so sweet," Amber said. "Have you ever killed a fallen angel?"

"No, but how hard can it be?"

Amber snorted at Scotty's flippant question. Fallen angels were extremely hard to kill. Not even the Horsemen went up against them if they didn't have to. And as accomplished a warrior as Scotty was, she was also half human, and a fallen angel might be a little out of her league.

Still, Scotty wouldn't let this slide. Somehow, Scorn would pay.

She turned back to Amber. "Are you going to tell Talon what she said?"

"No." Amber wrapped her arms around her knees, closing herself off. "He probably wouldn't believe me, anyway. Plus, I don't want him to think I'm lusting after him."

"But you are."

Amber's cheeks flushed a darker red. "Am not."

"Girl, you can lie all you want, but you're practically wearing a sign."

Horror filled Amber's expression. "You don't think Talon knows, do you?"

"Nah." Scotty glanced over at Talon. "Males are oblivious when it comes to shit like that."

"I hope so." Amber took a drink of her soda and replaced it on the table. "I'll die if he finds out."

"Why?" Scotty watched Talon fetch a beer from a cooler and toss it to his skanky girlfriend. "Maybe he'd feel the same about you if he knew."

"Yeah, right." Amber rolled her eyes. "He treats me like I'm his little sister."

"Well…duh. He's besties with your brother. He's never had a chance to see you as anything but his BFF's tagalong sis. Honestly, hon, you've never given him any reason to." Scotty raked her gaze over Amber and revised her statement. "Until now. I can't believe you're wearing a bikini." Normally, Amber was all baggy shorts and tees.

"Do I look stupid?" Amber curled in on herself even tighter. "I didn't want to wear this. Leilani made me."

"You look amazing! Lei's always right when it comes to fashion and girly stuff. You should listen to her." Scotty reached over and forced her cousin to sit up straight. "Show that shit off, girl. Talon can't ignore it."

"He wished me a happy birthday when I got out of the pool, but he didn't notice my bikini. He didn't even look."

Which, Scotty suspected, meant that he *had* noticed but was trying *not* to look. So maybe he realized Amber was no longer Logan's annoying little tagalong sister, but a beautiful, shapely woman ready for all the things that came with being an adult.

Like hot, sweaty sex.

Warmth flushed through Scotty as she remembered her time with Blade. The feel of his sinewy muscles under her palms lingered in her mind, and so did the sounds they'd made. The gasps, the moans, his deep, masculine roar that first time he came.

He'd called out her name.

She shivered with feminine appreciation, and her heart fluttered.

Then it came to an abrupt stop when she saw him crossing the lawn. Gods, he was perfection. His long, muscular legs, encased in worn jeans, carried him smoothly toward a gathering of people from work. Like that hussy werewolf, Nikki, who practically drooled as he approached. In the past, she'd been casual bedmates with both Blade and Mace, but Scotty suspected that she desired way more than casual sex. That ho-bag totally wanted to land one of them as a mate.

Over Scotty's dead body. Those males were hers. Not hers in the romantic sense, of course.

Liar.

She swallowed the lump of guilt in her throat. Until Scotty and Blade came clean to Mace, it would remain a lie.

Blade smiled at Nikki and gave her a hug, but as they pulled apart, his gaze shifted somewhere behind her and grew stony.

Scotty tracked his gaze to his brother, Stryke, who was talking with their parents, one arm slung around his pregnant mate, Cyan's, waist.

Now might be a good time to go over and…and what? Say *"Hi"* as if nothing had happened between them?

Damn, this sucked. Which was exactly why they'd made their pact. Sex changed things.

We'll get past this. We will.

We have to.

"Hey." Amber tapped her on her arm. "You're being summoned."

"What? Oh." Mace and a few other DART colleagues had joined Blade, and they were waving her over. Well, Blade wasn't. He looked like he'd rather be anywhere else.

Scotty knew the feeling.

She turned back to Amber. "Let's talk later, okay?"

Amber grabbed Scotty's arm as she stood. "Don't tell Talon what I said to you. Swear it."

Screw that. Talon needed to know that his psycho girlfriend had messed with Amber. But Scotty had broken enough vows this week, so she'd keep her word. Besides, there were always workarounds.

Fallen angels disappeared all the time.

"I swear, I will not say a word to Talon." Evil Barbie, however, was another story. Scotty jerked her thumb over at her friends. "Gotta go."

Leaving Amber to her sketchbook, she crossed the yard. Lyiah Zee, DART's Media Manager, ushered her into a gap between Mace and Blade. "Stand here," she said. "I want to get a picture of you guys for the company newsletter. We're highlighting the wendigo mission."

Scotty held in a groan. She didn't want to think about the wendigo mission ever again. Doing so made her think about a lot more than cannibalistic monsters. It made her think of sitting in Mace's lap while his fangs were buried in her throat. It made her think of being beneath Blade while his powerful body surged against hers. It made her wonder if any male could ever make her feel the way Mace and Blade had.

Lyiah made an impatient scooting gesture, and Scotty gingerly wedged herself closer between the two males, flinching when her hip brushed against Blade's hand.

Chill. He touched you a million times before you had sex, and you never reacted like that.

Gods, she needed to get control of herself.

Step back from the situation and look at it with logic. Not emotion.

Her father used to tell her that during training, back when she'd been a lot wilder and more impulsive. But he hadn't said it to her in years. He hadn't needed to.

The problem here was that she couldn't set aside her feelings, because she didn't even know what they were.

The party was rocking. The Horsemen had gone all out for Amber's birthday, including booking one of the most popular bands in the world. Well, Stryke had called in that favor, but it was still cool. They'd be starting any minute now. Maybe then, Blade would stop scowling at Stryke, who would leave as soon as the music started. Stryke had always been sensitive to sounds, but music was especially irritating because he could literally taste it, and for some reason, it always tasted bad.

That would suck.

"Can you guys scoot closer?" Lyiah gestured to Blade and Mace, urging them to move in on Scotty.

"Sure." Mace threw his arm around Scotty's shoulders and pulled her in with a playful tug as she wrapped her arm around his waist. He glanced over at his buddy, who had stiffly inched closer but still held himself half a foot apart. "Yo. Blade. Get in here."

Blade offered a brief, contrite smile and pressed up against Scotty, arm to arm, hip to hip. The whole thing was awkward as hell.

"Come on, Blade." Lyiah gave him an exasperated look. "Put your arm around them. You know, like you're buddies and not strangers on the street. The story is going to highlight your unit's camaraderie and teamwork."

Blade seemed bizarrely flustered as he nodded and gingerly brought his arm to rest just beneath Mace's on Scotty's back.

Maybe Blade had a thing for Lyiah? She was cute, smart, and, as a species of blood-drinking demon that took their nourishment during sex, she was probably a lot of fun in bed. But it wasn't like Blade to get weird around females. If he wanted one, he went after her with the self-confidence of a male who rarely faced rejection.

That was the awesome thing about being a Seminus demon. Females wanted you. Resistance was futile and all that. As lust demons, they'd been gifted with unnaturally good looks, powerful, seductive pheromones, and the ability to pleasure a female unconscious.

The tradeoff was that as much as females loved them, males hated them. Mace could deal with the jealous or pissed-off randos, but he had to watch out for the greedy fucking mercenaries. Bastards made a fortune selling abducted Sems to sickos—sickos who made black-market aphrodisiacs from enslaved Seminus demons.

Mace shuddered. Most of those poor males died a slow, torturous death, wrung so dry they were basically just husks at the end.

Not cool, especially when the aphrodisiacs could be bought legally.

Made by StryTech, of course.

Mace had never been to the facility where Sems could *pleasantly* donate semen for the legal creams, tinctures, and pills created and marketed by StryTech. Still, he'd heard they employed extremely talented females who coaxed every drop from a wrung-out male.

Sadly, and infuriatingly, there would always be a segment of the population who would believe the black-market stuff was better because of how it was harvested. Some people believed that the more the male suffered, the more potent the results would be. Fuckers. They were the same ignorant assholes who believed that fear and pain made the meat of animals tastier, when it was the exact opposite.

"Okay, smile! Gimme some fang, Mace." Lyiah brushed her finger over her wrist comms, and a holographic camera popped up.

Mace grinned into the subtle flashes, tilting his head a hair to the right. His left was his good side.

"Now look serious, but a little cocky." Lyiah sounded like she was trying to hype up a kids' soccer team. "You guys just identified a new species that was once believed to be mythical. You're rock stars!"

"We're doing Bigfoot and Nessie next." Mace grinned, then coughed out a half-baked apology. "Right. Serious. Got it."

He folded his arms across his chest and put on his second-most stern face. Steely, with a hint of mischief. He'd practiced it a lot in the mirror as a kid. There were only so many times people could tell you to be calmer, or quieter, or more serious before you got good at putting up a front.

He glanced over at Blade. Blade had the calm thing down, but he liked to mess around as much as Mace did.

"What do you think, Blade? Should we ask Ky to develop a new Cryptid department? We could start with Bigfoot. Then do like the Yeti. Or chupacabras—"

"I've had enough of the fucking wilderness." Blade's tone could best be described as *mood killer*. "I just want to get back to normal."

Now was the point where Scotty usually chimed in, steering things back to cheery.

But she didn't. She posed for the next photos, achieving the serious-but-cocky thing, but her gaze was distant.

"Blade," Lyiah huffed. "You keep inching away from Scotty. Close the gap."

Scotty tugged Blade back and gave him a knock-it-off glare.

What the hell was going on? Between this, the vibe between those two last night, and Scotty's bizarre behavior…yeah, they were keeping something from him. And it wasn't that Scotty was going to date Skoll.

"Dude." He tapped Blade's shoulder. "What's up?"

"Nothing."

"You're being weird. You both are. Did I do something to piss you off?"

Scotty looked up at him, startled, but Blade only shook his head.

"Come on, guys." Lyiah's tone was pleading. "I just need one picture."

Woodenly, Mace found his stern face again, but he couldn't muster the quirk of mischief. Something awful was stabbing at the fringes of his mind, a suspicion he was afraid to let develop.

"Finally," Lyiah said, looking pleased.

Guess she got her shot. Mace wasn't sure he cared at this point. The suspicion grew darker, penetrating his thoughts like a nightmare demon's long, spindly fingers.

No. Don't go there. Don't you fucking go there.

"Thanks, guys." Lyiah's camera winked out. "I'm hoping Ky will approve the story going public. Fantastic PR for DART. And you guys, of course. Congratulations!" She gave them a brief wave and took off to join her buddies.

Scotty and Blade sprang apart like lightning had struck the ground between them, their expressions masks of guilt.

No.

A sinking sensation in his gut nearly drove Mace to his knees.

No!

It couldn't be. They didn't sleep together. They didn't.

But what if they did?

Hot, searing rage boiled up, the fire stoking even hotter as he watched Scotty and Blade exchange more fleeting, guilt-ridden looks. The awkward kind that happened the morning after a shameful hookup.

Not that Mace had experienced it. But he'd seen it. And it looked just...like...that.

Nooooo.

His ribs tightened, squeezing the air out of his lungs as the truth sank in. The three of them had seen each other in every kind of situation, in nearly every state of undress, and they'd been tangled tighter together than a skein of yarn over the years, but they had never been this uncomfortable with each other.

Only one thing could cause that.

The image of Blade and Scotty together in a cabin scorched his mind. He could picture them rolling around in front of a fire, maybe on a bearskin rug or some romantic shit. He knew how Blade fucked—the guy liked it rough and intense. He'd tear Scotty up.

Mace reconsidered that last thought. Scotty was a wildcat who could hold her own. She wouldn't wilt under Blade's sexual assault.

She'd thrive.

The image of her flipping Blade so she was on top played like an erotic movie in his head. She was naked, her pale skin glowing in the light of the fire, contrasting with Blade's hard-cut, tanned body. Sweat glistened between her breasts as she rocked her hips against his, riding him, demanding more of him, her hair flowing down her slender back in a cascade of lava.

His rage hit a new level, so hot he could practically smell smoke.

He'd been best friends with Blade for as long as he could remember, and this was the first time he wanted to beat the guy to a pulp. But not here. Not in front of dozens of people, friends, and families. Mace might be an impulsive ass, but he wasn't a total loose cannon.

Mostly. It was taking an extraordinary amount of self-control to keep himself in check right now.

"Come with me," he growled to them, his words so warped with fury that he barely understood them himself.

Mace didn't give them time to ask questions. He strode toward the house, his fists clenched tightly at his sides, every footstep falling harder than the last. He figured he should be leaving burned footsteps in his wake, but he didn't look back to see.

The moment they were inside with the door closed, Mace slammed one of those tight fists into Blade's jaw so hard he heard his own shoulder pop. Blade stumbled backward, hitting the wall with enough force to leave a dent in the shiny steel.

"Mace!" Scotty leaped between them, blocking his path before he could nail Blade with another blow. "Holy shit! What are you doing?"

Mace ignored her, his focus fully on Blade, whose stunned expression and bloody lip almost made Mace feel bad for hitting him. Almost. The level of betrayal kept him firmly raged out.

"You bastard!" he snarled. "You broke our vow and fucked her!" He rounded on Scotty and jabbed his finger in her face. "And you. How could you?"

The air in the kitchen went still. Heavy and laden with layers of shock and shame that pulsed off them in waves.

Scotty's skin, already creamy pale, went sheet-white, her freckles standing out almost in defiance of the accusation.

Silence hung over them like a shroud.

"Answer me!"

Startled by Mace's roar, Scotty jumped. "Mace. Please. It wasn't like that."

The breath whooshed painfully from his lungs. It was true. Yes, he'd suspected, but a not-so-small part of him was sure he was wrong. That he'd imagined things.

Scotty swallowed dryly, but before she could explain how *it wasn't like that*, he lost his shit.

"But you don't deny it." No, of course not. They just looked down at the floor, so suddenly curious about the fucking, blue-stained cement. Level of his fury? Maximum. Totally pegged out. All he could think about was Scotty asking them to find her someone to screw. "What the fuck? What *the fuck*, Scotty? Were you so desperate to lose your virginity that you what? Seduced him while I was laid up in the hospital?"

"What? No!" Anger or, more likely, guilt, turned her face crimson. "Gods, Mace, we didn't have a choice!"

He stared in disbelief. "No…no *choice*? What, you had a virginity emergency? Did your hymen suddenly—?"

"Don't." Blade's voice was a low growl, rumbling with the threat of violence. "Don't talk to her like that, Mace. I'm warning you."

Blade could shove his warning up his ass. "Or what? You'll fuck her again?"

Suddenly, the fist of a pissed-off, redheaded daughter of a Horseman cracked into his cheek, knocking him into the fridge.

"Stop being a dick!" she shouted. "Blade was dying. We fell into this crazy cave system, and he lost his backpack. His suppressants were in it. Would you rather he be dead? Pretty shitty of you to automatically assume the worst too."

It took a few seconds for her words to penetrate his anger. Okay, sure, he'd gone too far. But dammit, knowing that Blade had slept with Scotty was like a spear to the heart. And knowing they'd kept it from him made it even worse. So, yeah, he'd fucked up, but not as badly as they had. And he wasn't going to let them turn this around.

"Maybe if you'd been honest and told me, I wouldn't have had to assume the worst! Why the fuck didn't you tell me?"

"Mace, we couldn't. Your health—"

Ignoring Scotty, he rounded on Blade. "And how the hell did you lose your injections?"

Blade dabbed blood from his lips. "What, you think I lost them on purpose?"

"I think you were being reckless. You hate wearing your pack. I've told you a million times that you shouldn't take it off every time we stop for two seconds."

"Fuck you!" Blade shouted. "You weren't there because *you* were careless and went off the trail. You don't get to accuse me of jack shit."

They all went silent at the sound of a door opening off the living room, but whoever came in left a moment later. Still, it was enough time to lower the temperature in the kitchen—and Blade's tone—by a few degrees.

"It doesn't matter anyway," Blade muttered. "What's done is done. She saved my life, but it was a one-time thing, and it won't happen again. Happy?"

No, Mace wasn't happy. At all. Okay, sure, logically, he could admit that Blade and Scotty had done the right thing. And maybe they even believed that this could be forgotten. But the cork was out of the bottle, and no one was putting it in again.

Putting it in.

Blade had *put it in*, all right. Anger and jealousy clawed at the raw wound gouged in Mace's heart. *Blade* had been the one to take her virginity. He'd gone through a unique experience with her, had given her a once-in-a-lifetime memory that Mace could never repeat or be part of.

"I'm sorry, Mace," Scotty said quietly. "But it wasn't any different than when you guys saved me from that sea demon a while back. Or when Blade restarted your heart that one time. Or when I gave you my blood a couple of days ago. We help each other."

Mace wanted to flip out. He wanted to break things. Punch things. Kill things. He considered what his parents would do. Wraith would probably go the kill-things route. But Lore and Idess would tell him to stay calm. Remove himself from the situation and think about it.

Unfortunately, that wasn't how Mace was built. He was more of a deflector than a thinker. He liked to rile others, but he didn't like being riled up himself. Yup, he was a Gargantua demon-sized hypocrite, but he didn't care. He didn't like conflict in *his* life. Keep shit simple.

There was nothing simple about this situation, which meant he had to be the one to simplify it. Fortunately, he could lie to himself as convincingly as he lied to everyone else.

Taking a deep, rattling breath, he nodded and pasted on a smile. "S'okay. All's forgiven."

Scotty's eyes narrowed into skeptical, glittering slits. "Really?"

"Yeah." No. He looked over at Blade and continued the lies. "Sorry about the sucker punch." No, he wasn't. "If it makes you feel any better, my knuckles hurt. You have a hard face." That part was true.

Blade reached up to test his swollen jaw. "It does make me feel better. But you know how you can make it up to me?"

Mace groaned. He knew what was coming. "You want to beat me in a game of Dragon Bait." The virtual reality game was one of the few in which Blade could kick Mace's ass, and he did it handily. So handily that it was humiliating.

"Better." Blade's smirk was downright evil. "I want you to spar with Ares next week when we train."

Scotty whistled, low and long. "Wow. That's harsh." Then she flashed a grin as wicked as Blade's. "But fitting."

Fuck. Mace hated sparring with Ares. Everyone did. The guy trained like he fought and gave no quarter. Well, he didn't kill you, so that could be considered quarter. Sort of. Because by the end of the lesson, you wished you were dead.

"I deserve that," Mace said with a lightness he didn't feel. He did, however, feel the need to drown himself in alcohol and forget that any of this ever happened. At least, temporarily. "We done here? Because the smell of the steak on the grill is killing me."

Scotty nodded. "Let's go."

He held out his fist. "Team up."

They touched fists, the same as they'd done a thousand times. Felt the same. Looked the same.

But it wasn't. Scotty's smile was too sappy. Blade's was too forced.

As they traipsed out the door, laughing and joking like everything was back to normal, he had a feeling that nothing would ever be normal again.

Chapter 17

The morning after the party should have been game day.

Usually, on Saturday mornings, Scotty would come to the compound to hang with Mace, Blade, and Crux—sometimes Sabre, and even more rarely, Rade—while they played old-school console games or modern virtual or mixed reality battles in their gymnasium-sized gaming room.

But Scotty had messaged saying she was working with Aleka to find Harvester's blood. She'd turned down Blade's offer of help, which meant he was home when Sabre called a last-minute house meeting. Which also meant he had to face Mace after all that fucking awkwardness last night.

Mace said he was okay with what had happened between Blade and Scotty. Said he understood. But when he thought no one was looking, Mace's expression had been one of sheer devastation. Then he'd paint on that big, happy grin and rejoin the party with ribald jokes, wild antics, and entertaining tales from their missions.

People who didn't know him like Blade and Scotty did would have seen the usual Mace. But no, that wasn't the usual Mace. It was the Mace who shoved everything deep inside and hid behind a devil-may-care mask. Blade was wary of that Mace, because eventually, the mask would crack, and the poisonous lava that seeped out would burn everyone it touched.

Blade's gut churned as he took the stairs down to the living room, where Rade, Mace, and Sabre were already seated. He greeted each with a nod, although he wasn't sure Mace saw. He'd averted his gaze so fast it probably put a crick in his neck.

Blade took the closest seat on the couch next to Rade, who was still in his sleep shorts and a tee.

"Cool, everyone's here," Sabre said. "I called this meeting because we need to decide who will take Masumi's bond."

Ah. Well, that explained why Crux wasn't here. As a pre-transitioned Sem, he wasn't capable of bonding with a mate or holding Masumi's bond.

"Give us time to figure it out." Mace stretched his long legs out in front of him and slumped back in his chair. "It's a big decision."

"We've had over a month to decide, and Stryke chewed me out about it for ten minutes this morning," Sabre said. "Now that he and Cyan are mated, his bond with Masumi is weirding them out."

Blade hated agreeing with Stryke about anything, but he'd be weirded out too. Every time Stryke or Cyan was aroused, Masumi would sense it through the bond, and she'd always know when they had sex. Not cool.

Sabre continued. "Stryke said that if we don't pick someone within the next twenty-four hours, he'll give the bond to Talon."

Talon? Interesting choice.

"He doesn't even live with us," Blade pointed out.

Mace dismissed Blade with a shrug. "It's no different than Stryke having her bond. One of her vases will always stay with us. Unless Talon decides to dick me over."

No way would Talon do that, but Blade still didn't like it. "Talon shouldn't be anywhere near Masumi's bond," he said. "Not while he's hooking up with Scorn. She's obsessed with Talon and sketchy as fuck. Who knows what she'll do to Masumi if she gets jealous?"

"Good call," Mace said, and everyone nodded in agreement. No one liked Talon's girlfriend…who he insisted wasn't his girlfriend.

Sabre gestured to Masumi's vase, where it sat on a corner table. "Why don't we ask *her* what she wants?"

There was a murmur of consensus, and Sabre summoned Masumi. She materialized from her little home immediately, her curvy body covered by a sheer pink robe that offered tantalizing glimpses of plump flesh and deeply shadowed places they all knew well.

A week ago, Blade would have been hard by now. But his mind kept flashing back to those precious hours with Scotty, and suddenly, Masumi didn't compare. The female who had literally been created to be every Sem's dream no longer appealed to him. Maybe it was because Scotty was forbidden fruit—now more forbidden than ever. Maybe it was because while sex with Masumi was always great, his time with Scotty had been the best ever, satiating not only his body but also his heart.

Now, being with Masumi felt empty. Worse, it felt like a betrayal. He'd been using his injections to avoid sex, jamming himself full of shit until his body felt like it was dying. Which was hilarious, given how he'd criticized Stryke for doing the same thing.

"What is it, my masters?" She slid her seductive gaze between all four of them. "Are we finally going to be together all at once? Perhaps we could invite Talon?"

Sabre coughed. "Ah, no. We're discussing your bond. Do you have any preferences on who should take it?"

"Why would you ask me that?" She tugged her robe's sash a little tighter, going from seductive to uncomfortable in a heartbeat. "It's not for me to decide."

Poor Masumi. She'd been born to be enslaved, had spent centuries with evil Sems before Stryke found her. It had taken years for her to learn to trust them, and she'd gone from a timid waif who was eager to please to a confident, bold seductress. But every once in a while, something triggered her old insecurities and fears. Blade hated every time he raised his hand too quickly, and she flinched. Or when she rejected the independence they'd given her, as she was doing now.

Gently, Blade caught her hand. "You should have a choice, Masumi."

"Choices are for free people."

Yep, that hit him right in the heart. Probably did the same to everyone gathered here. They all cared deeply for the female who had probably, at one time or another, saved each of their lives. She'd be saving Crux, too, when she guided him through his transition, which was a dangerous time for Seminus demons. But there was no one Blade trusted more to help his brother than Masumi.

"Masumi, you *are* free," Mace said. "As free as someone who requires a bond to survive is, anyway."

She gave them each a fond smile as she shook her head. "I cannot choose. I love you all, and I will be honored to accept any of you as my new master." She folded her arms across her chest and gave them all a questioning look. "Now, if none of you is going to use my services, I'm in the middle of a movie."

When no one took her up on her offer, she waved and dematerialized back into the vase.

Well, that hadn't been helpful at all.

"Why don't we draw straws?" Mace suggested. "Short straw is the winner."

"That's stupid." Rade idly spun the ring on his finger with his thumb. "We need to first rule out if anyone is unsuited to take her bond."

"You mean you," Mace said.

Rade's head swiveled around to Mace, his gaze unreadable and cold. Rade had always had dead eyes. "She would be miserable with me. Better to find someone else. Someone who won't be mated anytime soon."

"Then it should be Sabre," Mace said, his mouth quirked in a mischievous smile. "Since he's not in any danger of mating Aleka now."

Sabre shot Mace the finger.

"Mace," Blade piped up, "you could take her. You're probably the least likely person to ever get mated."

Mace was always saying he wouldn't mate until he was near *s'genesis,* when all Sems turned into evil, shape-shifting monsters with an insatiable drive to impregnate the females of any appropriate species by any means necessary. So, he'd be a great choice to take Masumi's bond.

Bullshit. You want Mace involved with a female so he'll take his focus off Scotty.

"Maybe *you* should be the one to bond with her," Mace shot back. "That way, if you ever lose your injector and get in trouble again, she'll sense it and can alert us."

You son of a bitch.

Heat rose in Blade's cheeks as Rade's and Sabre's heads jerked around to stare at him, clearly wondering what Mace was talking about.

The tension in the room thickened into a cloud that Blade could practically see as they glared at each other. Gold flecks began populating the dark irises in Mace's eyes, and Blade figured his peepers looked the same.

Even through his anger, he realized this was bizarre. When was the last time they'd been angry at each other? Hell, they rarely even got mildly irritated. Now, Blade was bracing for a physical confrontation and wondering if Mace would go for a head or body shot right off the fly. The chances of either were about fifty-fifty, but if he went for the head, he always followed with a sharp uppercut. If he went for the body, the next blow would be to the temple.

That was how well Blade knew Mace. He knew how he thought, how he fought, and how he liked his females. They were best friends, basically brothers, and now, they were facing off like the captains of rival teams.

Over Scotty.

Which was why they'd sworn the pact in the first place.

"Dammit, Mace," he growled. "You said everything was cool. If this is going to be an issue, let's deal with it now."

"Hey, boys," Sabre said, sounding so much like his father that Blade glanced over to see if Eidolon had snuck into the room. "Let's step off for a second. What's going on?"

Mace's nostrils flared as he clamped his jaw tight, never taking his smoldering gaze off Blade. "Nothing," he gritted. "It's fine." He shoved to his feet. "But I'm not taking Masumi's bond. I'm out." He made a curt washing-my-hands-of-it gesture and bounded up the stairs to his chambers.

Typical. Mace loved a good confrontation, but not if he was a main character. He liked to stir pots, but once the heat splashed onto him, he was out the door.

Rade leaned back on the sofa, watching Blade the way he watched the people he interrogated. With his ability to delve into people's minds, he was the most sought-after interrogator in the world, loaned out by DART on a case-by-case basis. But even without his specialized Seminus skill, his ability to read body language and situations meant he was always a couple of steps ahead of everyone else.

"What's his deal?"

"Let it go," Blade muttered. "It's not important."

Sabre snort-laughed. "Bullshit. In all the years I've known you, I've never seen you guys fight."

Blade spoke through clenched teeth. "I said, let it go."

There was a moment of tense silence. And then Rade's voice, low and gravelly, cut through it like a hot knife.

"One of you slept with Scotty." It wasn't a question. He knew. Rade always knew. He was unmatched at ferreting out secrets. Good thing he was also unmatched at keeping them. His accusatory, knowing gaze pinned Blade to his cushion like a bug in a display. "*You* slept with Scotty."

"Holy shit," Sabre said under his breath. "Is he right? You slept with her?"

"I'm not talking about Scotty," Blade said. "Drop it. I mean it."

They sat there for a moment, stewing in uncomfortable silence. Then, finally, Sabre cursed. "I don't think either one of you should take

Masumi's bond. Not right now." He took a deep, resigned breath. "So, I guess that leaves me. I'll let Stryke know."

Sabre took off, leaving Blade to squirm under Rade's shrewd stare.

"You're probably wondering why I was with Scotty," Blade said. "But—"

"I'm not. I assume it was a matter of life or death, but I don't give a shit either way."

"Gotta love your blunt honesty," Blade muttered. Sometimes, he felt like he was the only one of his triplet brothers with manners.

Stryke also lacked tact, but his arrogance made it a hundred times more infuriating. He knew he was an asshole and didn't care. Rade knew he was an asshole and *couldn't* care.

Blade didn't remember the incident as a baby that had changed Rade's life—and personality—forever, but he remembered how it had affected their childhood. Rade had been quiet, so quiet that, for a time, their parents worried he'd never speak. But he was always watching, and it wasn't until Blade overheard Rade talking to Crux a few years ago that he understood.

Crux had been twelve, half-heartedly tossing darts in the backyard of the rural New York home their parents had bought after Stryke, Rade, and Blade moved out of the house where they'd grown up.

Everyone except Stryke was there for their dad's birthday dinner, and Crux had quietly slipped out after dessert. Blade figured he'd see what was up, but as he took the corner around the tool shed, he saw that Rade had beat him to it.

He couldn't hear what they were saying at first, but he stopped, feeling like an intruder, the moment their words became clear.

"I feel different since Chaos died," Crux said, a dart dangling from his fingers, his gaze glued to the grass. "It's like something's missing."

Sems all felt the moment one of their brothers died, and a hole would always remain. But Chaos was Crux's twin, and they'd been tight. Tighter than Blade had ever been with Rade and Stryke.

"I've always felt like something is missing too," Rade said.

Crux looked up. "Always?"

"Ever since I can remember."

"Because that bad demon took you when you were a baby?"

"Maybe."

"What's missing?"

"Sometimes, I think it might be my soul." Rade shrugged. "I don't know. I struggle to feel…anything."

"You don't feel anything at all?"

"I sometimes feel anger. But that's all. So, I watch people to discern what others are feeling and thinking. I've never really been happy. Or jealous. Or afraid. The only time I was sad was when Chaos died. I think I can only experience an emotion when it's extreme. I don't think I can even love."

Blade sucked in a harsh breath. How could that be? Rade had parents. Cousins. Brothers. And why would he have admitted it to Crux, who still hadn't recovered from Chaos's death just five years ago? Poor Crux. He'd lost Chaos, might as well have lost Stryke, and now he'd learned that Rade didn't love him.

But Crux had always been wiser than his years, and he took a moment to think about what Rade had said.

"That's not true," he said softly. "You loved Chaos. Or you wouldn't have been in so much pain for so long when he died. I felt it, Rade. Yours was the worst of all."

"I think," Rade said, his voice thick with emotion he claimed not to have, "you're forgetting Stryke."

"But we don't know how he felt, because he severed our connections afterward." Bitterness and hurt infused Crux's words, adding more fuel to Blade's anger with Stryke. Stryke had wounded them all when he cut them out of his life by severing the mental connections all Sem brothers shared. Stryke could do what he wanted to Blade and Rade, but hurting Crux was unforgivable.

"Blade? You listening?"

Blade blinked, ripped from the depressing past and dumped into the depressing present. "Sorry. What?"

"I said I'm going to bed." Rade stood and started toward the stairs, but at the base, he turned back to Blade. "I don't understand relationships, but I know Scotty and Mace are important to you. I hope you work it out."

As stunned as Blade was to hear anything halfway caring from Rade, he agreed. But right now, he didn't see a way this could end well.

Not at all.

Chapter 18

The summons from DART came at five a.m. Brussels time, and Scotty was at HQ five minutes later. Mace and Blade showed up separately, which was odd. And as they waited outside Kynan's office for permission to enter, they stood silently, their expressions dark.

"What's going on?" she asked in a low voice.

"Nothing," they both mumbled, but the freaky, demonic guard bush in the corner rustled.

"Jealousy. Greed. Bitterness." Its whispered words were barely audible in the room, but they were clear.

Shit. Scotty jammed her hands on her hips. "I thought everything between us was fine."

"It is." Blade shot Mace a look. "Right?"

"Yeah. Sure." Mace kicked at the plant's stone pot. "Fucking bush."

"Anger. Frustration."

The door to Kynan's office opened, but instead of inviting them inside, he strode out and gestured for them to follow. "Come on. We're meeting Decker and a consultant."

They exchanged curious looks as they followed their boss to the smallest of the meeting rooms, where Decker, a human and one of DART's OG crew, and another dark-haired male sat at the table.

Decker stood, shaking their hands in greeting. He ran the Dublin chapter, but as one of DART's founders and the company's military liaison, he was often involved in operations at the main Brussels office.

He gestured to the new guy, who didn't offer any greeting beyond a curt nod and an icy stare.

"This is Dare." Decker gestured to the newcomer, who Scotty suspected would be even taller than Mace and Blade when he stood. "He's going to be helping out on this case."

As Scotty looked to Kynan for an explanation, Tayla walked inside.

"Hey, sorry I'm late." She gave Decker a hug.

They'd been buds for decades, but although they were the same age, Tay hadn't aged a day in over thirty years, thanks to her bond with Eidolon. Decker was probably in his sixties and still a good-looking guy. Even the silver in his dark-blond hair only added a distinguished air to his already commanding presence.

"I'll get right to it." Tayla tapped the comms unit in the center of the table, and a 3D projection map display popped up. A moment later, a realistic image of a stone building rotated next to the schematic. "This is Leap Castle. Its new owner, Patrick O'Hare, was brutally slaughtered in his bedroom one year ago. His murder was never solved, and since then, his estate has been contested by his three grown children. Also, since then, he's reportedly been haunting the place."

Mace sprawled in his chair like a lazy cat. "A.) Leap Castle has reportedly always been haunted. And B.) this sounds like a job for the Psychic Department."

"It is," Tayla said. "We'd like to send in one of our Mediums, but it's too dangerous. The vampire nest needs to be cleared out first."

A slow, malevolent smile touched the corners of Dare's lips. "I love smoking vamps," he said in a voice as dark and merciless as the char pits in Hell.

Whoa. That guy definitely did well with the females, and Scotty had to wonder if he was a lust demon of some sort. They were all stupidly attractive, had killer bodies, and voices that triggered female pleasure centers. That said, they didn't usually look so…cruel.

Mace bared his teeth at him, his fangs slicing downward. "Say what?"

"Sorry," Dare said, not sounding very contrite as he flashed his own, much bigger fangs. "I'm cool with bloodsuckers."

"Lemme guess." Mace's voice dripped with derision. "One of your best friends is a vampire?"

Dare matched Mace's sarcasm. "How'd you know?"

"You guys done?" Tayla popped her fists on her hips and gave them all a mom-look. Everyone shut up. "That's what I thought." She gestured to the castle blueprints. "This isn't a typical nest. It's Nosferatu clan."

Tension sapped the residual humor hanging in the air. The Nosferatu clan was slippery, the mobsters and terrorists of the vampire world, skirting the edges of human law. Sadistic, brutal, and powerful, the vampires who ran with the clan were the worst of the worst, forced to pass tests of strength, endurance, and savagery before being allowed into their tight-knit group.

"How many?" Blade asked.

Tayla shook her head. "Unknown. Intelligence from The Aegis and our own sources caps the number at around a dozen, depending on the day."

Mace snorted. "A dozen for just the three of us? Easy."

Easy? Mace was too confident. Nosferatu were vicious and not easy to kill. A team of four gave them good odds for victory, but not an easy one.

Mace gestured to Dare. "We don't need him."

"You do need him," Tayla said. "He's an expert on the Nosferatu clan."

Interesting. Scotty gave Dare a second, lingering look. Big dude. Thick, muscular arms, and she was pretty sure there was at least an eight-pack under that tight black tee.

Those eyes, though. Piercing and dark, they looked right through you.

"An expert?" Scotty asked. "How?"

"I used to hang with them." Dare's blunt answer stunned them all into silence. Except Mace, who was rarely silent about anything.

"You used to hang with them? Why?"

Dare shrugged. "Misspent youth."

"That's quite the misspent youth," Blade chimed in, watching Dare with hooded eyes, a predator assessing another predator.

Something niggled at the edges of Scotty's memory. This was all sounding vaguely familiar. Dare. Dare… *Dare?*

She gasped. Gaped at him like an idiot. "Are you—?"

"Cat and Hades' son," Tayla finished.

Mace and Blade both whipped around to stare too. Because holy shit. Yes, Scotty was the daughter of a Horseman of the Apocalypse. Yes, she was friends with the Grim Reaper's daughter. Yes, her grandfather was one of the most powerful angels to ever exist.

But come on. *Hades?* He and his fallen angel mate had lived in

Sydney for a few years while he worked to rebuild Sheoul-gra, and they'd visited her father's island a couple of times. But once Hades had constructed enough of his realm for them to live in, they'd all but disappeared.

"So, is that why Hades hasn't finished Sheoul-gra?" Mace asked. "Because you've been fucking around with Nosferatu instead of helping him?"

"Mace!" Scotty hissed under her breath, giving him a jab in the ribs with her elbow. He'd never been in control of his mouth, but antagonizing a complete stranger for no reason went too far, even for him.

"No, it's okay," Dare said, his voice as smooth and deadly as asp venom. "Sheoul-gra is close to completion. And I'd be honored to welcome Mace as our first…guest."

Ooh, nice one. *Guests* of Sheoul-gra were dead, spending their time in misery and torture until they were reincarnated—if they were lucky.

"Let's save the death threats for after the mission is successful," Decker said. "Back to the situation. There's a complication. The vampires have prisoners. Human prisoners. The Irish government wants them returned safely."

Mace held up his hand. "Wait a minute. Leap Castle isn't that big. I took a tour when I was a kid. It's too small and dilapidated to hold a nest of vampires and prisoners."

Decker shook his head. "The castle has been partially restored since then. And the vampires have tunneled through the hillside. They have multiple entrances and exits now, plus a lot of places to hide."

"Do the Nosferatu know they've been discovered?" Scotty asked.

"We don't think so," Tayla said. "But The Aegis has been tracking two different cells for about eight months, and one fell off the radar a month ago, so they may have an idea that The Aegis is after them. That said, The Aegis isn't exactly subtle. The Nosferatu won't see DART coming in." She glanced over at Dare. "And there's another complication."

Nodding, Dare turned to Scotty and the others. "Sheoul-gra's construction requires the use of dimensional crystals—" He broke off when they gave him blank stares. "They're rare elements leftover from the creation of the universe. When Azagoth destroyed Sheoul-gra, the crystals were scattered. It's why it's taking so long to rebuild. Not all the crystals have been located, and it's not like they're easy to replace. But," he said, "it seems that the Nosferatu are in possession of at least one."

"And what do these things do in the wrong hands?" Scotty asked.

"They can open rifts to other dimensions. Parallel and alternate realities. In the wrong hands, the damage could be catastrophic. Our one consolation is that the Nosferatu are unlikely to know what the crystals are or how to use them."

Grinning, Mace cracked his knuckles in anticipation. "Sounds like another opportunity to save the world."

"Or end it," Tayla warned. "So don't fuck this up."

"We never do," Mace said.

Yikes.

While Scotty wanted to agree, she casually reached under the table and knocked on wood.

Chapter 19

"Motherfuckingbastardassholes!" Mace bellowed, then added a few more choice expletives as the molten sting of a vampire's machete sliced through his jacket and nicked his shoulder. He fell back against a stone wall just as Blade swooped in like a damned superhero and lopped off the vamp's head in one powerful swing.

Blade landed in a crouch, and as he straightened, he gave Mace a scathing look. "Dumbass." He wiped his blade clean on the dead vamp's coat. "We told you not to enter a room without us."

Just a couple of days ago, Mace would have taken Blade's insult as friendly banter and would have responded in kind. But shit was different now. Ever since he'd learned what Blade and Scotty had done, Mace had been on edge, his happy-go-lucky personality taking a leave of absence.

"I told you I was going in," Mace snapped. "You were too busy joking it up with Scotty to hear me."

Blade wheeled around, his expression stormy. "You were being reckless, as usual—"

Scotty and Dare charged into the room. "Any sign of the hostages?" Scotty asked and then frowned at Mace's bleeding shoulder. "You okay?"

I'm horribly injured, so maybe you should have sex with me to make it better.

The bitter thought shamed him. A little. And it reminded him that he'd need to inject himself in an hour or so. "I'm fine."

"Where are we?" Dare poked his head around a darkened corner on the main level of Leap Castle. He'd entered from beneath the building, through a tunnel dug into the restored oubliette.

"We're in the old keeper's living quarters." Mace glanced down at his comms unit. He'd been checking the thing for nearby signs of life, but so far, he hadn't seen anything. This time, though, several little red dots appeared on the screen. "I got something. Ahead. Looks like they're coming from inside one of the tunnels." He gestured to his team. "I'll take the lead."

Blade stepped in front of him. "Better if I go first."

"I called it first," Mace snapped. Why was Blade being such a dick? Showing off for Scotty?

"I can cloak myself in shadows," Blade shot back. "In the tunnels, I have the element of surprise."

Okay, sure, that made sense. But Mace didn't feel like admitting it. "And if we run into trouble, the fact that I can pass as a vamp might help."

It was a lame argument, given that his only vampire trait was being able to convert blood into energy. He didn't need it to survive. Plus, vampires would sense his very-alive body.

"Whatever." Scotty shoved past them and started down the tunnel. "I'll go. The rest of you, take my six."

Blade shot Mace an accusatory glance, as if *he* was responsible for forcing Scotty into the lead. Not that Scotty couldn't handle any situation. She was as strong—if not stronger—than either of them and had the whole immortality thing going for her. But something kept both Blade and Mace putting themselves in harm's way instead of putting her there. And it was more than just chivalry.

It was Scotty's father.

If anything happens to my daughter because you guys fucked up, I'll make you wish your fathers had been eaten at birth.

Blade said Ares was exaggerating, but Mace took the Horseman's words to heart. Dude was scary as fuck.

Nothing was going to happen to his little girl on Mace's watch.

They fell in line behind her, Mace jockeying ahead of Blade and Dare as they started down the dark path.

The tunnels were crude, with deep gouges in the walls, seemingly dug by the vampires' own hands. The Nosferatu were like moles, preferring to capture their food and store it underground rather than hunt aboveground like normal vamps.

Damned freaks.

As they crept through the tight spaces, an oppressive, tingly sensation would occasionally sift through Mace's body, announcing the presence of a demon's soul. So far, he'd counted five. Whatever Medium DART sent in later would have their hands full.

They halted to check out the schematics Decker had provided, but they'd barely launched the 3D map when a bloodcurdling scream echoed through the caverns. Scotty darted ahead with no consideration for her safety. As usual. Which was why he and Blade were always sandwiching her between them.

If anything happens to my daughter because you guys fucked up, I'll make you wish your fathers had been eaten at birth.

Right. Because of that.

Blade swore under his breath and shoved past Mace. And wouldn't you know it? Blade wasn't wearing his fucking backpack.

Wheeling around, Mace swiped the pack off the floor. "Hey." He hurled it at Blade. "Guess you didn't learn your lesson in Alaska."

Snarling, Blade snagged the pack out of the air. "You know—"

"Stop it!" Scotty wheeled around, a spitting kitten with her claws out. "We are *not* going to blow this mission because you two can't put shit aside for a couple of hours. We lost the Reaper on the last assignment, and I'm not going to sit in Kynan's office and get my ass chewed again."

Shaking his head, Dare slipped by them. "Best special-ops team in DART, my fine ass," he muttered as he passed. "Fucking clowns."

Mace was really starting to hate the guy.

"Stay the fuck out of it," Blade growled.

Dare moved like a wraith, a smoky blur, and got right up in Blade's face, nose to nose. His eyes glowed, swirling with orange lava and murder, and Mace casually dropped his hand to the hilt of his favorite battle knife. Blade might deserve whatever beating Dare dished out, but Mace still wouldn't let that happen.

"You morons never even asked what my special powers are." Dare nailed each of them with his accusatory gaze. "You should fucking know every detail about the fucking weapons in your arsenal. Fucking amateurs."

The fact that he was right only made his words sting more.

Snarling, Blade stepped back and swung, but his fist went through empty air and a wisp of smoke.

Dare materialized at the tunnel entrance, shot Blade the finger, and took off into the darkness.

Blade snorted. "Guy thinks he's a fucking weapon."

Scotty rounded on them. "Don't get stupid, Blade. You, either, Mace." She jabbed her finger at him, and he gave her his best, what?-I'm-innocent look. "Dare's right. We fucked up. We're better than this. Let's get our shit together and do our jobs."

Welp, that was a mood buster. Never one to leave a mood in the shitter, Mace popped a salute, mocking her drill-sergeant tone. "Yes, ma'am. Getting our shit together, ma'am. Right, Blade?"

Usually, Blade played along, but now, his jaw was tight, his response even tighter. "Right."

"Okay." Scotty held out her fist. "We got this. Team up."

They did the whole team-up thing, but Mace couldn't help but feel that they were no longer playing the same game, let alone on the same side.

They caught up with Dare inside a bloodstained dirt chamber littered with rotting piles of human flesh and bones in various states of decay.

He held a finger to his lips in a gesture of silence. "I sense living souls," he whispered. "Human. We're getting close."

Blade glanced around in distaste at the three tunnels leading away from the chamber. The Nosferatu really were like spiny hellrats, living like vermin underground, leaving their waste scattered everywhere.

Blade was getting sick of tunnels. Their next mission had better be aboveground. Fuck this tunnel shit.

Then, out of nowhere, he thought about the time demons had rampaged through an outdoor theme park, killing dozens, including innocent children. Including Chaos.

No, aboveground wasn't any better. Evil needed to die, no matter where it chose to operate.

Blade glanced over at Dare. "Which direction?"

"I can't pinpoint it."

Blade started toward the closest tunnel. "I'll take this one."

"We need to stick together," Mace argued. "It's almost dusk. The vamps'll be waking up."

"Which means we need to hurry," Dare countered. "We split up to cover more ground."

"I'm with Dare," Blade said, hating to side with the asshole, but also wanting to get away from him. And from Mace. "We split up."

Mace threw up his hands in frustration. "Fine. Go ahead."

"Thanks. I will." Cloaking himself in shadows, Blade took off, moving silently along the rough-dug corridor. He slowed to peek into darkened recesses, most empty, a couple littered with the usual bones and body parts. A sleeping vamp was sprawled out next to a freshly dead human female inside one of the nooks, and Blade dispatched the monster with a shiv to the heart.

As he slipped out of the shallow cove, the sound of a sob echoed off the earthen walls. Ahead. A chamber.

He came to a stunned halt.

He'd found the humans.

Tied up like animals for slaughter, they were huddled against a wall, some crying, others frozen in terror. One female, who appeared to have been scalped, moaned into the ground, her arms and legs tied behind her back in a way that couldn't have been done unless the limbs were dislocated or broken.

Fury boiled in Blade's veins. Yes, he was a demon who had grown up with a slightly different concept—and, frankly, tolerance—of evil than humans. He didn't enjoy seeing people hurt, but generally, it didn't bother him overly much, either. But he'd also grown up with humans, like his mother, who was a werewolf but still human. Their father had taken him and his brothers to learn to fight. Their mother had made them volunteer at animal and homeless shelters, and three weeks out of the year, they'd had to help fundraise for food banks.

"Being human isn't about *what* you are," she always told them. "It's about *who* you are."

"But we're *demons*, Mama," Blade had argued once, when he wanted to play with his friends instead of ladling soup into bowls.

"That makes it even more important to learn empathy for those who aren't like you," she'd said and promptly buckled him into the minivan with his brothers for their soup-kitchen extravaganza.

So, yeah, he'd developed empathy, even if he had to keep it tamped down to preserve his sanity. But situations like this, where cruelty was the fucking point, made him lose his shit.

He took a silent step closer to the captives just as the scalped female rolled her head to the side and opened her eyes.

And screamed.

Shit!

Suddenly, there was movement. And sounds. Like a hundred death shrouds rasping across desiccated corpses. Nosferatu crawled from out of the shadows and unfurled from shelflike protrusions above, their gleaming eyes and razor-sharp claws promising a painful death.

They launched at him, sharp-fanged monsters that moved faster than Blade could track.

He spun like a whirlwind, flashing blades that cut into flesh and bone. But for every wound he delivered, he took two. He was badly outnumbered and, potentially, in a lot of trouble.

Retreat!

Fuck. The exit was blocked, and he was surrounded.

He'd been through this scenario a million times, though, in training and in real-life situations. Quickly, he dropped a holy water bomb, and the vamps scattered, their screams of fury following him as he ducked out of the chamber. Ahead, the sounds of battle reverberated off the walls, emanating from the direction where he'd left his teammates.

Vampires tore at his back as he bolted through the tunnels and burst into the room where he'd last seen his team. They weren't there, but a trail of fresh blood led back the way they'd originally come from.

In a near-panic, and with Nosferatu on his heels, he made it to the upper floors of the castle. Now that the sun had dipped below the horizon, the building was dark, the shadows long, and vampires were everywhere.

They were so, so fucked.

Chapter 20

"What *the fuck* went wrong?" Kynan's rage was palpable, a furious vibration that lashed at Scotty's skin.

"It was dark—"

"The vampires took us by surprise—"

"There were traps—"

"Bullshit!" Kynan's bellow no doubt tested the upper limits of his soundproofed office walls. "It's always dark, there are always traps, and you never get taken by surprise!"

"Except Mace, just the other day." Scotty's attempt to lighten the mood failed miserably, and she withered under Kynan's scorching glare. She didn't think she'd ever seen Kynan this angry.

Mace swallowed and became fascinated by one of his ancestor's symbols on his right hand. Blade stared at the bookcase next to him, but he wasn't fooling anyone. There was no way he was interested in Orwell, Hemingway, or any of the world history titles.

"So," Kynan said, punching his fists into the desk and leaning into them, "what the fuck went wrong? How did half a dozen Nosferatu escape with a powerful crystal, and three humans nearly die?"

Very slowly, Blade looked over at him. "I failed to identify myself to the captives, and one screamed. It woke the vamps."

"Everything happened really fast after that," Scotty said. "It was a huge cluster. We were separated and couldn't get together right away."

"Why were you separated? You're never separated."

Scotty squirmed. They were separated because Blade and Mace couldn't stand the sight of each other anymore. No biggie.

"Dare and I agreed that we needed to find the captives quickly and that splitting up was the best option," Blade explained.

"Yeah, well, Dare thinks you're all a bunch of squabbling amateurs. Real impressive." Ky looked between Mace and Scotty. "And what were you doing while Blade was traipsing off on his own? Did you try to stop him?"

"Yeah," Mace said, and Blade swore.

"You fucking told me to go."

Mace shot Blade a look of disbelief. "I wasn't fucking serious."

"Then don't say it," Blade shot back. "And it turned out I was right. I found the humans." The neener-neener undertone in Blade's voice made Mace sneer.

Kynan's denim eyes narrowed, and he straightened, watching them speculatively. The man didn't miss much. "What's going on between you guys?"

"Nothing we can't handle," Blade said. This time, Kynan swore.

"If you could handle it, we wouldn't be in this situation, would we?" He shook his head. "Is it safe to say that whatever personal issues you have with each other are responsible for this fucktastrophy?"

Yes.

"Sir," Scotty said, "this was a tough mission. It wouldn't have been a breeze even if everything had gone perfectly."

"That's fair," Kynan said, his voice leveling out a little. "But the fact is, people got hurt. We're already under the WCSG's microscope, and we can't afford for our finest elite team to go off the rails, especially when innocent human lives are at stake."

No, the World Council on Supernatural Governance wouldn't give DART the benefit of any doubt, not after the incident a couple of months ago that had ended in several dead DART and Aegis personnel. DART's funding was at stake, and Kynan was having to put out a lot of fires as even minor issues were now coming under extreme scrutiny.

"You guys need to get your shit together," he continued. "And you need to do it now." He paced behind the desk for a moment and then turned back to them. "I'm giving you a new assignment."

They all looked at each other, confused, but at least they were on the same page. They'd just gotten an ass-chewing and were getting rewarded with a new case? Made no sense.

"Starting immediately after this meeting, and then every day for the next two weeks, you are to report to Ares. You're going to train on his island from six a.m. to eight p.m. It'll be like the boot camp you never had and never wanted."

Okay, now it made sense. The worst kind of sense.

"So…torture," Mace muttered. "You're sending us to be tortured."

"You really want to get into it with me, Mace?" Ky asked, his gravelly voice rumbling with warning.

Mace slumped in his chair. "No, sir."

Kynan slid a challenging look over at Blade and Scotty. "How about you two? Got anything to say?"

They both echoed Mace's, "No, sir." They even matched his resigned and miserable tone.

Training with her father couldn't be called pleasant on a *good* day. It could be considered downright hell on the bad ones. Usually, it fell somewhere in the middle, but at the end of a session, you pretty much just crawled home and collapsed into bed. You might wash off the blood and treat your wounds if you had any energy left at all.

"This isn't a punishment," Kynan said, more gently. "Well, mostly. Maybe you'll remember it the next time you get stupid during a mission. This is about teamwork. Obviously, there's a problem here, and you need to work it out. And there's no one better than Ares to force you to confront the root of whatever has gotten between you."

Terror shot through Scotty like a lightning bolt. The root of their problem was *her*. There was no way her father could find out. No. Fucking. Way.

"What if we promise to work things out on our own?" she asked.

Please, please be cool, Kynan. She crossed her fingers.

"If you could work it out on your own, you would have done it already," he said, and her heart sank. "But I'll tell you what. If Ares thinks you guys are back to normal before the two weeks are up, we can cut this short."

Okay, that might work, but—

"And if he doesn't think that when the two weeks are up?" Blade asked.

Kynan's smile was grim. "I think you all know the answer to that." He gestured to the door. "You'd better hurry. Ares is waiting."

Chapter 21

The first day of training was brutal beyond anything Scotty had ever experienced. And she'd grown up in the damned arena. She'd spent countless hours sparring with demons, angels, and Horsemen. She'd nursed a thousand wounds and had broken several bones—most of which she'd kept from her mother.

Her dad had been the suck-it-up-buttercup kind of father, but her mom? Cara was tough as nails in many ways, but she didn't handle her daughters being injured well.

Her mother would have flipped out *hard* today.

Today had been like all those other days put together and distilled into nothing but carnage.

And her father hadn't even been there.

Nonstop waves of Memitim had come at Scotty, Mace, and Blade, and the angels had used not only physical weapons but also their angelic weapons. For four hours, the Memitim attacked, and when the onslaught finally stopped, Scotty and the guys fell to their knees in the bloody sand, unable to move, rendered quivering jelly.

They'd thought it was over. A handful of Memitim brought water and protein bars, and then Tavin, a Seminus doctor from UG, had come to heal them of their cuts, burns, and crush wounds.

After he left, the battle began again, this time, coming from Ares's Ramreel security staff. Three hours later, the water, food, and healing routine came again.

This time, though, when Tavin finished, her brother Rath came to tell them they could go home.

The one good thing about their hours of training was that they'd been either too busy or too exhausted to argue with each other, and as they limped in silence to the Harrowgate, they could barely breathe, let alone talk.

"See you guys tomorrow," she croaked as Mace and Blade stepped into the gate. They both nodded as it closed.

She leaned against a pillar and groaned. She didn't want to do this for two weeks. She didn't want to do it for another day. The problem was that both Mace and Blade were stubborn as hell, and she didn't know how long it would take Ares to beat them into compliance.

Granted, they'd worked together well today, fighting in practiced sync as if nothing had happened. But had it solved anything? She doubted it.

So, how were they going to get their shit together before Ares's training killed them all?

Maybe she should talk to someone. Instinct had her wanting to talk to Mace or Blade, but for obvious reasons, she couldn't.

Her mom was just on the other side of the courtyard, playing fetch with her hellhound, Maleficent, and it was tempting to see if she had a few minutes. But Scotty didn't want to put her mother in an awkward position with her father by confiding something she'd have to swear to keep from him.

Maybe Dawn or Leilani was available.

She sent missives, but they were both busy. Which left Aleka as her next best choice.

Okay, she could work with that. Aleka already knew about Scotty's idea to end her virginity, so the fact that she had wouldn't be a surprise. *Who* had ended it, however, might be. Scotty sent a message, and while she waited for a reply, she showered and scarfed down a plate of leftover spaghetti. Aleka replied as she was rinsing the plate.

I'm at the office. Come on by. I'll let security know to expect you.

Figured. Aleka was always at work. In a way, Scotty got that. She loved her job. But Aleka's job at the London Museum's Centre for Demon Anthropology and Archaeology was *so tedious*.

Scotty took the employee entrance to the building where Aleka worked, and as Scotty stepped inside her sister's office, Aleka looked up from her desk.

"You look like hell."

Scotty would have laughed if she wasn't so exhausted. "It's good to see you too."

Aleka plopped a book that had to weigh twenty pounds on top of a stack next to her chair. "I was surprised to get your message. You don't usually visit me in here."

Scotty glanced around the dark, dreary space. "It's creepy."

"You fight demons in haunted houses, but my *office* is creepy?"

So creepy. "Everything in here is old. As in, ancient. You can just… feel the vibes. Gives me the willies."

Aleka moved the delicate, steaming porcelain teacup she'd always treasured a little closer. "You are very strange, dear sister."

"I'm the strange one? You're the one who sits around in all this old crap all day."

Aleka sighed and removed the tea bag from the cup. There was no *Earl Grey, hot* with her. It was always *boring chamomile, tepid.* If she was feeling adventurous, a mild green tea. "So, why are you here?"

"To the point. Cool." Scotty took a seat across the desk from her sister. And then shoved aside a stack of books so she could see her. "I need some advice."

One perfectly manicured, reddish-blond eyebrow arched. She and Leilani had standing monthly *girl days* for manicures and whatever it was called when you had your eyebrows done. They'd invited Scotty a couple of times, but she was fine with her brows *going feral,* as they called it.

"Advice?" Aleka said. "From me?"

"Weird, right?"

"Yes." Aleka didn't miss a beat. "Is it about work?"

"Kind of." She sank back in her chair and tried to figure out how to begin. She finally settled on starting at the beginning. "Last week, Ky sent us to Alaska to hunt a wendigo. While we were there—"

"A wendigo? Seriously?" Aleka sprang forward in her seat, practically panting with excitement. "Did you actually see it? Did you get pictures?"

"Yes, yes, and yes," Scotty said. "But the images are of dead wendigos, and they're gruesome. You'll puke. Anyway, long story short, Blade and I got trapped together and had sex."

Aleka's eyes shot wide, and she sat there, stunned, before sinking back in her seat. "Um, okay. Wow. I guess you lost your virginity, after all." She took a sip of the tea. "So, are you together, then?"

"It was a one-time thing to save his life," Scotty said. "Nothing more."

Aleka pondered that as she watched Scotty from over the rim of her cup. "Does Mace know?"

"Yeah, and that's the problem. He's not handling it well. And Blade is being weird too."

The cup made the tiniest *clink* when Aleka set it on its matching saucer. She'd always been so freaking proper, and living in London had only made her waxed, stiff upper lip even stiffer. "You said this was *sort of* about work. I'm guessing the tension is affecting your job?"

One could say that.

"We let a bunch of bad guys escape and nearly got some people killed on our last assignment." Scotty let out a huff of air and flopped back in the chair. "Kynan is so pissed he's making us train with Dad for two weeks."

"Ouch." Aleka winced. "You *really* screwed up. That sucks."

One could say that too.

"We just spent all day in the arena. My hip is burning from a Memitim fireball, my leg hurts from being hamstrung, and I can barely move my arms. I don't want to do this for two weeks, and it'll only stop if we can all put this behind us."

"How are you going to do that?"

The hell if I know.

"That's why I'm here. I need some ideas. I mean, this is why we made that pact in the beginning. To prevent exactly this." Scotty shook her head, unable to comprehend the mess they were in. She and the guys had been a solid trio, a well-oiled unit, for as long as she could remember, rarely going more than a few hours without touching base with each other. Which made what she was about to say almost inconceivable. "Maybe we need some time apart. I don't want to break up the team, but right now, we can't work together."

Aleka picked up the cup, but instead of drinking, she gazed thoughtfully into her flower broth. "Oh, I know!" she chirped. "Maybe you should sleep with Mace and make it even."

Scotty rolled her eyes. "Very funny."

"Sorry," Aleka said, still looking a little amused. "I've never been in this kind of situation, so I'm not sure what advice I can give you."

"Yeah, well, sleeping with one of them is what caused this. I don't think doing it again would help."

Aleka thought on that for a minute, finger on her chin the way she'd always done when she worked on puzzles. Word puzzles, crossword puzzles, jigsaw puzzles…Aleka loved them, and she always did the finger thing.

"You know," Aleka said slowly, "I was kidding about sleeping with Mace, but honestly, what could it hurt?"

Scotty gaped at her utterly dense sister. "*What could it hurt? Are you serious? That could destroy our friendship.*"

"It's already in jeopardy, Scotty. Do you honestly think Mace will get over it? I don't know him that well, and even I can tell you he won't let this go."

Aleka was probably right, but there was more to consider.

"And what do you think that would do to Blade?"

"Well, let's look at this from his perspective." Aleka set down her cup. This time, the *clink* was louder. "Do you think Blade wants you? Romantically?"

"Ah…" Scotty really hadn't thought about that. Seemed unlikely, given their oath—their broken oath. "I don't think so." Which, she had to admit, kind of hurt, even if it was for the best.

"Then he shouldn't be jealous if you sleep with Mace once."

"I guess…"

"Look," Aleka said, "Blade hasn't been his normal self, either, right? He probably feels guilty about what happened. *You* probably feel guilty. If you sleep with Mace, no one has any reason to feel guilty or left out. Everything will be equal and fair."

Okay, maybe her sister had a point. Actually, the more Scotty thought about it, the more sense it made. She, Mace, and Blade had always shared everything. There were no secrets between them. They'd all been equal in every way.

Until now. Maybe the way back to the status quo really was to sleep with Mace.

What's the worst that could happen? Their friendship could be put in jeopardy? It already was.

The best that could happen, though, was that things would go back to the way they needed to be.

She could practically hear her father demanding she calculate the odds of success, as one did before any conflict.

Okay, she was game. She pooled all her knowledge, all her data, everything she knew about Mace and Blade…and she got her answer.

The odds, she figured, were fifty-fifty. It would be a coin toss.

And for some reason, she never won those.

Blade looked around in surprise as he entered the forensics lab on Underworld General's second floor. The usually pristine space looked as if it had been hit by a tornado.

"Sabre, damn, this place is a disaster."

His cousin shot him the finger. "No shit."

Blade took in the overturned furniture, shattered equipment and glass, and destroyed containers leaking various-colored liquids. "What happened?"

"A Darquethoth mental patient escaped his ward and made his way to my lab."

Blade considered that. "How the hell would you know that a Darquethoth demon has mental issues?"

Sabre shrugged. "I dunno. Maybe he doesn't enjoy killing people?" He sighed and gestured to several smashed boxes. "And it figures that I'd just gotten twenty cases of material from a demon attack in Lisbon."

"Don't you have staff to help clean up?"

He barked out a bitter laugh. "It also figures that I gave my entire staff the day off for a colleague's wedding. Fuck love, man."

Blade felt that like an icepick to the heart. Fuck love, indeed.

"Here, let me give you a hand." He bent over to pick up some bagged-evidence boxes, wincing at the million stabs of pain shooting through him. The training session today had been beyond brutal. The hot shower afterward had helped with the tension and pain, but he wouldn't feel better until morning.

When they'd start the bullshit all over again.

He wanted to be pissed at Kynan for making them do this, but really, it was Mace's fault. He'd said he was fine with what had happened between Blade and Scotty, and he'd lied. Then he'd let it fester until it erupted.

Where was Mace's apology for that?

He loved Mace, he really did. But the guy had never apologized for anything in his life. He lived the way his bio-dad, Wraith, always had. As if the world revolved around him. The impulsive, devil-may-care shit made him the cool guy, the Seminus demon all the young ones wanted to emulate.

It was wearing thin on Blade in a way it never had before.

Sabre nodded at Blade as he plopped the evidence boxes on a desk. "Thanks, man."

"No problem. I'm just glad you're taking the time to see me."

"You said it couldn't wait until I got back to the compound."

"That's because you don't get off work for four more hours, and I need to get to bed."

"Bed?" Sabre glanced at his watch. "You must have a female waiting for you."

Blade reached back and rubbed his sore neck. "Nah. I'm just beat." Literally. "Kynan sent us for two weeks of boot camp at Ares's place."

"Dayum." Sabre cringed. "Why?"

"Because we fucked up. Bad. And he thinks torturing us will fix it."

"Ouch." Sabre sank down onto one of the stools and gestured to another, but Blade had too much nervous energy to sit. "Does this have anything to do with what was going on between you and Mace the other night?"

"Yeah."

Sabre settled back on the stool and eyed Blade with the analytical gaze he'd inherited from his father. "So, this is about you sleeping with Scotty? Are you two together?"

"No. Hell, no." Blade blew out a long breath. He didn't want to talk about this, but damn, he needed help. "We aren't together. It was an emergency situation during a mission. A one-time thing. Not romantic at all."

She'd deserved so much better than what amounted to rutting in the mud like animals.

Sabre scrubbed his hand over his face. Dude was an expert in forensics, and no doubt he'd already done the postmortem on this situation. "I'm guessing Mace isn't handling it well?"

"You saw how he was when we met about Masumi's bond. He seemed cool when we told him, but he's been an asshole since."

"Mace has always been an asshole," Sabre said, a note of affection toning down the exasperation in his voice. Everyone loved Mace, but only in small doses. Blade and Scotty were the only two who saw the real Mace, the guy who would give his life for those he loved. Who was loyal to a fault. Who hated being alone. "But yeah, I can see the problem."

Blade leaned against a metal bookcase, and it groaned as it absorbed his dead, exhausted weight. "I don't know what to do."

Sabre considered Blade's predicament as he swiveled back and forth on the stool. He was the spitting image of his dad, his lab coat lending him that same air of authority. Talking to Sabre was like talking to Eidolon…but without as much of the intimidation factor.

Which wasn't to say that he didn't have an intimidation factor. The guy was a quarter Soulshredder demon on his mom's side, and when it came out to play, it was time to run. Fortunately, he kept the beast fed with cage matches and pit fights at skeezy, demon-run establishments. Blade had patched him up afterward more than a few times.

"How would you feel if the situation was reversed?" Sabre asked.

The idea that Mace could have been the one with Scotty in the cave instead of Blade felt like a hot coal in his belly.

"I'd like to think I'd understand."

"Bullshit." Naturally, Sabre called him on it. He was so like his old man. "You guys have been best friends for as long as I can remember. You've managed to keep your hands off Scotty all this time…I mean, you *swore* oaths, and you're telling me you'd be totally chill if Mace banged Scotty?"

Blade didn't answer. How could he, when he wasn't sure?

Sabre tried another tack. "How do *you* feel about Scotty?"

I love her. "My feelings are irrelevant," he said gruffly. "I can't be with her. It would destroy our friendship."

"Sounds like that might already be happening."

A sour taste filled Blade's mouth. He didn't want to lose his friends. His team. Scotty.

"It's not," he insisted. "We can fix it."

"How?"

Fuck Sabre and his hard questions. Deflated, Blade leaned more heavily against the bookcase. "I don't know."

"Is that why Ky sent you to Ares?"

Fuck Kynan too. "He thinks teamwork will get us back on track."

Sabre shrugged. "Doesn't sound like a terrible idea."

"Really?" Aaaand, fuck Sabre again. "Fourteen hours a day in Ares's battle arena doesn't sound like a terrible idea?"

A few seconds ticked by, and then Sabre nodded. "You're right. I take it back. I actually can't think of much worse." Something next to Sabre beeped, and he ended it by pushing a button on the nearby computer. "Does Kynan know about you and Scotty?"

"No. He just knows something is going on between us that made us fuck up an assignment."

Sabre looked skeptical. "I wouldn't count on that. He doesn't miss much." He wiped some broken glass onto the floor with the rest of the mess. "And you'd better pray that Ares doesn't find out."

Blade scowled. "Why would I worry about him? He's always taught us that we have to do whatever it takes to survive."

"Yeah, well, he won't consider doing his *daughter* part of that."

Ares was a master tactician who understood survival. He'd probably be proud that his daughter had saved a life. "You really think he'd rather I die in misery?"

"Than defile his little girl? Uh, yeah. Duh."

Shit. What if Sabre was right? Ares wasn't stupid, and he'd eventually figure out why their team was malfunctioning. They needed to get this fixed before that happened.

"So, that's all you've got? Don't let Ares find out?"

Sabre shrugged. "Unless you guys can sit down and hash it out together. Maybe get counseling. Or have Rade get in your heads and snip that thread."

Counseling wasn't a terrible idea, but getting Mace to sit still for more than ten minutes wasn't easy, especially if he had to talk about his feelings. And as far as Rade getting into his head? That was a hard no. He wasn't letting his brother anywhere near his mind. Mace and Scotty wouldn't, either.

"How about a spell that would reduce the animosity between you?" Sabre offered.

Interesting proposal. "Spells can be that specific?"

"Sure." Sabre shrugged. "You just need to find a trustworthy spellcaster. Good luck."

He seemed to be enjoying Blade's predicament a little too much. That was the Soulshredder in him. They could see emotional wounds and scars, and they got off on exploiting them.

"The hospital employs some spellcasters," Blade said. "They'd be trustworthy."

"True." Sabre reached for a handful of M&Ms in a bowl next to the computer. "But they'll tell our parents, and you know it'll get back to Ares. And then you'll die horribly."

"That's so helpful."

"I try." Sabre tossed a piece of candy into the air and caught it in his mouth.

Blade heaved a sigh, cutting it short because his ribs were killing him. Exhaustion tugged at his eyelids. He needed to go. He'd heal fully in his sleep, just in time to start all over again.

"I'm gonna bounce." Blade looked around at the destruction. "Unless you need help cleaning up."

"Nah, thanks. Some staff from the morgue are coming up to lend a hand."

Blade nodded. "Thanks for listening."

"Anytime," Sabre said. "Let me know if there's anything I can do."

Nice offer, but unless Sabre had secretly developed a time-travel machine in his lab, there was nothing the guy could do.

Unfortunately, Blade had a feeling there was nothing anyone could do.

Mace always liked going home. His mom kept his favorite hazelnut butter cookies on hand for visits, and his dad would share all the crazy crap going on in the hospital. Man, Mace was glad he hadn't gone into the medical field. His dad's job poking around inside dead demons was probably interesting, but being stuck in one place would drive Mace nuts. He needed to be active and busy all the time, even if he was just playing video games.

"Hey, son," Lore said as Mace stepped through the front door of his parents' Italian villa. He'd grown up here, among the clementine groves and vineyards. Had learned to appreciate good food, good wine, and good friends.

And right now, his good friends were in trouble.

"Hi, Pops." He gave his dad a hug and had to hide a wince at the way Lore unintentionally squashed Mace's pulverized shoulder. He'd taken several crushing blows from blunt weapons on that side of his body. Not that the other side was much better.

"You okay? You look beat." Lore peered closer. "Is that a black eye?"

"Yup." It was mostly healed, barely a shadowy crescent now, but his dad noticed everything. At least Mace had gone home, showered, and changed, so he didn't look like he'd been dragged through a slaughterhouse anymore. He'd also gotten in half an hour with Masumi, but he'd been too exhausted to do anything but lie there while she did all the work.

And during the entire thing, all he could think about was Scotty doing that to Blade, which pissed him off and gave him the energy to come talk to his dad.

"Where's Mom?"

"She's at the hospital."

"Working?"

Lore nodded. "She's looking for a spirit that's been evading her for days."

Well, good. Mace wasn't sure he wanted his mom to hear this. "Is Wraith here yet?"

"He's out back." Lore gestured with his gloved hand toward the open glass doors behind him. Mace could only recall seeing his dad's bare right hand a few times in his entire life, which was fine. The glove kept everyone safe.

It must suck to have to wear the thing all the time, though. That, and the faded *dermoire* on his right arm had to be a constant reminder that he was a half-breed Seminus demon with all the things that went wonky when a Sem bred with a human. Lore and his twin sister, Sin, were anomalies. Demon DNA gone wrong. But they'd gotten beyond their dark and twisted past, finding respectable jobs, mates, and family.

Pretty cool. Mace had always admired their strength.

Outside on the stone patio next to the fire, Wraith was waiting, his blond hair rustling in a smoky, citrus breeze. "Hey, kid," he said as Mace took a seat at the round table. "What's up?"

Lore grabbed a couple of beers from the outdoor mini-fridge and handed them out. "You okay?"

The bottle hissed as Mace wrenched off the top of his brew, crafted by Stryke's company to allow Seminus demons to get a buzz. There really wasn't anything StryTech didn't have its fingers in. "I need some advice, and you both come at things differently." He paused, unsure how to broach the topic.

"Female trouble, guaranteed," Wraith tapped his bottle against Lore's as they exchanged knowing looks.

Mace peered down at his own beer and blew out a long breath. Fuck. "You know how I've been best friends with Blade and Scotty since we were kids, right?"

"Obviously," Lore said.

Wraith took a swig of his beer. "I still don't know how you and Blade have kept it platonic with her."

"We made a pact."

"Really?" Wraith studied him for a second, and then one corner of his mouth raised in a knowing smirk. "You want to break it, don't you?"

Mace stared into the longneck, wishing it promised a trip back in time instead of an alcohol high. Why wasn't Stryke working on time travel instead of space travel?

He'd be willing to bet that Blade was having similar thoughts.

"It's already broken," he rasped. "It was Blade."

"Ah, shit," Lore muttered.

Wraith drained his beer and reached for another. "Is your shiner part of the story?"

Mace tested the tender tissue beneath his eye with a finger. Still hurt. "In a way."

"What the hell?" Lore chucked his bottle cap into the trash. "How could they do that to you?"

"It's not like that," Mace said, hating that he had to defend Blade. "It wasn't intentional."

Wraith snorted. "What, Blade accidentally fell on her while they were both naked?"

That was not a vision Mace needed in his head right now. "They were trapped together on a mission, and he didn't have his suppressant."

"Nuh-uh. No way. How did he not have his injector pen?" Wraith demanded.

That was a sticking point for Mace, as well. Pun not intended.

How could Blade have been so careless? "He says he took his backpack off for just a minute. Some sort of flood happened or something, and he lost it."

"Do you believe him?" Lore asked, but Wraith was clearly in the skepticism camp.

"Of course, I believe him." *Of course.* Blade had never lied to him.

Except when he kept what had happened between him and Scotty from Mace.

Lore seemed to consider that. "So, are they together now? Are they a couple?"

"They said they aren't." Mace forced himself to unclench his jaw. "They swear it won't happen again."

Amused, Wraith tossed a piece of wood on the fire. "Yeah, right."

"It won't," Mace insisted.

Lore arched an eyebrow. "If you believe that, then what's bothering you?"

"Things are weird now." Mace toyed with the label on his empty beer bottle. "And I know Blade's in love with Scotty. He has been for a while. He sucks at hiding shit."

"What about you?" Wraith asked.

"I'm great at hiding shit."

Lore tossed him another beer and took the empty. "You know what Wraith meant. Do you love her?"

As Mace set the new bottle on the table, he focused on the tightness in his chest. "I don't know," he admitted. "I love her like a friend. I always have."

"But?" This time, it was Lore coaxing more information from Mace.

"But…it just…I don't know. It seems like things have changed. We did that mission to Stryke's oil rig, and after that, everything felt different. I knew Blade had a thing for Scotty, but it didn't really bother me because of our pact." He threw his head back and focused on a lone cloud in the night sky, its wispy extensions forming arms and legs. Looked like a damned wendigo. "And then that fucking Alaska assignment. I wish we'd never gone."

"Have you guys talked about it?"

"Yeah. And I thought I was fine. I thought we were all cool." He took a swig of his beer, relishing the cold liquid soothing his raw throat. "But I guess not. Blade acts like I'm a dumbass for letting it bother me, but I can't help it. Everything was cool between us, and now it's all broken. It's affecting our job too. We fucked up a huge mission, so Kynan is making us train with Ares until we get past this."

"What about Kynan and Ares?" Wraith asked. "Do they know what happened between Scotty and Blade?"

"Gods, I hope not." Mace tried not to think about the possibility. "But Ares will eventually beat it out of us. We need to get our shit together before that happens."

"Sounds like you guys need to talk it out," Lore said, but Wraith scoffed.

"Talk? Fuck that. You need to fight it out."

"Don't listen to him." Lore kicked his booted feet up onto the brick planter holding Idess's prized lemon tree. She babied that sucker, spritzing the leaves and bringing it inside during storms. "Pummeling each other won't help anything."

"Hey," Wraith said, "you parent your way, and I'll parent mine.

Talon turned out great."

Lore laughed. "Only because of Serena."

Wraith tossed his empty bottle into the bin next to the door. "You're probably not wrong."

"Come on," Mace said tiredly. "I need real advice. No one is pummeling anyone, and talking hasn't gotten us anywhere."

"Maybe you guys need a break from each other. Let things cool down," Lore suggested. "Give it some time and perspective."

Not a terrible idea. "How long of a break?" They'd not been apart for more than a couple of days, and even then, they'd kept in near constant contact.

Lore shrugged. "A month or two, maybe?"

Months? They were a work team. There was no way they could avoid each other for that long.

Wraith looked up at a moth circling overhead. "Or you could do the obvious."

"I know you're not going to tell him to eliminate the competition," Lore drawled.

"What?" Wraith looked scandalized. "Blade's family. A broken nose and fractured jaw?" He shrugged. "No big. But killing him? That's a little extreme."

"Then what's the obvious thing?" Mace asked.

Wraith looked at him like he was an idiot. "Sleep with Scotty."

Mace nearly choked on his beer.

Lore gave Wraith an are-you-kidding-me look. "That's insane."

"Completely bonkers." Mace coughed again, blinking his watering eyes.

"Why?" Wraith lounged in his chair, his new beer settled on his abs. "You and Blade would be on equal footing. Balance restored."

Yep. Bonkers.

Or was it?

Hmm. Both his dads had presented totally different bits of advice. Lore's was probably the best. But Wraith's was…intriguing.

It was also unrealistic. Blade would go ballistic if Mace suggested it, and who knew how Scotty would react? She'd probably laugh in his face. Or punch him in said face. Said face that had already been beaten into a pulp.

He blew out a resigned breath. "I think Dad's right," he said. "We should stay in our separate spaces for a little while. I'll talk to them after training tomorrow."

Of course, that was assuming they were in any shape to talk.

Chapter 22

Day two of Horseman Hell Boot Camp was worse than the first, and in Mace's opinion, it wasn't even close.

Ares, wearing his hard leather armor and astride his blood-bay warhorse, Battle, had been waiting for them when they arrived. In retrospect, it should have been the first clue that their day was fucked. Ares didn't release his stallion from his arm and go full Horseman unless he was planning to make someone regret all their life choices.

His hawklike gaze had unnerved them as they assembled in front of the warhorse, and by the time he asked them why they were there, they'd been as jumpy as a hellrat in a hellhound den.

Their bumbling, stuttering responses had only pissed Ares off.

"We had a bad day."

"We, uh, screwed up."

"Kynan is overreacting."

"But we've learned our lesson."

"Enough! If you can't tell me the truth," he'd growled, in his deep, uncompromising voice, "I'll beat it out of you."

And, sure as shit, he'd made good on his threat. Their day had been divided between sparring with the Memitim in five-on-three battles that forced them to work together and obstacle courses designed to force cooperation.

They'd started off well. When they arrived, everyone seemed ready to cooperate. The tension between them had been nearly non-existent, even if they weren't exactly joking around and back to normal. Still, for a couple of glorious hours, they'd fallen back into the familiar groove, fighting as one highly coordinated and efficient machine.

Then Mace noticed the way Blade hovered near Scotty, taking ridiculous chances with his body to block strikes meant for her. And naturally, instead of taking the noble high road, Mace had gone full, pothole-laden low road, stepping in to take more blows meant for Scotty than Blade. Eventually, she just stood there, glaring at them while they played punching bag.

Shit went downhill from there.

And when the grueling *training session* ended, they'd collapsed to the arena floor, not caring that the sand and dirt beneath them had been churned into sticky mud by sweat and blood.

"You guys should be ashamed." Ares towered over them, looking no worse for wear after four solid hours of going against the three of them by himself. By. Him. Self. "Get your shit together. I mean it. Because every time I even sense a crack in your teamwork, I'm going to add an hour to your sessions, and with the way you've been going, we could be here for days straight. Got it?"

"Fuck." Mace fell back onto the ground and stared blankly at the multicolored twilight sky.

"See?" Ares said. "He gets it." Then he smiled down at Scotty. "Love you, sweetheart."

"Love you too, Daddy," she moaned.

Laughter hung in the air, and heavy footsteps reverberated on the ground as Ares strode away. Sadistic prick. Mace loved the guy, respected the hell out of him, but he didn't always like him. Right now, for example.

Mace felt the familiar warmth of Blade's palm come down on his chest, and a heartbeat later, healing energy surged through him. Tavin had healed them all twice today, but Ares hadn't summoned the guy after their last round. Mace was too exhausted to wonder why.

"Thanks," he said, genuinely grateful. Although Blade always healed them as best he could after a battle, this time felt...different. "Why'd you do that?"

"Tavin didn't come. No doubt it's a test of teamwork. Ares probably wants to see if I'll do it."

"Ah." That made sense. It was also a little disappointing.

"I don't hate you, Mace," Blade said softly. "Things might be shit right now, but I could never hate you."

Startled, Mace looked up, saw pain lurking in his buddy's shadowed eyes. "Same," he croaked. "Same."

"Guys?" Scotty came to her feet with a wince. "Maybe now would be a good time to talk."

Agreed. Mace glanced around, suddenly uncomfortable in the middle of the arena, exposed to anyone with exceptional hearing. "Not here."

"Let's go back to the compound." Blade offered Mace a hand, and Mace didn't hesitate. They locked their grips, and Blade pulled Mace to his feet.

Despite the new camaraderie, shit was a little awkward as they headed to the Harrowgate. They entered in silence, programmed the thing, and exited through their private gate.

The walk to the main building was just as silent. Inside, Rade and Crux were playing in the soundproofed game room, and Sabre was still at work, so they had the living room to themselves.

Naturally, now that they were somewhere they could talk, they just stared at each other. Fuck. This needed to be settled, and it needed to happen now.

"We can't keep going like this," Mace said. "We'll be dead by Wednesday if we have to keep this shit up with Ares."

"Wednesday?" Blade snorted. "Tuesday by noon."

The brief moment of amusement gave Mace a reprieve from the tension that had been pressing in from all around him. Around all three of them. They'd been stewing in a damned pressure cooker for days, and cracks were forming. It wouldn't be long before things went critical.

Then Blade got all serious again and ruined it. "I talked to Sabre yesterday." He hooked his thumbs in his bloodstained pants pockets. "He thinks maybe we need some time apart."

"Dad said something similar," Mace called out as he fetched them water from the fridge. When he returned to the living room, he passed out the bottles. "I don't know how that'll help, though. It's not going to change what happened."

"Well, we can't take it back," Blade said. "So, we need to learn to deal with it."

"*I* need to learn, you mean." Mace swore. "You really don't get it, do you?"

"Get what? You're the one who said you were cool with it, when you really weren't."

"I meant it when I said it," he snapped. "But it turns out I'm not, okay?" Reining in his anger, he continued, a little calmer. "I know I shouldn't have accused you of being careless with your injections. That was a dick move. But you've been weird, and don't you dare deny it."

"What?" Blade stared at him. "I haven't been weird."

"Yes, you have," Scotty said, backing Mace. "We all have."

Blade looked like he was going to argue, but a few heartbeats later, he blew out a breath and looked down at the floor. "Scotty? Do you regret—?"

"No!" Scotty took his hand, and a flare of jealousy heated Mace's chest…until she grabbed his hand too. "I love you guys, and I would do anything to save your lives. We can never have regrets about that. But we do have to find a way to move on."

"I just don't think spending time apart is the answer." Mace concentrated on the feel of Scotty's warm hand in his. How right it seemed. And yet, it was so wrong. "I know this is mostly my issue. I get it. But if I'm alone, it's just gonna fester inside me. It's what I do."

For a long moment, no one said anything.

"Lore suggested time apart, right?" Blade asked. "Did you talk to Wraith?"

Mace laughed. "You don't even want to know what his solution is."

"I'm willing to try anything if it'll help get us back to where we were," Blade said.

Anything? Okay, challenge accepted. Blade was so going to regret saying that. "He said I should sleep with Scotty and then we'd be even."

Man, he couldn't have dropped a bigger bomb if he'd been in command of all the world's nuclear arsenals.

Silence lingered in the aftermath. Scotty didn't look as stunned as Blade did, but her cheeks burned crimson beneath the smattering of freckles.

She took a deep breath and blurted, "Aleka said something similar." When Blade's head whipped around to her, she closed her eyes and took another bracing breath. "Look. Maybe Aleka and Wraith are onto something. This all started because Blade and I slept together. Maybe we can fix things if Mace and I do the same."

Mace's heart thudded against his ribs so violently he was sure they both heard it. He'd considered Wraith's idea, but more as a fantasy long shot than as part of any tangible reality. It hadn't occurred to him that Scotty might think it was a genuine solution to their predicament.

No one said anything for so long that Mace started counting Mississippis in his head. He got to nine Mississippis when Blade finally spoke up in a voice so devoid of emotion that he must have used the silent stretch to suppress everything he felt.

"I don't think it's a good idea."

"Oh, what a fucking surprise," Mace muttered under his breath.

Anger flashed in Blade's eyes. "Don't be a di—"

"Hey," Scotty snapped, cutting off Blade and glaring at them both. "This is exactly why we need to do something. You've never fought like this. You've never been jealous of each other about anything. You've shared everything from your darkest secrets and fears to holidays and females. This won't be any different."

It was *so* different.

"No way." Blade swung around to Scotty. "You don't throw gas on a fire you're trying to put out."

Mace's temper flared as he pictured the heat between Blade and Scotty as they went at it in the Alaskan wilderness. "So, you're saying what's between you and Scotty is a fire?"

"You know that's not what I'm saying."

Mace stared in disbelief, his brain recalling the sight of Masumi in Blade's room, her coloring so closely resembling Scotty that there'd been no doubt about Blade's kink. Then there was the way he looked at Scotty. And it wasn't just since they'd returned from Alaska. Mace was only now realizing how far back Blade's crush on Scotty went.

"Do I?" he asked. "Do I really know that?"

Blade glanced away.

Yeah, you know what I'm talking about.

"Scotty," Mace said, trying to keep his voice steady, "are you sure?"

She nodded, and for a split second, excitement and joy made his heart leap. He hadn't admitted it until this moment…but he loved Scotty. He'd just never allowed himself to think, even for a heartbeat, that his feelings went deeper than friendship.

But the wrongness of what he felt cast a pall over it. He'd been devastated when he learned that Blade and Scotty had slept together, and as much as he wanted to make love to her, he didn't want Blade to hurt the way Mace did.

"Guys," she said softly, "I love you. I don't think I can separate who I am from who we are together. Blade is my right arm, and Mace is my left." She gave an impish smile. "And I'm ambidextrous, so you are both equally important. But right now, I feel like both arms are broken. Time apart would mean losing them altogether."

"It wouldn't be forever," Blade said, his voice rough. Wrecked.

"I think it would be," she whispered, agony lacing every word. "And even if we could eventually get past this, it won't be the same. There will always be a scar."

"If you do this with Mace," Blade warned, "there will be two."

Scotty's smile was both sad and wry as she murmured, "Symmetry."

Symmetry. Something told Mace that Ares would regret teaching his daughter that particular lesson.

Blade couldn't believe this was happening.

Sure, he knew where Scotty was coming from. He knew she wasn't using this as an excuse to get Mace into bed. She truly believed that by making everything fair, they could restore some balance in their relationship. Reluctantly, he had to admit that it even made some sense.

But that didn't mean he had to like it. And it certainly didn't mean it was the right way to go.

He swept his gaze over Scotty, his mind taking him back to the cave, her body against his as they became one. Yeah, it sounded cheesy and flowery, but they'd forged a bond that day, as if their very souls had touched. He'd have done anything for her before, but now? Now she *owned* him.

What he wouldn't give to have her again, to take the time to make love to her instead of rutting like beasts in heat. He wanted a do-over. A chance to show her how much she meant to him. To revere her the way she deserved, wake up every nerve ending slowly with his fingers, his tongue. He wanted to spend hours worshiping every inch of her toned, lithe body.

Fuck.

Mace had every right to be angry, didn't he? Blade had been yearning for Scotty, and of course, Mace knew. Begrudgingly, he could admit that he got it now. He really got it.

What had happened between Blade and Scotty had saved Blade's life, and Mace could probably get past that. Eventually. But he—rightly so—wouldn't be able to shrug off Blade's obvious pining for Scotty.

Fuck, fuck, *fuck*.

He swung around to Mace. "Can I talk to you for a minute?" He gestured at the door to the backyard. "Alone?"

Scotty blocked them, fists on her hips, her freckles standing out angrily against her pale skin. "You are *not* taking Mace outside to beat him."

"It's okay, Scotty." Mace shot Blade a warning stare as he scooted around her. "I'll be fine."

"If I see one drop of blood," she shouted at their retreating backs, "I'm making a lot more of it!"

Blade would have chuckled if his mind wasn't swirling with images of his two best friends fucking each other's brains out. Ruthlessly, he shoved his jealousy down into the empty cavern of his chest. It could hang out with the acid reflux that was currently burning a hole in his esophagus.

Once they were out on the patio, Mace took up a watchful position next to a steel-plated pillar, folded his arms across his chest as he waited for Blade to talk. Or deck him. Which was tempting.

Blade didn't know where to start. This was a situation he couldn't have prepared for, and he hated navigating unknowns. Frustrated, he shoved his hand through his hair and let out a growl.

"Look," he said gruffly. "I think you sleeping with Scotty is a bad idea."

"No shit?"

Blade ignored that. "But I'm not going to stand in the way."

"Okay…" Skepticism gleamed in Mace's narrowed eyes. "Let's assume you actually mean that. You didn't bring me out here to say it. So where, exactly, is this going?"

Good question. This was so fucking uncomfortable.

"When I was with Scotty," he began, pausing as he gathered his thoughts, "you know, in the cave…" He drew in a long breath. "Things were…frantic. I'd waited for as long as I could, so…I mean, you know how it is." It was pain and lust and desperation all scorched around the edges by the danger of knowing you'd stepped too close to the fiery edge of death. "What I'm saying is, I wasn't in the right mindset to…to make it, um, you know…good. For her." Dammit, he sounded like an idiot. "It was Scotty's first time, and it wasn't what she deserved." He scrubbed his hand over his face and looked down at the stamped concrete pad, letting out a curse after a few pounding heartbeats. "You need to make it right."

Mace stared in disbelief, and when he spoke, his low voice dripped with doubt. "Are you saying that you want me to—"

"Show her how it should be." Jealousy made Blade's words sharper than they should have been, but Mace didn't seem to notice.

"Damn," Mace breathed. "I don't know what to say."

Blade jabbed a finger at him. "Nothing freaky."

"Freaky?"

"Come on," Blade said. "You know how you are."

"I'm not sure if I should be offended or not." Mace's voice was both droll and amused, almost like he was back to his usual self.

"There's nothing wrong with your assortment of toys and…tools, but they have a time and place."

"And you don't think Scotty strapped into my sex swing is the right time or place?"

"Don't." The sudden vision created by Mace's words made Blade growl with a combination of lust and anger. "I'm not in the mood."

"Hey, man." A rare note of contrition bled into Mace's voice. "I would never hurt or disrespect her. You know that, right?"

They locked gazes, and as lit up as Blade was at the situation, he trusted Mace. Trusted him with his life. And with Scotty.

"I know."

There was a strained pause as Mace searched Blade's face, getting a bead on his emotions. Blade wished him luck with that, because they were all over the place. "And you know I don't want to hurt or disrespect *you*, either."

"Yeah," Blade croaked.

Mace moved closer and lightly dropped his hand on Blade's shoulder. "If you truly don't want me to do this, I won't."

A comforting, warm sensation spread through Blade's chest. Their friendship had never been tested until now…and Mace was trying to make it right. "Seriously?"

"Yeah."

Relief filled him, and for a long moment, Blade considered taking Mace up on that. But man, what a selfish, greedy move. He wanted Scotty for himself, even while knowing that she wasn't his and never would be. She couldn't be. All he would ever have was one small piece of her. One frantic but amazing night of bliss.

How could he justify keeping Mace from having the same?

He couldn't. Blade loved Mace and Scotty too much to say no to something that might set them all right. And once it was over, they never had to think about it again.

He just had to get through those couple of hours of knowing what was happening in Mace's bedroom.

Closing his eyes, he shook his head. "I want you to do it. Just… don't tell me about it, okay? No details."

"Me?" Mace said lightly. "I never kiss and tell."

Blade rolled his eyes. "You *always* kiss and tell."

"Only when things get kinky."

"And I repeat, you *always* kiss and tell."

Before Mace could think of a comeback, the door opened, and Scotty poked her head outside. "Everything okay?"

Mace and Blade nodded in unison. "We're good," they both said, and Blade felt a rush of relief. They were already falling back into sync.

"For real," Blade added.

He didn't like the glint of doubt in Scotty's eyes. For this to work, the three of them had to be all-in. Mace's mother had always touted the power of the mindset, the idea that one could manifest their wishes through positive energy and action. Of course, she'd been a Memitim, a guardian angel for those deemed critical to the future—for good *or* bad—so she was full of light and sparkles and cheery affirmations.

But Idess's father was also the Grim Reaper, so when she wasn't unicorns and rainbows, she was fire and fury. Mace had gotten a touch of that. Slow to anger but scorched-earth vengeance in an instant.

"Thank gods." She stepped out. "I'm meeting my sister and Raika, so I'm gonna go." She grinned, the first genuine one he'd seen since Alaska. And he knew they were doing the right thing. "I'm glad we talked. See ya!"

They watched her take off, and then Mace punched Blade in the shoulder. "Wanna play some old-school GTA?"

He shrugged. "Sure." Getting some aggression out with Grand Theft Auto sounded good. Plus, he could beat Mace about half the time. "We should invite Crux too."

"You go get him. I'll make some popcorn."

Sounded good. Finally, something sounded good.

Chapter 23

Aleka and Raika were waiting for Scotty when she arrived at Pizzeria Inferno in downtown Sydney. Since Australia had been ceded to demons by humans, it now flourished as a demon Disneyland, its provinces divided into five Tiers according to the Ufelskala scale of evil. Sydney sat squarely in Ufelskala Tier One territory, considered generally safe. Even a handful of humans lived there.

"We ordered for you," Raika said as Scotty took a seat. "Your favorite. Onions, lard, and blood clots."

"Gross." That was Raika's favorite. Scotty loved Raika to death, but growing up in a realm drenched in evil had definitely impacted her life. Or maybe it was being born in Sheoul. Or perhaps her Grim Reaper DNA. Whatever. She was weird. "Aleka would never let you order it for me."

"To her credit," Aleka said as she put aside her ever-present planner, "she did try to order it for us. But we settled on a pepperoni to share, and she got a nasty pizza to take home with her." She looked across the table at Scotty. "Sounded like you wanted to talk about something. Does it have to do with what we talked about the other day?"

Scotty nodded and glanced over at Raika. "Short version: I slept with Blade to save his life," she explained. "Now, our entire team is falling apart, and I asked Aleka for advice on what to do."

"Wow." Raika reached for a pretzel bite, spearing one with a pointed black fingernail. "But that's easy. Fuck Mace."

"That's what I said." Aleka grinned. "See? I told you it could work."

"Yeah, well, Mace and Blade agreed."

"No way." Aleka's eyes shot wide. "You're kidding."

"Nope."

"Damn." Raika smiled darkly, the tips of her fangs glinting in the torchlight that contributed to the restaurant's hell theme. "You're playing with fire, girl." As if on command, flames flickered in Raika's eyes for a few heartbeats before winking out as if they'd never been there. Scotty was just glad she could control it now. Raika's teen years had resulted in a lot of burn injuries, scorched furniture, and full-blown fires.

"This could either be a giant success or the biggest mistake ever." Scotty groaned. "What would you guys do?"

Raika swallowed her pretzel bite. "I'm his aunt, so I wouldn't go the sex route. But *you* should ride Mace like a bucking hell stallion."

Scotty scowled at her friend. "But you've always said he's an ass."

"He is." Raika shrugged. "But I respect his ruthlessness. And let's face it, he's a Seminus demon, so he's got to be godlike in bed. You'll have a great time. I mean, as long as he's wearing a ball gag and you don't have to listen to him talk."

Now, Scotty was picturing him with a ball gag, his fangs penetrating the ball, his cock penetrating *her*.

She took a few gulps of her ice water, but that didn't stop the perspiration from beading on her brow.

"I'd meet him in a hotel," Aleka said, reaching for her drink. "You can't take him home, because, duh, Dad. And you definitely can't do it at his place."

Scotty agreed with not taking him home. She had a house with all the privacy she'd need, but her parents rarely knocked when they came over. Plus, her father had a way of knowing everything that went on within the boundaries of his island.

"Why not Mace's place?" she asked. "All the bedrooms are sound-proofed."

"You didn't do it in Blade's bedroom," Aleka pointed out. "So, to be fair, you shouldn't do it in Mace's. The compound needs to be off-limits, because if this thing goes south, you don't want anything to taint their living spaces."

Sometimes, her sister made sense—more than sometimes, but Scotty would never admit it.

"So…let me get this straight," Raika said. "After you and Mace do the deed, you think everything will go back to normal? You're not going to have feelings for either of them?"

"That's the plan."

Raika laughed, a deep-throated, head-back laugh that made her corset bounce and her breasts practically pop out. Every male in the place was staring and drooling.

"You are so naïve," she choked out between laughs.

"Oh, yeah? And what makes you an expert on relationships? I've never seen you with a male. Ever."

They waited for the server to deliver the pizza and plates. When he left, Raika snagged a piece.

"I don't date," she said. "I don't have time. Too many bad guys to catch."

Poor Raika. She'd been cursed by Heaven to capture the worst demons her father had released. She had a quota, and if she didn't meet it, the harsh punishment left her in agony for hours.

"Still," Aleka began, "I can't believe you've never met someone who interests you."

"Never."

"Not even a little?" Scotty prodded. "I don't believe you."

Raika scrutinized them both, and Scotty wondered if Aleka's skin felt as flayed as hers. No one could maintain eye contact with her for long, not without increasing discomfort, and Scotty was relieved when Raika finally glanced down at her glass of bloodwine.

"I'm going to tell you something," Raika said. "But if you tell anyone else—"

"You'll throw us into a pit full of mind-flayers and sword spiders," Scotty finished. "We know that. It's your standard threat. Spill."

There was a moment of hesitation, and then Raika blurted, "I sneaked a peek into one of Amber's sketchbooks." She took a big swig of her wine. "Hoo, boy, was she pissed when she caught me. Have you ever seen her angry? I mean, really angry?"

Scotty and Aleka both shook their heads. Amber had inherited her father's ability to explode like a bomb, sending lethal shockwaves out in all directions. As a result, she worked hard not to let herself get lost in fury.

"She didn't kill anyone," Raika said, "but she blasted me so hard my skin burned off. Hurt like a motherfucker until I healed. I advise you not to go through her sketches without permission."

"Okay, that might explain why you didn't date for a couple of days, but not for your entire life."

Raika ignored Scotty, her gaze locked onto a guy a few tables over. "That male is staring at you, Aleka."

Aleka sniffed dismissively. "He's not staring. He's leering. He's probably a demon, and he looks like an asshole."

He did. His cocky leer and puffed-up chest gave him a douchebag air. "You'll never know unless you talk to him," Scotty teased.

"This is a Schrodinger's Asshole situation," Raika said. "Is he an asshole? Is he a demon? Both? You won't know until he opens his mouth."

Scotty laughed, and they turned back to their food—and the previous topic. No way was she letting Raika get away with not filling in the gaps of this juicy story.

"Well?" Scotty prompted. "What does your lack of a love life have to do with Amber?"

"It was her sketches. There was one of me in a dirt grave. A faceless male was shoveling dirt onto me. When I asked her, she said she didn't know who he was. Just that he was my lover."

Scotty blinked. "So, you haven't been with a guy because of that?"

Raika took another swig of her bloodwine. "If I don't take a lover, I won't end up in a grave."

"Amber's visions don't always come true," Aleka said. "Not in the way she sketches them, anyway. Remember that time she tranced out and said Uncle Reseph would be in a plane crash, and he scoffed because he never flies, even with Aunt Jillian?"

He had tried to get Jillian to stop flying, though. Amber had assured them that Jillian hadn't been involved in her vision, so she'd continued with her job as a pilot and head of DART's air transportation department.

Raika rolled her eyes. "How was anyone supposed to guess that a plane would crash on top of him?"

As a Horseman of the Apocalypse, he'd survived the freak accident, but it had taken weeks for him to fully heal.

"Still," Aleka said, in that haughty way she had when she was sure she was right, "you can't live in fear of relationships."

"Says the girl who spends every waking moment by herself in a dusty old office, and who won't attend an event if Sabre is going to be there," Scotty said, which earned her a sharp glare.

"I—" Aleka broke off and glanced down at her comms unit. "Oh, my—oh, my gods!"

Alarmed, Scotty glanced down at her own comms. "What is it?"

Breaking news? Nope, nothing.

Aleka looked up, her eyes wide with shock. "They did it."

"Great." Raika rapped her long nails impatiently on the table, getting Aleka's attention. "Who did what?"

"Wraith and Serena." Aleka's emerald eyes grew liquid, but she was smiling, so it couldn't be bad news. "I asked them to help look for Harvester's blood. I can't believe I didn't think of it sooner. And they did it. They have her blood!"

"No fucking way!" Scotty leaped to her feet, uncaring that everyone in the joint was staring at her. "You're serious? We can bring back G-ma?"

A slow, victorious smile spread across Aleka's face. "And save Eva. I just need a couple of days to prepare."

Scotty grinned, finally feeling like her life was back on track. In just a couple of days, Eva would be healthy, G-ma would be alive, and her team would be back to normal.

Things could only get better from here.

The morning sun was already blistering-hot when Mace and Blade arrived at Ares's training arena, ready for whatever torture he'd devised to put them through today. Oddly, Scotty was late, and they were surprised when she showed up in the archway with Ares.

Their surprise turned suspicious real fast, though.

Scotty and Ares were smiling.

Sure, that was normal for Scotty, but it was really unsettling on Ares. The dude's perma-scowl was practically iconic.

"What's wrong with him?" Blade whispered to Mace. "He looks insane."

"Right?" Mace was really freaked out.

"Guys!" Scotty ran across the expanse of groomed sand, practically bouncing. "Guess what? You'll never guess. We have Harvester's blood!"

"Hell, yeah!" Mace high-fived her, and Blade did the same. "This means Eva is safe, right?"

Ares's grin slid off his face. At least he no longer looked demented. "Only if we can bring back Harvester."

Confused, Mace looked between them—down to meet Scotty's gaze and up to meet Ares's. "You mean there's a chance we can't?"

There'd been a plan in place to bring Harvester back almost from the moment they'd learned that the blood that fell on Limos's party and the Dome of the Rock belonged to the angel.

"Unfortunately, yes." Scotty's grin had faded, too, but she perked up again. "But Aleka's done the research, and she believes that we can do it. With Raika's help."

"Why Raika?"

"Because she has some of the same powers as her father, and the ceremony requires manipulating souls and Sheoulic energy."

"There's still a chance it won't work—"

"Daddy!" Scotty jammed her fists on her slim hips and rounded on Ares. "It's going to work. Think positive."

Ares was the size of a fucking building, and his intimidation factor was off the charts. But in the stare-off contest between him and his precious little girl, he backed down first, with the slightest twitch of amusement on his lips.

"I prefer being realistic," he said, his voice a low growl, "but I want this as badly as you do, so I'll be…positive."

"Look at you and your personal growth." Beaming, Scotty bounced on her toes and patted him on the shoulder. "And people say you're resistant to change."

"No one says that." Ares swiped his fingers over a crescent mark on his neck, and his leather armor, the breastplate embossed with the same horse symbol as his forearm, clacked into place. A summoned sword appeared in his fist. "Now, are we all ready to work some shit out?"

"Everyone says that," Scotty chirped, clearly enjoying poking the bear, "and we got all our shit worked out already."

One reddish eyebrow came up. "Did you, now?" He grinned. The one that made you shit your pants because you knew there was a whole lot of pain and humiliation coming your way.

"Aw, come on, man. We—" Mace didn't get to finish his sentence. Nope. Instead, he took a full body slam from the shield Ares must have pulled out of his ass. He flew backward, over the low arena wall, and crashed into the stadium seating.

"He's your teammate," Ares yelled at Blade and Scotty. "And you let him get hurt. What are you going to do about it?"

Mace knew the answer to that. They'd come to his defense like a pack of hellhounds, just as he'd done for them countless times.

And yep, in an instant, Blade and Scotty launched at Ares. Fuck, yeah. "Get him, guys!"

Ares defended himself almost casually against their coordinated attacks, but for the first time since the punishing training had begun four days ago, Ares gave up ground. Sure, he regained it with his powerful offensive pushes, but Scotty and Blade, working together in a seamless, coordinated combat dance, made him work for it.

Mace loved watching them fight. Blade's decisive, high-octane blows could shatter bone and skulls or sever heads and limbs, while Scotty's quick, graceful style distracted their enemies and left them vulnerable to attack from Blade or Mace. Although she was physically stronger than they were, she preferred lightning-fast, crippling strikes with her blade or high-speed hand-to-hand.

Mace's style was a blend of both, but he liked to play with his prey more than they did.

And he was ready to play.

He leaped nimbly over the retaining wall and came at Ares from behind. Blade and Scotty joined forces to distract the Horseman while Mace landed a devastating kick to the kidney. His brief moment of surprise left an opening, and as a unit, they swarmed him, giving no quarter. Once, a sword-blow to the legs took Ares down to his knees.

They fought hard, and three hours, multiple broken bones, and lots of blood later, they lost the battle but still won the war. The outcome was expected, but what made it a victory was that losing took three hours instead of twenty minutes like last time. Yes, Ares had held back—he could have killed them all in a matter of minutes if he'd wanted to—but he'd been forced to fight harder than he likely expected, and after they all collapsed to the ground, their lungs burning and their cuts stinging, Ares congratulated them.

"I'm releasing you from training," he said. "You never told me what got you sent here, but you seem to have fixed it. Did you?"

They exchanged looks. There was no doubt in anyone's expressions. Just determination.

Mace turned back to Ares.

"We did," they said in unison.

Team. Fucking. Up.

Chapter 24

So? Did you and Mace do it?

Scotty nearly choked on her moussaka as she read the missive from her sister, who was sitting across the family dinner table from her. Thursday dinner had been a thing in her family since she was born, and if you missed it, you'd better have a good reason.

Having sex with Mace wasn't a good reason.

Not that it would happen anytime soon. They hadn't talked about it since they, well, talked about it. And after their workout with her father this morning, they were too tired—and too thrilled—to discuss it. Mace and Blade had gone home to rest and heal, and she'd done the same. A two-hour nap and a relaxing swim in the crystal sea surrounding the island had her right as rain again.

Just in time for dinner.

No, Scotty sent back. And to keep her sister from prying more, Scotty asked her a question. Out loud, not in an annoying holo-missive.

"What time is the ritual tomorrow?"

Aleka looked over at her. As usual, she was elegant and classy in dress pants, heels, and a white silk blouse. A jeweled band held her hair in a shiny cascade of rose gold to the middle of her back. Meanwhile, Scotty's was up in a tangled, frizzy ponytail, her tank top was inside out, her denim shorts were ratty, and she'd kicked off her flip-flops half an hour ago.

Sometimes, you just had to not give a shit.

"One p.m.," Aleka said. "Greenland time. We'll do the ritual at Uncle Thanatos's."

Scotty both dreaded it and couldn't wait. What if it didn't work? No. She couldn't think that way. Not after scolding her father for the same thing. "How much more prep do you have?"

"Not much. If Eva worsens, we can do it earlier. Mainly, I just want to make sure we get this right, because we've only got one shot."

Dinner grew quiet as the brutal reality sank in.

Cara quickly changed the topic. "Did you girls hear the big news?" she asked as she reached up to pet the massive hellhound lying next to her.

Hal didn't usually hang out in the house, but a member of his pack had recently been slaughtered by a fallen angel, and he was "feeling vulnerable." Scotty had no idea how a hellhound could feel vulnerable, but for the millionth time, she gave thanks that she hadn't inherited her mother's gift for either healing the beasts or communicating with them as Aleka had.

"Is it about Gabriel?" Aleka asked. "An Archangel losing their wings is news that travels at light speed."

"He'll need to watch his back." Scotty put down her fork and took a piece of pita bread from the pile in the center of the table. "Demons will want to drag him to Sheoul, and everyone else will want him in their possession. Can you imagine what could happen to him if The Aegis got hold of him?"

"No one is getting hold of him," Ares said. "I've granted him asylum. He's under my protection so long as he stays on the island."

"So," Scotty said with a wry smile, "*we* got hold of him."

Her father gave her a proud wink. "He's a treasure trove of information. Even disgraced, his value is immeasurable. He's already given us some good intel on Lilith and the fallen angel we've been after."

"Fearr?" Scotty gave a satisfied nod. "Uncle Thanatos has been obsessed with killing her for years."

As Wraith's BFF, Thanatos held a grudge against the fallen angel for her part in killing Wraith. Didn't matter that Azagoth brought him back. Fearr was on borrowed time.

"Has Gabriel said what happened in Heaven?" Scotty asked. "What does he know about Gramps?"

Her father's expression was troubled. "As we've already heard from Azagoth and Stryke, power changed hands. The Thrones are in charge, and Reaver is being held prisoner, along with all the Archangels."

"I don't understand," Aleka said. "How can they hold Grandpa prisoner? He's a Radiant. He's the most powerful angel in existence."

Anger made a vein throb in Ares's temple. "They're using the Archangels' power to hold him. But Gabriel thinks he might have given Reaver a little push to free himself."

"Someone needs to get word to Revenant," Scotty said. "He could bust Gramps out."

Ares stabbed a juicy slab of roast lamb on the serving tray and hauled it to his plate. "Heaven sealed Revenant inside Sheoul. My sources say he's under constant attack by Satan's sympathizers, and he's isolated himself in the B'lal region, where no one can reach him."

"Grandpa managed to get inside Satan's fortress and rescue Harvester once," Aleka pointed out. "Maybe we can figure out a way to get in."

"Reaver had to cloak himself in evil to do it. We can't do what he did. Only Reseph has ever set foot in the heart of the B'lal region, and it was when he was Pestilence."

Scotty suppressed a shudder. She'd heard the stories about her uncle's time as Pestilence, when he'd gone so evil that even all these years later, her family still hadn't fully recovered. To this day, he avoided most family gatherings, and he'd never attended them when Harvester was there. Scotty wasn't sure what had gone down between the two back when Harvester was a fallen angel, but the hatred in her eyes when she looked at Reseph had been hard to miss.

"Surely, we can get a message to him," Cara said. "Your spy network is extensive."

"Stryke tried." Ares carved into his meat, making the horse glyph on his forearm dance. Or maybe Battle was restless, needing to run. Her father had to release the warhorse from his arm daily, or Battle got twitchy. "Twice. The first try ended with an entire thread in his intelligence web being snipped. He suspects one of Satan's loyalists."

It seemed insane that, despite Satan not being around—and wouldn't be until he was freed in another nine centuries—he still had powerful demons doing his bidding. Revenant wasn't as much ruling Sheoul as he was just barely clinging to power.

"And the second attempt?" Scotty asked.

"Stryke got a lot of heads in boxes."

"Unbelievable." Aleka stabbed her fork into her roasted eggplant. "What's the Thrones' endgame? Has Gabriel said?"

"He hasn't." Ares shoved his plate aside. "I don't know if he even knows. Sounds like they kept him in the dark about most things." He took a swig of iced tea. "We won't get any more out of him for a bit. He's in some sort of recuperative sleep. Could last a while, I guess. I have Z keeping an eye on him. He'll alert me when Gabriel wakes."

Zhubaal had once been Azagoth's right-hand man, but after Sheoulgra's destruction, the fallen angel and his mate had come to the island with the Memitim. He'd proven to be a valuable asset.

Scotty's comms beeped. No doubt her sister again. But when she accessed the message, her heart almost stopped.

It was Mace.

Wanna come over? Blade's hanging with Stryke and Crux in the game room, so you can sneak in and he won't see you.

They'd agreed that Blade shouldn't know anything until after it was over, but she hadn't brought up the hotel idea to Mace yet.

She sent a return message. *I'd rather get a hotel.*

Mace's missive came a moment later. *I'll book a room at the Ritz Paris. Meet me tonight.*

The moussaka in her belly soured as her nerves kicked in.

"What's wrong?" Rath's rumbling voice carried from the end of the table where he sat opposite her father. "You look troubled."

Now, everyone was looking at her. Great. "Nothing's wrong. I just have a lot of work stuff on my mind."

"Are you still in trouble with Kynan?" Aleka asked, and Scotty shot her a glare. She'd managed to avoid the topic of work all night, mainly to keep their dad from asking more invasive questions, and Aleka had just blown it.

Sure enough, Ares turned his intense gaze on Scotty. "You never said why Kynan sent your team to me for training."

"*Sorry, sis,*" Aleka mouthed.

Scotty took a big swig of iced tea, buying time to compose herself. "It wasn't a big deal. We screwed up a mission. There were hostages, and a crystal artifact that got away, and it got kind of messy."

"Yeah, I know that." Ares swallowed a bite of pita bread. "But you never said *why* the mission went south."

Because I had sex with Blade. "Poor communication."

His eyes narrowed. "Why? And don't tell me you don't know. Your team is held up as a model for how well you work together."

Dammit. She glanced at her comms and Mace's message. She needed to get out of here.

"It's just…things got a little tense after Mace got hurt and Blade and I had to finish a job without him. Kynan chewed our asses. We're fine now." She stood and looked at her mom. "Thanks for dinner. Great as usual. I need to go."

"Scotty—"

"See you at Thanatos's tomorrow. Bye!" She darted out of there, raced down the staircase, and hopped into the island's Harrowgate, where she stood for a moment, her heart and mind racing.

She was about to go and have sex with her best friend. Her other best friend. The one she *hadn't* had sex with yet.

She should change her clothes. At least put her top on right. Maybe she should shower again. She'd showered before dinner, but she probably smelled like Greek food.

What was Mace like in bed?

The thought interrupted her panicked fear of smelling like Mediterranean herbs. Excitement filtered through her, quelling her nerves a little. She'd loved being with Blade, even though things had been frantic, and the setting had been less than ideal. She couldn't imagine a better way to have lost her virginity. He'd been perfect.

So, how would that experience differ from the one she'd have with Mace?

You're not going to have one with Mace if you don't get moving.

Right. She hurried to her villa, showered, and spent half an hour trying to decide what to wear. She finally settled on a matching green panties-and-bra set, black leggings, the gray cashmere sweater Aleka had gotten her for her twenty-ninth birthday, and sneakers. Casual, but classy...and still practical for battle.

You never knew when you might have to kill a demon or kick a groping guy's ass.

Gut churning, her palms sweating, she waited for Mace to send her the room number. Five minutes later, she was standing in front of the door.

Am I really going to do this?

Her heart pounded, all fight-or-flight, and she was on the verge of choosing *flight* when the door swung open.

Mace stood there, barefoot and in worn jeans and a black tee, the long, ropey muscles of his arms flexing beneath the bronzed skin.

She didn't have to wonder about his underwear. He didn't wear them. She'd seen him undressed—or nearly so—a million times. At the time, she'd thought nothing of it. Now, it was all she could think about.

"Hey," he said, sounding confident and sexy, and not at all like his nerves were eating him alive the way hers were.

"Hey." Okay, she sounded cool too. Maybe she wouldn't come across like a nervous dork. "Nice place."

He'd gotten a suite, complete with a couch, a couple of leather chairs, and a kitchenette. A bottle of wine was chilling on the counter, along with a tray of chilled, chocolate-covered strawberries.

Wow. Something about his thoughtfulness caught her off guard. Not that he couldn't be thoughtful, but she hadn't expected it. Not for her. This wasn't a date. This was just supposed to be sex. Sex to match what had happened between her and Blade.

Sure, they didn't need to do it in a cave, but this went too far.

"It's okay," he said. "I mean, it's not the floor of a cave, but…"

She laughed, somehow unsurprised that they'd both been thinking of the cave. "Okay, so how do we do this?"

He blinked. "Wow. Right to it."

Yeah, she'd even surprised herself there. The awkwardness was making her twitchy. "Sorry. I'm just nervous, you know?"

There was a heartbeat of hesitation, and then he twitched his broad shoulder in a shrug. "I am too."

"Really? I can't picture you ever being nervous with a female."

"I'm usually not," he admitted, his cheeks going adorably pink. "But this isn't a normal situation. It's you."

That, she understood. "You'd think we would both be comfortable instead of jumping out of our skin, right? I mean, we know each other so well."

He took her hand and led her to the couch. "Were you nervous with Blade?"

She didn't sit. Instead, she turned to face him. "Not really. It was different. He was in pain, and I just wanted to help."

Why had she never noticed how truly magnificent Mace was? This close, he smelled a little woodsy with a hint of rain, as if he'd been walking through a forest during a storm. His shirt stretched across his broad chest, defining hard muscles she was dying to touch. To explore. To commit to memory, since this would be the only time she'd have the chance.

"Maybe we should just get it over with." All this unfamiliarity was making her mind spin out of control. She needed action, something to make her stop thinking. And wanting.

She started to lift her shirt over her head, but he seized her wrist.

"Not like that." His voice was husky. Smooth. Intoxicating. "Undressing each other is part of the fun."

Oh. Heat flooded her face at the way his fingers slid down her arm to grasp the hem of her sweater. He hesitated, something she rarely saw him do. His gaze met hers, his eyes glittering with gold arousal, dark hunger, and a silent question.

Are we really going to do this?

She knew the answer to that.

Very slowly, holding his gaze with hers, she nodded.

A shudder went through him, and like a wave, it passed through her too.

He lifted her shirt and tugged it over her head. He'd seen her in swimsuits a million times, but she'd never seen his gaze linger. Neither he nor Blade had ever looked at her with desire. Not that she'd noticed, anyway.

But right now, the gold in Mace's eyes grew molten as he slipped her bra straps off her shoulders. She'd always been self-conscious about her breasts, which weren't as voluptuous as her sister's. Or any of her cousins.

"Beautiful," he whispered as he deftly flicked the front catch open and let the bra fall to the floor.

Suddenly drowning in self-consciousness, she covered up with her arms. "Don't lie."

His dark brows snapped together. "I'm not, I swear. I'm not above throwing out flattery to get what I want, but I would never lie to you."

"It's just…I know you like females who are especially…endowed."

He gave her an impish grin. "Yeah, I'm a breast guy. But," he said, as he gently pulled her arms away from her chest, "I also like an athletic body, and yours is perfect. You wouldn't look right in a D-cup."

"Or a C-cup," she muttered, and he laughed again.

"I was being generous. Because," he said with a wink, "I'm charming like that."

If his goal had been to put her at ease, it worked. This was so much easier than she'd imagined it would be.

Eagerly, she helped him out of his shirt, revealing his chest, layered with sinew and thick muscles she'd seen a thousand times, but in very different situations. She wanted to run her palms over his smooth skin, but she was on a mission, and she wouldn't be deterred.

His jeans were next.

He let her unbutton them, her knuckles brushing his rock-hard abs as she worked the buttons. His cock burst free, all unabashed and "Hey, how ya doin'?"

Oh, my.

Her nipples tingled, but it was nothing compared to the delicious ache that began to pulse between her legs,

Her mouth watered, and her hand shook as she feathered her fingers across the smooth head, amazed by the silky texture. There hadn't been time to explore with Blade, and a pang of guilt dampened her lust a bit. She was trying to make this fair for both of them, so maybe they should just get to it.

"Hey." He caught her hand as she moved to pull away. "What's wrong?"

"Nothing. Not really. I was thinking that maybe we should just do it. Like with Blade. I don't want either of you to feel cheated."

His sensual smile took her breath away. "It's okay, Scotty. Blade and I talked about this. He wants us to enjoy ourselves."

Whoa. She blinked, unable to imagine that. "Really?"

"Yeah. He was concerned that you got cheated out of losing your virginity the way it should have been. He wants you to have a better experience with sex."

Oh, gods. Blade was so sweet and considerate. It made her love him even more.

Stop! Don't! You can't love him. Not like that.

No, she couldn't. Ruthlessly, she shoved those unwanted romantic feelings down.

"What else did he say?"

Mace's fingers went to the waistband of her leggings. "He said I can't be freaky with you."

"Freaky?"

His smile was all kinds of naughty as he shoved her pants down. "I'm pretty open to anything when it comes to sex."

A warm sensation curled between her legs at his words as her imagination took flight. She'd seen his sex swing and handcuffs, his assortment of crops and toys, but she'd never really thought about him using any of it. It had always been best *not* to think about either him or Blade in a sexual way.

Now, she was imagining all kinds of stuff.

"But what if I want to get freaky?" she asked, and he laughed, which kind of annoyed her.

"I think we should get the basics down first."

"I did the basics with Blade—"

"Really?" He sank to his knees and tugged down her panties. "Did he do this to you?"

Leaning in, he dipped his tongue between her legs. She sucked in a harsh, startled breath as his tongue slipped deep and stroked her core.

"Mace," she whispered. "Oh, damn."

"So that's a no," he murmured against her hot flesh before spearing her with his tongue again.

Pleasure swamped her, crashing into her with so much force that her knees nearly buckled. He massaged her thighs, his hands slowly moving upward as he kissed her deeply, his lips sucking and doing sinful things that made her arch into him. His fingers reached the top of her thighs, and he used his thumbs to spread her wide, exposing her to his touch and his gaze.

"I could do this to you for days," he murmured.

Oh, gods. She'd let him.

She knew about oral sex, of course. She was almost thirty years old, best friends with lust demons, and she lived on an island full of horny Ramreels. More than one assignment had taken her to BDSM clubs, human and demon brothels, and underworld vice dens. She'd seen everything. But seeing and experiencing were two different things. Now, she understood what she'd been missing.

Suddenly, Mace lunged to his feet, hauled her into his arms, and carried her to the bedroom. She barely had time to catch her breath and kick her underwear off her feet before he tossed her onto the bed. As she bounced, her legs flopped open, and like the predator he was, he growled, dove between her thighs, and continued what he'd started.

His hot tongue pierced her, and she cried out as a rumble of ecstasy tore through her very center. He circled her clit with his thumb as his tongue filled her, sliding in and out in a torturous, wonderful rhythm. He built her to climax slowly, masterfully, like an artist painting a scene. He used short strokes, long strokes, and applied different textures and pressures.

"That's it, sweetheart," he whispered against her clit. "That's it..."

Yes, it was. He flicked his tongue over the tip, and she lost her mind. The orgasm took her apart at a cellular level, turning her thoughts to confetti as waves of pleasure pumped through her.

He kept licking her, long, deep laps from her core to her clit, prolonging the pleasure to the point that she nearly had to pull away just to catch her breath. But she rode the orgasm and his tongue until there was nothing left but watery muscles and straining lungs.

"I think," she croaked, "I'm a big fan of the basics."

Mace's grin was heart-melting. "Good. Let's get even more basic."

This was the best sex of Mace's life, and he hadn't even come yet.

His cock jerked, reminding him of that fact. A stab of pain followed—a gentle prod from his Seminus genes, telling him he needed to get on it. He needed to get on *her.*

Fuck, yeah. He couldn't wait. Not after watching her climax like that. The way she'd arched her back and rolled her hips as she gripped the bedspread for dear life had been the most erotic sight ever. He'd tasted her orgasm, savoring the spicy tang as it charged him up. He was made to make females come, and in return, their desire fueled him. The more they came, the longer he could go between having to bed another female.

He was going to set a record with Scotty. He hadn't been lying when he said he could eat her for days. And now that she'd caught her breath, he'd do it again.

Parting her toned thighs once more, he leaned in, anticipation making his heart pound. She rolled her hips eagerly, and he accepted her silent invitation by stroking his tongue over her glistening core.

"Mace," she groaned, "that's so…good."

He smiled against her, male pride swelling in his chest. Yeah, he was good at this. Females begged him for this. But suddenly, he no longer cared about those other females. What he was doing to Scotty was for her, and for her only.

Never again would he give another female this kind of pleasure.

That's a weird hill to die on.

It was. But he didn't care. This was like indulging in a luxurious, decadent dark-chocolate gelato after a lifetime of having nothing but vanilla ice milk. He was ruined now. Never going back.

Ravenous for what only Scotty could give him, he dove into her, licking and sucking, dragging his tongue through her slick flesh and flicking it across her swollen bud. She writhed, bucking against his mouth as he lapped at her, working her into another frenzy.

She came hard, and as she came down, he shifted his weight and moved up her body, licking and kissing as he went. He spent extra time nuzzling the soft skin between her hipbones before worshipping his way upward, teasing her navel and breastbone with his tongue.

And then he reached her breasts.

He'd seen them several times over the years, but only quick glimpses while she was changing clothes or tearing them away from wounds. And he'd lost count of how many times he'd seen her in a bathing suit. Her breasts were on the small side, ideally sized for her athletic body.

He'd known they'd be the perfect handful, and he'd guessed the nipples would pucker when he nibbled them. But he hadn't known she'd orgasm when he sucked them.

"Mace!" The way she shouted his name as she came again filled him with fierce male pride, and he smiled as he drew a nipple deep into his mouth, letting his fangs put dimples in her perky flesh.

"Are you ready for me?" He teased the nipple with his tongue. "Or should I play more?"

The little vixen grinned down at him. "Play."

Arousal ripped through him like a wildfire, and he regretted asking the question. He needed her. Sooner, rather than later.

Rising up, he straddled her, loving how her lust-glazed eyes sharpened with curiosity. He gripped his shaft and stroked in long, slow passes from the base to the tip. She liked that. Her eyes glittered with greed as she watched, her back arching and her hips rocking.

"I know you can't make yourself come like that." She reached up and cupped his sac, and he groaned. "But what if I touch you?"

"Doesn't matter." He moved his hand aside when she took over, pumping her fist up and down, creating an almost unbearably pleasant friction. "I have to be inside a female when my orgasm starts." He sucked in a harsh breath when she circled the head with her thumb.

"When it starts." She sat up, scooting out from under him. "But what about when you finish?"

He swallowed dryly. She was bending forward, her lips getting closer… "I can finish anywhere—ah, *fuck*!" She took him into her mouth and sucked him like a straw in a thick-ass milkshake.

He couldn't take it. He'd wanted her like nothing else in his life. He'd wanted *this* like nothing else in his life. Didn't matter that she didn't know what she was doing. What she was doing was the best thing ever.

The climax struck like a bolt of lightning, searing him from the inside. Then Scotty did the sexiest thing, releasing him to lean back, bracing herself on her arms as he spilled on her breasts. Her sexed-up eyes went heavy-lidded as she dragged a finger through the pearly liquid. When she put her finger to her lips, his spent cock got instantly hard again.

Sems were capable of multiple orgasms, dozens in a single session. But he had a feeling he was going to break some records tonight.

"Suck it," he growled, and then he growled again when the pink tip of her tongue flicked over her fingertip, catching a drop of his cum. Fuck, that was sexy. Even more so when she moaned as the aphrodisiac took effect.

"Mace," she whispered, her gaze clinging to his. "I want you. Please."

She didn't have to beg. He'd never make her do that. Besides, he wanted her, too, with a fierce possessiveness he'd known he was capable of but had never thought he'd experience. Not when the one female he'd truly always wanted wasn't available.

She still wasn't. But at least he had right now.

Impatient, he positioned himself between her legs, the tip of his cock at her slick entrance.

I love you.

He didn't say it, but he thought it as he slid inside her welcoming heat. Closing her eyes, she arched up to meet him, taking him deep. Her tight walls squeezed him, rippling along his shaft with every pump of his hips.

He wanted to break loose, to give her everything he had, to claim her, but he held back. In part to give her the passionate, gentle experience she'd missed out on with Blade, and partly to keep from losing himself to obsession. She was a match, and he was tinder, and this friction was dangerously close to sparking a fire.

But as their bodies entwined and their kisses grew hotter, he couldn't help it. He pounded into her, coaxing another orgasm out of her. And another. And another. He lost count of his own climaxes, each one tearing him apart until they crashed into a pile of panting, moaning exhaustion.

He recovered first, fetching the sparkling wine and strawberries, which they scarfed in bed, tangled in the sheets.

"Wanna get some real food?" he asked, as he poured the last of the bubbly into their glasses. "Or go to a movie?"

She laughed as she reached for one of the two remaining strawberries. He loved her laugh. Deep and melodic, she'd always been so free with it, unafraid to find the humor in almost any situation. "Can't you just relax for ten minutes?"

"Relax?" He scoffed. "Do you even know me?"

Stretching out on the mattress like a great, sleepy cat, she propped herself up on one elbow and regarded him with curiosity. The sheet covered her hips and waist, but it had slipped, exposing her breasts, and he had to force himself not to stare like some kind of perv.

But they were just so perfect.

"Your bird suits you, you know."

He nudged the remaining strawberry closer to her. "My bird?"

She nudged it back and then pointed to his neck. "Your personal symbol. The eagle is in perpetual flight. Just like you."

He'd heard that a few times in his life. "My mom swears that I'll settle down someday, but I don't see that happening."

"Oh, come on. Someday, you'll meet a female, and you'll finally perch somewhere."

Ouch. Okay, yes, that was the plan. There was no way he'd let himself turn into a monster after his next transition, and mating would prevent that. But he didn't *want* to meet a female to settle down with. There was only one he wanted. Scotty was part of him, and he supposed she had been since they were kids.

Part of him, but not his.

Deep thoughts and yearning threatened to take him down, so he did what he always did when shit got too serious, and he shoved the tray and glasses aside, not caring that they spilled.

"Mace!" Scotty sounded positively scandalized.

Grinning, he pounced on her, wedging himself between her legs. "You didn't think we were done, did you?" Lowering his mouth to hers, he kissed her, a playful, teasing kiss that made her giggle. "We have this room for ten more hours, and we're going to make the most of it."

They did, and afterward, as Scotty snored softly in the wee hours of the morning, he lay awake, thinking that this had been the best night of his life.

And also, a huge mistake. They might have put their friendship back into order, but his heart would never recover.

Chapter 25

Blade was heading out as Mace was coming in. They met on the back porch, and Mace looked like he'd had a rough night. Blade felt that. He'd been juicing up with sexual suppressants since his time with Scotty, and his body felt like it was starting to fall apart.

It *was* falling apart. That was the danger of the injections. The effectiveness wore off sooner with each one. Eventually, they wouldn't work at all. By then, a Sem could be half-dead. Or *all* dead.

Stryke knew all about that.

"Hey." Mace raked his fingers through his hair, but it didn't help.

"Hey."

"Where're you off to?"

Blade hefted his catch bag, which he used to haul his tools for making or disarming physical and magical traps. "I have a class today."

"Ah, yeah. DART's new recruits. Good luck."

"Thanks." He eyed Mace, taking in his rumpled and spent appearance. "Where have you been?"

"Um…" Mace reached up and rubbed the back of his neck, his gaze getting all squirrely. "Ah…Scotty and I…you know. It's done."

Pow. Right in the fucking heart. Blade had dreaded hearing those words. But following the blunt force trauma of Mace's admission came a sense of relief. The lancing of a wound. It was over. They were all cool now.

He swallowed, and when he spoke, his voice was raw with emotion he couldn't contain. "Okay. Thanks for telling me."

Mace met his gaze. "Are you?"

"Am I what?"

"Okay."

No. "Yes."

"You're lying," Mace said quietly, and Blade didn't deny it. "You love her, don't you?"

Blade drew in a shuddering breath. "Yeah."

Mace's shoulders sagged. "Me, too."

Figured. And Blade couldn't blame him. She was extraordinary. She was so much a part of their team and their lives that she might as well be an appendage.

Same with Mace. He was just as important to Blade as Scotty.

"What are we going to do?"

"We're going to get past this," Mace insisted. "And we're going to get back to normal."

As much as Blade wanted things to go back to the way they'd been, the reality was more complicated than that. "What are we going to do when Scotty gets a boyfriend? I don't know if I can watch that."

"Dude, that's easy." Mace flashed fangs and a sinister smile. "We kill him."

And that fast, all residual tension between them fled. Blade laughed, freed from the burden of jealousy and greed. "Sounds like a plan."

"Cool." Mace grinned and held out his fist. "Team up."

"Team up, man. Team up."

Chapter 26

One of Blade's favorite tasks at DART was teaching new recruits how to disarm traps. Every second Tuesday of every month, he taught a class, and without fail, he had to use his healing powers to patch people up.

Except today.

For the first time ever, the students listened and were careful. It made class boring, but Blade would take it as a good sign. Especially because, in just under three hours, the Horsemen were going to attempt to bring Harvester back and save Eva.

"Thanks for offering to help," Logan said as Blade entered his friend's family castle. Hidden from humans in a remote part of Greenland, the keep had housed Thanatos—and now his family—for centuries.

"Anything for Eva." Blade helped Logan spread a sheet over the massive oak table in the castle's dining hall. "Scotty said she and Aleka will be here in a couple of hours with the blood."

"Are you staying for the ceremony?" Logan asked. "Is Mace coming?"

"I wish." The three of them rarely missed important events that affected any of them. They were a package deal. Everyone knew that. So, he hated that Scotty had to face whatever happened without him and Mace. "Scotty said they only want immediate family in the vicinity. Something about diluting the powerful connections or whatever."

She'd explained it, but Blade's understanding of magical and mystical crap was limited, and he'd zoned out the way he always did when Stryke talked about science stuff. But give Blade a murder scene, a survival scenario, or a fight, and he was in the game to win.

"Ah, yeah." Logan dragged a dining room chair away from the table. "Dad mentioned that not even Mom will be there. Except for Raika and Idess, they're keeping the circle limited to Reaver's blood relatives."

Blade studied his friend as they moved the heavy chairs aside to create more space. Logan looked like shit. Stress had dulled his eyes and pulled his mouth tight, and he probably hadn't slept for days. Blade could only imagine how terrified he must be.

"How are you doing?" Blade asked. "How's Eva?"

"Not good. That's the answer to both questions." Leaning heavily on one of the chairbacks, Logan closed his eyes. "I'm scared, man. If this doesn't work…if I lose Eva…"

"It'll work," Blade assured him. "Harvester is too mean to stay dead, and Eva is too awesome to die."

Which was funny, because he'd been skeptical about Eva at the beginning. Everyone had. Not only did she work for the enemy, but she'd also been part of an Aegis team that murdered two of their friends and led to the death of another, Logan's best friend, Draven.

"I hope you're right," Logan said, his voice thick with emotion. "I can't lose her, Blade. After everything we went through. After Draven…" He took in a shuddering breath. "She's the woman of my dreams, and I haven't had enough time with her."

Blade understood in a way he wouldn't have before that night in Alaska. No, that wasn't true. A few months ago, they'd come close to losing Scotty to a churning ocean full of sea demons. It would have killed him.

And she wasn't even his.

The idea of losing her—to death or another male—filled him with terror. He'd gone toe to toe with monsters ten times his size, but he couldn't face losing Scotty.

The reality was like hitting a brick wall, sending him to the verge of hyperventilation. Because someday, he *would* lose her. Not to death, hopefully, but to a male. And even if she never hooked up with a guy, it didn't matter. In around seventy years, Blade would go through his second maturation stage and turn into a violent, raping monster if he didn't take a mate before that.

So, yeah, this thing the three of them had was amazing, but it had an expiration date.

And he didn't take loss well. When his little brother, Chaos, died, he'd fallen apart. Had gone to a dark place for a long time. No one noticed, because everyone had been focused on Stryke, but Blade had suffered, and only Mace had paid any attention. Mace, with his goofy antics and upbeat sense of humor, had brought Blade back from the brink. His work with DART had helped keep him busy, and then Scotty had joined the team. And, just like that, the darkest days of his life had faded away.

No, he couldn't lose her. He couldn't lose anyone again.

"Logan?"

"Yeah?"

Blade gazed absently at the portrait over the great fireplace, an ancient painting of Thanatos. It was slightly off-kilter, which meant that someone was messing with Regan's OCD. Probably Thanatos, but Logan and Amber sometimes got in on the fun. Once, during a sleep-over, Logan, Blade, Talon, and Sabre had gone on a spree, moving furniture and knickknacks slightly out of place, misaligning multiple light switches, and generally being dickheads. Stryke had refused to participate and undid everything they'd done while they slept. He'd always been a wet blanket.

"When did you know Eva was *the one*?"

The tension in Logan's expression melted away, his mouth curving into a secret smile. "After we slept together for the first time. There was just something about her. It felt right, I guess. Like it was meant to be." He gave Blade a sheepish look. "Yeah, I'm a sap."

Blade thought about his time with Scotty, how being inside her had felt so, so right. Like she was a part of him, and he of her.

"S'okay," he said quietly. "I get it."

Logan cocked an eyebrow. "Yeah? Anything you wanna tell me?"

"Nah." Blade got back to clearing the space for the ritual. "Just curious."

Logan gave him a speculative look, but he didn't press. Good. Because Blade hadn't sorted shit out in his own head, let alone well enough to talk about it.

But he knew one thing for sure: He'd come to a crossroads. He loved Scotty, and he was afraid to lose her. He was afraid to lose Mace too. And the horrible thing was, losing one or both wasn't a matter of *if*. It was a matter of *when*.

Mace's mouth watered at the savory scent of the white chicken chili wafting through the compound. Sabre cooked something for the entire household every Wednesday night, and no one missed dinner. Like his father, Eidolon, he was a great cook.

Usually, Scotty came, too, but she would be busy with Harvester's reanimation. Assuming it worked.

Please let it work. Logan would be devastated if he lost Eva, and the Horsemen needed Harvester back.

"Yo, Mace." Sabre replaced the lid on the giant pot of chili as Mace walked into the kitchen. "Will you keep an eye on this for a little while? I need to send Aleka some files that might help with the ritual."

"You two are speaking?"

Sabre made a frustrated sound. "I'm her last resort when she needs something tested at a lab."

"Why doesn't she just ask Stryke?"

This time, the sound Sabre made was both amused and derisive. "She says Stryke is even more of an asshole than I am."

She was right. But still. "What did you do? Come on. Spill already."

Usually, Sabre just told them all to fuck off. Now, though, he paused in the doorway and looked back over his shoulder. "*I* didn't do anything."

That was the most he'd ever said about whatever had gone down with him and Aleka. Mace wasn't letting this opportunity slide.

"So, what did *she* do?"

Angry gold flecks glittered in Sabre's eyes. "She accused me of something and then refused to give me a chance to explain."

"What did she accuse you of do—?"

The back door banged open, and Blade walked inside. He tossed down his bag and looked between Mace and Sabre. "Did I interrupt something?"

"Nope." Sabre waved in both greeting and goodbye and took off for his quarters.

"Damn." Mace lifted the lid off the pot and took a big, hungry whiff as Blade fetched a couple of beers from the fridge. Crux would be happy. He loved anything with green chilis. "I almost got him to tell me what happened with Aleka."

"Seriously?"

Mace replaced the lid and turned to his buddy. "He said she accused him of something, but he didn't say what."

"Don't know what he could have done," Blade said as he opened the bottles and handed one to Mace. "Dude is as straitlaced as his dad."

Mace laughed. "And he doesn't even see it. I called him Eidolon Junior the other day, and he acted like I was an idiot."

"You are an idiot."

Mace tapped his beer against Blade's bottle in salute. "Love you too, bro." Blade smiled, but it was half-hearted. "What's up? You seem distracted."

Blade propped his hip against the counter and stared absently out the window for a moment before speaking. "I went with Logan to help set up for the Harvester ritual. I feel bad for him. He's terrified he's going to lose Eva."

"I can't imagine what he's going through." Heck, Mace didn't even want to *try* to imagine it. Nope. He preferred to keep negative emotions like fear and sorrow at arm's length.

"I can," Blade said roughly. "I thought we were going to lose Scotty on the way to the oil rig."

The terror Mace had suppressed since that day surfaced like one of the sea demons that had grabbed her off the boat. How easily she could have been dragged to the ocean floor and torn apart. Immortality only went so far. If they hadn't been able to wrench her free, she'd have been gone forever.

Mace slammed his bottle down. "I don't like to think about that."

"It's all I *can* think about lately," Blade murmured.

The sound of simmering chili filled the room, alongside a sudden, oppressive mood.

Mace was afraid to ask. But he had to.

"What's really going on, Blade?"

Blade lifted his gaze to Mace's, his dark eyes troubled. "I want her, Mace."

It was as if an infection had been lanced, releasing the poison. Months—if not years—of lying to themselves had come to an end. In a way, it was a relief. Everything was out in the open now. Or, it would be, once Mace confessed as well.

"I know," he said. "So do I."

"Fuck." Blade sank down onto a barstool, his hands in his hair as if he wanted to tear it out. "She's all I can think about. I can't be with anyone else…not even Masumi. I've been shooting myself up with so much suppressant that my balls are going to fall off or some shit." He barked out a bitter laugh. "I used to think Stryke was a fool for using suppressants until he almost died. Now, I'm standing at the edge of that same hellmouth."

Mace got it. He so got it. "I've been doing the same," he admitted. But he'd only needed one injection since being with Scotty. Blade was a week in, a point where the injections would be barely effective. He had to be strung out. And now that Mace was paying attention, yeah, Blade's hands were shaking. "Scotty is the only female I want."

"We can't continue like this." Blade looked up. "It'll kill us both."

He was right. The injections would, eventually, kill them. But so would having sex with another female who wasn't Scotty…just in a different way. "So, what do we do?"

Blade blew out a long, ragged breath. "She has to make a choice. She's got to choose one of us, so the other can move on."

Mace stared at his friend—his friend who had lost his mind. "Are you serious?"

"Yeah."

The lid on the pot of chili began to rattle, but Mace ignored it, unable to comprehend Blade's line of thought. "Are you saying you'd be okay with her choosing me? Like, totally cool? No problem?"

Blade white-knuckled his beer. "Obviously, I want her to choose me," he said, his voice and fingers relaxing in slow increments as he spoke. "But, Mace, I'd rather she be with you than some rando. At least my two best friends would be happy, and I could stop obsessing."

It made sense, but Mace was still having a hard time processing it. "I think it's better if we're all on the same team, still friends, and everything is back the way it was."

"You know that's not possible," Blade said quietly. And yeah, Mace did know that. But sometimes, he was really good at glossing over the bad stuff and burying his head in the sand.

"You're just like Dad."

Talon had said that to Mace more times than he could count, often when Mace did exactly what he was doing now: burying his head in the sand. So sure, good old Talon had a point sometimes, but Mace also excelled at ignoring his brother.

Woodenly, Mace went to the stove. "So, what do we say to Scotty?"

"We tell her what we just talked about."

Mace tasted the chili, not because he was hungry but because he needed a distraction. "You don't think we'll be blindsiding her?"

"She's smarter than both of us combined. She knows we need to do something."

No doubt Blade was right. And the chili needed more salt. "Let's do it, then. Let her know we need to see her."

And then, gods help them all.

Chapter 27

Everyone was there.

Everything was in place.

Eva, with Logan at her side, sat curled up in a blanket in Thanatos's great leather chair—a relic he'd maintained for a gazillion years. Aleka knew the exact number, but Scotty had never listened to the boring stories from the past that all her relatives seemed to delight in sharing.

All four *Horsepeople*, as Wraith called them, stood near the head of the great hall's dining table, and Idess had placed Scotty, along with her cousins Amber and Leilani, at the four corners.

The bowl of dried blood Wraith and Serena had procured sat in the center of the table, where Aleka, Raika, and Idess had placed a bunch of mystical crap that, again, Scotty didn't care about. Dried herbs, vessels containing various-colored liquids, some crystals, a shard of bone, and a couple of bowls of stinky organic matter Scotty didn't ask about, because, ugh, *just get on with it, already.*

"Everyone," Aleka called out. "We're starting. We need you all to step straight back but remain relative to your positions at the table. It's possible that if this goes wrong, there could be an explosion."

An explosion?

No one seemed overly concerned, so Scotty leaned against the archway between the kitchen and the living room and waited for her sister, Raika, and Idess to do whatever it was they were going to do.

It started with chanting—Idess in an ancient angelic language, and

Aleka in a Sheoulic dialect. Then little fires sparked in the organic matter. Aleka poured liquids into the stinky bowls while Raika, her eyes glowing garnet, watched. They mixed stuff and chanted, and it was all so banal…until the dried blood in the big bowl began to liquify and bubble.

Raika, arms outstretched and palms up, pivoted to face Eva.

Suddenly, an oppressive thickness settled over them, and everything went still.

Except Raika's hair, which whipped around as if she were caught in a windstorm.

Eva gasped, and curiously, Scotty felt a weird tug in her chest. As if something inside her was being pulled.

"It's working," Raika rasped, lifting her palms higher as Eva's head fell back, her mouth open as if in a scream, but nothing came out.

Nothing that Scotty could see, anyway.

Logan clung to Eva, his expression a mask of worry and fear, his eyes bloodshot and glistening with unshed tears. Poor guy—

Pain, as if a fist or an alien had punched through her rib cage from inside, absolutely wrecked Scotty. She couldn't breathe, couldn't cry out, couldn't even collapse to the floor. She just stood, frozen, as a sensation of losing a part of herself, like an organ—maybe her heart—held her in place.

Then it was over, and she slumped back against the wall, exhausted and shaking, just as Eva collapsed into the chair, her head tucked against Logan's chest.

The blood in the bowl sloshed upward, spinning into a funnel that made grotesque wet sounds. It started to form limbs, a vaguely female form…a head.

It rose higher and higher, becoming more recognizable as a female. Long hair, slim waist, breasts.

Harvester.

"No!"

Reseph's roar drowned out the wet, squishy sounds. Scotty wheeled around in time to see him charging the partially formed body, his summoned sword raised, poised to lop off the head.

"Kill her!" he screamed.

Limos blocked his path. He wheeled hard to the right, only to get tackled by Ares and Thanatos. They took him to the floor, Thanatos pinning his shoulders and Ares straddling his legs.

"It's not Harvester's blood!" Hatred burned in Reseph's eyes, his struggles growing more violent. "It's Lilith's!"

Oh, shit.

Scotty tasted bile as she looked at the figure. It was solid now, skin forming on the feet and spreading upward. The thing twisted and writhed, its eyes, now fully formed, gleamed with dark evil.

"I destroyed Harvester's blood," it said in a raspy hiss. "And now I will have her power and her—"

Scotty finished what her uncle had started. She hadn't even realized she'd moved until she stood there, her summoned blade dripping.

Lilith's nearly fully formed body turned to liquid, and her blood splashed to the floor.

For a few heartbeats, everyone stood still as the growing implications of what had just occurred sank in. They'd failed.

"How?" Aleka croaked. "How could this have happened?"

Ares helped Reseph to his feet. "Lilith must have found Harvester's blood before you did and swapped it for hers. She probably arranged for Wraith to find it exactly where and when she wanted him to."

"I don't understand," Aleka said. "What was her plan? Is she dead now?"

"No." Raika, her eyes and skin back to normal, crouched on the floor and dragged her finger through a splash of blood. "Harvester's Grace mixed with Lilith's blood, and she was controlling it from afar. Like an avatar. The plan was probably to join it with her physical body. The power Lilith would have wielded..."

Scotty didn't even want to let her mind go there. She turned, a bit unsteadily, to Eva. "How's she doing?"

Eva smiled weakly, her eyes still closed, her head still resting on Logan, who held her so tightly it was a wonder she could breathe. "I feel better. Tired, but better."

"So..." Limos absently rubbed her forearm, where the glyph of her hell stallion used to be. Scotty couldn't help but feel sorry for her. Like her brothers, Limos had been linked to her warhorse for thousands of years, and even though it had been a carnivorous monster, its death at Lilith's hands had been hard for Limos. "Where is Harvester's Grace?"

"I can't see it." Idess sounded worried. "I can feel it, though."

Aleka paled. "But we don't have Harvester's blood," she croaked. "We're done. She's gone."

A pall fell over the room as months of hope crashed and burned.

Tears stung Scotty's eyes, and exhaustion sapped her energy. She barely made it to the couch before her legs gave out.

"This can't be happening." She wished Blade and Mace were here.

She should have insisted that they be allowed to attend.

Raika studied the blood on her finger, fascinated by a drop that dripped down her knuckle. "Lilith just went to the top of my Most Wanted list."

"She wouldn't be on any list if your father had destroyed her soul instead of releasing her from Sheoul-gra," Scotty snapped.

Raika turned, her body taut, her expression unreadable. "I know."

Dammit. Scotty knew that what she'd said was unfair, but the pain was so raw that when she opened her mouth to apologize, all that came out was a sob.

"It's over," Aleka said numbly. "We've lost her forever. All we needed was a drop. Just…a drop." She covered her face and wept.

Scotty wanted to hug her sister, but Aleka spun and rushed for the door.

"Wait!" Reseph caught Aleka by the elbow. "I think I can help."

Scotty leaped to her feet. Well, she tried, but she felt so slow. This was hitting her hard. "How, Uncle Reseph?"

He swallowed. Looked down at his boots. "When I was Pestilence…" He took a deep, ragged breath. "Pestilence drank a lot of blood. It's how I knew Lilith was here tonight. Some blood splashed on my mouth. I…tasted her."

The horrors her uncle had committed when his Seal had broken, unleashing the evil Horseman, Pestilence, upon the world, never stopped. Scotty had a hard time imagining him capable of some of those atrocities, but she knew they'd happened.

"I carry the blood of everyone Pestilence fed from inside me. Harvester…she was one of them. If Harvester's Grace can find it, I'll gladly drain my body of every drop."

With that, he slashed his arm open from elbow to wrist.

Idess let out a surprised breath, her gaze locked upward. "The Grace is forming again." As Reseph's blood poured out onto the floor, her gaze followed what Scotty assumed was Harvester's Grace. "It's swirling around Reseph. I think it's looking for what it needs."

As one wound healed, Reseph made another. And another. His slashes grew more vicious with every slice of his blade.

"Reseph?" Scotty stepped toward him, but Limos snagged her shoulder.

"Don't," she said quietly.

"But—" Holy shit, he was literally hacking at his arm now. His expression was one of pure anguish, and his eyes burned with unholy hatred. Hatred of himself. On his knife arm, his stallion raged, the glyph bucking and kicking. "What's happening?"

"Something that's been coming for a long, long time."

"I don't understand."

Her father's hand came down on her other shoulder. He looked sad, but he made no move to stop his brother. "He's purging his sins. One of them, anyway."

Reseph crashed to his knees in the rapidly expanding pool of blood. Head bent, he sagged, the knife falling from his fingers. Blood ran from dozens of wounds in his arm, on his torso, and even his chest. How many times had he stabbed himself? How much pain was he in, both physically and mentally?

"Idess?" The layered, 3D tats on Thanatos's throat writhed as he looked over at Mace's mom. "What's happening?"

"It's circling," she murmured to no one in particular. "Circling…"

Suddenly, a thin stream of blood rose into the air the way it had earlier. Anxiety shot through Scotty. Last time, Lilith had tried to steal Harvester's Grace. Now, Scotty was afraid to hope. Afraid to be crushed once again.

Please, please let this work.

The form took shape. Scotty held her breath as the skin began to solidify. Long, black hair flowed down its back, growing longer…just as it had when Lilith appeared.

But as the facial structure solidified, Scotty couldn't hold back her excitement.

"Harvester," she whispered. "It's her. It's really her."

Harvester's limp body lowered to the floor. For a heart-stopping moment, there was silence. Stillness. Not a single twitch or breath.

And then she took a huge gulp of air.

They all rushed her, laughing, cheering. Crying.

She opened her eyes, taking each of them in in turn, but when she got to Reseph, on his knees next to her, the color drained from his face, his blue eyes tortured, she paused. Their gazes met. She reached up, her hand trembling, and placed her palm on his cheek.

"I forgive you," she murmured. "I forgive you."

Chapter 28

Scotty was both exhausted and excited as she headed to the compound. She couldn't wait to tell Blade and Mace about Eva and Harvester. She'd have gone straight to their place, even if they hadn't sent her a message saying they wanted to see her.

She wished she'd been able to spend more time with her grandma, but Harvester had passed out shortly after being reconstituted, and everyone agreed that she should get some rest before they overwhelmed her with questions and hugs.

The important thing was that Eva would live. By the time Scotty left, she looked better than she had in weeks. Unfortunately, she was also back to being mortal.

They'd find a way to fix that, though. Surely, Harvester would help, once she was up and running again.

Even though it was well after midnight, Scotty found the guys on the well-lit basketball court, shooting hoops with Crux, who spotted her first and shot her a big grin.

"Hi, Scotty!" He loped over to her, enthusiasm radiating off every inch of his tall, gangly body. He wasn't looking forward to his transition, but she knew he'd be pleased with what would happen to his physique. "Wanna play? We can do two-on-two. You and me against those two jerks."

"Another time," she said, wishing she wasn't drop-dead tired. "I need to talk to the *two jerks*."

Crux shrugged, then smiled again. "Tomorrow?"

"We'll see."

That seemed to satisfy him, and he took off for the house, leaving her with the guys. Dressed in shorts and tees that showed off sinewy muscles and rock-hard bods, they moved toward her with smooth, lethal grace that reminded her of predators.

A mere week ago, she'd have thought nothing of how incredibly sexy they were, but now, all she could do was remember how they touched. Kissed. Licked.

And she wanted more.

Gods, how was she supposed to survive the next assignment with them if she imagined them naked every time she looked at them?

Sex with them was supposed to fix things—and it had. But it also created new problems.

Like perma-lust.

They'd awakened something inside her. They'd introduced her to new sensations and emotions, and they'd forever altered how she would look at them. They were still friends, closer than ever, but now, she saw them as lovers too.

Swallowing dryly, she met them at the edge of the court.

"Everything went great," she said, and they both looked relieved. "Well, Lilith tried to interfere, but we sent her packing."

Blade tossed the ball into the storage bin. "How the hell did Lilith get involved?"

"Long story," she said, nearly buckling under a new wave of exhaustion. "I'll tell you later." Casually, she reached out and braced herself against a nearby bench. "What's important is that Eva is going to be fine, and Harvester is back."

"Did she say what happened?" Mace plucked a couple of hand towels off the bench and tossed one to Blade. "What's going on in Heaven? Where's Reaver? Is there going to be—?"

"I can't answer any of that. She only said a couple of words before she passed out. Than and Regan are keeping an eye on her. They'll let everyone know when she wakes up."

Blade wiped his face and then scrubbed the towel through his sweat-dampened hair. "Awesome news. I've been worried about Eva, and I'm glad you have your grandmother back."

"Me, too." Mace gestured toward the back door. "Wanna come inside? We need to talk to you about something."

"Oh." She frowned. "I thought your message was about the ritual."

"It was," Blade tossed his towel onto the bench. "But we also wanted to talk to you."

Mace shifted his weight, the way he always did when something became uncomfortable. "We can do it later. She looks tired."

Scotty didn't care how tired she was. She needed to know what was going on. "Talk to me. I'll sleep later."

They exchanged glances, and a sinking sensation filled her belly. She wasn't going to like this, was she?

When they just stood there, waiting for the other one to speak, she prodded them. "What's going on? You're freaking me out."

"It was Blade's idea," Mace blurted. "But I think he's right."

"Okaaaay…" Now, she was *really* freaked out.

Blade took a deep breath. "I…well, *we*…want, I mean, after being with you, we both, uh, well—"

"Oh, for fuck's sake," Mace broke in. "We're in love with you, Scotty. Both of us."

Stunned, Scotty just stood there, not quite comprehending. But as Mace's words sank in, her strength flagged, and she sat heavily on the bench. What was she supposed to feel right now? She wanted to be happy, but this didn't seem to be a happy moment. The guys looked troubled.

Questions. She had so many questions.

"Why are you telling me this?" She barely heard herself speak through the roar of activity in her brain. Heck, she didn't even know if that was the question she should have started with. She seemed to be operating on autopilot.

"Because we need you to choose," Blade said. At what must have been her confused expression, he elaborated. "Choose one of us."

She blinked at them, still not understanding what was happening. Heck, she hadn't even finished processing what Mace had said yet. Then, her brain caught up, and she surged to her feet, ignoring the sudden wave of vertigo.

"Are you guys crazy? What is *wrong* with you? I'm not choosing!"

They both looked baffled. "Why not?" they asked in unison.

Had they always been this dense, or was it a new affliction? "Did you think this through at all? What happens when one of you has to see me with the other one? Imagine seeing us cuddled up on the couch watching movies, or kissing goodbye, or…whatever. I mean, really?"

"Better than seeing you doing any of that with someone else," Blade said. "We can't watch that."

"I thought it was nuts at first too," Mace admitted. "But the last week and a half has been a clusterfuck, and we managed to get through it. We're in a good place now, all of us, and—"

"Exactly," she said. "We're in a good place. Why ruin that?"

"We wouldn't be ruining anything," Blade said. "We'll be saving us."

Had she crossed into another dimension or something? Should she look around for that crystal Dare had been on the hunt for? Because seriously, what was wrong with these two?

"I suppose you want me to flip a coin or some shit." She jammed her fists on her hips instead of using them to strangle the idiots. "And did it occur to you that maybe I don't want *either* of you?"

There were the baffled looks again. As if they couldn't even conceive of the idea that she might not want to be with one of them.

Gods help her, she *did* want to be with them, but that was the problem. She wanted them both equally. And there was no way that could work. Temporarily, maybe, but at some point, they'd need to take mates, or they'd go insane after their next transition. Which meant, again, she'd have to choose which one to keep. There was no way in hell she could choose just one.

So, it had to be *none*.

"I won't do it," she said.

Blade nodded solemnly. "Then when Kynan gets back from the conference, I'm going to request a transfer to another unit."

Mace and Scotty both wheeled around to Blade, and she wondered if she looked as shocked as Mace did. "What?"

Fists clenched at his sides, Blade closed his eyes and took a deep breath. When he opened them again, they swirled with shadows.

"I've spent too long pretending I wasn't in love with you, Scotty," he said, and his words—and the vulnerability behind them—plucked at her heart and made tears sting her eyes. "I told myself I didn't care if you dated, but I seriously wanted to kill Jon and Skoll every time they looked at you. The idea of one of them…" He shook his head. "I can't work like this anymore."

He started for the stairs, the finality in his words and body language sending a stab of panic through her. She couldn't lose him. She couldn't.

"Blade." She grabbed his arm, but he refused to look at her, keeping his gaze on his destination. "Give us a chance. Please. Our team has been through a lot. We can get through this."

"Can we?" he asked softly. "Because I'm not so sure anymore." Gently, he freed himself from her grip and took the stairs two at a time, every footfall sounding like a death knell.

"I can't believe this." Blood throbbed through her every pulse point as the fear of losing everything gripped her. "What about you, Mace? Do you want to get transferred?"

Suddenly, he was inches from her face, her hands in his. Heat flared in his eyes, little flecks of gold that seemed to wax and wane to the beat of her heart.

"I want the same thing Blade wants," he said softly, with a hint of breathlessness. "You. Gods, Scotty, I want you so bad it hurts. And so does Blade. You can make one of us happy."

The tears in her eyes spilled over, burning hot, miserable paths down her cheeks. "And destroy the other one," she rasped.

"No." He leaned in, his heat scorching her as his lips touched her cheek, kissing away one of the tears. "You would set them free."

Her throat closed as he drew back, his gaze searching her face. For what, she didn't know. All she knew was that she'd never been in so much misery.

"I want to kiss you," he said, his voice deep, husky, tortured. "But I won't take anything from Blade."

So. Many. Feels.

Overwhelmed by this—by *everything*—she wheeled away from Mace with a cry, her eyes burning with unshed tears.

"Scotty—"

"Go!" she cried. "Just go."

He stood there.

"I said, go!"

"Uh, this is my home…"

At her glare, he grinned, that playful scamp grin he'd perfected to disarm females, and she fell for it. She fucking fell for it when she'd always rolled her eyes at other females when they did the same thing.

Angry with herself, she glared harder.

"Okay, okay, I'll go." He jerked his thumb toward the back door. "See you later."

He took off with a cocky swagger, and he didn't look back. Just gave her the space she'd demanded. Irrationally.

A wave of dizziness washed over her, and she sank onto the bench. She tried to look around at the yard, where she'd spent countless hours swimming in the pool and playing tennis with Blade and Mace, but she couldn't see through her tears.

Would they ever be able to hang out like that again?

She had a feeling she knew the answer, and she wanted to vomit.

She had to get out of here. Needed to scream or cry or—

Her wrist comms vibrated, and a message popped up. It was from Amber.

Harvester is awake. She wants to see you. And she's acting weird, so hurry, okay?

Closing her eyes, Scotty thanked the Fates. She'd needed a distraction, and this was perfect.

Tell her I'm on my way.

Harvester was waiting for Scotty inside Thanatos's library, a gothic-themed monstrosity that suited a Horseman called Death. Suited Harvester too. She might be an angel, but she liked to say that she had especially dirty wings.

G-ma was so funny.

"Grandma!" Scotty threw herself at Harvester and sank into her hug. "I still can't believe you're back."

Harvester laughed and drew away, but something about her subdued manner made Scotty's alarm bells chime. "If not for you and your sister, I wouldn't be." She frowned. "You've been crying. Why?"

Because I'm in a no-win situation, and I'm about to lose my team and at least one of my best friends.

The thought threatened to bring back the tears, but she ruthlessly shoved the problem aside for the moment. Right now, her grandma was back, Eva was safe, and there was too much to celebrate.

Her father had taught her that.

"No matter how badly you lose the battle, no matter how much you lose in blood and treasure, celebrate everything, every chance you have. Celebrating even minor triumphs is a step forward during times when you've slid backward. Morale matters."

"It's nothing, G," Scotty said. "I'm just tired." As if to prove the point, a wave of exhaustion hit her, making her sway hard enough that she had to brace her hands on Thanatos's desk. Instantly, Harvester whisked her to a chair.

"Sit," she ordered. "I'll get you some water."

Scotty waved her off. "It's okay. I'm fine." But it was weird. As an immortal, she felt exhaustion, but usually only after serious physical activity or days without sleep.

Harvester, wearing one of Regan's black sweatshirts and pink sweatpants with the word *Hot* on the ass, scrutinized Scotty for so long she started to squirm. "When did it start?"

Scotty shrugged. "It was the ceremony to bring you back. It really wiped me out. Probably wiped all of us."

"Did you feel anything odd? Like a tug?" The concern in Harvester's expression made the alarm bells chime louder. "Or like something was being pulled out of you?"

Um, yeah. "How did you know?"

Closing her eyes, Harvester sank down in the chair next to her. "Oh, Scotty."

The alarm bells were no longer chiming. They were clanging. "G? What's going on?"

Harvester took her hand, and Scotty's gut sank. Nothing good would come of this conversation. "You probably don't remember much of this, but when you were little, you were attacked and nearly killed by demons…"

Harvester continued, each word leaving Scotty reeling in shock, even as they knocked loose memories she hadn't known existed.

The Harrowgate.

A new memory clawed at her mind. "I opened a gate for the demons. But it wasn't the island gate. That was the day I learned to open gates with my blood. Lilu—she was my invisible friend, wasn't she?" More memories crashed through her mind in a flood. "Holy shit, Lilu told me how to open the gate, and it let all those demons through! *That's* why I hate opening gates." Twenty-five years of stress over opening gates was finally explained. But she had so many more questions. "What the hell, Harvester? Why did you take away my memories? Do my parents know what happened? Do they know I didn't remember any of it?"

"I didn't *take away* your memories," she said with a defensive sniff. "I just…buried them a little. I wanted them accessible if anyone ever brought it up. And yes, your parents know what happened."

"What about Lilu? Who was she?" Scotty racked her brain, searching for answers. "She must have been a demon."

"Not *a* demon. *The* demon. It was Lilith," Harvester said. "I suspect she was behind several attacks on your cousins, as well."

Of course! "The *tempestus* demon that attacked Logan when he was little."

"And, I believe, the attack at the theme park that killed Chaos."

Scotty blinked. "Blade's little brother? What would Lilith have against Blade's family?"

"I don't believe they were the target. Logan was at the park with them."

Holy shit. Chaos's death had wrecked the entire Seminus clan and caused a huge rift between Stryke and his family that lasted for decades. It wasn't until just a few months ago that the healing had begun…for everyone except Blade. There was still a lot of tension strung between the two brothers.

"All this time, we believed it was a random demon incursion." They happened all the time. Hence, the existence of The Aegis and DART. "Why are you telling me all this now?"

"Because one of the demons that attacked you that day was a *mordaemon*."

"A *mordaemon*? Why have I never heard of those?"

"They're very rare, and like the *tempestus* demon that attacked Logan, they're usually restricted to the demon realm. They feed off only one thing. Immortality."

"Meaning…?"

"They steal immortality from immortals."

Scotty shuddered in horror. "Nasty critters. But I'm still immortal, so obviously it starved that day, right?"

"I wish. Oh, how I wish." Harvester's voice, normally forceful and confident, often a bit vicious, caught on little jags of emotion, and a tremor of foreboding shot up Scotty's spine. G-ma wasn't one to get emotional. She hoarded her feelings the way orcs hoarded enemy skulls. "I didn't get to you in time, darling. It took your immortality."

No. That wasn't possible. Scotty would have been dead a million times over if that was the case. Harvester was confused. She'd just been reassembled from a drop of blood and a few miracles, so of course, she wasn't all there.

"You almost died," Harvester continued, her eyes glistening with unshed tears. "We nearly lost you."

"Well, obviously I didn't die, so my immortality is just fine—"

"No." Harvester reached out and gripped Scotty's arm. "I gave you a tiny bit of my Grace. Enough to restore your immortality."

Whoa. Okay, so the demon *had* gotten a meal that day. Scotty sagged into her chair. This was a lot to deal with. "Why didn't you tell me?"

"Because what I did is forbidden. But it doesn't matter now." The emotional warble was back in Harvester's voice, and once again, fear gripped Scotty in its icy fingers. "When Raika's incantation drew my Grace out of Eva…it drew it out of you as well."

Oh, gods.

Without Harvester's Grace, Scotty was no longer immortal. Her supernatural healing abilities would be affected, too, maybe even nullified. How could she do her job now? How could she fight demons and protect her team?

"Can't you give me the Grace back?"

"No," Harvester rasped. "I'm cut off from Heaven. I might as well be an Unfallen. I have no powers, no ability to transfer Grace to you."

Panic frayed the edges of Scotty's control. "Heaven could be closed off for decades! Centuries, even!" This was a disaster, and not just for her. "What about you? How are you going to get Reaver out of his prison if you can't get into Heaven?"

"We'll worry about your grandfather and me later. Right now, we need to buy you some time," Harvester said, sounding more like her usual self, now that she was in planning mode. "You can bond with something that will lend you its life force or lifespan. One of your mother's hellhounds, perhaps."

Scotty recoiled. "Those disgusting things? No way." There wasn't even a guarantee that it would work. Not everyone had the genetic makeup required to communicate properly with the beasts. Scotty's mind spun as she contemplated her new reality. "I'll just be extra careful until you get your powers back—"

"You said it yourself. It could be decades."

Okay, sure, that would put a dent in her career plans, but she could manage. Maybe she could take more of a supportive role on the team. She wasn't sure how that would work, but the idea of giving up everything wasn't acceptable.

"But we don't *know* it'll be decades," Scotty said. "Heaven could open its gates in a couple of weeks. I say we play it by ear."

Her grandmother spun away, but not before Scotty saw a tear fall. A tear. In all of Scotty's years, she'd never seen Harvester cry.

"G-ma?" Scotty pushed to her feet, alarmed by how shaky her legs were. "What is it? What's wrong?"

"When the *mordaemon*s take immortality from someone, it drains their life force too. My Grace plugged the drain. But now that it's gone…"

"I'm dying." Scotty caught herself on the back of a chair as a wave of nausea crashed over her. "I am, aren't I?" she croaked. "How much time do I have?" When Harvester didn't answer, Scotty's blood congealed in her veins. "G-ma?"

Very slowly, Harvester turned to her, her face pale and streaked with tears. "Days, darling. You only have days."

Chapter 29

When Scotty finally left Harvester, her first instinct was to go to her mom.

Scotty had always been a daddy's girl, and as Aleka liked to say, Scotty was their father's *mini-me*. To be fair, Aleka was their mother's.

From the moment Scotty could talk, she'd followed Ares around, asking questions about battle tactics, weapons, and combat. Then she'd try to impress him by setting up intricate battle plans using plastic army men. Or set traps around the house and island—balloons filled with glitter that would explode on the victim…fun stuff like that. The violet fur dye that splashed all over one of the Ramreels had not been met with humor, however. But Ares *did* give her points for creativity.

And while Scotty practiced swordplay and setting traps, Aleka helped their mom cook and assisted with her veterinary work. They had tea parties and took field trips to museums. *So boring!*

But even though Scotty preferred hanging out with her father, it was her mother she wanted when she was sick or hurt. It was her mother's hugs and soup that made things better.

Unfortunately, comfort food and cuddles wouldn't fix Scotty's mortality problem. More importantly, she didn't want her parents to know about it. They'd freak. Justifiably, yes, but there would be crying—and terror—and then her mom would be searching for a hellhound to bond with Scotty. Ugh. No. A hellhound was a last resort.

She'd have to come up with another plan, though. And fast.

Harvester gave her twelve hours to solve her problem. If she failed, G-ma was going straight to Ares and Cara.

But the solution was obvious.

She'd have to bond with either Mace or Blade.

And then she'd lose the other.

Somehow, she kept herself from crying as she messaged them, asking them to meet her in the pavilion in their backyard. She'd always loved the outdoor space, lit with strings of fairy lights and decorated with hanging and potted plants, some of them from the demon realm. The octagonal space offered a great view of the pool and the manicured garden paths across the acres of land that made up the complex.

She used to wonder why Stryke, who spent ninety-nine percent of his life indoors and hated water, had created such beautiful surroundings. Especially when the buildings were sterile and industrial, given character only by all the males who had lived here over the years.

But recently, she'd visited the new StryTech complex in downtown Sydney, and the amenities put this place to shame. Coffee shops, grocery stores, food carts, and even hair salons. Turned out Stryke knew the importance of keeping his employees happy. Who would have thought?

She waited impatiently in the pavilion, her stomach churning when Mace and Blade started down the path. They were both in sweats and T-shirts, Mace in flip-flops and Blade barefoot.

"Is everything okay?" Blade hurried up the steps. "How's Harvester?"

"She's fine," she said, and they both seemed relieved, if confused about why they were here. "This is about earlier."

Now, they looked nervous. She could relate. Her anxiety had her playing with her hair, chewing on her lip, and she even caught herself pacing in circles around the firepit at the center of the pavilion.

"Did you make a decision?" Mace asked quietly.

She shook her head, still pacing. "You guys asked me to choose. But choose what? What are we talking about here? Casual dating and sex? A permanent relationship? Or—?"

"A bond," Blade said. "We know each other too well, and we've been together too long to waste time." He gestured to Mace. "He might feel differently, but I want a mate."

I want that too.

She wanted to say that. Wanted to say it to both of them. But where did Mace stand? Maybe she wouldn't be forced to make a choice after all.

Mace's gaze burned into hers, and she knew his answer wouldn't make this any easier. "I'm in line with Blade on this. When I know I want something, I want it all, and I want it *now*. You know me. Instant gratification."

Her heart swelled with the purest kind of happiness. So much love filled her…to the point of hurting. Because the truth was that she would only be able to have half of what she wanted.

But how was she supposed to make the decision? Maybe she didn't have to. She could shove this problem at *them*, and she knew exactly how to force their hands.

Her father had taught her to fight dirty, and she was about to get into the mud.

Mace held his breath.

He and Blade had both asked Scotty to make a lifelong commitment to them, just hours after telling her to make a decision that would change all their lives.

"I said I wasn't going to choose." Scotty finally stopped pacing. She squared off in front of them, crossed her arms in that stubborn way of hers, and said, "And I'm still not going to. You are."

Mace and Blade looked at each other. What kind of crap was that?

"That's…not going to happen," Blade said.

"Agreed," Mace chimed in. "Also, does this mean that you actually *do* want us?"

She huffed. "Of course, I want you. I've wanted you since before we made the stupid pact. But I can't possibly make a choice. And here's the thing." She clasped her hands in front of her so fiercely that her knuckles turned white. "Apparently, I'm no longer immortal."

"What?" Mace and Blade both blurted, but before they could ask anything else, she held up her hand, silencing them.

"It's a long story, and I don't feel like telling it right now. But what it comes down to is that, not only am I mortal, but I'm also actively dying. Harvester suggested bonding with a hellhound."

It wasn't often that Mace was speechless, but right now, he had no words. Thankfully, Blade was not stricken by the same affliction.

"If you bond with one of us, you'll get our lifespan. And in five hundred years, when we die, you can still bond with a hellhound."

The sadness in her eyes made Mace want to pull her close, and he suspected that Blade was having the same thoughts. "I told you, I can't choose. So, either you guys choose, or I'll pick a smelly hellhound."

Fuck that. "What if there's another way?

"I'm all ears," she prompted.

Gods, he couldn't believe he was going to say it. "I've heard there's a way to let fate decide."

Scotty and Blade frowned, but he figured it out a heartbeat later. "The bonding ritual."

Mace nodded. "The three of us could engage in the bonding ritual. Fate would decide who to bond Scotty with."

Scotty's freckled face turned beet-red. "You mean…?" She swallowed, probably attempting to make her voice less squeaky. "You mean, all three of us at the same time? Like, simultaneously?"

"Yeah." It would be the last time with Scotty for one of them, and the beginning of a lifetime with her for the other.

Blade's gaze flipped between Mace and Scotty and then settled on the wooden deck. "I'm in."

"So am I," Mace said.

Scotty stood there, cheeks burning, both hope and fear glistening in her eyes. "Me, too." Her voice was quiet, but steady. "When?"

Mace shrugged. "I'm free now."

"Now?" Panic replaced the hope in her gaze. "I can't. I need…I don't know. I just need some time. A shower. I'm not sure—"

Blade, always the steady one, stepped into her, gripping her upper arm with one hand and tilting up her face with the other in a gesture so tender that Mace could almost feel the love and trust flowing between them. And the thing was, he wasn't jealous. The exact opposite. This was the way it should be.

His grandfather, Azagoth, had once told him that all beings walked paths full of crossroads, shortcuts, and dead ends. He said the right way wasn't always clear, but there would be signs to guide you if you just paid attention. Well, Mace was paying attention. Probably for the first time in his life.

"Do what you need to do," Blade murmured to Scotty. "Then let the Fates decide. No matter what, we will both be here for you. Always."

Very gently, he dipped his head and touched his lips to her cheek. Scotty reached for Mace, pulling him close, and because it seemed like the right move, he kissed her other cheek.

She smiled at each of them and stepped away. "Give me an hour."

One hour. It sounded like forever away. And also, too soon.

In one hour, all their lives would be very, very different.

Chapter 30

One hour later, Blade met Scotty at the back door, his stomach in knots, his palms sweating. He couldn't remember being this nervous in his entire life. To be fair, though, the sexual suppressant left him strung out and shaky, which made his anxiety worse. He was at the very limits of the suppressant's effectiveness, and if not for Scotty, he'd be forced to summon Masumi in the next couple of hours.

With any luck, after tonight, he'd never have to hunt for sex partners or summon Masumi again. He'd be bonded with Scotty and wouldn't so much as think about another female for the rest of his life.

Scotty stepped inside, looking incredible in a black miniskirt, a green-and-black-striped tank top, and high-heeled boots that made her muscular calves into art. She usually wore her fiery mane in a ponytail, but now, her shiny waves flowed down around her shoulders as if begging for him to take them in his fist.

He'd dressed up too, just a little. Instead of tactical pants, jeans, or leather pants, he'd put on black slacks, the ones he'd worn to his mother's birthday party a few months ago. He'd been able to remove the bloodstains from his beatdown with Stryke, at least. Not so with the shirt he'd worn. So, tonight, he'd thrown on a new one he'd purchased… burgundy, Scotty's favorite color, but one she swore she couldn't wear because her coloring was wrong.

Whatever that meant. She looked good in any color. And in nothing at all.

"Hey," he said.

"Hey." She fidgeted as he closed the door, messing with her fingernails and playing with her hair. She was about as anxious as he'd ever seen her. *Join the club.* "Where's Mace?"

"Come on." Blade took her hand, giving it a comforting squeeze as he led her to the staircase. "Mace will join us in a few minutes."

His heart pounded as they climbed the stairs, but at the mezzanine at the top, instead of taking a left toward his and Mace's rooms, he took a right. Scotty gave him a confused glance, but it wasn't until he opened the door to one of the spare suites that she finally asked a question.

"What's going on?" She stepped inside the room, lit by candles for a soft glow. Soothing music played in the background, and on the table, a bottle of champagne chilled in a bucket of ice. Three glasses sat nearby.

Blade ignored her question as he popped the champagne cork and poured two glasses.

"Blade?" She narrowed her eyes at him. "You didn't murder Mace or chain him up or anything, right?"

Laughing, he handed her a glass. "He's in his room, and no, he isn't duct-taped to a chair. We agreed to do this in a neutral place, and he wanted us to have some time alone."

"Really? Why?"

Blade had asked Mace the same thing when he'd brought it up. Mace's answer had only reinforced Blade's love and respect for the guy. Truly, if fate chose Mace, Blade wouldn't question it. He'd be wrecked, for sure. But he would also know that Scotty was with a male she deserved.

"Because we didn't get that in Alaska," Blade replied. "I didn't get the chance to date and seduce you the way you deserved." He clinked his glass against hers. "So, this is me seducing you."

Flares of pink spread across her cheeks, and her lashes fluttered, making soft shadows play under her eyes as she glanced, almost shyly, down at her glass. "You don't have to do that, you know."

Gods, he wanted to wrap her in his arms and protect her from everything. She might be brash, hardcore, and as tough as a lava beast's scales in a fight, but she was utterly defenseless in matters of relationships.

"Yeah, I do." There was a humiliating hitch in his voice, but he had more important things to worry about. "I might not ever be able to do it again."

The reminder of how much was riding on this night threatened to bring him to his knees, but he put his meltdown on hold because nothing was going to ruin this. Nothing.

Her hand shook as she took a delicate sip of her bubbly, leaving a single drop on her bottom lip. Slowly, because she looked like she was ready to bolt, he reached out and caught the sparkly drop with his thumb. Her lids flicked up in surprise as he took her glass, set it and his down, and swept her into his arms. Her soft, feminine gasp hit him in the heart as he pulled her to the center of the room, which he and Mace had turned into a dance floor.

"What are we doing?" Scotty looked up at him with big, beautiful eyes that he could peer into for the rest of his life.

He moved against her, easing her into a slow sway to the rhythm of the music. "Did you know I like dancing?"

Those gorgeous eyes flared. "I know everything about you, and somehow, I didn't know that."

Her lips, still damp from the champagne, drew his gaze. He was parched, his body wrung out from days of injections, and he was tired of behaving. Of being a gentleman. But at the same time, Scotty was mortal now, and no matter how desperate he was to have her, he needed to stay in control.

It wouldn't be easy. Something inside him wanted to fight for what it wanted. It recognized his mate, and it wanted her with a savage ferocity that borderline frightened him. Having grown up in the human realm, he'd muffled his baser self and rarely felt like the demon he was.

Now, the demon wanted out, and it wanted him to claim her. Quickly, before Mace got in the way.

He growled softly, a warning to himself. *Keep that demon restrained.*

Then, slowly, so slowly, he lowered his head and kissed her, a light, controlled brush of the lips, but it ramped up his libido faster than if she'd been naked.

"It's my little secret." So secret, in fact, that he only practiced with Masumi.

"I love that about you," she whispered against his lips. "Show me more."

He'd show her anything she asked for. He'd crack his chest open and show her his heart if that's what she wanted.

He twirled her around the room, their feet moving in sync as he held her close, his eyes locked on hers. She caught on quickly, and by the third song, they danced as if they'd been doing it forever.

They swung past the table, and without breaking stride, he swept up their glasses.

"To the future," he murmured, tapping his glass against hers.

Take her. Bond with her now!

The primal need to make her his nearly made him stumble. He'd been hard from the moment she walked through the door, but now, his cock ached where it was pinned between their bodies but still not close enough to her.

As much as he didn't want his private time with Scotty to end, if Mace didn't get here soon—

There was a light tap at the door, and Blade was torn between being relieved and disappointed.

"Come in," she called out, and Blade reluctantly pulled away from her.

As she greeted Mace, Blade poured another glass of champagne.

"Thanks, man." Mace took the flute, looking uncomfortable as hell in gray slacks and an untucked, black button-down. Blade had always liked dressing up, but Mace was a jeans-and-T-shirt guy to the bone.

The music became unnaturally loud as they stood there, all kinds of awkwardness winging between them. Scotty fidgeted with her glass, Mace drained his, and Blade just concentrated on the growing need throbbing in his groin.

"Is this weird?" Mace asked. "Because it feels weird."

Scotty laughed, though not a nervous laugh. It was genuine delight, and whatever anxiety Blade had felt for the last hour melted away.

"If it didn't feel weird," she said, "*that* would be weird." Boldly, she set down her glass and swung around to them. "Do you guys remember what Dad taught us about handling an awkward situation?"

"Either extract yourself from it..." Blade began.

"...or confront it and take control before it gets *out* of control," Mace finished. "Also, bringing up your murder-machine of a father at this exact moment is not the sexy flex you might have been going for."

She laughed again, and Blade revised his earlier thought about her being defenseless when it came to relationships. She'd just grabbed the reins of this one, and Blade would let her lead him anywhere.

"So, let's confront this," she said. "Battle plan. First, I take off Blade's clothes. Then I take off Mace's." Crossing her arms over her chest, she looked at them in turn, practically daring them to argue. No, ma'am, that wasn't going to happen. "Then you both strip me."

Blade's mouth went so dry he splashed more champagne into his glass and chugged it. "Then what?" he croaked.

"I'm guessing we'll have figured it out by then." Scotty came to him, her hips swinging, her hard nipples pressing against her top, and Blade was practically panting by the time she stopped in front of him and started on his shirt buttons.

He kicked off his shoes as she slid his shirt off his shoulders, her soft hands leaving tingles wherever they brushed his hypersensitive skin. When she got to his pants, a tremor of anticipation went through him, and he hissed when her knuckles brushed his shaft as she shoved the slacks and his boxers down his hips.

Slowly, she went down to her knees in front of him, and he was pretty sure the brush of her cheek against his cock on her way down was intentional. Clenching his fists at his sides, he waited for her to finish with his pants and socks. As she returned to her feet, her cheek caressed him again, and he had to bite back a groan of pure, hot lust.

Then, with a flirty grin, she repeated the ritual with Mace.

Amazingly, Blade didn't feel even a shred of jealousy, not even when his inner demon demanded that he flip up her skirt and take her when she knelt to remove Mace's pants.

Patience. It'll be worth waiting for.

But his patience had a limit, and he reached it the moment she was back on her feet.

Mace must have reached the same threshold because, in a coordinated sweep, they moved in, Mace going for her top, and Blade coming in from behind. He gripped her hips, intent on removing her skirt, but it felt too good to press into her, his erection cradled against her firm ass. Inhaling her spicy, feminine scent, he kissed her neck, nuzzling her nape as he slid one hand beneath the fabric of her skirt.

Her soft moan sent a shock of desire through him. He wanted to drag this out, to enjoy every single second, but anticipation had hijacked his senses, and he ground his cock into her, letting it slip beneath her skirt as his fingers breached the elastic of her panties.

She was wet already, and she arched into his touch. Mace swallowed her gasp with his mouth, kissing her as he removed her bra.

She made a sound of impatience and tried to shove down her skirt, but Mace gripped her wrists, pinning them to her abdomen.

"You said we get to undress you." His voice was dark, rough with restraint. "Let Blade do it."

"But he's *not* doing it."

The petulance in her voice made Blade smile as he nipped her skin and pushed a finger inside her tight heat. "So, you don't like this?"

"Yes," she moaned as she rode his hand. "So much."

"You should put her out of her misery." Mace flicked his tongue over one of her nipples. "I want to hear her come."

Blade wanted to *taste* it.

There'd been no time for that in Alaska. But there was time now. His cock twitched painfully, reminding him that there wasn't *much* time.

In a quick, coordinated surge, he moved in front of her as Mace moved behind. For a heartbeat, she seemed confused, but the moment Blade sank down on one knee, taking her skirt down with him, glorious understanding brightened her eyes.

She wants this.

He dragged his gaze down, from her plump, moist lips, past her breasts, which Mace was caressing from behind, to her slender waist, and finally, to the red vee of curls that made his inner demon wild.

Mace, ever Blade's wingman, gently nudged her feet apart with his, widening her stance and exposing her glorious, glistening flesh to Blade's hungry gaze. Gripping her upper thighs, he used his thumbs to open her even more, and when the tip of his tongue dipped between her swollen lips, she shouted his name.

And that was the end of his restraint.

He surged against her, lapping at her like he was starving. And he was. Starving for her. Starving for everything he could get for as long as he could get it. He penetrated her with his tongue and swirled it deep inside as Mace alternated gently caressing her breasts and pinching her nipples.

She was getting close, the air filling with her pheromones and the sexual energy sparking between them. Her panting breaths came faster, until they were little more than sharp gasps, and when he dragged his tongue through her slit to concentrate on her silky nub, she screamed the way Mace had wanted her to.

Her orgasm jacked Blade up, her unique zest making his tongue tingle and his body tighten.

He knew she'd be spicy.

In a surge of impatience, he shoved to his feet and swept her into his arms. He felt like a bit of a caveman as he hauled her to the bedroom and set her on the floor at the end of the king-size bed.

Mace tugged her against him, kissing her senseless as Blade climbed onto the mattress and fetched the knife from the bedside table. He and Mace had chosen the dagger, a gift from Reaver following their first training session with Scotty. The word *FATE* had been etched into the bone handle, and since fate would be choosing Scotty's mate, the dagger seemed appropriate.

"Are we ready?" Blade's voice was so ragged with lust and the gravity of the situation that he barely recognized it as his own.

Scotty nodded and held her hand out to him.

Taking it, he lay back on the bed and pulled her down on top of him. Gods, she was beautiful as she mounted him, her breasts swaying gently, playing peek-a-boo with her long, silky hair.

Mace stayed back, his gaze hot as she straddled Blade's hips. His shaft slid through her slick valley, and they both moaned as she rocked against him. He ran his palms up her muscular thighs, letting his thumbs slip between them to stroke the place he'd just tasted.

The entire time, her gaze was locked with his. This was what he'd missed in that cold, wet cave in Alaska. Because even though he'd felt their connection then, it wasn't like this. Her gorgeous eyes burned with intensity that went beyond lust. There was so much riding on this, not the least of which was her very life.

"I love you," he murmured. "No matter what happens tonight, I will give my life for you. And for Mace."

Her throat worked on a hard swallow, and her eyes grew misty. "Same." Her voice was husky and shredded by emotion. "No matter what, you will both always be part of me."

His heart clenched in a bittersweet reaction, but before he could go down a deflating path in his head, Scotty took him in her hand and guided him to her entrance.

"Yes," he whispered harshly, his pelvis rocking upward to meet her.

She was so ready for him, taking his head into her smooth, tight core.

Gods, he wasn't even inside her yet, and he was about to come.

Slowly, she lowered herself on him, and every inch was exquisite torture. Sensation spread from his cock to his chest, then to his extremities, wrapping him in erotic vibrations. It was as if their souls had touched, and suddenly, as she sat fully on him, he felt the most complete he'd ever felt. This was right. So right.

Fate *would* choose him. He knew it as surely as he knew his name.

Poor Mace.

He arched upward as possessive instinct took over. This female was his, soon to be awarded to him by the Fates themselves. He ran his hand up her waist, over her ribs, and to her breast, loving how she arched into his touch with a soft little gasp. But it was her hand he was after. He needed to twine his fingers with hers and begin the mating ritual.

Wait. Not yet.

Mace.

Scotty looked over her shoulder at the other male, a sultry invitation that would no doubt live in Mace's fantasies forever.

The ritual that would determine the course of their lives was about to begin.

Fuck, yeah.

Scotty giving him the *come-on* look was the sexiest thing Mace had ever seen.

They were really doing this. Two of them would walk away from the bed with a mate. The other would just walk away.

She held out her hand and beckoned him with half-lidded, desire-glazed eyes, and his incubus instincts overrode his reservations, disappearing them in a cloud of lust. He took her up on her invitation, let her lead him toward her, and as he stepped up to the mattress, she pulled him down for a kiss.

Her lips met his, gently at first, and then with growing urgency. Hungrily, he took her mouth, tangling his tongue with hers. At her moan, he positioned himself behind her as he kissed his way down her throat to the back of her neck. He wanted to bite her, to hold her steady when he entered her, but now wasn't the time.

Once they were mated, though…

A twinge of guilt managed to pierce his lust, but he ruthlessly shoved it down. He could deal with the fallout of fate giving him Scotty later. Because as much as he didn't want to see Blade hurt, he wanted this so badly right now.

His cock pressed into the small of her back, her smooth skin gliding against his as she rocked on Blade.

"Are you ready?" he whispered against her ear, and she nodded.

Blade reached over to the nightstand and tossed him a bottle of lube.

This is it.

His hand shook as he spread the silky liquid on his cock and then guided it to her rear entrance. Carefully, he pushed against the tight ring of resistance. "Relax, baby."

Blade must have done something to her because she cried out with a soft, "*Yes*," and released the tension in her muscles.

Mace nudged inside with slow, easy motions that took him a little deeper with each punch of his hips.

Gods, this was incredible, a rush of physical and emotional pleasure unlike anything he'd felt before. Love and mating hormones filled the room with a honeyed scent, and it was as if that honey flowed through his veins, as well. Right now, nothing but bliss existed.

Two of the most important people in his life were with him, sharing one of the most consequential moments a Seminus demon could experience.

He didn't want it to end. Ever.

"I love you so much, Mace," Scotty said, reaching back to caress his face, her slim fingers stroking his jaw. "You will always have part of my heart."

"Ditto," he croaked against her shoulder, cursing his lack of pretty words that would be appropriate right now.

Her hand dropped to Blade's face. She tilted her head, allowing Mace to nibble the curve of her shoulder unimpeded as she stroked Blade's bottom lip with her thumb.

"I love you too, Blade," she murmured. "So much. Part of my heart will always be yours."

"And you'll always have mine," Blade said roughly, managing to sound a lot less idiotic than Mace. Which was unusual, because Mace was usually the one accused of having a charmed tongue.

And a talented one.

Blade reached for the dagger next to him, and with a quick flick of his wrist, he nicked his sternum and handed the weapon to Mace.

"You need to taste us," Blade said, and Scotty didn't hesitate.

She bent forward, her hair spilling across Blade's chest as she swiped a drop with her tongue. Then she straightened and looked back at Mace, her eyes gleaming with greed. "Now you?"

Anything for her. She could take his blood from his jugular if she wanted. But he figured she'd settle for a little from his forearm.

He made a cut and then groaned when she cleaned it up with the tip of her tongue. He'd watched that tongue work on him before, and his body craved more. But too soon, Blade took her left hand in his right, and Scotty reached up with her right to twine Mace's fingers in hers so that each of them held her on the side of their *dermoires*. When this was done, she'd take the arm markings of her new mate, including his personal symbol.

She'd look good with an eagle in flight on her throat, but he had to admit that Blade's broken blade wouldn't look out of place. But then, she'd look good in anything. Or nothing.

Blade's big body surged under her, lifting her on Mace's cock, and he groaned as a slow, rolling rhythm moved them together as one. Just as it was when they were in battle, they began an organic, synchronized dance, their bodies becoming one. Their *emotions* becoming one.

All around them, erotic energy crackled, skating across Mace's skin and adding another layer of carnal sensation. Scotty arched, crying out, clenching around him as she came.

"The next one," Blade breathed. "Let's shoot for the next one."

They'd need three simultaneous orgasms for this to work. Plus, a blood infusion at the same time.

Panting, Scotty rotated her hips, seeking more, and Mace clenched his teeth, trying to hold off until—

"Almost there," she gasped. "Oh, so close…"

Blade and Mace locked gazes, and Blade gave a nod. Mace returned it. They were both there.

Go time.

Blade picked up the dagger again, and as he nicked Scotty's breast, Mace bit into her throat.

Blood hit his tongue in a sweet, syrupy rush. Holy hell, Scotty tasted electric, bold, and he knew the second Blade put his mouth to the tiny cut because he made a sound of ultimate satisfaction.

And then the sexual bomb exploded.

Mace came so hard his brain shut down, leaving his body to absorb the pleasure, the ultimate orgasm that hit every part of him, right down to his very soul. He felt Scotty's peak, and he felt Blade's erotic surrender, all of it wrapped in devotion to the relationship they all shared.

And that was when Mace understood that even if he could never be with Scotty again, this one night, this one moment, would always be worth it.

Chapter 31

Scotty wasn't sure she would ever recover from what had just happened. Not that she wanted to.

Waves of pleasure surged through her, over and over. It was like it had been the two times with Mace and Blade individually, except it was…more. More pleasure, more intensity, more connection.

Filled by both males, it was as if she was connecting a circuit, and along with her own orgasms, she felt theirs, too. She felt *everything*. Their emotions, their desires, their very life forces.

This is how my life is meant to be.

The thought hit her like a blow upside the head. Like how Rath used to whack her with a hoof when he didn't appreciate her attitude. She'd always hated that, but honestly, his hoof whacks always knocked some sense into her. Ramreels were nothing if not brutally honest. Neither deception nor tact was in their DNA. If they thought you were an idiot, you knew.

And now she knew that everything she'd ever done was destined for this moment. This, she understood, was in *her* DNA. This didn't come from her mother's human side. No, this was a transmission from the Fates, neither good nor evil, and she could thank either Reaver or Lilith for the bone-deep knowledge she'd just gained.

This was a crossroads in her life. Had she taken another path, the world would have changed in some way. What she'd just done would change the world in another way, yet to be determined.

Another orgasm tore through her, and she carried the guys with her. Another. And another. They kept up with her, and by the time the intervals between peaks left them able to speak, they were just a knot of pleasure piled on top of the mattress.

She had yet to open her eyes. What if she saw the mate rings on Blade's neck?

What if she didn't?

"I don't think I can move," Blade rasped.

Mace kissed the nape of her neck between panting breaths. "Me, either."

They lay there in exhaustion, the love they shared blanketing them in post-coital bliss.

And then.

A distinct shift filled the room with tension. She felt it in the way Mace's leg muscles tensed, and Blade's fingers tightened on her waist.

"Do you guys feel that?"

Behind her, Mace stepped back, allowing her to lift off Blade. But unlike the times she was with them, there was no feeling of emptiness. No feeling of being…bereft.

She could still feel them. In her body. In her heart. In her *soul*.

Mace brought her a robe and wrapped her in it as she stood on wobbly legs. "When will my markings appear?" But even as she spoke, she felt a tingle in her right arm. Shadows formed on the back of her hand, and as she watched, they spread, exact replicas of the markings on Mace and Blade. "It's happening!"

She looked at the guys, but they were busy watching each other.

They were looking for the rings that would form around the throat of her new mate.

Blade reached over and pushed the edge of the robe away from her shoulder. The marks were just now working their way up her arm, light shadows forming on her pale skin. Now, they were at her collarbone.

She climbed off the bed and ran to the full-length mirror on the back of the door.

Halfway up her neck, the squiggle that marked Blade and Mace's grandfather appeared.

The next glyph would belong to the father of whoever she'd bonded with. But shouldn't she feel it? Shouldn't she know who she'd bonded with by now?

Blade's father's symbol was an open eye. Mace's father's symbol was an hourglass.

Which one would manifest?

A shadow formed, just under the skin. An…eye? No, an hourglass. No…an hourglass superimposed over an eye?

Mace and Blade flanked her, the way they always did. Blade on the right. Mace on the left. Each took one of her hands, and an instant, warm sensation flooded her veins. Gods, she could feel *both*. Was that normal? Would the sensations focus on only one when the *dermoire* was complete?

She glanced over at Mace and Blade's reflection…and was it her imagination, or were mate rings forming on their throats? *Both* of their throats.

"Guys…"

"I see it," Mace gasped, his fingers feathering over the taut skin of his neck.

Blade's hand shook as he reached up to his own throat. "My sword…holy hell…the blade, it's not broken. It's…whole."

It wasn't just whole. Another shadow was forming along with it.

"What the—?" Mace gaped at the mirror. "My eagle."

Scotty's entire world shifted.

Just below her jaw, a glyph appeared. The same one that now graced both Mace and Blade's throats.

An eagle—Mace's eagle—was now perched on Blade's once-broken sword.

Mace squeezed Scotty's hand. "Does this…does it mean what I think it means?"

Warmth flowed through her, mixed with a flood of emotion coming from both Blade and Mace. There was relief, wonder, and a little trepidation…but mostly a sense of rightness and love.

Someday, you're going to face an impossible decision. There will be no winner if you choose. So let fate make the choice.

Her grandpa Reaver's words, from so long ago, made sense now. And the dagger. The one he'd given the guys on that day of training so many years ago. He'd known, hadn't he?

"It means you're mine. Both of you." Hot tears stung Scotty's eyes as reality hit home. These males, whom she'd loved for as long as she could remember, were hers in every way.

Chapter 32

Scotty was still flying high when she met Aleka at her London apartment that overlooked the museum. Aleka had gone full Brit since moving there, and she had tea, scones, and finger sandwiches set out in her quaint little dining area.

"What was so urgent that you—?"

Scotty whipped off her coat, revealing the sleeve of glyphs on her arm and throat.

"Holy…*shit*, Scotland." Aleka had been holding a cup of tea, but it was now forgotten, its contents spilling onto the floor as Aleka stared.

Scotty paraded past, feeling a little sassy. "I'd have thought congratulations would be more appropriate, but 'holy shit,' works." She plucked a little sandwich from the plate and popped it into her mouth. She was starving. Sex did that to a girl. Which she now knew.

So cool.

Aleka was still gaping. "I don't know what to say. Who did you mate with? I don't recognize that symbol."

Scotty plopped down in a seat and shoved a couple more sandwiches into her face. "You're gonna need to sit down."

For once, Aleka didn't argue. She just took a seat and stared at Scotty's new decorations. "Tell me. Tell me everything."

Scotty did. And by the time she was done, Aleka was shaking her head in disbelief. Between the two of them, they'd eaten every sandwich, every scone, and had drained the teapot.

"This is unbelievable," Aleka said as she leaned back in her chair, exhausted by the story. Scotty got that because she was exhausted too. But she was also energized. This had gone from the worst day of her life to the best, and all it had taken was a bonding ritual with her two best friends.

"And what's really crazy is that I think Gramps knew all along that we were supposed to end up like this."

Aleka got up to heat more water for the tea. "Have you told anyone else? What about the guys?"

"They went to talk to their families," Scotty said. "I wanted to tell you first."

Aleka whipped around. "Me? I'm the first person you've told?"

"You're my sister," Scotty said. "I know we haven't always been—*oof*."

She broke off as Aleka hauled her into a huge hug. "I'm so happy for you." She pulled back, her eyes brimming with emotional tears. "And somehow, I'm not surprised by this." Abruptly, her eyes shot wide in horror. "But what about Dad?"

Right. That might be a problem.

Aleka took the teapot to the counter near the stove. "How do you plan to handle him?"

"I was hoping you had a suggestion."

Aleka considered that as she poured steaming water into the pot. "Did you know that Stryke has a new division that's going to start a colony on the moon?"

"What? Who the fuck cares?" Scotty surged to her feet and opened her sister's fridge, looking for more food. Sex definitely worked up an appetite. "I have real problems."

"Yeah. I know. And Dad is the biggest one. So, if I were you, I'd buy Mace and Blade tickets on the first moon flight. Because he is going to freak. The. Fuck. Out."

"Oh, come on." Scotty slammed the door closed. "Dad will be happy—"

"Two lust demons are banging his little girl."

Shit. Yup. The guys were as good as dead.

Mace's gut stirred a little as he entered the Charnel House, a demon club in a rinky-dink town in what used to be called Australia's Northern Territory. Now, it was known as Scaldera, named after a river in Sheoul.

The former Northern Territory was home to Ufelskala Tier Three demons and lifestyles, and as far as demons went, it wasn't...awful.

Still, no human was safe outside of what used to be New South Wales, now New Horun, where the Ufelskala Tier One demons ruled.

Good thing Mace wasn't human. But he wasn't Tier Three evil, either, and he watched his back as he sought his target.

He wasn't even sure why he wanted to talk to Talon, and frankly, if his parents hadn't basically ordered him to, he would have let Talon find out the news through the family grapevine.

Man, his parents had been funny, though. The moment they'd seen his mate rings, they'd freaked.

"Who is she?" Idess had been over-the-top thrilled, because her little boy getting mated meant he wouldn't go insane in the future.

But Dad's tone had been more wary. "Who is she?" Same question, but a whole lot of concern in that voice, probably worried that his little boy had gotten himself tied for over four hundred years to some heinous bitchbag like Talon's girlfriend.

It had been his mom, though, who immediately saw the change in his personal symbol. "Mace," she'd gasped. "Your eagle!"

He grinned. "Yeah, look at that. It finally perched."

Lore got in closer. "It's not perching on a branch." His brows drew together. "A sword. Funny, that looks like Blade's sword."

Mace nodded. "Because it is."

His parents stared in a combination of surprise and confusion. Mace considered drawing the whole thing out just for fun, but he decided not to keep his parents in suspense.

"I bonded with Scotty," he said, and his parents erupted in smiles. Idess even squealed and threw herself at him in a big hug.

"I'm so excited," she said. "Congratulations. It's about time. And—" She frowned. "Wait. Why do you have Blade's sword?" She gasped. "You didn't...do something to him, did you?"

Apprehension darkened Lore's eyes. He no doubt remembered the conversation he'd had with him and Wraith about how bad things were with the team. "Son, what's going on?"

Mace laughed. "I didn't kill Blade, if that's what you're thinking." He turned to his dad. "Blade and I are both in love with Scotty, so we told her she had to choose—"

"And she chose you?"

Mace wasn't sure if he should take offense to the surprise in his mom's voice or not. "She couldn't choose, so we let fate decide."

"And fate chose you," she said, clearly anxious to get to the end of the story. He'd watched his mom fast-forward to the endings of movies and read the last chapter of books before the first all his life.

"Fate chose all of us."

Lore and Idess shared baffled glances. Finally, Lore said, "What, exactly, are you saying?"

"I'm saying that both Blade and I are bonded to her."

It took a few heartbeats for his parents to grasp what he'd said, but when they did, their slow, genuine smiles were worth it. They'd been thrilled.

But now it was time to tell Talon.

"Why should I have to tell him in person?" he'd argued. "He won't give a shit."

Idess sighed. "You two haven't had the easiest relationship, but it's not going to get any better if you don't share important moments like this with him."

Ugh. Whatever.

An acrid stench from the kitchens assailed him as he moved through the club, making him thankful he'd grown up in the human realm, eating human food. Demon diets were nasty.

Finally, his eyes adjusted to the low, hazy light, and he saw Talon at a table near the fight pit. A fight must have just finished, because the pit was empty of competitors, and a crew of imps was scrambling to clean it up.

Mace walked up to the table, forcing his brother to look up at him. "Mace. What are you doing here?"

"Crux said Sabre was meeting you somewhere. I figured Sabre needed to fight, and you usually come with him to patch him up."

Nodding, Talon leaned back in his chair and stared down at his drink. "I just finished healing him. He's cleaning up in the back."

Mace pulled out a chair and sat. "First fight of the night?"

"Yeah."

Mace shook his head. "Damned Soulshredder genes." Sabre's mother, Tayla, was half-Soulshredder, a species of demon that could see emotional scars and exploit them, and they lived on the pain of others. Sabre had to expend his violent tendencies now and then to keep his inner Soulshredder satisfied.

A few demons of various species, from ugly, skinny things to ugly, lumpy things, skittered or lumbered by, and once they were past, Talon looked over at Mace. "So, you figured out where I was, but you haven't said why you're here." Narrowing his eyes, he sat upright. "You're mated."

"That's why I'm here. To tell you in person."

Somehow, Talon's eyes got even narrower. How could he even see between those lids? "Why? You avoid talking to me in person."

"Other way around, bro."

Talon didn't argue. "So, who's the girl?"

"Scotty."

"Whoa." Talon had looked vaguely bored, but that got his attention. "It makes sense, but what about Blade?"

"Blade's mated to her too."

Now, he had Talon's complete interest. Dude sat straight up so fast he nearly knocked his drink off the table. "Seriously? In two different rituals? That shouldn't be possible—"

"One ritual. We were trying to let fate decide."

"Huh. I guess it did." He kicked his feet out and crossed them at the ankles, practically daring anyone to trip over them. "So, how is that gonna work? Who's she going to live with? Are you all moving in together? Same room? Same bed? Hot threesomes?"

"We still need to work all that shit out." But no to the threesomes. Mace would be happy if he never saw Blade naked again.

"Well." Talon raised his glass. "Congratulations."

"That's the nicest thing you've ever said to me."

"Is it?" Talon looked out over the fight pit. "Maybe it's because I'm trying to hide the fact that I'm a little jealous."

"What?" Mace teased. "You wanted Scotty?"

"I want a mate." Talon shook his head. "And I can't believe I just admitted that to you."

Mace couldn't believe it, either. His brother rarely confided anything to Mace, especially if it was highly personal. "Are you thinking of mating your fallen angel?"

Talon snorted. "I haven't seen her in days."

"You broke up?" Wraith would be elated. Everyone would be.

"We got into a fight, and she stormed off. Haven't seen her since."

"Is that a good thing?"

Talon ran the tip of his finger around the rim of the glass. Typical of glass made in Sheoul, it made a screaming sound instead of a musical note. "Probably."

"What did you fight about?" Mace asked, expecting Talon to tell him to fuck off, so he was shocked as shit when that didn't happen.

"She's jealous of Amber. Swears Amber wants me, and that I'm encouraging her. It's ridiculous."

"And yet, it's true."

Talon's gaze snapped up. "I don't encourage her."

"But she does want you."

A slinky female walked by, shooting them winks with one of her three eyes. "Has she told you that?" Talon asked after she was gone.

"No, but I've seen the way she looks at you."

Talon scoffed. "Bullshit.

"Whatever." Mace shrugged. "It's best you don't mess with her anyway. Thanatos would skin you alive."

"Me?" Talon laughed. "What's Ares going to do to you and Blade?" He held up his glass again. "Been nice knowing you."

Mace reached up and massaged the back of his neck. It was pretty tight. Mainly because of exactly what Talon had just said. "Yeah, Scotty is trying to figure out how to handle that right now."

"Good luck."

Mace grinned. "I don't need luck. I have fate on my side."

"You sound like Dad. That attitude got him killed once."

Fuck, that had been a terrible time. Wraith had confronted fallen angels in Underworld General's parking lot, believing himself to be invincible.

He wasn't. And he'd died. Mace had been devastated, more for Talon than for himself. Mace still had Lore. The Horsemen had killed two of the fallen angels, and it all worked out in the end, but Talon had never been the same.

"You tell me I sound like him all the time," Mace pointed out. "Why?"

Talon looked at him like he was a moron. "Because you do. Your mouths and your recklessness get both of you in trouble, and you don't care. You don't care what that does to everyone around you."

That was the first time Talon had ever given Mace a reason for his hostility, and it blew away everything he'd ever believed. He sat back in his chair, stunned.

"Holy shit. That's why you hate me, isn't it? I always thought you were jealous of me because Wraith loves me too. But that's not it. You hate me...because you hate *him*."

Mace used to avoid family gatherings to spare Talon pain, but now…now, he realized that the problem was never about Mace. It was about Wraith.

"I don't hate him," Talon said, sounding tired. "We're just different people. And he loves you more than me."

"What? That's not—"

"It's okay. I accepted that a long time ago."

Mace scrubbed his hand over his face, feeling like a piece of shit. It must have sucked to grow up believing that your father loved another kid more than you. But it wasn't true.

"Why would you think that?"

"Are you kidding? You were wanted, Mace. You were planned, and the entire family helped to make sure you were conceived. Wraith didn't even know I existed until I was shoved into his hands. He didn't even know my mother's name. It's Swatha, by the way. I found her. She tried to kill me. Again." He let out a bitter laugh. "It doesn't matter. The past is the past."

It didn't sound like the past was in Talon's past at all. But this was the first time in, oh…ever, that he and Talon had talked about anything substantial, and Mace wasn't going to ruin it by pointing that out.

But there was something he *could* do. It sucked, but it was probably overdue.

"Hey, uh…I'm really sorry for being a shithead."

"You?" Talon gaped, being overly dramatic in Mace's opinion. "*You* are apologizing?"

"Miracles do happen," Mace drawled.

"Yeah, well, you'll need to be more specific. You're a shithead a lot."

That was probably accurate. "At the hospital," he clarified. "I shouldn't have stirred the pot."

"What makes that time different from any of the other times?" Talon's voice was wry, matching his sardonic smirk.

Mace's first instinct was to stir shit up again, but a strange flutter on his neck, right where his eagle perched on the sword, stopped him. No idea why. But it suddenly felt important to make Talon know he was sincere.

"That's fair." He shrugged. "I guess I've just always felt rejected, and it's fun to get back at you by riling you up. You have to admit, it's easy as fuck."

Talon had taught him a lesson about rejection. Mainly, that it sucked. Sucked so much that he kept relationships casual and kept his heart behind a wall of impulsivity, fun, and a fuck-off attitude.

At least, until Scotty and Blade. They'd bonded over the fact that they all had brainiac siblings who were giant pains in the ass.

"Blade was close with his brothers," Mace continued. "Back then, anyway. I wanted that with you. I didn't know you didn't feel the same way. Not until you broke my model planet."

He hadn't merely broken it, either. He'd smashed it against the wall and then stomped it into a million pieces, all the while telling Mace how he wished he wasn't his brother and to stay away from him.

Talon's head whipped up, then he looked back down at his drink. "I was pissed. You brought it over to show off to Dad when you knew I was trying to get him interested in my biology project. Instead, he was all about helping you paint your plastic planet."

Mace stared. "Talon, I didn't bring the model over to show him. I brought it over for *you*. I thought it would help you with your project."

Talon frowned. "Why would you bring a model of a planet to help with a biology project?"

"I was six years old, man. Give me a break. You were what, eleven? I didn't even know what biology was, but I heard you say you needed something round to make a virus. I thought you could paint it however you wanted." Mace shifted on his chair. Demons didn't believe in comfort. "It's no big deal. I screwed up the bottom of the model when I put it together, anyway."

"Ah, fuck." Talon threw his head back and ground the heels of his palms into his eyes. "I'm sorry. I didn't know. Shit was so messed up back then." He looked over at Mace again, his eyes bloodshot and swimming with regret. "It's still messed up. My relationship with Dad feels so forced when it's always been so easy for you."

The thing was, Talon was right. Mace and Wraith shared the same interests. They had similar personalities. But Talon and Wraith had clashed a lot, and it made sense that Talon would have grown resentful of Mace's relationship with his father. Especially if he hadn't felt as wanted as he had been.

Years of conflict ran through his brain like a movie, and so much was making sense now.

"Maybe we could…" Mace began, but Talon wasn't listening. He was staring at his comms, the color draining from his face. "What is it?"

"It's Scorn." Talon looked up, shock glazing his dark eyes. "She's dead."

Holy shit. Not that Mace was all that surprised. She'd probably had a million enemies. But very few of them would be capable of killing her.

"I'm sorry, man."

Talon didn't appear to hear. Gold flecks began to swirl in his eyes as anger stirred. "She was murdered."

"Yeah, that's rough—"

"Whoever did it is going to die," Talon growled. The gold flecks turned red as his fury built. "I swear."

"Talon?" Mace leaned forward, keeping his voice calm and level. Talon's birth mother was an *iradiaboli*, a demon species notorious for their anger turning to obsession. "I get that you're upset, but you need to chill."

Where the hell was Sabre? He should be here helping.

Activity began near the fighting pit as the crews prepared for the next battle, and Talon's gaze sharpened. "My turn."

"Talon, don't—"

Talon surged to his feet and took off toward the pit. Mace sat back in his seat and signaled for a drink. This was going to be a long night.

But not necessarily a bad one. He'd made some headway in his relationship with his brother. They'd connected for the first time since they were kids, and Mace felt like he finally understood Talon a little better.

He grinned as he watched Talon leap into the pit. The guy was a physician, but like the rest of the Sem and Horsemen crowd, he'd grown up learning to fight, and he could hold his own. And now that his evil girlfriend was out of the picture, maybe he'd find someone decent to mate.

The very word made Mace's heart swell. He'd started the night thinking that he could lose it all, and instead, he'd gained everything.

"Mace, hey, what's up?" Sabre, his face shadowed with half-healed bruises, sat across the table from him. "Where's Talon?"

Mace gestured to the pit. "Have a seat and order a double. Scorn's dead."

Sabre's head whipped around to where Talon was stripping down for the fight. "Shit. I feel like this is going to be the start of his villain arc."

Mace laughed, but yeah. Talon wouldn't take this well.

It was definitely going to be a long night.

Chapter 33

Blade's parents were thrilled with the news.

After their initial shock at learning that two Sems could bond with one female, Shade and Runa had offered their congratulations, and they'd immediately started planning a party. And when Mace, Idess, Lore, Serena, and Wraith showed up, the planning turned *into* a party. Then his aunts, Sin and Tayla, arrived with his uncles, Eidolon and Con, and shit got wild.

Blade and Mace had been lucky enough to be raised by very sex-positive people…which made sense for Seminus demons. But humans were tricky. Fortunately, even the humans who had joined the clan had adapted to—and even celebrated—the sensual part of life. Some things just made life worth living.

Everyone was happy. And everyone was sworn to secrecy until Scotty's parents—mainly, her scary-ass father—were told.

Now, a couple of hours later, Blade arrived home, disappointed that Scotty wasn't there. She'd said she was going to talk to her sister to get some advice, and that she'd come straight back.

They'd all agreed that the three of them would be present when she told her parents at their ancient Greek manor. Ares wouldn't respect anything less.

Blade and Mace might wait outside, though. Near the Harrowgate.

He paused in the living room as a warm sensation flowed through him. It was strange but comforting, and he drew in a startled breath when he realized what it was.

Scotty.

He'd been so busy that he hadn't noticed the tingly sensation of awareness in the back of his mind and in the center of his chest that belonged to his mate. It was different than the brother link he shared with Crux and Rade. And Stryke—before he'd broken the connection. Those links were based on the intensity of emotions. Or death. When Chaos died, breaking their connection, Blade had felt as if a hole had been drilled through his core. One that had never been filled.

Until now.

The back door squeaked open, and he wheeled around, his pulse pounding in anticipation. But the hope of seeing his new mate died a painful death when the pounding footsteps didn't belong to her.

Stryke stopped at the threshold between the kitchen and living room, the twitch of one dark eyebrow the only giveaway of his surprise to see Blade. As usual, when he visited family, he was all business-casual in black slacks and a half-tucked, purple button-down that screamed of his mate, Cyan's, influence. She was the light to his dark, the sparkles to his drab, the fun to his boring.

Blade nodded in greeting. "You here to see Crux?"

"Good guess." Stryke brushed past Blade and headed toward the game room.

"Wait." Blade caught up, cutting him off at the entrance. "He says he's going to ask if he can be there for Chasm's birth."

"So?"

Gods, Stryke could be difficult. "I just wanted to give you a heads-up so you don't crush him when you say no."

Stryke scowled. "I wouldn't do that. Cyan and I both think his presence might be the best thing for him and the baby. Maybe their souls can reconnect."

Something clogged Blade's throat. A lump? Why, yes, it was. He'd grieved the loss of Chaos for so long, and while he'd never get his little brother back—not the child he was—Blade welcomed his return to the family.

"That's actually really cool," Blade said.

"Approval?" Stryke gave Blade a quizzical look. "From you? Miracles do happen."

Blade snorted. "Like you give a shit about my approval."

"No, I never have," Stryke said with his trademark brutal honesty. "But this time, yeah. I might not care much about what you think, but I do care about you, Blade."

What a joke. "Do you? Do you really care about me or my life?" Blade reached up to touch the new rings around his neck. "You haven't even said anything about my mate mark."

"Why should I bother? You'll just tell me to fuck off."

Blade's head snapped back as if he'd been punched. Stryke had never been one to hold back, and he'd just let Blade have it with a knock-out blow of truth.

Stryke was right, the bastard.

Just a few weeks ago, Stryke had apologized to the family for pulling away from them following Chaos's death and had offered to restore the brotherly link he'd severed. Rade and Crux agreed, but Blade had refused.

All this time, Blade had blamed his brother for all the tension between them. He'd blamed him for not engaging with his family after Chaos's death. But in truth, Blade had shut him down every time he tried—not that he'd tried often, which was also part of the problem. But for the first time, Blade understood *his* role in the estrangement.

You pushed him away.

Rade's words from a few months back rang in his ears. That brother was right too. All he needed now was for Crux to come downstairs and deliver an ego-crushing judgment.

"Well?" Stryke prompted. "You gonna tell me about your mate, or are you gonna tell me to fuck off? I don't have all day."

Blade sighed. Stryke would never *not* be Stryke. "It's Scotty."

For a long moment, Stryke stared. It wasn't the dead-eyed stare Rade had, but it wasn't the one Stryke usually had, either—the one that looked right through you, as if he was looking at an insect. This one was contemplative. Curious.

"How does Mace figure into it?" Stryke asked. "Isn't that his eagle perched on your sword?"

"We're both mated to her."

"Hmm." Stryke studied Blade's new symbol even more closely. "I didn't know it was possible for two males to bond with the same female."

"I don't think anyone did."

Stryke's eyes went dark and focused, the way they always did when he went into a hyperfocused thought mode that would distract him even if the world was crumbling down all around him.

"I need to look into this," he murmured. "If I can isolate the—"

"Yeah, I'm outta here," Blade said, figuring Stryke wouldn't even notice. So, it shocked the shit out of him when his brother stopped him with a firm hand on his shoulder.

Stryke smiled, just a twitch in the corner of his mouth, but it counted. "Congratulations. Scotty suits you. She suits you both. Somehow, I'm not surprised that it turned out this way."

Blade had heard that more than once today.

Not one to stick around for personal conversations, Stryke started past Blade, but he stopped his brother again.

"You should know..." Blade took a deep breath. Bringing up this topic was like lighting a fuse. "The day Chaos died—"

"I don't want to talk about this. Not again." Stryke wheeled around.

"Stryke, listen. Please." It killed him to beg his brother for anything, but this was important and long overdue. Stryke paused, but he didn't turn around. "We've always wondered why. Why the demons attacked *that* day. Why they were so driven to kill. Why they were even in the human realm. We know now."

Stryke swung back to Blade, his features tight. Guarded. "Tell me."

"Harvester figured it out. You know she's back, right? She thinks it was Lilith's doing."

"Why would—?" Stryke snarled. "Logan. Lilith was after Logan."

"Yeah."

Stryke's demeanor turned dark. Murky. Deadly. "Tell whoever needs to know that my company will provide any assistance necessary to find and end her."

"I will." Blade shoved his hands into his jeans pockets and shifted uncomfortably. So much more needed to be said. And yet, what *could* be said? They'd lost so many years to anger and bitterness, leaving a gulf of separation between them. Bridging it wouldn't be easy. Maybe even impossible. At this point, words meant little. "Hey...I was thinking."

"Trying something new?"

Had...had Stryke actually attempted to use humor? "Look at you, making a joke. Talk about trying something new." He nearly fell over when Stryke smiled. Well, it was a smirk, but that was close enough.

"You'll find that being mated comes with personality changes," Stryke muttered, but there was an underlying affectionate note in his tone. "So, what were you thinking?"

"It's about your offer to reconnect our brother link. Um...if it's still good, I'm cool with it."

A few moments passed, enough to make Blade feel like an idiot for bringing it up. But when Stryke finally spoke, his hesitation made sense.

His voice was thick with emotion.

"I'll have Cyan do it today." He reached out and gave Blade's shoulder an affectionate squeeze.

In Stryke's world, that was a hug.

Stryke took off before shit got weird, but Blade's eyes still stung with almost two decades of pain being flushed from his system.

He skimmed his fingers over his sword glyph, truly understanding it now. There was still a lot of work to be done in his life, but like his sword, he was finally whole.

Chapter 34

They'd all agreed that Mace and Blade would be present when Scotty told her parents about their bond.

But for the boys' safety, Scotty insisted they wait outside the manor. That way, if Ares took the news badly, the guys at least had room to maneuver. They wouldn't run, but they might need to dodge.

Still, Scotty didn't think her father would freak out, despite what Aleka said. He loved Mace and Blade, and he would want his daughter to be happy.

And she was.

As she stood in her parents' great room, she could feel her mates, a comforting, faint awareness that they were alive and well. And maybe a little nervous.

No doubt they could sense her anxiety as she waited for her parents' response to what she'd just told them.

"Congratulations, honey," Cara said as she crossed the room to give Scotty a hug. "I don't understand how it all works, but the three of you make sense." Cara pulled back and turned to her husband. "Don't you think so?"

Ares had yet to say a single word. Or have any expression besides an unreadable blank one.

"Darling?" There was a note of alarm in Cara's voice, so subtle that anyone who didn't know her well might miss it.

But it made Scotty's hackles rise.

Crap.

Ares pushed out of his chair, rising to his full, imposing height. His size had never intimidated Scotty, but right now, he was a mountain casting a huge shadow. Had his shoulders always been so wide? Surely, he had never been that tall, either.

On his arm, Battle reared up. The stallion sensed his mood, and it was ready to fight.

This was so not good.

"Where are they?" he demanded. "If they were too cowardly to come with you—"

"They're right outside, Daddy," she said quickly. "They wanted to come inside with me, but I made them stay."

Wordlessly, he stormed out the door.

In a panic, Scotty chased after him, her mother on her heels.

Mace and Blade were standing near the base of the stairs, but they backed away as Ares charged down the steps like a rampaging bull.

"To the arena. Now!" His command boomed like a thunderclap, scaring birds out of the trees and drawing the attention of the Memitim who were currently sparring in the arena.

The Memitim scattered as Mace and Blade entered, jogging just ahead of Ares.

"Weapons," Ares snapped as he summoned a sword.

"Daddy!" Scotty caught up to him. "What are you doing? I told you, they saved my life. You can't hurt them!"

"How much they hurt depends on them." He glanced over at Cara. "Take her."

"What?" Scotty croaked. "No—"

Cara gripped her hand and drew her away. "It'll be okay, Scotland," she said in a soothing mom-voice that might have worked if Scotty had been sick with the flu, but not when her mates were about to be slaughtered.

"But—"

"Let him handle this."

Mace and Blade scrambled to arm themselves from the weapons rack. A sword and shield for Blade, a pike and chain for Mace. Scotty knew the strategy; Blade would distract Ares with a tank assault while Mace used his speed and agility to knock him off his feet. It was a good plan that would be effective against most opponents.

But not Ares.

"I need to help," she whispered, and her mother gave her hand a comforting squeeze.

"Did it occur to either of you to talk to me before you trapped my daughter in a lifelong bond?" Ares shouted.

"She was dying," Blade argued. "We didn't want to waste time or risk something happening to her."

Good answer.

And yet, her father only got angrier. "So, you're saying you only mated her because she was dying?"

Oops.

"Hell, no." Mace planted his pike in the sand and propped himself against it as if he didn't have a care in the world. That was his disarm-the-enemy move, and it was born of desperation, because he knew full well that Ares wasn't easily disarmed. "We love her."

Ares swung his sword in a motion so fast that Mace didn't have a chance to react before his pike was sheared in half, and he landed on the ground.

"How long have you loved her?"

It's a trap. Every question is a trap. Scotty held her breath. *Be careful, guys.*

"For years," Blade said, and Scotty's heart melted.

Her father had a different reaction. "So, you're telling me you've been lusting after my daughter for *years?*"

"Well, yeah." Mace picked himself up off the ground. "Look at her."

Oh, Mace. Wrong thing to say. But she knew why he'd done it. Ever impatient, he wanted to get this over with. Antagonizing a Horseman was certain to jumpstart a battle.

Ares lit into him so fast and hard that Mace, forced to retreat, went down twice more before Blade distracted Ares with a shield bash into his flank.

"Prove you're worthy of my daughter," Ares growled, intensifying his relentless attack, knocking Blade back with mighty swings of his sword and flinging Mace around with his bare fist.

"Prove it?" Mace yelled, his temper sparked, his eyes going gold. He was magnificent in his fury, and Scotty's chest expanded with pride. "We've been proving it to you for thirty fucking years!"

Mace launched into Ares like a linebacker, a move her father didn't see coming. They tumbled to the ground, Mace's fists pounding into Ares's face. Blade pinned his legs, and for a heart-stopping moment, it looked like Mace and Blade might actually claim victory.

But with a roar that shook the arena, Ares exploded to his feet, knocking Mace and Blade off him as easily as if they'd been nothing more than pesky insects.

Blade stood, brushing sand off his shirt, but his gaze was locked on Scotty. She'd always been able to read him, and it was no different right now.

I won't let you down.

Gods. Of course, he wouldn't.

He held out a hand to Mace. Their hands clasped in a strong grip, and in an instant, they were side-by-side, forming a wall in front of War, Second Horseman of the Apocalypse.

And they weren't afraid.

Her heart swelled to near bursting. After all these years, those breathtaking males were hers.

As a unit, they advanced on her father.

"We love her," Blade said, his deep, rumbling voice dripping with truth that could only come from the soul. "If I have to die to prove it, I will. Because I'll know that Mace will still be here for her."

"Same." Mace wiped blood from his nose with the back of his hand. "I will die for her. I will die for Blade. I will die for this entire *family*. And you know that. So, if you're going to kill us for loving your incredible daughter, do it. But know this. We won't make it easy. Because we fight for *her*."

Tears filled Scotty's eyes, and when she looked at her mom, her eyes were brimming with tears too.

"Fate chose well, Scotland," she murmured.

Scotty swallowed the lump in her throat. "I know."

Silence stretched. The air stilled. The Memitim watching from the sidelines were frozen in place.

Ares regarded Mace and Blade with cold, battle-hardened eyes.

But as they moved toward him, he smiled.

"You have my blessing," he said, his voice echoing through the arena. "And my respect."

With a sob of relief, Scotty threw herself at him. "Thank you, Daddy." She wrapped herself around him for the biggest, tightest hug ever. "I love you."

His big arms caged her against him. "I love you, too, my littlest warrior." He hadn't called her that since she was a child, and the hitch in his voice put a lump in her throat. "And those two knuckleheads." He pulled back and smiled down at her. "But don't think this means I'll go easy on them when we train."

She laughed. "No one would *ever* think that."

After that, there were hugs and "I love yous" all around. Her parents contacted the Sem families and offered to join in with the existing party planning. An hour later, Scotty found herself back at the compound with the guys, snuggled on the couch to play some video games.

She'd once dreamed of this, of Mace leaning over to kiss her, and Blade doing the same, and now, here they were.

"Maybe we should discuss living arrangements," Blade said, after he shot a couple of pixelated bad guys.

That was probably a good idea. "I've thought about it a little." She bit down on her bottom lip as she considered her next words. "I loved being with both of you, but I don't think I want that on a daily basis, you know?"

The memory of being between them, of being engulfed in so much sensuality, made her flush hot and reconsider what she'd just said.

"Agreed," Mace and Blade said at the same time.

"But maybe like, once a year on our anniversary, we can be together like that." She took their hands in hers, loving the instant comfort and affection that linked them. "You know, strengthen the mate-bond magic?"

"I don't think that's how it works," Blade said, his voice going a little huskier at the topic of sex, "but it can't hurt. If that's what you want, we can work something out."

Mace shifted on the couch to face her. "But what about the rest of the time?"

She inhaled a ragged breath as a wave of love and arousal washed over her, transferred through the bond from the guys. They were going to need her soon, and she couldn't wait.

"What if you guys got adjoining suites?" she suggested. "We could have a door installed between them. We can just kind of play it by ear and need then."

"I like that," Blade said.

Mace agreed. "I do too."

Another wave of desire rolled through her, and she realized that the guys were no longer paying any attention to the game. Their eyes, smoldering with banked heat, were on her.

She shivered with delight. "Technically," she murmured, "it's still our mating day. We could strengthen the bond even more—*oof!*"

She laughed as Mace hauled her into his arms and kissed her. Then her laugh turned to a moan as the kiss got hotter. A moment later, Blade was there instead, kissing her senseless.

Winding her arms around his neck, she held on as he lifted her off the sofa and carried her to the suite where they'd changed their lives forever. Mace kicked the door shut and prowled toward them, stripping off his shirt as he crossed the floor.

Smiling with anticipation, she let Blade put her down on the bed, where she admired her new *dermoire* that announced that she belonged to not one, but two of her best friends.

They'd all known that nothing would ever be the same after the bonding ritual. And they were right.

Just not in the way they'd expected.

But now that she knew what to expect, she lay back on the mattress to watch the guys strip and soak up her good fortune. Someone Aleka could probably name had once said that greed wasn't a money issue. It was a heart issue.

If that's the case, she thought as two big, naked warriors descended upon her, *I'm very greedy, indeed.*

Epilogue

Revenant's heavy footfalls echoed through the dark, narrow hallways, his gore-drenched boots leaving a trail of demon blood on the icy stone floor. People always associated Hell with heat, but the cold that permeated some of the underworld was, in some ways, even worse.

His black armor, shiny with the disgusting wetness associated with the butchery of battle, creaked as he strode past three dozen guards representing as many demon species.

The passageway seemed endless, so many demons—physical and mental. Revenant had grown up in these grotesque, twisted halls, raised by Satan himself in the bowels of this hideous stronghold.

He hated it here. Too many memories at every turn. He'd have razed the palace to the ground decades ago if it hadn't been a strategic fortress at the apex of three regions run by warlords united only by a hatred of him. Those warlords were, in fact, why he was here. And why he was covered in gore.

"My lord." The demon standing at the end of the hallway, his broad body blocking the entrance to Rev's private residence, raised his clawed hand in a gesture of deference. "I assume the rebel leaders' heads are gracing the fortress walls on spikes, and that their corpses are being boiled with root vegetables in my clan's cook pots?"

"That's…disturbingly specific." Specific, but accurate. Gringe's clan, in return for their mercenary services, demanded first pick of any dead enemies. Other clans and other demons got to scavenge the leftovers.

Gringe grunted. "Those rebellious heathens need to know what happens when they challenge the King of Hell."

Whatever. Gringe and his entire clan wouldn't hesitate to challenge Rev if they thought they could win or gain favor with Satan. Not that Satan could bestow any favors. Not right now, anyway. Revenant and his brother, Reaver, had locked that fucker up for a thousand-year sentence.

Thirty years later, Rev had managed to keep his enemies at bay, but he was no fool. As the centuries passed, and Satan's release date drew nearer, Revenant would be contending with more frequent coup attempts. They'd grow larger in scale and involve more cooperative demon clans and factions.

"Sir." Drudge, Rev's Archon in charge of his intelligence and security apparatus, jogged up to him, his scaly feet clacking on the stone floor. "What did you want me to do with the traitors in the palace?"

Rev paused while reaching for the handles on the giant iron doors leading to the private living chambers he shared with his mate, Blaspheme. "How many did you root out?"

"Three dozen from our fighting forces. They planned to plant explosives in the barracks."

"Any others?"

Drudge hesitated, his long, dragon-like snout flaring. "My lord…"

Fuck. "Tell me. I won't kill the messenger," Rev said. "Probably."

The crimson slits in the dragon-demon's yellow eyes flickered with anxiety. "We discovered one traitor in your cabinet. Sir."

"Who?" Rev growled, his gut sinking. He didn't trust anyone except his mate, but he'd hoped the people he kept near him could at least be counted on to not betray him.

"Noctus," *Drudge* said, his voice grave. "It was under some… intense…questioning that he admitted to conspiring with the Sythh clan to poison your mate."

Revenant hissed, his fangs punching down as a fresh rush of fury flooded his veins. Enemies and allies alike had plotted not to kill him, but to kill his mate. Most of those involved had paid in blood—theirs, and that of their loved ones.

"Is he still alive?"

"Yes, my lord."

"Bring him to me. Put him in my personal holding chamber."

A slow, malevolent smile spread across Drudge's angular face. "What shall we do with the remaining traitors?"

"Kill them," Rev said. "Kill them all. However you want. But no one lays another claw on Noctus. He's mine."

"Yes, sir." Drudge fled, eager to get on with his grim work. Revenant wished he had time to watch, but Blaspheme was his highest priority, especially now that he knew she was a target of his enemies.

As soon as the male disappeared around a corner, Revenant threw open the doors and burst inside. Blas's maidservant, a willowy Drekevac demon, yelped in surprise, dropping a cup of what he assumed was tea.

"Where is she?"

"In her chamber." She knelt to clean up the mess on the floor, but glanced up at him, concern clouding her black eyes. "Milord…she needs to eat."

Alarm shot through him. Blas hadn't been doing well lately, as the effects of full-time Sheoulic evil on a heavenly angel began to take their toll.

Fucking Heaven. His fury boiled anew.

When Heaven initially locked him inside Sheoul, Blaspheme had still been free to come and go. As a doctor at Underworld General, she'd run one of its clinics in the human realm, which limited her exposure to the toxic effects of Sheoul's evil. But recently, the Heavenly pukes had changed their minds, and she'd been trapped down here, just like him.

Just like his mother.

His wings exploded from his back, and he shot upward through the gaps in the floors that allowed him to get from the bottom floor to the top in three flaps. Servants scattered as he landed at the top floor staircase and strode to the entrance to their private chambers.

He could have just flashed into them, but he didn't want to startle Blas. In her weakened condition…well, he didn't want to think about what surprising her might do to her frail body.

Gently, he tapped on the door and swung it open. A fire burned hot in the great fireplace, once a hideous, twisted monstrosity that served as a source of amusement for the keep's previous owner. Rev could still hear the shrieks of the victims who'd burned—sometimes to death—inside.

Now, the glossy, ghoulish thing had been replaced by white marble from the human realm, shot through with silver and gold veins that Blas said vibrated with heavenly frequencies.

Revenant wouldn't know. Heavenly frequencies usually weakened or died in his presence.

Blaspheme stood facing the flames, her back to him, and the sight of her nearly brought him to his knees in shock.

Her ivory gown hung limply from her gaunt frame, the dirty hem pooling around her bare feet. Her wings drooped against her back, the feathers dull and frayed, curling at the tips. Several feathers lay on the floor around her.

Rev's entire body trembled at the sight of his beloved, his once-vibrant, glowing angel, now so diminished.

"Blaspheme," he croaked, his voice sounding rusty, as if he hadn't been screaming commands for…how long had it been? Weeks? Months?

Slowly, she turned to him, and he forced himself not to react to her pale, hollowed, gaunt face and sunken, dull eyes. Both palms pressed into the concave expanse of her lower abdomen, her wrists resting on prominent hipbones.

"I lost the baby," she whispered. "Again."

Grief shattered him, and in three strides, he had her in his arms. He hugged her tightly, hating how it felt as if his embrace would break her into pieces.

"I'm so sorry, darling. But if—"

"I can't do this anymore," she wailed, breaking away from him. She collapsed onto the stone floor, burying her face in her hands. "I'm sorry. So sorry. I'm not strong enough for this life. I thought I was, but…"

Sobs racked her as he gently gathered her in his arms and carried her to their bed. He didn't bother undressing, even though he reeked of battle and blood. All he could think about was wrapping her in a cocoon of comfort.

The bed creaked under their weight, and in moments, he had her tucked against him, her face buried in his chest.

"I will find a way to get you out of here," he swore.

She looked up at him, tears streaking her red-splotched face. "Did I lose our baby because I'm being punished?"

His heart, usually hardened and encased in ice, always thawed and got squishy when his mate was in pain. "You're not being punished," he rasped. "I am. Heaven fears me, so they trapped us both, and I'm willing to bet that they're not sending any souls to bring life to our children."

"We can't try anymore," she whispered. "I can't do this again."

"I know." He'd made that decision before he left to fight the most recent war brought against him. Blaspheme was too frail to withstand another pregnancy. He'd only capitulated the last time because she'd begged him. And seduced him. And there was nothing he wouldn't do for her.

But he also knew what Sheoul did to angels.

Technically, Revenant was an angel, but he'd been born and raised in Hell, corrupted from birth and tortured for centuries. There wasn't a trace of Heavenly angel left in him.

But Blaspheme was a full-fledged angel who drew her powers from Heaven itself. Since being cut off from that power, she'd become a shadow of what she once was. Unable to draw from Heaven, she was withering away—the way his mother had during her captivity in Satan's dungeons.

But unlike his mother, Blaspheme wasn't going to die. He wouldn't let her. Somehow, he'd break out of this prison and save his mate.

And when he did...

Heaven would fall.

The Demonica Birthright series will continue with *Legacy of Gabriel.* Read on for an excerpt, plus a drawing of Scotty, Mace, and Blade by Steffani Christensen.

An excerpt from Legacy of Gabriel, book four in the Demonica Birthright series...

Raika stared at the summons.

The summons from *Heaven.*

Why would she be ordered to go to Heaven for a meeting? Usually, angels communicated with her through the H-portal app on her comms device. Angels had finally joined the twenty-first century. Very rarely, if it was necessary to meet in person, they came to her.

You have been given a special pass to access the realm. At precisely noon, press the green button.

What green button? Noon? What freaking time zone? Angels were morons of the highest—

Another message popped up. *The green button will appear when the hour strikes noon on Temple Mount.*

"Hmph." Feeling a little sheepish, she checked the time in Israel.

11:58 a.m.

Shit. Those bastards. What if she'd had plans? Or had been in the middle of a battle? Or any of a thousand possible scenarios?

With an irritable huff, she used one of the gifts Heaven had bestowed upon her when she was formally appointed as a Reaper and traveled to the Mount in a blink, wondering what would happen if she didn't push the button.

She was tempted to find out, because screw those arrogant jerks. But she was also insanely curious about why she'd been summoned instead of getting a message or a visit from some self-righteous Celestial.

The button appeared as a 3D projection in front of her at exactly noon. She skimmed her finger over the little dot and instantly touched down in a gold and crystal chamber, being stared at by three female angels in white satin robes.

"There you are," the chick with the purple sash and yellow hair said brightly. "Let's get you ready."

Ready? "For what? And isn't Heaven on lockdown? No one in or out because of your civil war?"

"You were given special permission from the very top." The statuesque, dark-haired angel with a crimson sash sniffed. "You should be extremely honored and grateful. And there is no civil war."

"Really? Because the Heavenly goon squad gave Gabriel the boot, and the rest of the Archangels are being held prisoner after they were overthrown by—"

Abruptly, Raika found herself clothed in an ornate ivory gown that flowed like a majestic waterfall to her feet. The delicate, jeweled bodice tapered down the front, and then spread in a web of glowing crystals all the way to the hem. Weightless and sparkly, it was exquisite, unlike anything Raika had ever seen.

It would look great on her mom.

A mirror appeared in front of her, and she barked out a shocked laugh. The getup was so not her. She'd never once tamed her hair into a glamorous updo, she'd never worn a pair of open-toed high heels Cinderella would envy, and she'd certainly never donned a sparkly, diamond-encrusted tiara.

No, those weren't diamonds. Not with the way they gleamed as if lit from within. Hypnotically beautiful, maybe they were stars. Actual stars. Whoa.

The whole thing was ridiculous.

"Are you kidding me?" She spun around to the angels. "I look like a unicorn took a shit."

Crimson Sash peered down her narrow nose at Raika. "You couldn't very well meet the Angelic Council in what you were wearing."

"I was wearing clothing appropriate for killing demons, which *you* guys force me to do, and excuse me…who am I meeting?"

The purple-sash chick took her hand and guided her to the door. "The Angelic Council. You're being presented."

"Presented as what? A cupcake?"

Raika didn't have time to ask any more questions. Not that they seemed inclined to answer any. They whisked her down a massive, arched hall to a set of emerald doors wide enough to allow the tallest angel with the widest wingspan to enter.

"Wait." Red Sash studied Raika, her turquoise eyes raking her from head to foot. "This won't do. How's this?"

The other two angels nodded in approval.

"Perfection."

"Superb."

Raika stared at Red Sash. "What did you do?"

Suddenly, the mirror appeared again, and Raika stared at herself. A slightly different herself. Chestnut hair instead of black. Slightly smaller nose. Rounder eyes.

"We want you to look more like your mother than your father," Purple Sash explained. "No sense in reminding people who sired you."

"*Who sired me?* You wretched sacks of ass mucus! Change me back!" She rounded on Red Sash. "This is bullshit—"

An invisible blow caught her on the cheek, and she stumbled back a step, nearly losing one of the high heels.

Red Sash transformed from a radiant beauty to a vision of fury, gaining a couple of feet in height and a booming voice. "You will not use foul language or insults in the presence of your superiors. You *will* behave." She threw out her arm and pointed to the doors as they swung open. "Go."

Raika thrust out her chin in stubborn defiance. "And if I don't?"

"Then you will join the Archangels you seem to care so much about." Purple Sash made a sweeping gesture with her arm and spun Raika toward the opening. "It won't take long."

What bitches.

Some sort of shimmery veil concealed whatever was on the other side of the doorway. They could be sending her into a hell realm or a butcher shop, for all she knew.

Actually, either would be better than this glowy, sparkly place full of talking bags of ass mucus.

"Wait." Raika turned to the angels, but they were gone. She was alone in this strange place, expected to blindly follow orders.

Not that she had a choice. Well, she did have a choice, apparently. Face the unknown or become a prisoner in this horrid realm of gleaming walls and weirdos. It was creepy, and her sense of unease increased when she finally figured out why.

There were no shadows.

Everything was light and bright, with no variations in shade caused by the positioning and strength of the lights. The place was magnificent, glittery, and architecturally stunning, and yet…it was sterile and, dare she think it, soulless. Bizarre.

Flexing her hands and wishing she had a weapon in each of them, she stepped through the doorway.

And came to a stunned halt.

She was standing in the sky. Not even on a cloud. Just…hovering in the air above a brilliant city, with buildings the colors of gemstones. Bridges of polished pearl stretched across crystal blue rivers that cut winding paths through verdant meadows and multi-colored forests.

Such beauty.

Such *boredom*. What did people do here? Have picnics and ride Pegasi?

"Welcome."

What the—?

Raika nearly jumped out of her skin. She'd been so busy being appalled that she hadn't noticed the people materializing all around her. At first, there were only a few, including the tall, dark-haired speaker decked out in a deep-blue suit of some shiny material. But as if a veil were being lifted, she realized she was in a glass-floored room in a tower that rose high above the city below.

Music swirled through the room as Celestials, all in their finery, mingled, some carrying chalices filled with the rose-colored liquid flowing from a fountain in the center.

The male who'd spoken strode forward. "I'm Galad." He made a graceful sweeping gesture with one bejeweled hand. "And everyone here is anxious to meet you."

She frowned, feeling like a cornered mouse as the crowd closed in. Man, she *really* wanted a weapon right now. "Meet me, why?"

The angel seemed confused. "Your handlers didn't tell you?"

"Obviously not."

Looking deeply troubled, he stepped back and conferred with another dude and a female in a plain gray dress that somehow didn't look drab.

Raika took the opportunity to look around, but the more she did, the more anxious she became. Everyone was watching her, some with speculation, some with open hostility, others with disgust. Whatever. As the daughter of Azagoth, the Grim Reaper, she got that a lot.

But too many of the males were regarding her with appreciation and lust.

Instinctively, she reached for her powers, but hit a wall. Fuckers had blocked them.

Raika had spent most of her twenty-nine years either in the hellscape realm where her parents lived, or hunting demons in the hell realm known as Sheoul, and very little frightened her. Most of the time, she was the meanest monster in the room.

But not this time.

This must be what my prey feels like when I've got them cornered.

Galad turned back to her. "We brought you here today to find you a match."

She wasn't sure she'd heard him right. "Did you say…a match?"

The female in the gray dress stepped forward, chin high, cool, steel-colored eyes drilling into Raika. "As Azagoth's daughter, you are of special interest to us. So today, you are being presented into our society," she said in a voice as cold as her gaze. "To find a mate."

About Larissa Ione

Air Force veteran Larissa Ione traded in a career in meteorology to pursue her passion of writing. She has since published dozens of books, won numerous awards, and hit several bestseller lists, including the New York Times and USA Today. When she isn't writing, she's traveling overseas or in her RV, playing on her VR headset, or watching Big Bang Theory reruns. She believes in celebrating everything and would never be caught without a bottle of Champagne chilling in the fridge…just in case. She currently lives in Wisconsin with her retired U.S. Coast Guard husband, her son, and her very own rescued hellhounds, a Belgian Malinois named Duvel, and a Belgian Tervuren named Draak.

For more information about Larissa, visit www.larissaione.com.

Discover More Blue Box Press Authors

Go to www.TheBlueBoxPress.com for more information.

Dylan Allen
Jennifer L. Armentrout
Kristen Ashley
Xio Axelrod
Steve Berry
Lexi Blake
Audrey Carlan
Marie Force
C. W. Gortner
Heather Graham
Donna Grant
Larissa Ione
Suzanne M. Johnson
J. Kenner
Randy Susan Meyers
Jennifer Probst
Christopher Rice
M.J. Rose
Kennedy Ryan
J.R. Ward

On Behalf of Blue Box Press

Liz Berry and Jillian Stein would like to thank ~

Steve Berry
Benjamin Stein
Kim Guidroz
Chelle Olson
Hang Le
Chris Graham
Tanaka Kangara
Jessica Saunders
Stacey Tardif
Suzy Baldwin
Grace Wenk
Trinity Shain
Steffani Christensen
Dylan Stockton
Peggy Boulos Smith
Richard Blake
and Simon Lipskar